This book should be returned to any branch of the
Lancashire County Library on or before the date shown

THE

MISMADE

GIRL

LANCASHIRE COUNTY LIBRARY

3011813447897 7

THE

MISMADE

GIRL

Mark Lock

Published by Accent Press Ltd 2016

ISBN 9781783758159

Copyright © Mark lock 2016

The right of Mark Lock to be identified as the author of this work has been asserted by the author in accordance with the Copyright, Designs and Patents Act 1988.

The story contained within this book is a work of fiction. Names and characters are the product of the author's imagination and any resemblance to actual persons, living or dead, is entirely coincidental.

All rights reserved. No part of this book may be reproduced, stored in a retrieval system, or transmitted in any form or by any means, electronic, electrostatic, magnetic tape, mechanical, photocopying, recording, or otherwise, without the written permission of the publishers: Accent Press Ltd, Ty Cynon House, Navigation Park, Abercynon, CF45 4SN

LANCASHIRE COUNTY LIBRARY	
3011813447897 7	
Askews & Holts	13-Feb-2017
AF CRM	£7.99
HAC	

PROLOGUE

Shoot You Down

Summer 1999

Constable Jimmy Colgan always seemed to draw the short straw and luck was never, ever on his side. For years he'd done the pools and hadn't won a thing and now the lads in the station had kicked him out of their lottery syndicate. Over two years they'd only won a poxy tenner which, between eighteen of them, didn't exactly go far.

'I think the balls can smell your involvement, Jim,' Patterson had said to him just the other day. 'I think they're deliberately coming out wrong to spite you.' And, to Unlucky Jim Colgan, they probably were. The last five years had not been kind to Jimmy. Wife leaving with their son and daughter, an uncontrollable house fire, several small car accidents, parents both dying within a month of each other, that incident of gross misconduct. It had all combined to give him the aura of a man with a curse on his head. So, that morning, when the sergeant handed him his first job of the day, he wasn't fazed – he always ended up with the shittiest jobs going.

'There's a nonce – convicted nonce – over in Collier's Wood. Bartholomew Kurtz. Phones his sister in Newcastle every week apparently. Only not this week. She's worried, wants us to take a run out and check everything's OK.' The sergeant gave a dismissive little nod. 'Won't be much. Just tell him to give the old girl a ring if he's there. OK?'

Colgan had shrugged and shoved the piece of paper with the name and address into his jacket. He'd turned to go but the sergeant wasn't finished.

'Oh, and by the way, you're taking the graduate.'

'Eh?'

'Our new blood. Take him with you. Show him what a convicted nonce looks like. He'll need to get used to nonces if he's going to work for the Met.'

'Oh, great,' Colgan huffed as he went back into the main office. 'Lovely jubbly.'

Colgan said nothing during the eight-minute drive to Boundary Road. He'd spent most of the time peering out of the corner of his eye at the graduate sat next to him. Bloody students, he thought. Think they can walk into a nice cushy little detective role, skipping all the pavement-pounding that makes you a proper copper. Colgan thought this one looked a bit too well-heeled. Hair and teeth a little too perfect. Kept grinning over at Colgan like he was on a bloody Sunday school trip. The one major consolation was that the uniform looked far too stiff and starched, like a block of cardboard squashed around him, and the graduate kept shifting in the seat, fidgeting with it.

'You get used to it. In the end,' Colgan eventually said, as he pulled the handbrake on hard and turned the engine off.

'I'm sorry?'

'The uniform. It's a bit itchy at first but you get used to it.' Not that the student would ever have to get used to it. Fast-tracked onto the graduate scheme, this was nothing more than a couple of weeks' work experience for him, before heading back up to Hendon to sit poncy exams. 'The helmet, though. That's a different matter.' He picked the two helmets off the back seat and threw one of them over to the graduate. 'Now keep your mouth shut and let me do the talking.'

They shoved the rusting garden gate aside and strolled up the path to the door. The smell of paint was overwhelming, as though somebody had only recently given the door an extra coat or ten of Postbox Red Dulux. Colgan pressed the doorbell and from somewhere in the house the first few jangly bars of *The Blue Danube* could be heard. After a few seconds, he banged on the glass with the side of his fist.

'Police. Open up. Come on, Kurtz, open up.'

The graduate shifted uncomfortably and gave Colgan a look from the corner of his eye.

'What?'

'Hmm?' The graduate stared down at his feet.

'What's the problem?'

'Nothing.'

'Look, son. When you've spent twenty years on the job like I have, you'll find that all the social graces you learned at finishing school will have disappeared right up your arse. *Kurtz*!' He banged on the glass one more time. 'Come on, you nonce. Open up!' Colgan looked at his watch. 'He's not here. Come on, let's go.' He started to move away from the door but the graduate stayed put.

'Shouldn't we ...'

Colgan stopped. 'What?'

'Shouldn't we, perhaps ... you know ...'

'No, I don't know.'

'Shouldn't we go around the back and take a look?'

Colgan sighed for the billionth time that morning. That was the problem with taking on overeducated kids. They were always so fucking keen and yet didn't have a fucking clue.

'What's the point in going around the back? If he's not there, he's not there. Doesn't matter what angle you take it from.'

'But the sister – the sister was worried. Says he always phones her from the phone box. Every week, she says.'

'Listen, kid. One of the things you need to understand is that nobody gives a flying toss about nonces – or paedophiles or pederasts or whatever bloody Latin-derived name you choose to call them. They're the scum of the earth. The last thing you want to do is to break your back over a piece of shit like Kurtz here. The sister's probably just a dotty old bint worried he's off molesting again. Now come on, let's go.'

'No.' The graduate stood his ground. 'I mean ... I'd feel better if we went around the back. Just to check.'

'Oh, you'd feel better, would you? Well, pardon me. I didn't realise this was all about your peace of mind. For a minute or two there I thought you were simply showing concern for a fellow human being.' Colgan shifted his weight from one foot to the other. 'Well, in that case,' he spat, 'why don't *you* go and have a look around the back. Set your mind at rest. *I'll* stay out here and have a fag and a little think about other ways in which we can waste the day away. I know,' he was digging the cigarette packet from out of his trouser pocket, 'what about we go up west and count the number of "Golf Sale" signs on Oxford Street? Or shall we go find a bridge and play bloody pooh sticks?' He lit up and sucked on his Lambert & Butler.

'I'll go on my own, then.' The student went through the gate and walked towards the lane leading around the back.

'That's it,' Colgan muttered out of the side of his mouth. 'Go and have fun.'

Constable Harry Luchewski made his way along the rocky footpath at the rear of the houses. He was finding Colgan to be a total, platinum-plated, prize-winning tit. No wonder everybody else at the station avoided him like the plague. He was poison. The sort of colleague to make you want to fake a brain haemorrhage just to get a couple of weeks off on the sick. Vile. Still, he had to grin and bear it, even though he secretly wanted to smack the bloke on his stupid fat nose.

Most of the back gates had numbers on, so it was easy for him to find Kurtz's scrappy little yard. He let himself in. A few broken pots stood in one corner and a worn brush was propped up against a badly stained plastic bin. The paving stones were mossy and slippery and Luchewski nearly lost his footing more than once. He crossed the small yard and knocked on the back door of the house.

'Mr Kurtz? Hello?' No answer. 'It's the police, sir. We're here to make sure you're all right. Mr Kurtz?' Still nothing. 'Your sister contacted us. Says she's worried.' Silence.

After pulling his uniform jacket into shape and running his finger under the strap of his helmet, Luchewski twisted the handle of the door and pushed.

It opened. Bracing himself, he walked into the dimly lit kitchen.

'Mr Kurtz? Hello, sir?' Some unopened tins of Heinz tomato soup sat on the worktop; the sink was full of unwashed plates and dishes. 'Mr Kurtz? Are you there?' He made his way around the table and saw a man sitting on a dining chair in the middle of the room beyond.

'Mr Kurtz?'

The man looked at Luchewski and shook his head. He had heavy rings around his eyes and a face full of gritty stubble. 'You've missed him.'

He pointed directly in front of him and as Luchewski came into the room ...

'Agh!'

Harry felt his chest tighten and his feet superglue him to the spot. Lying face down on the floor in front of the man was a body. Its arms were extended and the wrists had been tied to pipes which led from either side of the radiator. The body was wearing nothing but a pair of greying underpants, and along the back and the legs were vicious red slashes. Puddles of blood had seeped out of the wounds onto the parquet flooring.

'He died a couple of hours ago. I used that in the end.' The man on the chair dangled a piece of cord from his hand. 'Strangled him.'

'Did ... er ...'

'Lost my rag with him. Couldn't take no more. He wasn't saying nothing, so ... I just lost my rag with him.' The man gave the cord another little shake.

Luchewski nervously pointed at the body. 'Kurtz?'

The man on the chair nodded. 'He wasn't saying

nothing. Refused to tell me where she was – what he'd done with her. Kept denying it all. Over and over again. He kept denying it all.'

Luchewski could see that Kurtz had been gagged and that one of his legs had clearly been broken. The foot at the end of the leg had swollen up to the size of a small football, and as well as the cuts to the torso there was some major bruising and what looked like burn marks.

It was the first dead body Luchewski had ever seen.

'Nothing I could do would make him talk. Nothing. So. In the end ...' The man rubbed his tired eyes with the back of his fists. His T-shirt was drenched with Kurtz's blood. 'You might want to bag this up. For evidence.' He held out the piece of rope in his hands. 'There's stuff down there you might need to watch out for too.' He gestured to an area on the floor next to the body. 'Couple of knives. Blowtorch. All that stuff.' Luchewski still couldn't move from the spot. 'My fingerprints are all over it all.' The man lifted his fists and held them out towards Luchewski. 'You might want to handcuff me. Take me in. I'm tired now.'

'JESUS CHRIST!'

Luchewski jumped out of his skin at the sound and spun around to see Colgan coming into the room behind him.

'WHAT THE FUCK ...?' Colgan stabbed his finger towards the man. 'Stay there! STAY RIGHT WHERE YOU ARE! Jesus Christ! DON'T YOU FUCKING MOVE!' Colgan tried pulling out his radio from his belt but was jerking so quickly that he dropped it onto the floor. 'Fuck! I'm calling for backup! YOU FUCKING

STAY THERE!' He scooped the radio up and held it to his face.

The man on the chair looked at Luchewski. 'He always like that?'

Luchewski glanced back at Colgan. 'Dunno.'

'Sorry about all this,' the man whispered. 'Are you all right? You look a bit pale.'

'What? Oh. Yeah. Yeah.' Luchewski found himself feeling oddly numb. 'And you?'

The man smiled sadly.

'Been better, you know? Been better.'

Seventeen Years Later

It had been a long shift. Twenty hours straight with a couple of naps snatched here and there and the occasional bite of an increasingly stale sandwich. The daytime had been pretty quiet – a handful of broken bones, a detergent accident and one quite serious head injury – but the night was always so much busier in A&E. Especially after chucking out time. She never understood why young men felt the need to fight each other. It was as if the booze let out some sort of primeval urge to kill anything in sight. Alpha males, with nothing to be alpha about, latching on to some infinitesimal reason to be kingpin. A girl, a spilled drink, a funny look. None of it worth the pain and suffering that followed. It didn't help that the young men that stumbled in drunk and dazed were always so obnoxious and leery. All the dirty comments and touching up that she had to endure. She and all the female nurses. Sometimes it could be very satisfying to apply a dressing just a little too tight.

Exhausted, she drove out of the car park at St George's onto Blackshaw Road. It always made her smile that the powers that be, in their infinite wisdom, had built a hospital – one of the major teaching hospitals in London – directly opposite a massive cemetery, as if to remind the public that sometimes there was nothing any doctor could do. She wondered how many patients went straight from the one to the other.

The drive home was endless. It would normally take around forty minutes to get to Bromley, but tonight it seemed to drag on, with roadworks after roadworks and red light after red light. Learner drivers blocking up lanes with their stuttering and stalling, delivery lorries backing up streets not designed for delivery lorries to back up. Seething, she eventually found herself pulling onto Bromley Avenue more than an hour after setting off.

The sun had all but disappeared as she unlocked the door and made her way up the stairs to her first-floor flat. She put on the television and poured herself an enormous glass of white wine, then stuck a frozen pizza in the oven. Waking the computer up, she checked her emails – just some rubbish about reclaiming PPI – and Facebook – a short message from her mum reminding her not to forget her dad's birthday that weekend – before curling up on the sofa with the wine and pizza to watch the news, followed by Graham Norton.

After running an extra-hot bath with plenty of Radox, she eased herself in and tried to forget the day, which was difficult when its events had been burned onto her retinas by too much artificial light. The blood was always there. Every day, gallons of blood and twisted limbs. The cries of pain and shrieks of horror. It all seeped into her psyche and was hard to shake off. Scalding hot baths helped, but not enough.

She dried herself down and slipped on her pyjamas. One last flick through the channels told her that there was bugger all worth watching at this time of night, and she turned everything off before crawling under the duvet. Flicking on the bedside light, she tried reading the book she'd bought in the hospital shop last week – a trashy piece of nonsense filled with hormonal housewives and practically pornographic descriptions of how to eat chocolate – but her eyes were set against the idea and kept pulling down the shutters on the page. Giving up, she threw the book on the floor, switched off the light and snuggled down into the soft, warm blankets. She tossed and turned, restless, for twenty minutes or so before finally succumbing to the irresistible fug of sleep.

Seventeen minutes after she started snoring, the man who had been hiding in her wardrobe all evening silently pushed open the door and stepped into the room.

PART ONE

Elizabeth My Dear

One

Detective Inspector Hal Luchewski knew straight away. As soon as he saw the way her body was positioned, he knew, and a strange shivery sick feeling rushed up his chest and seemed to linger around his throat, clasping his Adam's apple like a vice.

'Been dead for about twenty hours now, I'd say – that's a very rough guess of course. Little more than a random number picked out of the air to make myself sound impressive.' Dr John Good smiled at both Luchewski and DI Burlock.

Burlock grinned back at the forensics officer through his unkempt beard. 'Who is she exactly?'

DS Green heard the question and came into the doorway from the hallway beyond. 'Guy downstairs owns the house. Rents it out … *rented* it out to …' he pointed to the body on the floor. 'Alice Seagrove,' he read the name off a notebook. 'Junior doctor in St George's Hospital, Tooting. Says he saw her getting back around nine thirty last night.'

'Sexual?' Burlock frowned over at Good.

'Doesn't appear to be. No sign of any sexual assault. Underwear still intact.'

'Then why's she tied to the radiator pipes like that? And the gag. What's that about?'

'Bartholomew Kurtz.' Luchewski spoke for the first time since he came into the bedroom.

'Eh?' Burlock looked up at him.

'Bartholomew Kurtz,' Luchewski repeated.

'Who the hell's Bartholomew Kurtz?'

'You'll find her left leg's broken.' Luchewski ignored Burlock. 'And cause of death was strangulation.'

Good gave Luchewski a bit of a look. He squatted next to the body. 'I think you're right. Left leg could well be broken – it's certainly badly bruised. And there are definitely ligature marks around the neck. Also,' he gestured at Luchewski to join him, 'what was the name again? Bartholomew Kurtz?'

Luchewski bent over the cadaver. The whole room stank of blood. He wished that he could get used to it, but he never really did. No amount of exposure to death ever really got you used to it. You just found different ways of tolerating it. Different ways of holding it all in.

He stared at Good. 'Yes. Bartholomew Kurtz.'

Good pointed to the dead girl's back. 'As you can see, before he killed her, he spent some time cutting her up. Look at this …' With a gloved hand, he lifted the flimsy pyjama top up slightly. Her back had been sliced up badly, dried blood – some patches darker than others – covered its length and had soaked into the carpet below. 'Can you see?'

'See what?'

And then he saw it.

'What is it?' Burlock edged forward.

'Christ.'

The slices along the back hadn't been random, aimless slashes. Scratched deeply into the skin, Luchewski could make out the letters:

BART
KURT

Pulling the top up a little further, Good managed to reveal the whole of the message.

BARTHOLOMEW
KURTZ

'Bloody hell.' Burlock's face look liked a hairy, crumpled tissue.

'I need some air.'

Good looked up to see Luchewski marching out of the room and down towards the stairs.

'Sixteen ... seventeen years ago, over in Merton,' Luchewski began. All three of them were sat on the wall in front of the large, bay-windowed house. The street was suburban beyond being suburban. A road filled with families, Land Rover Discoveries and twice-yearly holidays in Florida. 'A twelve-year-old girl disappeared. Her name was Louisa Gaudiano. She'd been at a local youth centre with her friends.' Burlock and DS Green were listening intently. 'There'd been a disco or something like that – I can't quite remember. Anyway, I think she'd argued with her friends and left before they did. Nobody ever saw her alive again.' Luchewski watched the white-uniformed forensics team photographing and fingerprinting Alice Seagrove's Fiat Punto. 'Police did all the usual things: door-to-doors, appeals in the media, reconstructions. But running a check on local sex offenders, it turned out there was one who lived not two hundred yards from Louisa Gaudiano's own front door.' Luchewski picked a stone out of the pebble-dashed wall and flicked it onto the road in front. 'Bartholomew Kurtz.'

'Where's Kurtz now?' Burlock bustled, his grey beard twitching.

'Bartholomew Kurtz had served a prison sentence for abusing young boys,' Luchewski continued. 'On the evening the girl disappeared, neighbours had seen him pacing up and down the street. As if he was waiting for something. Or somebody. Kurtz had a club foot and walked with a stick. All his neighbours knew him. But they didn't know his past. So, obviously, police take him in, ask him all about Louisa Gaudiano, search the house from top to bottom. But nothing. He knows nothing, they find nothing. There's nothing at all to link him to the disappearance of the girl.'

'He's dead, isn't he?' Green got up off the wall and dusted the back of his trousers down.

'And all the while, Louisa Gaudiano's dad is tearing his hair out. Frustrated and confused. Not knowing what to do. He walks the streets from morning to night calling out for her. Looking for her. Trying to find her.' Luchewski thought about Lily, and had to swallow hard to stop himself from starting to well up. 'The poor bastard can't sleep for worry. He can't eat. He's desperate to find his little girl. Then they take in Kurtz for questioning, and everybody in the area starts talking about the local paedophile. How it must have been him that took the girl. So, one day, Nino Gaudiano pays Kurtz a visit – only with a bag of tools by his side. Pliers, knives, sledgehammer. That kind of thing. He ties him to the radiator then spends the next three days slowly torturing Kurtz, trying to find out what he did with his daughter.'

Burlock and Green looked at each other. Further along the road, a silver Peugeot pulled up.

'Cuts him, burns him, smashes his leg. But Kurtz says nothing Nino wants to hear. He doesn't admit to anything.

4

Denies all involvement. Just begs for his life.' Luchewski got up from the wall and started to walk towards the Peugeot. 'Then, on the third day, Nino gets annoyed and uses the cord from Kurtz's pyjama bottoms to strangle him.' Green and Burlock slowly followed behind Luchewski. From the car stepped a slender Indian girl in a perfectly ironed blue suit. She spotted the officers and, waving cheerily, clip-clopped along the pavement towards them. Luchewski smiled at her. 'A trainee constable discovered the body. It gave him nightmares for years. Hello, Priti. It's bloody good to see you.' Luchewski swung his arms around the young woman and crushed her in a gigantic hug.

'Steady on, sir,' Priti Singh squeaked from somewhere inside Luchewski's smothering cuddle. 'People will talk.' She patted him on the back firmly and Luchewski responded appropriately by letting her go.

'How are you?'

'Good. Really good, actually.' Luchewski wondered if it was the anti-depressants talking. 'I feel really good.'

'Well it's good to have you back, Sergeant.' Burlock came forward and gave her a quick squeeze of his own.

'Cheers, Freddie.' The three months' sick leave had flown by and she was at least giving the impression of having got over it all.

'Hi, Priti.' Green smiled shyly at her.

'Rob,' she nodded in response.

'We're about to ruin your day, I'm afraid,' Luchewski put his hand on her shoulder. 'Come inside and have a look. See what you think.'

'Howdy doody!'

'Corrie, love, it's Hal.' Luchewski had left the rest of them to it and was wandering down towards Farnaby

Road, his phone clasped to the side of his head, pleased to get away from the scene for a few seconds at least.

'Hi, Hal. Another day in paradise by the sounds of it.'

'Mmm. Look, I need you to dig some stuff out of the system for me ...' Corrie was an expert on using the HOLMES2 database. It was something Luchewski didn't have the slightest clue about. It might as well have been a bloody space shuttle for all his ability with the thing. 'Run the name "Alice Seagrove" through and tell me what turns up. I also need you to find all the notes on a case from about twenty years ago – everything you can get your hands on. *Regina vs Gaudiano*. That's G-A-U ...'

'Yeah, yeah, I know. I can spell.'

'And try the name "Bartholomew Kurtz". You can spell that too, can't you?'

'You cheeky sod, of course I can! Kurtz. That's like Marlon Brando in *Apocalypse Now*, isn't it?'

'Eh? Is it?

'Yeah. You know, a cow getting sliced up at the end.'

Luchewski shook his head to himself. 'Whatever. Just see what you can dredge up, OK?'

'Okey dokey. Pig in a pokey.'

Someone was having a good day at least.

Good was pointing to the wardrobe as Hal re-entered the bedroom, but the inspector's eyes couldn't help but keep falling back upon the lifeless young woman on the floor.

'Think he might have been hiding in there.'

'What?'

'We found a footprint – well, a couple of smudges more than footprints. Clothes had been moved aside, and the door was wide open when we arrived. I'll get Spound to see if we can match the tread to any particular make. Unfortunately, the footprints aren't especially big or small so all I can really tell you at the moment is that you're looking for an average-sized person – not much help, I know.' Good pulled the hood down from his white spacesuit. His leonine mass of grey hair spilled out and Luchewski found himself rubbing his sparse shaven head in response. 'How're things going? With Stevie, I mean.'

'Oh … it's fine.'

'Fine?'

'Yes. Fine.'

'"Fine" is not a very enthusiastic word to use about your relationship, Inspector Luchewski!'

'No. No, honestly. It's all good. Started the teacher training course on Monday – seems to be enjoying it.'

Good squinted at him disbelievingly. 'Hmm. OK.'

'Sir.' Luchewski spun around to see Singh waggling her phone at him. 'Sir. Corrie's been trying to get hold of you. Seems your phone is turned off.'

'Oh, shit,' he muttered to himself as he fumbled about in his pocket for the phone. 'Tell her I'll call her back in a minute or two.' Using it as an excuse to escape Good's questions, he started to leave the room, but the forensics officer called after him.

'Come around one night – you and Stevie. Be good to finally meet him.'

'Tut, tut, Inspector. Knocking your phone off like that. Could make a girl think that you didn't want to speak to her.'

Luchewski smiled at the idea of Corrie as a girl – she was well into her forties, as roly-poly as a butterball and waddled whenever she walked – which was hardly ever. Her main love affair in life was with the boxes of cream cakes from Greggs that she always came to work with, and avoided sharing around at all costs.

'That was quick.'

'You know me. The Quick-Draw McGraw of the Beckenham squad.'

'Have you been helping yourself to some of the confiscated drugs down in Vice again?'

'Might have been. What of it? A girl's got to have a hobby.'

Luchewski smiled again. 'Will you please stop referring to yourself as a girl, Corrie. It's unbecoming in a woman for whom the menopause is a memory.'

'Oooooh! Below the belt, Inspector,' she joked. 'If I wasn't such a lady I could say a few things about … well, let's just say your hairline, for a start.'

'I'll have you know I choose to have my hair this way.'

'Oh yeah?'

'Oh yeah. If I didn't – if I let my hair grow with its normal sweeping, beautiful thickness – I'd be making most other men my age feel inadequate and consumed with jealousy. So, I sacrifice my own looks for the greater good.' John Good's delicious head of hair made a sudden appearance in his mind.

'How very noble of you!' Corrie laughed. 'I'll try to remember that when I can't stop staring at it in some meeting or other.'

Luchewski laughed. 'Touché. So, what have you got?'

'I put Alice Seagrove through the system – nothing more than three points on her driving licence about six months ago. Speed camera just outside of Chislehurst snapped her doing forty-five in a thirty zone one evening. Then I did a search on Nino Gaudiano.'

'Oh, yes?'

'Turns out he was released from Belmarsh last November.'

* * *

All the photos, measurements, swabs and dustings had been taken and it was time for the body to be removed. Luchewski hated that bit. It was the moment where the body stopped being a pretend thing – a Madame Tussauds wax model, all still and lifeless – and became a somebody. The way the body flopped when lifted, the roll of the skin, the liquid in the eyes – it hammered home the fact that this 'thing' was, in fact, a someone. Or, at least, *had* been a someone. It was always the saddest moment of all.

Luchewski decided it was better not to watch, and went through to the sitting room where Singh and Burlock were helping the forensics team go through the contents of Alice Seagrove's life.

Burlock was sat at a small table, working his way slowly through a box of correspondence.

'What's that?' Luchewski asked.

'Bills, mostly. Some letters from family. Not much.'

Singh had pulled out a stuffed lever arch file, and was flicking through with her rubber-gloved fingers.

'Singh?'

'Oh. Certificates.'

'Let's see.' Hal took the file from Singh and looked through from the beginning. Grades one to four piano – one pass, two merits, one distinction. A gold swimming proficiency certificate. The details of a life, thought Luchewski. GCSEs – 5A*s, 3As and 1B. A-Levels – Biology A, Chemistry A, Physics B. A bright girl.

Then he spotted the name of the school that Alice Seagrove had gone to.

'Oh, God.'

Singh arrived alongside him. 'What is it, sir?'

'She went to Longley Road Secondary.'

9

'What?'

'Longley Road Secondary.' He looked Singh in the eyes and pointed in the direction of the body. 'How old was she?'

'Erm … twenty-nine. I think.'

Luchewski sighed hard. 'I think she was in the same class as Louisa Gaudiano.'

TWO

As he drove onto the hardstanding in front of his house, Luchewski knew he was in trouble. What with the stresses and strains of the day, he'd forgotten that Stevie was coming over, and even the way that Stevie's beaten-up old Corsa was parked at such an awkward angle made Luchewski feel that he'd be treading on eggshells tonight. He looked at his watch. 10:25. Shit. Definitely in trouble.

'Hello,' he tried to sound perky as he closed the front door behind him. He could hear the television babbling away in the sitting room, and he threw his keys and wallet down onto the hallway table. 'Hello,' he gave it another go. Again, there was no reply.

Luchewski pushed the door to the sitting room open. Stevie was crouched on the sofa staring at the television, a large glass of red wine in hand.

'You all right? How was your day?' Luchewski was trying to keep the mood light.

'Your dinner's in the dog,' Stevie slurred back without turning to look at Hal.

'I haven't got a dog.'

'Well, if you did, your dinner would be in it now. Which would be a shame, since it was a very nice dinner that I cooked, specially. Shame to waste it on a dog.'

The volume on the television was too high and, even though Stevie was only watching snooker, the occasional clack of the balls and mumbling commentary was enough to interfere with the conversation that Luchewski was trying to impose on them both.

'I didn't realise you liked snooker.'

'Oh, there's *lots* you don't know about me, Mr Harry fucking Luchewski, king of the fucking Metropolitan hip-hip-hooray Police. Lots and lots you don't know. In fact, you hardly fucking know me a' all.'

Luchewski pulled off his jacket and sat alongside Stevie, who seemed to recoil slightly.

'OK, then. As you like snooker so much, tell me who's winning.'

'That one there.' He pointed to the screen. 'The boy with the spots.'

'What's his name?'

'Er ...'

'What's he doing now? I never really understood snooker,' Luchewski lied. 'Tell me what he's doing. What are the rules?'

'He ... that one there. He's knocking the balls with his stick.'

'Cue.'

'Cue. It's like pool, but none of the little balls have numbers on.'

'So, do they have to hit particular balls? Why are they different colours?'

Stevie finally turned to face him. 'You can fuck right off.' He took an enormous glug of the wine and twisted his entire body away from Luchewski.

Levity obviously wasn't the way forward tonight, so Luchewski tried a different approach. 'Look, I'm really, really sorry I missed your supper – I forgot you were coming over –'

'Oh –'

'I've had a really difficult day at work,' he continued

quickly before Stevie could jump on him. 'We found a young girl – a junior doctor. She'd been strangled. A horrible business. Entire life in front of her. It all got on top of me, and I'm sorry but I forgot you were cooking dinner for us tonight.'

'You could have phoned. You *do* know how to use your phone, don't you?'

'I'm sorry … I just lost track of time.'

'If you'd let me know, I might have understood – well, no, I'd still have been pissed off, but … this not knowing … it's not right.'

The audience were now applauding one of the snooker players and the noise made Luchewski's head rattle.

'Look, can we turn this fucking television off? It's too fucking loud.'

Without warning, Stevie suddenly got up and walked towards the door. 'I'm going to bed. One of the other rooms tonight. Don't try and come in. I need to be alone. Think a bit about things.'

And with that he was gone, footsteps thumping on the stairs and the dying applause of snooker fans on the box.

The door opened and suddenly it was as though the last seventeen years had not happened. Admittedly, Nino Gaudiano looked a little less lean and a lot more lined than he had the last time Luchewski saw him, sitting, head bowed, across the courtroom. The hair a little more salt-and-pepper, the features somewhat heavier, but it was still undeniably one-time murderer Nino Gaudiano. He waved Luchewski and Singh inside.

'Been a long time,' Gaudiano smiled to himself. 'Been a long, long time.' He held out his hand to Luchewski who instinctively took it and shook it. 'How are you, Const … I was going to say "Constable", but that's probably not right any more, is it? What is it now?'

'Inspector. Detective Inspector.'

'Detective Inspector, eh? You've done well for yourself. Good. I knew you would. I just knew you would.' Gaudiano turned to Singh. 'And I'm sorry, my love, you are?'

'This is Detective Sergeant Singh,' Luchewski replied before realising what he was doing. Singh gave him a filthy look in return.

'Detective Sergeant Priti Singh, sir.' She proffered her hand to Gaudiano, who gave it a gentle shake. 'Metropolitan Police South, Major Incident Squad.'

'Lovely to meet you.' Nino Gaudiano had a glint in his eye and Luchewski remembered how, all those years previously, he was always charming and flirtatious with the female officers. A stint in one of the toughest prisons in London had obviously done nothing to tarnish that sheen. At fifty-four, he still had it.

Gaudiano looked past them and saw the uniformed officers on the stairs behind. 'What's this, back-up?' he laughed.

'There are a couple more out front and a car full of them around the back, I'm afraid,' Luchewski apologised. 'Just in case?'

'Just in case what?' Gaudiano frowned.

'We need to talk, Nino.'

Luchewski sipped the far-too-hot coffee that Nino Gaudiano had placed on the kitchen table before him. He just about managed to stop himself from crying out in pain as the scalding liquid hit his tongue and, struggling to swallow, he put the mug back down on the wickerwork coaster. He noticed Singh doing exactly the same thing.

'Tuesday night?' Gaudiano asked before having no

14

problem whatsoever drinking his own coffee from a cracked mug with a PG Tips chimpanzee on it. 'At work. I start at seven o'clock when all the office workers have gone, and clean right the way through until six, before they start creeping back in again. I have to clock in, if you need proof. All the other cleaners will vouch for me too. Why? Why are you asking this, Inspector? What's happened?'

'Nino.' He leaned in a little closer. 'We found a body. A young woman. She was murdered in exactly the same way you killed Kurtz. She was strapped to radiator pipes and gagged in a similar way. The killer had gone to the trouble of breaking her leg. He'd also cut some words into her back.'

'Words?'

Singh grimaced. '*Bartholomew Kurtz.*'

'Hold on ... what? He cut that man's name into her back?' Gaudiano slumped back into his seat. He looked stunned. 'Why ... why would he do that?'

'That's what we're trying to find out. Obviously, you're our first port of call.'

'I don't believe it. I mean ... I really can't believe it ... who was this poor woman? Do you know?'

'She was a twenty-nine-year-old doctor.' Luchewski looked very closely at Gaudiano. 'Her name was Alice Seagrove.'

A sharp intake of air and then a hand to the mouth. Gaudiano's eyes were wide with confusion. 'No.'

'What's that, Mr Gaudiano?' Singh asked.

'Alice Seagrove. I know Alice Seagrove – I *knew* Alice Seagrove. She went to school with my Lou. They were best friends.'

Seventeen years earlier

Everyone was nervous. She knew that. Even the cocky kids like Darren Westlake and Conrad Phillips were nervous despite all the strutting about and gum-chewing. She could see it in their eyes. Pulling her new bag over her shoulder, she looked about for somebody she knew. All the older kids were running about and kicking footballs, but the new Year Sevens were floating around like little lost dogs. Some of them had come with their parents – which was a bit pathetic, she felt. There was no way Alice was going to have *her* mum or dad come into the yard with her. She wasn't that useless. That was an open invitation for the older kids to swoop in and start picking on you – the boys with the fat tie knots and the too-tight blazers. She'd heard the stories.

'They stick your head down the toilet if you don't give them your dinner money,' Lucy Heaton had said. 'And in the science lessons, they put dead frogs in your school bag while you're not looking.' Lucy Heaton, though, was stupid and thought that Spiderman was real and that television was invented by the Queen, so you couldn't really trust anything she said.

She fiddled with her tie and went back to stand near the gate. Everything about her smelled new. The blazer, the blouse, the stupid little tie. Even her bag had that plasticky whiff of newness about it. The maths set that her mum had got her from Smiths rattled about inside, and her shoes felt all unbendy and squeaky. It was like being one of those dummies in shop windows. Unable to move.

Then she saw Katie Thompson from her old school being dropped off by her dad. She looked a bit scared too, so Alice walked over to her, pleased to have found someone to latch herself onto.

'Hi,' she said as coolly as she could manage. 'You frightened?'

'Yeah. A bit.' Katie's eyes tried to take everything in. 'What about you? You scared?'

'Nah,' Alice tried to lie. 'I'm fine. I'm all right. Come on, let's go in.'

Some of those Year Elevens *do* look a bit big, she thought to herself as the bell started to ring and they made their way towards the main door.

Three

It was like a dam had burst. Moments before the buzzer had sounded the yard was virtually silent. Luchewski, Singh and Brian Lawson were the only ones strolling across from the main building to a collection of Portakabins. Then … a vicious *BZZZZ*, followed by a bubbling throb of voices before –

CRASH!

The first door flew open with hundreds of chattering, squabbling kids streaming out of it, quickly followed by the CRASH! of another door at the other end of the building. Within seconds, the yard was smothered by what seemed to Luchewski to be millions of the little fuckers. A tsunami of teenagers. Sweaty, spotty, spitting horrors pouring their way out of the main gates and down the road or onto buses. Luckily the three of them had managed to clamber up onto the rickety steps of one of the ramshackle Portakabins before the madness unleashed itself.

'Noisy.' Luchewski found he had to raise his own voice to be heard.

'Tell me about it,' Lawson replied, mouthing the words clearly. He pushed the door to the classroom but it was stuck, so he gave it a second, harder nudge with his shoulder and practically fell into the building. The two police officers followed him in.

'Watch where you're standing. The floors are rotting. Put a foot in the wrong place and you'll come a cropper.'

There were still desks in the room and a pile of chairs stacked up against one wall. 'We're getting rid of these old dinosaurs. At last. They were only meant to be a temporary measure – only supposed to last for seven or eight years at most. But, of course, LEAs being LEAs, we've kept them in service for far longer than we should have.' He tested out the floor just in front of a dusty desk, before resting his backside on the table. 'It's only because we're becoming an –' he made air apostrophes with his fingers, '*academy* that we're scrapping them. Flavour of the month now, and we can access all the funding going. All the kids are getting iPads too. Not the staff, mind. Just the kids.'

Brian Lawson was in his mid-forties and wore a suit far too smart for a deputy head. Luchewski noticed that his shoes looked new and expensive too – John Rocha, perhaps? – and his aftershave seemed to fill the small room like a kind of thick soup. His beard was trimmed back to Gary Barlow stubble, and his hair given a slick, spiky life of its own with gel or mousse. Brian Lawson *was* Mr Male Grooming Products.

'I remember rooms like this at my old school,' Singh looked around to find another desk with the requisite number of legs to lean against. 'They'd have to bring in little gas heaters in the middle of winter. Then the windows would steam up and everybody'd get too hot. And the rain would bang on the roof so you could hardly hear the teacher.' She shivered. Luchewski couldn't tell whether it was due to the memory or the fact that the room was sodding freezing.

'The main building's not much better. An old Victorian cesspit, basically. Roof's shot to pieces. Windows all need replacing. Drains block whenever nobody's looking – and with twelve hundred kids on site, you can imagine the smell. A boiler that thinks it's Keith Moon. No,' Lawson gave a little smile to show perfectly veneered teeth, 'bomb the place, that's what I say! Level it and start again.'

'Yes.' Luchewski wiped a smudge off a window with the cuff of his jacket. He was keen to get the conversation back on track. 'You've taught here for how long, Mr Lawson?'

'All my career. Started here twenty-two years ago. A lowly history teacher, given all the classes nobody else wanted to teach.' He straightened up on the desk, and the whole room appeared to stagger underneath him. 'Became deputy head three years back.' He smiled a self-satisfied smile that made Luchewski want to tie the man's shoelaces together.

'Tell us about Alice Seagrove, sir. If you please.'

'Yes, of course. I'm sorry. Poor girl.'

'What sort of a girl was she?'

'Well, before you arrived I dug out her file – just to put a face to the name, so to speak. As soon as I saw it, I remembered. She was pretty. Very bubbly. Very confident. One of those girls who knew that she was going to go far. In fact, everybody knew it. An outgoing sort of girl.' He sighed. 'Of course that all changed when poor Louisa disappeared.'

'What happened then?' Singh repositioned herself on the wonky table.

'She became very withdrawn. Shied away from most things. Just concentrated on her schoolwork. You couldn't blame her, really. One of her best friends had just vanished into thin air. A difficult thing for a twelve-year-old girl to handle, I'd've thought. I think the parents tried counselling, therapy. But, as far as I can remember, she just kept her head down and worked her socks off.'

'You say *one* of her best friends. Were there many others?'

'She was very popular. Most of the other girls liked her. A couple of years later most boys would have liked her too, I'm sure of it. But boyfriends were never a part of her life after Louisa Gaudiano had gone. She'd have had no time for them.'

'Any girls in particular you can think of?'

'There were a couple. Being their personal tutor you get to know who likes who and who dislikes whoever else. Yes. Yes, they were a foursome. Alice, Louisa, and ...' His brow creased for the first time and Luchewski was secretly pleased to see that Lawson had not resorted to Botox. 'I ... er ... the names escape me – too many pupils over the years, I'm afraid – they start to blur after a while. Even the faces start to look the same. One year morphs into another. I'll try to get one of the secretaries to dig out a list of my tutor group for that year and get it emailed over to you, if you'd like.'

'Please.'

Singh fished a crumpled tissue out of her pocket before giving her nose a massive blow. 'It must have been difficult,' she said. 'For the whole school, I mean. Louisa Gaudiano's disappearance. Must have been a very difficult time.' She slipped the tissue back into her pocket.

'It was hell, Sergeant. The teachers and sixth formers organised search teams. We split the area up and combed the streets trying to find any sign of her, handing out pictures. That kind of thing. The police said that we shouldn't. That it was their job to do the searching. But what else could we do? You just feel useless. Impotent. And we weren't related. Imagine how Mr and Mrs Gaudiano felt, knowing that there was nothing they could do but sit and wait for the police to find their daughter.

Horrible. It's no wonder her dad did what he did in the end. I might have done the same thing had it been my child that had disappeared.' He looked to Luchewski. 'Wouldn't you, Inspector?'

As they made their way out of the Portakabin – the door wedging half-shut behind them – Luchewski spotted a couple of youngish-looking teachers smoking around the side of one of the other soon-to-be-demolished buildings. Lawson spotted them too.

'Mr Potter! Ms Wilkinson! You know the rules – smoking on school property is illegal,' he barked as though they were kids. 'Now stub it out!'

The woman sheepishly dropped her cigarette and looked up with apologetic eyes while the man tossed his fag churlishly to the ground, tutting as he did so. Luchewski tittered to himself, and Singh raised her eyebrows as the two teachers sloped off towards the main block.

'Tch. Art teachers,' Lawson mumbled to himself as he came down from the rotting wooden steps. 'Damned art teachers.'

Suicide was becoming inevitable. Everything was stacked against him. Everything. Even the bloody Job Centre was putting pressure on him to find a stupid bloody job. The woman behind the desk had given him a list of three jobs that she said were suitable, and that, this time, she wanted to see some evidence that he'd actually applied for them. Silly cow. Didn't she know that he didn't have time to let his life get all sucked away by the meaningless monotony and drudgery of work? Work was for morons. People with no spirit, no life. People whose only thoughts were of money, television and ready meals. Ants in a fucking ant farm. He could never become one of them.

Eating was not much of an issue – you could live quite well on brown rice, B vitamins and the occasional tin of beans. The problem was that canvases and paint were expensive. Seventy quid a week from the dole was barely sufficient to maintain his stock. And as they paid you in one big chunk every other week, he was finding that by the middle of the second week, the money had gone. Then the electricity meter would die and he'd be left cold and in the dark, waiting for the giro to be paid into his account.

Of course, he kept telling himself, that was the way that the truly great artists lived their lives. Spartan. In the very bosom of poverty itself. Gauguin, Vermeer, Van Gogh. All of them starving and desperate. It was the way of the true artist. The struggle. Those for whom it all came so easily were never *real* artists. They just got lucky, and luck had nothing whatsoever to do with real art.

Rejection was also *de rigueur* for the true creative genius. He'd spend days touting his work around the galleries of east London, but so far they had all turned him away. Especially that one up the road in Shoreditch. Three times he'd been back there with three different sets of work, but the greasy-looking man with the spray-on tan had smirked and shaken his head each time. Idiot. He'd choke on his fucking smirk when the name Andrew Cornish was famous.

Cornish got up from his unmade bed and slouched across to where the new canvases were stacked. Selecting one – a twelve-by-twelve-inch – he positioned it on the floor. This new collection of his was going to be the one to do it for him, he was certain. Positive. At least, it was this or nothing at all. He pulled off his jumper and knelt in front of the canvas. Looking up, he caught sight of himself in the wardrobe mirror. There was so little left of him. His ribs were jutting out from under his skin, and his neck looked as though it could snap given too much of a push. His face was now so sunken that the flesh had become virtually an irrelevance. Peel it all away and you wouldn't spot much of a difference. Gingerly, he touched the wounds running along his bony arm. Some of them were healing well. Others were taking their time, the scabs thick and risen. Reaching up to the table, he pulled down a razor blade.

'Prelude To Suicide Number 12,' he absentmindedly named the piece as the blade cut into his skin and the blood ran down his arm, dripping onto the canvas.

Four

It was Indian-summery and a couple of the constables had come in wearing short-sleeved shirts. Luchewski always thought that wearing short-sleeved shirts with ties looked ridiculous and ended up making you look like a real estate agent from Arizona. The sort of guy to say 'Phew-ee! It sure is hot today,' before wiping his sweaty brow with a neatly folded handkerchief. It wasn't the impression that Luchewski particularly wanted to create, so his light cotton jacket stayed firmly in position over his long-sleeved linen shirt.

Behind him, on the board, were four photographs. In the centre, an old mugshot of Bartholomew Kurtz, taken five weeks before his murder. His middle-aged face fat and slobbery. Alongside that was the original police shot of Nino Gaudiano, his handsome eyes sagging and bloodshot, his chin covered in dirty stubble. Below both was an old school photograph of Louisa Gaudiano – bright, smiling, fresh-faced in her newly ironed school uniform. And at the top of the board, a hurriedly acquired snapshot of Alice Seagrove. Taken on a sunny day in front of some trees. All teeth and hair and intelligence and confidence. Blissfully unaware of her impending appointment with a psychopath.

'What about the wife?' Detective Chief Inspector Woode had ventured far enough out of his office to attend the briefing. 'Teresa, is it? What does she say about it?'

Luchewski felt his hands slipping into his trouser pockets. 'She's been informed, of course. We've a PC over there with her now. Singh and I will take a run out this morning.'

'They had a son as well, didn't they? Where's he?'

Luchewski turned to Singh who dutifully opened her notebook and started to read off what she had previously written. 'Flight Lieutenant Angelo Gaudiano. Thirty-three. Served in Afghanistan with the RAF, 39 Squadron. Something of a hero by all accounts. Received the Distinguished Flying Cross for rescuing some children caught in crossfire. Flew his Chinook straight into the action and lifted them out.' The notebook slapped shut.

'What about the crime scene?' Burlock growled in his broad Yorkshire accent.

'What about the crime scene?' Luchewski replied.

'Are we looking for a copper or somebody close to the original investigation? I mean, whoever it is did a pretty bloody good job of recreating the Kurtz crime scene. Even down to the way the legs were positioned.'

Singh flipped open her notebook once again and cleared her throat. 'Before going home last night, I spent a little time with my very good friend Mr Google. It took about forty minutes, but in the end I managed to find at least eight different websites with images of Bartholomew Kurtz's dead body. Crime scene photos that had obviously been leaked some time over the last seventeen years.'

'Jesus Kid Jensen.' Woode shook his head.

'It was just a quick search. There are probably other sites that I didn't see. So, in answer to your question, Freddie, no. I don't think we can narrow it down to people involved in the Kurtz investigation. It could be anyone.'

Burlock nodded his head, impressed.

'I'm arranging for all the police notes from the original

investigation to be shipped over here. The school are also going to be sending over class lists from seventeen years ago. Might be a line of enquiry worth following. We'll also need to talk to her colleagues at the hospital. Everyone who knew her.'

The group of detectives in the briefing room went quiet and it was a particularly keen-looking one – tie and short-sleeved shirt intact – that edged forward and asked the question that everybody else was thinking.

'Is … is this a one-off, sir? D'you think? Do you think there … there might be others?'

'Other killings, you mean?'

The man nodded.

Luchewski shrugged his shoulders. 'I don't know. I hope not. But I don't know.' He turned and found himself staring into the happy face of Alice Seagrove.

Teresa Gaudiano – as was – had traded up. Big time. The house in Old Coulsdon was a long way from the rundown council flat in Collier's Wood that she had shared with Nino and their two children, and the clothes she wore were clearly expensive. Luchewski even thought that she looked younger than the last time he'd seen her. Creams and procedures, he told himself. Her face was particularly immobile, and she seemed to find it difficult to move her lips.

'I filed for divorce.' She strained to make the syllables as clear as possible, and Luchewski and Singh found themselves struggling to catch the words as they slightly whistled out of her mouth. 'Six months after Nino was sent down. Best thing I ever did, I'm afraid to say. I mean, poor Nino. He always found it difficult to control his emotions. When our little angel disappeared …' She paused, swallowing hard. 'When she disappeared, it was

29

the worst thing in the world. The worst thing in the world … it still is.' She tried a smile which Luchewski found unconvincing. 'What Nino did was unforgiveable. Absolutely unforgiveable. But he was always so impulsive. So bloody gung-ho about things. It's the fiery Italian in him. Do things first and think about the consequences later. That's what life was like with him. It could be very draining.'

Luchewski looked across the long garden to where a boy of about nine was busy kicking balls into a miniature football net. The boy was dressed in the red kit of a team that Luchewski – who knew absolutely nothing about football – couldn't identify. Arsenal? Liverpool? Could have been anything.

'As soon as the decree nisi came through, I handed in the notice on the flat and moved with Angelo to Balham. We just needed to get away from Collier's Wood. It was a place of bad memories. We needed a break.' She sipped some of her orange juice before putting the plastic cup back down on the garden table. 'That's when I got the job with Fredericks'.'

'Your husband's company?' Singh was still trying to catch each oddly sibilant word.

'Mmm. Robin's company. Well, I'm an executive now, of course, but back then it was pretty much just Robin's baby.' She seemed to swagger in her seat with pride. 'When I joined, there were only three offices. One on the Balham High Road – where I worked – one in Tooting and one in Streatham. Now we've got twelve offices all across south London. Winners of the London Independent Estate Agents Trophy three years running. Regional champions of the United Kingdom Property Service Industries Award in 2012.' She gave a smug little smile which looked as though it could rip her cheeks in two.

'How long have you and Mr Fredericks been married, Mrs Fredericks?' Hal stepped in to try and stop her face from splitting open.

'Eleven years, this October.'

'And you've the one son?' Luchewski nodded towards the soccer-playing boy.

'Yes. George. Our pride and joy. Robin has two daughters from his first marriage, of course. And I've got my Angelo.' She sighed. 'And my Louisa. Wherever she may be.'

'Mrs Fredericks,' Luchewski leaned forward in a sympathetic kind of way. 'I know it's difficult to talk about, but,' he lowered his voice a little, 'what do *you* think happened to Louisa?'

Her hand shook as she lifted the orange juice to her lips one more time. 'I don't know. I don't think that Kurtz ... took her life. I think that's pretty obvious to everyone except Nino. I hope ... I hope she's still alive somewhere. Happy. You know. It's not impossible, is it? Someone took her and she's been happy with them. A couple who couldn't have children. They've raised her as their own. Something like that.'

Singh frowned. 'Mrs Fredericks, Louisa was twelve when she disappeared. I don't think –'

Luchewski patted the sergeant on the knee as a way of shutting her up. 'You never know. You never know.'

They sat in near-silence for a short while, the only sound the occasional thud of a football being booted into a net. Luchewski was the one who kick-started the conversation again.

'Tell us about Alice Seagrove, Mrs Fredericks. How well did you know her?'

'Not at all, really. Alice and Louisa became friends at

31

secondary school. She came around to the flat a few times, but then after Louisa vanished, I don't recall ever seeing her again. It's only because of this awful business that I found out she'd become a doctor. Her mother must be devastated.'

Back in the car, Singh leapt on Luchewski before he'd even had time to plug in his seatbelt.

'What was that about, sir?'

'What?'

'That knee-tapping business back there. What was that for?'

Luchewski started the engine of the TT and they roared off the drive. 'Sorry, Singh, but I thought it best you kept quiet at that point.'

'Why?'

Sometimes she seems to have quite mad eyes, thought Luchewski. 'Because ...' His voice tailed off while he tried to think of a decent reply. 'Look, Singh. When you have kids, you'll understand.'

'Bit dismissive, sir. Don't you think?'

Luchewski found himself cringing. 'It's difficult to explain, Singh. The poor cow has managed to keep herself alive for the last seventeen years clinging to that thought. Who are we to disillusion her?'

Singh stared out of the window and tutted gently to herself. 'I thought we were the police. I thought we were the purveyors of truth and justice. Not just some sweep-it-under-the-carpet brigade. I thought that no matter how brutal reality can be, we have to face it – and help others face it – head on.'

Luchewski clicked the indicator to the right. 'Believe me, Singh. There's a time and place for the truth. And that wasn't it.'

* * *

The lecture room was packed full of the PGCE students, every one of them keen as mustard. Give it another month or two and a couple of weeks on teaching practice, thought Stevie, and they'll start dropping like shit from a birdcage. It was bound to happen. It always did. Over ten years ago now – Jesus, was it *really* over ten years ago? – he'd seen it happen on his degree course. Students with fresh folders, quirky pencil cases, and blemish-free DMs. All carefully constructed nonchalance and devil-may-care attitude. All sucked dry in a matter of months. Young people with little understanding of pace. Rush at something too hard, too fast, and you'll drop down flat. Quickly. But take your time and get there easily, gently, and you'll be fine. Pace yourself. That was the key to life. Knowing what speed to move at and when to move at it.

It helped that he was several years older than most of the students on the course. They all looked like children to him. There were even one or two – not too many, thank God – that still seemed to be having a bit of a ding-dong with acne, and some students looked no more than about fourteen to him. He half expected their mums or dads to pick them up at the end of the day, or to pop in with the packed lunches that they'd forgotten to bring. That was why he and Liz seemed to latch onto one another from the very first moment.

Liz was in her early thirties and wore one of the weirdest hats that Stevie had ever seen. It was brown and shapeless with what looked like those little fly things that fishermen have stitched into the fabric. And she never took it off. Even during the tutorials, it was still wedged permanently onto her head so that anybody sitting directly behind her had to keep looking around it to see. Her face was round but pretty, her eyes large and deep-set. Her

33

hair – what you could see of it – was sliced into a dominatrix-type bob, and her make-up was perhaps a little too much.

And she was mad. Completely and utterly, unrestrainedly mad. Sitting next to her on the first day, Stevie found himself crippled with stifled laughter as she opened up and told him everything about herself. One broken marriage to someone she referred to as 'The Bastard'; two kids – eight and six – who lived on bars of Dairy Milk; a mother with the first signs of dementia who kept leaving the fridge open at night 'so the little cows can get in'; a desperate feeling of having wasted her life, hence the Open University degree in English Literature; the part-time job in a doctor's surgery; the way her next-door neighbour lined up his garden gnomes on the wall so that they looked as if they were watching her every move; a pet cat with a diseased ear that winced each time it came in through the cat flap. Everything.

'Aye, aye. Here he comes. Mr Trousers.' Liz had started to refer to one of the lecturers – Dr Danborough – as 'Mr Trousers', though Stevie didn't quite know why. 'Be prepared for an hour and a half of monotonous droning.'

It was true. Danborough did have an incredibly tedious voice. The fact that he was supposed to be showing students how to teach made it all the more horrific. Surely one of the first things you should be able to do as a teacher was to make your voice as varied and as audible as possible? Raise it a little? Danborough just mumbled on, seemingly with a sense that there was no point in bothering any more. His lectures were, more or less, just an extended sigh of despair. Everybody's heart seemed to sink when they saw who was going to be taking the class.

'Biro at the ready, Stevie boy.' Liz gave him a wicked

wink. 'He won't be handing out any notes. He's too depressed to remember how to use the photocopier.'

Stevie looked across the throng of students. Pens were primed over Hello Kitty stationery. Massive, cool spectacles were perched on noses ready to take in the inevitable, endless round of Powerpoint slides. Death by Powerpoint, another lecturer had described it as – not that Mr Trousers would pay any attention to that.

Suddenly, from across the room, slightly to the left and further down the tiers of seats, a young guy turned back and caught Stevie's eye. Neither of them looked away, and the guy gave Stevie a gigantic smile. Stevie grinned before the boy with sweeping blond hair and dazzlingly blue eyes winked at him.

Stevie felt an immediate shiver up his spine, a cold spasm in his belly and the air rush out of his chest. The boy smiled again before turning to face the front where Mr Trousers was struggling to get the computer to work properly.

If the room hadn't had air-conditioning, Stevie felt, he would have melted.

Alice Seagrove's killer was eating chips. Lovely big fat juicy chips with plenty of salt and vinegar on – like chip shops used to make before they got all lazy and bought in bags of ready-cut frozen ones.

Poor little Alice, he thought. She'd struggled hard. When the time came to slip the cord around her neck, she'd struggled like a demon. Twisting and kicking out with her one good leg – it had been tempting to break that one as well. But in the end she gave up. Like a good girl. Let the rope do its magic and take her out of this dreadful world. It was the best thing for her. For all of them, in fact.

A pigeon strutted along in front of him, its head bobbing back and forth like a Nazi's. He resisted the urge to kick it across the road and continued on his way. He couldn't be distracted. Not now. Not when he had so much work ahead of him.

Five

Luchewski picked up the catalogue that was blocking the front door, slammed the door shut and wandered through to the sitting room. He tossed his jacket over the back of an armchair and took off his tie. His whole body felt knackered and it was tempting to just lie down on the sofa with a couple of cushions behind his head and allow himself to doze off.

But he didn't.

Instead he went through to the kitchen and poured himself an unhealthily large tumbler of whisky before sitting back onto the sofa and ripping off the plastic cover of the catalogue.

Firmin's Auctions
Purveyors of the Unique
Articles and Items from the Worlds of Radio,
Theatre and Television
Next Auction – Saturday December 18th

Luchewski was on the mailing lists for loads of catalogues like this. Auction houses that dealt in the miscellaneous rubbish that floated about – the detritus of show business. Costumes and broken props from stage shows that never got anywhere, yellowing scripts from politically incorrect old radio comedies, reels of unused footage from dodgy old television programmes.

He flicked through the glossy booklet, tutting and snorting at some of the ridiculous old crap they were trying to palm off on people. After a few minutes he flicked it aside. There was nothing of his father's in there.

Bored, he leant over and pressed the 'Play' button on his answer phone. It beeped and told him there were five messages on it for him.

Beep. 'Harold. It's Elizabeth.' His sister always called him Harold nowadays and always referred to herself as Elizabeth. Had done ever since the accident. It was as if by using their full names she could keep him at bay, avoid having to deal with him. He was after all, in her mind at least, partly responsible for their parents' deaths. 'Harold ... if you're there, pick up the phone.' She hardly ever phoned him these days, and he was just starting to worry that something must be wrong when – 'Has Lenny Schinowitz spoken to you?' He sighed. It was just some stupid rubbish about his father's estate. Someone wanting permission to use one of his tricks or something. Nothing much. Nothing to worry about. On the message, his sister sighed before putting the phone down.

Beep. 'Harry, my boy. Lenny here.' Speak of the devil. 'I ... er ... need to talk to you. In person, my boy. Shouldn't be done over the phone.' There was something uncertain in the old man's voice that made Luchewski frown. 'You and Elizabeth. Together ... er ... I think. I'll try again later.'

Beep. 'Harold? Are you there, Harold?' His sister again. 'Pick up if you're there. Lenny needs to talk to us about something. Something about Dad. Says it's something big.' Another long pause. 'Oh for Christ's sa –'

Beep. 'Look, Harold, I've booked us an appointment with Lenny tomorrow evening at six. At his offices. He's going to stay behind to see us. So whatever you do, make sure you're there. Right?'

Beep. 'Er ... hello, Harry. Elizabeth's going to come and see me tomorrow night. After the office has closed. Be a good idea if you'd come along too. OK, my boy? Yes?' A pause, as if Lenny Schinowitz was expecting an answer. 'Erm ...' – a slightly embarrassed 'erm', Luchewski thought – 'see you then. Maybe.'

Click.

Luchewski leaned back on the sofa and took a large gulp from the glass. Something big? About Dad? What was going on?

Normally, he would have ignored any message from his sister and only paid the slightest bit of attention to whatever that old shyster Lenny Schinowitz had to say. But something in their voices ... the way they were both so desperate to get hold of him. It made him uneasy. A little bit scared.

He got up and went back to the kitchen to fill the tumbler for the second – and probably not the last – time that night.

Seventeen years ago

The room smelled of paint, Alice thought, as she bustled in through the door with the rest of the kids. Paint and Alpine Mountain air freshener. You could almost taste it on your tongue and at the back of your throat. It was as if the caretaker had been busy all summer straightening up the tired old classrooms, desperate to trick the Year Sevens into believing that the school was flash and new and free of germs. One look at the soggy brown water stain on the ceiling and you weren't fooled for long.

'That's it. Come on in,' the teacher bellowed over the squeaking of chairs, the mutter of voices and the rustle of brand new blazers. 'Find somewhere to sit. That's it. Hurry up.' He was young with a smooth face and a stiff quiff on top of his head. Alice wondered if the smell wasn't so much air freshener as the excessive amount of hairspray used to keep the man's quiff fixed in place. It almost glistened under the glare of the lights.

The tables were arranged in even rows and Alice looked around to see if there was an empty one for her and Katie. Spotting one on the other side of the room, she poked Katie's arm and made her way across, squeezing past chairs and schoolbags. Just before they got there, however, a tallish girl with long, straight black hair slipped onto one of the seats and gave Alice a triumphant little grin. Alice sighed. Sitting at the table in front, another dark-haired girl – this one with a friendlier smile – proffered the empty chair next to her.

'You sit there. I'll sit back here,' Katie said, taking up the seat next to the triumphant girl. Alice nodded and dumped her bag on the floor, kicking it under the desk.

'Busy, isn't it?' The friendly girl next to her gave another warm smile. 'I knew it would be ... they always tell you it will be busier than your old school, the teachers, I mean, but this is mad.'

'What school are you from?' Alice fidgeted with the starchy skirt her mother had picked up from Primark.

'Oldcastle. What about you?'

'High Park.'

'Oh.'

Clap. Clap.

The teacher was trying to retake control of the mumbling masses.

'OK. Settle down. Settle down. We've got lots to get through.' The noise subsided. 'Could you all get a pen out please. I'm going to hand out your timetables and I'd like you to make a note of certain things on them – room changes and stuff. So, pens out.'

Everybody shuffled down to the bags lying at their feet and unzipped them, fishing around for pencil cases.

'What's your name by the way?' the girl asked as she slapped her pencil case on the desk.

'Alice. What's yours?'

'Louisa. People just call me Lou. You haven't got a pencil sharpener, have you?'

41

Six

Big Issue had seen him before. He was sure of it. No, he was certain of it. He didn't know how or where from, but he was certain he'd seen him before.

The morning was warming up and he'd picked out the pennies from his threadbare pockets and dropped them almost one by one onto the counter. The man in the shop rolled his eyes as he slid them into his hand, adding them up as he went.

'Ten more.'

'Wha?'

'Another ten. You need another ten.'

Big Issue huffed and managed to find a few more sticky coppers somewhere in his clothing. After he'd finished counting them, the man behind the counter wiped his hands on his trousers.

'OK.'

Big Issue snatched up the bottle of White Ace and teetered his way out of the shop. The Mile End Road was busy as always and people swerved to avoid him as he made his way along to his favourite spot. Squatting on the ground in the alleyway between Betfred and a bathroom tile shop, he grasped the top of the bottle and twisted hard, making the cider fizz as it opened.

The first mouthful was always the best, he thought, as he slugged the bottle upwards. No matter what time of the day. Everybody else was off to work, but here he was at quarter to nine in the morning starting the day as it meant to go on – an increasingly hazy round of begging, drinking and vomiting. Punctured by the occasional punch-up. It was just how he liked it. No more nine to five for him.

It was as he was taking his seventh or eighth swig of the cider that he saw him. It was barely for a second as the man passed the alleyway, but in that insignificant blip of time, a spark somewhere in the deep dark recesses of Big Issue's fuggy brain leapt across synapses and he thought: *I know him.*

Stumbling up, White Ace bottle gripped in his right hand, Big Issue made his way back onto the pavement. The man was moving quickly. Too quick for him to follow at this time in the morning, so he watched as he disappeared into the crowds further along the road.

Big Issue wondered where it was he knew the man from. He couldn't have been in the unit with him, could he? No. He was far too young. Perhaps from one of the awful jobs he'd had after falling out? There were too many of them to count, and most of them he simply couldn't remember.

But he definitely knew him. No doubt about it.

Shrugging to himself, Big Issue retreated back into the alleyway to finish up his bottle of cider just as the man from Betfred cast him a filthy look as he unlocked the shop door.

'That's vree! Vree men on bikes! Ha ha ha!'

Josh was doing his best Count-from-Sesame-Street impression as he cut through the ambers and swerved past the bikes trying not to be late for school for the eighteenth time that week. 'Vree cyclists! Ha ha ha!'

Neither Sophie nor Zak were impressed.

'Dad,' Zac looked up at him from the passenger seat. 'Er … what are you doing?'

Josh spotted another cyclist. 'Four! Four cra-zee bikers! Ha ha ha!'

'Dad?'

'The Count. From Sesame Street.'

'Who?'

'What?' Sophie leaned forward from the safety of her booster seat.

'Sesame Street. You know.' He realised they wouldn't know what he was on about. 'Oh. Just a programme. An old programme. From the telly.' He zoomed past an old woman climbing out from her car.

'Er, Daddy,' Sophie's voice had a tinge of the critical about it. 'The sign said "thirty". Thirty miles pen hour. You're going …' she leaned forward again. 'You're going more than forty miles pen hour.'

'*Per* hour,' Zac corrected his little sister. 'It's forty miles *per* hour.'

Josh looked down and saw he was going about forty-three. He thought it best to lie again. 'No. No I'm not, darling. It's the angle you're looking from. I'm only really going about thirty-five.'

'That's still more than thirty miles pen hour, Daddy.' The tut-tut look she gave him in the rear view mirror made him feel a momentary spasm of guilt. 'A policeman can still arrest you and put you in prison.'

'Anyway, she's right,' Zac gave him a wry smile. 'You *are* going over forty miles an hour.'

'Am not.'

'You are.'

'I'm not, I tell you. It's the angle you're sitting at. I'm sitting directly in front of the dashboard and I can see that the little hand is pointing at about the thirty-five mark.'

Everybody felt the car jolt as Josh deliberately took his foot off the pedal.

'Daddy!'

'Look! There's another one.' A courier in a shiny black helmet and even shinier Lycra shorts crossed their path. 'What's that now? Six is it?'

'Five,' Sophie replied sounding bored.

'Five! Five fantastic cyclists! Ha ha ha!'

'Are we going to be late again?'

'Late? No. Not if we can get through the next light without stopping.'

They turned the corner, the next set of lights directly up ahead of them.

'Oh, shit.' The green had turned to amber.

'Daddy!'

Zac laughed. 'I'm going to tell Mum you swore. *Again.*'

The car rolled to a stop behind a large white Lexus.

'Bugger and balls!'

'Daddy! That's rude.'

Josh swivelled about in his seat. 'I know. Shit, shit, bugger and balls.'

Sophie gave a big, wet raspberry snort and clamped her hand to her mouth. Zac wriggled with laughter, nearly banging his head on the glove compartment.

'Shit, shit, bugger and balls! Shit, shit, bugger and balls!'

'Shit, shit, bugger and balls!' The children joined in with the chant. 'Shit, shit, bugger and balls!'

'Shall I put the window down so that everybody outside can hear us?' Josh taunted.

'No!' screamed Sophie.

'Yes!' shouted Zac.

'SHIT, SHIT, BUGGER AND BALLS! SHIT, SHIT,

BUGGER AND BALLS!'

By the time the lights turned green again, Josh was wiping the tears from his cheeks. So what if they were going to be a few minutes late for school again? So bloody what? School wasn't *that* important.

Luchewski couldn't believe how many meeting rooms there were in this particular part of the hospital. If only they would strip out the leather swivel chairs, smash up the oak-veneer tables and burn the flipcharts, they could easily fit in another couple of dozen beds. If every hospital in the country did the same thing, the pressures on the NHS would disappear overnight, he thought. All part of the arse backwards, upside-down world we now find ourselves living in.

Teams of detectives had taken over the rooms for the morning and were slowly working their way through the staff. Interviewing them. Questioning them. Running over Alice Seagrove's last few days and weeks. Piecing her last known movements together.

Luchewski and Singh seemed somehow to find themselves in one of the pokier meeting rooms with a window that stared out at a grubby looking brick wall and not much else, and a table with so many coffee cup stains it looked like a gathering of Olympic flags. The nurse in front of them shifted in her seat.

'So ... er ... Nurse Defalco. The last time you saw Alice Seagrove? When was that?'

The nurse was plump and pretty in a way that made it difficult to pinpoint her exact age. She could have been in her early twenties or her mid-forties. A quick glance and you'd never tell. But her voice gave her away.

'Last week. Monday, I s'pose,' she answered in a growl that betrayed years and years of smoking. As

47

Luchewski looked closer, he could see the mass of tiny red broken capillaries that outlined the top of her cheeks. 'On the evening shift. The "moron" shift we calls it, on account of the idiots who come in covered in cuts and stabs and broken noses and the like. The morons.' She grinned like it was a good joke. 'Late nights. Exhausting. Knock yer for six.'

'And how was she? In herself?' Singh gave that tilt-of-the-head-type show of concern that Luchewski noticed she sometimes did. 'Was she her usual self?'

Nurse Defalco shrugged. 'S'pose. Dunno.' Her eyes scanned the room. 'Dunno. S'pose. Didn't seem no different to me. Always kept herself to herself. Friendly enough, y'know. Worked hard.' She looked down at the floor and tried to kick something sticky up off the parquet with her foot. 'Seemed … OK.'

'Any incidents with staff or patients recently that you think we should know about?' Luchewski scratched an itch on the tip of his nose.

'Er … no. No. Not that I know of.'

'How long have you worked here, Nurse Defalco?'

'Too long.' She grinned and showed a row of yellow teeth, before allowing her face to fall into a frown. 'Terrible, ain't it? Poor girl. Like I said, seemed nice enough. Can't believe anyone'd wanna do her over. Don't seem right. Prob'ly an old boyfriend.' She pointed towards Singh's notebook. 'You wanna write that down. Bet I'm right. Usually is, ain't it? Jealous boyfriend or husband. Jilted or summat. Can't take rejection. Like all men.' A flick of the eyeballs to Luchewski. 'She moved on. He finds out. Smashes a few beer bottles. Goes round late one night and … bang. One less junior doctor in the NHS. Classic.'

Luchewski sighed to himself. Everyone was a

detective. A bog-rate Bergerac with bad breath. Everyone. He knew that many people in the hospital, no matter who they were – from the yawning orderlies through to the silk-suited consultants via the bedbound, spewing terminals – would have their own opinion on what had happened and that sometimes even the most solid and undeniable of evidence would not be able to change their minds.

Nurse Defalco was one of them.

'Thank you, Nurse Defalco,' Luchewski stood up and straightened his jacket. 'Let us know if you think of anything else.' He grinned his best fake grin before turning to stare at the brick wall outside the window.

'I wouldn't want her looking after me when I'm ill,' Singh said, slapping the notebook onto the coffee-stained table. 'Completely off her head.' She came alongside Luchewski and watched a cloud of steam rising up from an air vent far below. 'You'd think the NHS might actually vet the people they have working for them.'

'The people who run the NHS don't actually care who works for them. Not nowadays. As long as waiting lists and overheads are down, they wouldn't care less if Genghis Khan took up residency as an Ear, Nose and Throat specialist. They let just about anybody in. And if the doctors have MBAs and experience of running their own auditing firms or tax consultancies, even better.'

Singh smiled. 'Still. Best if your nurses aren't mad. Like that one clearly was.'

'Mad, yes.' Luchewski turned to face Singh. 'And a liar too.'

Down in the small room where the kettle was always on the boil and the biscuit tin always empty, Nurse Defalco poured herself a hot cup of the nastiest coffee that the 99p Shop stocked. There was no one else in the dayroom and she was glad of the quiet. Usually there was a huddling cluster of nurses, chattering and giggling around one of the tables. But not at the moment. Thankfully.

That copper had shaken her up. No reason why. He just had. His eyes peering inside her. That was how it had felt. Pushing straight into her, trying to spot her lies. Digging under her skin until she wriggled like a worm. She'd come out of the boardroom shaking.

Not that she'd really *lied*, of course. Just sort of skirted around the truth. Yes, that was what she had done, she told herself. Just skirted around the truth. Edged herself along the kerb and turned her back to the truth. It was surprisingly easy to avoid.

Feeling pleased with herself, she fell back onto one of the institutional grey chairs, took an over-enthusiastic swig of her coffee and spilt it all down the front of her uniform.

Chapter Seven

Nino Gaudiano was finding it difficult to sleep. And it wasn't just the sun streaming through the tightly pulled curtains that was responsible.

He had left work just after six – an hour after the sun had started peering over the horizon – and as soon as he had left behind the monotonous comfort of emptying bins and wiping down desks and hoovering office floors, his mind had slipped back to thinking about it. About her. About them both. His Louisa and Alice Seagrove.

He couldn't remember anything about the bus ride home, nor the two-hundred-yard walk from the bus stop to his flat. He couldn't remember the half-burned cheese on toast he'd ate at the kitchen table. He couldn't even remember the strip wash he'd had before slipping into his bed. All the while his mind had flittered about like a leaf in the breeze, snatching at any thought or memory of those two little girls together.

And he just couldn't fall asleep.

Thoughts of them in the flat he'd shared with Teresa and the kids, listening to some terrible song on the radio. Thoughts of them being picked up from sports day in the back of his dodgy old Astra. Thoughts of them skipping about in the yard together whilst the adults all sat inside waiting for the teachers during a parents' evening. Relentless, never-ending memories.

He sat up and threw a pillow across the room. He felt

as useless now as he'd felt all those years ago. Useless. Like a withered limb.

That had to change. He had to do something. The police were never any good. They were as useless as he felt. They'd poke about a bit, make it look as if they were doing something, then give it all up and go back to lining their own pockets. No, they'd never really helped when it came to his Louisa, and they wouldn't really help now.

He was going to have to do it all himself.

Again.

Hard-boiled, heartless journalist Laurie Frasier – tough uncompromising truth-seeker with a steely eye and a bloodthirsty determination to get to the centre of any story – was crying.

Sitting in the editing booth she watched the footage her colleague was putting together for tonight's edition. She'd overheard the story and managed to sneak in to watch the film while her colleague had gone for lunch. Over and over she watched it.

'… have named the victim as twenty-nine-year-old Alice Seagrove, a junior doctor at –'

Whirr.

'… the victim as twenty-nine-year-old Alice Seagrove, a junior –'

Whirr.

'… twenty-nine-year old Alice Seagrove –'

Whirr.

'Alice Seagrove –'

The tears came hard and quick, running down her cheeks and dripping onto her black trousers. It was horrible. Who could do such a thing?

It was like being twelve again.

Seventeen years ago

'Firstly, let me introduce myself. My name is Mr Lawson, and this,' he gave an elaborate little wave, 'is my classroom. B1:29. Make a note of that. Mr Lawson. B1:29.'

The girl with the long dark hair sitting behind Alice snorted. 'What a tosser!' she whispered.

'Now I know that many of you are feeling a little bit scared, a little bit "whooooa, hold on, I'm a bit frightened!" sort of thing.' He wobbled his hands in the air.

'Fucking hell!' the long-haired girl whispered again. Alice stifled her laugh.

'But I want you to know that, being your personal tutor, I am here for you. All of you.' He smiled and seemed to concentrate his smile in the direction of Louisa. 'If you feel a bit lost or worried, or just not sure where you should be or when you need to be there, simply track me down – I'm usually here, room B1:29, if I'm not mainlining coffee in the staffroom, that is – and let me know.' He seemed to wink at the entire class.

'This guy thinks he's got a stick of rock up his arse,' the long-haired girl hissed. 'Thinks he's the dog's nuts. Fucking tosser.'

'Erm, sorry ...' Mr Lawson was pointing at the girl. 'It's Miss ...' he consulted a sheet of paper on his desk.

'It's Miss Frasier, isn't it? Laurie?'

'Sir.'

'Sorry, Laurie, but would you mind not talking while I'm addressing the class? It *is* a bit distracting, you know, hearing you mumbling away there.'

'Yes, sir. Sorry, sir.'

'That's all right.'

Then, under her breath, 'Knob.'

Chapter Eight

Back at Hartshorn House, Luchewski found a small pile of folders sitting on his desk with a Post-It note stuck to the top one.

"As requested, Mr L.

C –. big kisses!"

Corrie had had the folders dug out and shipped over to Beckenham. Luchewski scrunched up the little yellow sticky note and tossed it at the bin, narrowly missing it. He picked up the top file and started reading.

"Missing Persons – Louisa Gaudiano (No. 9763654/A) – Ongoing"

Ongoing? Yeah, right. In *theory* the case was ongoing but in practice it was long dead. Left to rot on a shelf along with all the other embarrassments that the Met deliberately chose to not remember.

Luchewski pulled the elastic band from around the file. It was thick and full of photographs of the youth club where Louisa Gaudiano was last seen by her friends, and of the streets around Collier's Wood and Wandle Park. Luchewski recognised many of them. There were statements given by the friends, and documents making reference to the CCTV footage logged away in another basement somewhere. Luchewski made a note to ask Corrie to chase that up too.

As he pulled the miscellaneous sheets of paper out of the manila file, he noticed that many of the documents were not in the right order, as if they had been rammed back in without any thought. Luchewski tutted. He wasn't the most ordered of people and usually couldn't really give a monkey's about the anal pettiness of such things, but seeing this young girl's file so ... well ... deflowered in that way made him feel oddly sick. So before reading them through he spent a few minutes straightening them up.

As he read he kept a list on a sheet of A4 of all the important facts that he felt he should have at his fingertips. By the time he got to the end of the file, the sheet of A4 looked like this:

Louisa Gaudiano Disappearance

08/06/1999
All Saints Road Youth Club – Collier's Wood

Longley Road secondary pupils in attendance:

- *Louisa G.*
- *Kathryn Thompson*
- *Alice Seagrove*
- *Laurie Frasier*
- *Darren Westlake*
- *Joshua Woodington*
- *Leon Derry*
- *Conrad Phillips*

(Another 24 local children accounted for. Six other adults, inc. Pastor and his wife)
Disco – Mr Zippy (DJ)

Disco starts 7 p.m.
Around 7:30/7:45 – argument with LF over money – storms out.
Seen walking towards Wandle Park – crying – by Mrs Jean Smith – then never seen again.
?????????

Luchewski sat back in his chair and tapped the rubber part of his pencil against his teeth. How could a bright, street-smart twelve-year-old girl walk out of a busy disco on a sunny June evening and just disappear?

The pictures in the file were dull-looking. Flat and uninteresting. It was only seventeen years ago but the technology had moved on so much. Cameras on mobile phones were much sharper than that these days. It all looked so oddly dated. So old-fashioned. So wrong.

Luchewski jumped up from his chair and opened his door onto the large office filled with besuited coppers.

'Singh!' he shouted. 'Finish that sandwich. We're going for a drive.'

Luchewski parked the TT on All Saints Road, near to the old church hall that nearly two decades ago hosted teenie discos and children's birthday parties. A couple of deflating balloons sellotaped to the top corner of the services board showed that, at least in that respect, nothing much had changed.

They got out of the car. The air felt warm and Luchewski slightly loosened his tie and threw his jacket back onto the driver's seat. Leaning in, he scooped up the manila file on the rear seat.

'So this is where she was last seen?' Singh didn't seem to notice how warm it was and pulled her jacket closer around her.

'Not quite.' He opened the file and fished out a sheet of paper. 'Let's walk it.'

They made their way down All Saints Road, the cute, window-boxed Victorian houses on their right. Traffic was light at this time of day and they talked easily and with hushed voices, as if talking of these things too loudly in these parts might stir up unwanted ghosts.

'At around 7:45ish, a ... Jean Smith spotted her crying around about ...' they walked a little further to a junction, 'here. Smith says it looked as though Louisa was carrying on down towards East Road at the end.'

'Who was Jean Smith?' Singh asked. 'I mean, was she reliable?'

'Dunno. She was a sixty-one-year-old florist at the time. That'd make her about eighty now. So if she's not dead she's probably losing her marbles or her memory, or both. No point even thinking about chasing it up. You'd probably just waste an entire afternoon finding out about the best way to freshen up wilting carnations or something.'

They carried on until they came onto East Road. Brand new houses – big flash double-garaged ones – had sprouted up on one side and opposite those was a row of Dutch-roofed 1960s terraced houses. Both sides of the street seemed to be staring angrily at each other as if neither thought that the other should be there.

'She would have gone north here ...' They turned and wandered slowly up the street. A couple of net curtains twitched. 'And turned just here. None of these buildings would have been here then. It was mostly rundown industrial units.'

They slipped down a turning into the small lane that ran alongside the northern end of Wandle Park. 'Now, it's unlikely she actually went *into* the park – it would have taken her the wrong way home. And anyway, according to the CCTV records, there was no footage of her coming out at the main entrance on the High Street. So all we can assume is that she carried on past this gate along the road towards home, which isn't all that far away now.'

After a short while they stopped outside a block of shabby flats. 'And that's where she lived. With her family. Louisa and her brother Angelo, dad Nino, mum Teresa.' He lowered the manila file and looked around the street. 'How long did it take us to walk that?'

'Er … seven minutes? Eight?'

'Not even that, let's face it. Five or six at the most. A five- or six-minute walk. So how can a healthy, intelligent young girl like Louisa Gaudiano disappear from view over such a short distance and in such a short amount of time?'

'Robert Black.'

'Eh?'

'The paedophile Robert Black. It couldn't have been him, of course. He'd been arrested years before the Gaudiano girl disappeared. But someone like him. Somebody who could snatch a child off the street in a matter of seconds without anybody noticing.'

Luchewski remembered Black. Child rapist and murderer, given four life sentences for the murders of young girls. He would pull alongside them in his van and push them into the back, stuffing them inside sleeping bags. The whole affair would take him no more than thirty seconds. Brazen daytime kidnapping.

'Was it someone she knew?' Singh continued. 'Did she get into the car willingly? Without thinking?'

Luchewski looked up then down the road. A new Polo was struggling to slot itself into a tight parking space just outside the flats.

'Yes. She must have done. It must have been,' he answered. 'It's the only explanation.'

Luchewski started walking away from the flats, past the turning down which they had just come and along Denison Road. Singh eventually caught up with him.

'Where're we going?'

'You'll see.'

They both carried on down Denison Road before turning onto Carter Road. The whole area was slightly more suburban and rundown than the flashier flats that had been erected the other side of the park. It was clearly collection day, as Luchewski and Singh had to negotiate the stinky green wheelie bins that straddled the pavement, and the little black boxes filled with empty wine bottles and Chicken Tonight jars.

Eventually they came onto Boundary Road and, after a minute for Luchewski to get his bearings, found themselves standing outside one of the houses. Luchewski felt oddly pleased to be back, like reliving some horrible nightmare that you'd managed to overcome, staring it in the face and showing it who was boss. What had happened here had plagued his sleep for years afterwards. He hadn't gone for counselling – hadn't even been offered it – but after a while he had moved on. Too many other horrible things to see and hear about.

'Kurtz?' Singh guessed.

Luchewski nodded.

The house looked different. The door was now a uPVC white effort with roses twisting up the glass. The windows, too, had been replaced at some point over the last seventeen years. The front garden was neat and trimmed, with toddler toys lined up neatly along the path.

'He lived this near to it all?'

'Yeah. Yards away.'

'Jesus …'

'I know.'

Singh's brain was whizzing. 'Maybe he *did* have something to do with it. If he lived this near.'

'Living next door to Joseph Goebbels doesn't make you a Nazi, Singh.'

'No, I realise that, but … Jesus.'

'There's something else.' He marched off again.

'Are we ever going to stop walking?' Singh asked, finally feeling the warmth and unbuttoning her jacket.

'One more stop, I promise.'

At the end of the street, a railway bridge took pedestrians over onto a different road. They both went over the bridge and down a short lane before coming out onto a busy main road.

'Where are we now?' Singh tried to see a street sign.

'Look over there.'

Luchewski pointed to a massive building just opposite. It was one of a number of ramshackle buildings, together with a spiky green fence around it and cars dotted around the edges.

'What is it?'

'It's where we were this morning,' Luchewski replied. 'The hospital. St George's Hospital. Where Alice Seagrove worked.'

'Again. It's so close.'

Luchewski nodded. 'Yeah. I know.' The cars sped by and buses hissed their doors open and shut before jutting out into the traffic. 'I think the answer to all this lies somewhere in these small streets.'

Back at Hartshorn House, Burlock's sergeant Robbie Green nabbed Luchewski as he strode through the office. He flapped a sheet of paper under the inspector's nose.

'Alice Seagrove's mobile phone records.'

'Anything?'

'Well …' Green always looked like he'd had a really good scrub and the scent of carbolic soap hung around him like a Doctor Who scarf. His desk was always perfectly set out, too, and Luchewski and Burlock had, in secret, expressed their concerns to one another. 'OCD' was a phrase that always crept up in those conversations. 'The typical things, you know. Mum, Dad, work, couple of friends, couple of colleagues. But there is one number that comes up a few times and only in the last month or so. A mobile. It's unregistered. She phones them, never the other way around.'

'Did we ever find her phone?'

'No. He must have taken it with him. Probably had his name in her contacts folder.'

'Can the network access her contacts folder? Get at the names?'

'Wouldn't have thought so. That would have been stored on the phone itself. I'll check it out.'

'How many calls?'

'Seven.'

'Have you tried it yet?'

Green shook his head. 'Waiting for your say-so.'

Luchewski took the sheet of paper from him. 'Let me.'

Green followed Luchewski into his office where Luchewski grabbed his phone, pressed '1' for an outside line and then tapped the phone number in. A pause. A single solitary ring and then –

Welcome. The person you are calling is busy at …

Luchewski hung up. 'Answerphone.' He handed the paper back to Green. 'Chase it up with the network. See what information they can give you. Try to find out where it was bought and when. That kind of thing.'

'Sir.'

Green turned and left, opening the door handle with the sleeve of his jacket as he went.

Laurie Frasier's mind was not on her work. Not at all. She was supposed to be reporting from the site of an industrial accident in Esher – a worker's leg had been crushed when a roll of sheet metal had come off its mooring – but she could barely string the script together. The cameraman and the soundman were starting to look a bit pissed off.

'What is it, Laurie?' Jack the cameraman with the ridiculous hipster beard asked with false concern. 'You're not focusing today.'

'Yeah,' Leo the runty little boom operator agreed. 'You're not right today. You don't seem right, my love.'

Laurie rubbed her eyes with the back of her wrist.

'Oh and now you've gone and smeared your mascara all over your face ...' Jack was finding it difficult not to tut out loud.

'Bit of bad news ... not really up to this at the moment.'

'Yeah, but we still got ninety seconds of airtime we need to fill, don't we, Jack?'

'We've got to get it down. I've filmed all the external shots we're ever going to need. We just need you to do your bit now.' His eyes were trying to egg her on. 'Need to get on if we're going to edit it all nicely for tonight's edition.'

She sniffed hard. It was embarrassing being all girly and hopeless. Letting them see her like this. It wasn't the side of her she liked the world to witness. She was tough and hard and a force to be reckoned with. Not a snivelling mess.

'OK. Just ... just give me a minute.' She found her bag

and pulled her phone out. 'Five minutes. I want to make a phone call to someone. After that, we'll go for it. Get it done. Knock some shit into this story.'

She pretended to be tough once again and she could tell by their reaction that they were relieved. That was the problem with trying to be something you weren't. People get used to it, then they don't like the real you whenever that leaks out. They come to depend on your alter ego.

And so do you.

'Five minutes,' Jack said.

She tottered off on her heels to a place just around the corner, where she proceeded to dial the same number Luchewski had dialled not half an hour before.

Chapter Nine

Luchewski lifted the pile of files from the Louisa Gaudiano disappearance case and moved them to another less cluttered part of his desk. As he did so, a sheet of paper that had been hiding underneath them fluttered down to the ground. He bent over and picked it up. It was a printout of an email that Corrie had left on his desk even earlier in the day.

To: Met Police Force (DI Luchewski)
From: Brian Lawson

Mr Luchewski,

I've gone through the records of the year that Louisa Gaudiano joined the school. If you remember, I was the form tutor for the group she was in, so if anybody can tell you who she was friends with at the time of her disappearance, it'll be me.

Luchewski recoiled a little at the smugness of that sentence, remembering the overly groomed teacher with the wafting aftershave, before realising that it was entirely suitable.

I'll give you the whole list of pupils in the group but I'll stick an asterisk next to the girls who were part of Louisa Gaudiano's close circle of friends.

> Martin Aldridge
> Leanne Berling
> Damon Burgh
> Andrew Cornish
> Leon Derry
> Jade Elmington-Wilson
> Serena Evans
> Laurie Frasier (*)
> Louisa Gaudiano
> Lucy Heaton
> Robert James
> Baxter Perry
> Conrad Phillips
> Alice Seagrove (*)
> Vivienne Thomas
> Kathryn Thompson (*)
> Wayne Trigg
> Darren Westlake
> Joshua Woodington
> Leon Young

I'll get one of the secretaries here to scan through last known addresses of everyone – if that'll be useful.
Brian Lawson

Luchewski leaned over and picked up the other piece of paper he'd scribbled on earlier that morning. Thompson, Frasier, Westlake, Woodington and Derry. Members of the same tutor group and all of them present at the disco. Seagrove too, of course. And she was dead.

He ticked the names and set it aside once more.

* * *

Brian Lawson got up from his desk to stretch his legs. It had been an annoyingly busy day. For a start, there had been two disciplinary meetings with parents in the morning. The first one had gone predictably well – a Year 8 pupil caught urinating in the playground gutter for a dare – with the parents all embarrassed and finger-wagging. 'Sorry, Mr Lawson, he'll never do it again. We'll make sure of it. That's no Xbox for a month now. So very sorry. Ever since he's started hanging around with X and Y he's been playing up. Even at home he answers back and doesn't always do as he's told. Rude to his sister too.' Lawson had nodded sagely and patronisingly and waved them all out of the office once things had begun to get a bit repetitive.

The second meeting though hadn't gone so smoothly. A Year 11 lad with a shockingly bad case of acne had messed about in Chemistry, nearly setting fire to the lab *and* the lab technician. What should have been another simple slap on the wrist had turned into a slanging match between Deputy Head and parents.

'Well I don't see what the problem is,' the thick-as-a-brick-of-shit mum had said, though he could tell that having to say a word with as many syllables as 'the' was causing her some difficulty. 'Issa chemistry lesson. Issa good thing to be getting stuff to explode, ain't it?'

'Not if it entails a member of staff almost losing their face in the process,' Lawson said, happy to know that bitter sarcasm was going to be easily lost on this pair and that he wasn't going to get into trouble. 'As it is, her eyebrows will take some time to grow back.'

'Look, Mista ...' the Buddha-headed dad leaned forward in his seat and nearly broke it as he did so. The strain of having to move away from the front of his

67

television was obvious, and Lawson almost hoped that the poor chap would have his impending and unavoidable coronary there and then to spare him the pain of having to miss an episode of *Celebrity Coach Trip*. 'Look, Mista ...' The huffy, laborious breathing was almost too much to bear. 'I don't know your name but my Jake ... my Jake, he don't do fings like what yous sayin' to me now.'

'I'm sorry?'

'He's a good boy. Don't get no trouble. Never done nuffin ... wrong ... always doin' good ... helps downa charity, doncha, boy?'

The boy sitting next to him nodded.

'Mr Lewis, this is the fourth time this year I've had to call you in for a meeting. And it's only October. That's not to mention the five meetings we had last year. I think Jake needs to reassess his position in the school. We've virtually run out of formal warnings for him now. Anything else would tip him over the edge and we'd be looking to move him into the referral unit.'

'Don't want my Jakey in no referral unit,' the mum shuffled oddly in her seat. 'He don't deserve to be there. That's where bad boys go. Kick 'em outta school and put them down there to rot.' She shuffled again. Lawson found the stench of chip fat overwhelming. 'No way my Jakey going there.'

'Ain't my fault.' Suddenly the spotty kid who had no idea of how to do up a tie swivelled forward. 'Always picking on me you lot are.'

'What?'

'Singlin' me out. All of yer.'

'Who?'

'You. The teachers. All of yer. See me as some sort of fret.'

Lawson couldn't help but smile. The thought that he would see Jake Lewis – greasy little Jake Lewis with his sticky hair and inability to read properly – as some sort of threat made the corners of his mouth turn up.

'See! Worra you laughing at?' Jake frowned and a couple of spots caught in the ridges of his forehead seemed to ooze. 'Don't you laugh at me.'

The dad put his hand on the boy's arm. 'Keep it calm ... Jake. Don't let him wind ... you up. He wants ... he wants you to break so he can ... get rid of you.'

'Mr Lewis. All I want is for Jake to behave in an appropriate manner whilst at school. That is all. Every other pupil at –'

'That's right, Jakey.' The mum half stood. 'All they wanna do is make you one of them.' She cast a filthy look at Lawson. 'One of them nine-to-fivers in suits and wiv mortgages and stuff. Try to snap you in two, they do. Did the same to me when I was in school. So I left and it didn't do me any 'arm.' She tried to look proud but only looked even more stupid than she was. 'Keeps you down in school, they do. Come on!' She straightened up. 'Let's go. I've had enuff of this.'

The boy pushed his chair back behind him and smirked at Lawson.

'I'm sorry, where are you going? We still need to discuss –'

'We've discussed quite enough, thank you very much. No way is my son gonna have the stuffin' knocked out of him by a bunch of turds like you. Come on, Pete. We're off.'

If the mum had hoped it would look like an enormous, dramatic gesture then she hadn't bargained on the idiot dad who found it almost impossible to get up out of his chair. He pushed down on the arms and tried to lift his bulk before collapsing back with a horrible nasal rasping. A few difficult seconds passed as he regained his strength before trying again. This time he managed to clear the chair but almost stumbled as he leaned forward out of it. One hand on Lawson's desk kept him upright for long enough though. A few more huffs and puffs and –

'Nah. We're not goin' … goin' to hang around here an' be … insulting.'

'Come on!' The mum pushed open the door, the boy followed her through and eventually the dad caught up with them and managed to roll himself through the door frame.

That had been the type of day Brian Lawson had had. Paperwork with the occasional intrusion by idiots and a sandwich for lunch.

He stretched and looked at his watch. 3:27. Nearly the end of the school day.

Lawson got up and went to the window. The good thing about his office, he always thought, was its position. It overlooked the yard and, more importantly, the entrance to the sixth form centre.

He looked at his watch once again and waited.

Perhaps he might go for a run tonight.

Stevie didn't know who was picking up Liz's kids from school and it looked as though Liz herself didn't care. As she knocked back her third gin and tonic – shapeless brown hat still wedged firmly onto her head – and tapped the table along with the music playing over the speakers, she suddenly looked like somebody who was trying to hide away from the rest of her life. Drowning it all away in the overcrowded student bar.

'S'great still being a student,' she slurred, her eyes

glossy. 'Being able to drink yourself half to death on a weekday afternoon and not feel guilty about it. Look at them all.' She swept her arm out in front of her. 'Not a care in the world.'

Stevie drained the last of his Peroni and dropped the glass bottle back on the beer mat.

'They should probably all be doing essays or calculating atomic masses or something, shouldn't they? Something the taxpayer thinks they're paying them for?'

'Nooooo,' Liz shook her head like a hippopotamus. 'Nooo. That's not the point of university. The point of university is to escape the real world. Leave it all outside where it belongs. Life comes along all too bloody quickly and forces itself upon you, arse-raping you with its unrelenting rules and regulations. Making you suck the cock of social acceptability and respectability. Look at them all.' Her arm swept over the table again, knocking the empty green bottle over onto its side. 'Oops. Sorry. Look at them. Poor bastards. Haven't got a clue what's about to happen to them once they step outside and leave the lovely warm cloistered environment of "Higher Education".'

She ran her tongue around the rim of her glass before pushing it alongside the Peroni bottle.

'You want another?' he asked.

'Wouldn't say no,' she drooled and turned to look at all the young people in the dimly lit bar, huddled around tables and propped up against the little shelves that went all the way around the room. 'Poor bastards.'

Stevie picked up the glass and the bottle and went over to the bar. It was relatively free and he managed to get served within seconds of plonking the empties down on the laminated surface. Along with the two drinks, he bought four packets of crisps – two cheese and onion, two salt and vinegar – hoping the salt might eventually sober Liz up.

'Need a hand?'

'Hmm?'

Stevie turned and found himself staring directly into the pale blue eyes of the young man who'd made him melt just the day before.

A slight flutter in the stomach.

'Looks like you've got your hands full.' The young man smiled his wide, beautiful smile and took a couple of the packets of crisps from Stevie. 'I'll carry these for you.'

'Oh. Er … thanks.'

They walked over to the table where Liz was sitting and Stevie dropped the drinks down a little too quickly, making the G&T slop and spill over the side of the glass.

'Stevie!' Liz cried before looking up. 'Oh. Hello.'

'Hi,' the young man replied proffering a packet of crisps to her. 'Cheese and onion or salt and vinegar?'

'Oh.'

'Thanks for that,' Stevie found himself slightly short of breath.

'That's OK. You're both on the PGCE course, aren't you? I've seen you in the lectures.' He seemed to be staring at Stevie. 'I'm Mike, by the way.' He stuck his hand out towards Stevie who, after wiping his wet fingers on his jeans, took it and shook it warmly.

'Stevie.'

'Good to meet you, Stevie.'

'And I'm Liz.' Liz's hand jutted up towards Mike.

'Hi, Liz.'

'Well … er … thanks for that. Er… can I buy you a drink? Would you like to join us?'

Mike smiled again. He seemed to do a lot of smiling.

'Not at the moment. Maybe another time. I'm afraid there's somewhere I have to be in an hour. And if I don't get going now, I'm going to be late.'

'Oh.' Stevie hoped he didn't come across as too disappointed, but Liz's darting eyes had obviously picked up on it. 'Oh well. Never mind.'

'Sorry. I'll … er … I'll probably see you in lectures tomorrow, anyway. Yes?'

'Yes.'

'Good. Right, I'd better be off. Good to meet you both and I'll see you tomorrow.' He moved away from the table. 'Bye.'

'See you.'

Mike made his way through the clusters of students and out through the door.

'You're in there,' Liz grinned, waving her G&T in front of her face.

'What? No. Shut up.' Stevie scooped up his bottle and rammed it into his mouth.

'You are. And what's more,' she glugged down nearly half of the drink, 'you *soooooooo* want it.'

He swallowed his beer. 'I do not.'

'Do.'

'Do not.' Stevie could barely control the smirk on his face. 'Now shut up.'

It was October and the evenings were starting to nudge themselves earlier into the day. Slowly, bit by bit, inch by inch, they were nibbling away at the sunlit hours. Give it another month, thought Hal, and you wouldn't be able to see a thing without streetlights after about three in the afternoon. He always found autumn a strange time of year. A sort of seasonal halfway house. Not warm enough for T-shirts, not cold enough for winter coats. And the

73

bloody leaves could make a simple act like walking along the pavement a treacherous business. Rotting yellowing leaves, mushy and slimy, soft and slippery underfoot. Thankfully, this particular part of Soho was completely free of trees.

Luchewski parked the TT in the first available spot he could find and stuck his Metropolitan Police card on display in its window. He strolled down Berwick Street, turned left into Broadwick Street and then right onto the much wider Wardour Street. The early evening was full of people in a rush to get home, tourists, and the semi-inebriated. Soho was never quiet. Never peaceful. A rattling mass of humanity, it buzzed of despair and hope twenty-four hours a day, seven days a week. And nobody noticed anyone else. That was the odd wonder of the place. An area so full of so many different people, and each of them in their own separate world.

Luchewski quite liked that.

Huddled away down the thin alleyway that was Bourchier Street, you would never spot the offices of Lenny Schinowitz. Bought for a song way back at the start of the seventies, Lenny could probably have sold the building for around five million pounds and moved out to some cheaper place away from the centre of town. But instead, the decrepit old talent agent was hanging on in there. And it wasn't because he didn't want the money. Oh no, Lenny's life was ruled by the almighty dollar. The reason he didn't sell the building was because he always felt that if he held out just one more year, he could get even more for it. Always just one more year. Because of that, Luchewski knew that Lenny would never live to see a penny from the sale of the offices. That was a pleasure awaiting his children.

Luchewski pushed open the long, glass-fronted door

and stepped into the small reception area. The receptionist behind the desk recognised him straight away.

'Ah, Mr Liddle ... er, Luchewski. How good to see you. The Schinowitzes are expecting you. If you'd just take a seat and I'll let them know you're here.'

Hal smiled and sat on one of the extremely expensive, avant-garde leather armchairs. On the walls were large black and white photographs – stills some of them – of Liddle and Moore. The one just behind the head of the receptionist showed Moore – or 'Uncle Barry' as Luchewski always called him – dressed as Robin Hood, the ridiculously tight costume and the far-too-tiny Lincoln green hat emphasising Moore's plumpness. And just over his shoulder, Liddle – or 'Dad' to Luchewski – dressed as Maid Marian, a long, pointy hat perched on his head with a flowing, silky frock and a miserable, what-am-I-doing-wearing-this-stupid-costume look stuck on his face.

Next to that was a still from the 1978 Christmas Special – Luchewski recognised it straight away. The two comedy magicians busy with one of their larger-scale tricks. He recognised that too. It was called 'The Mismade Girl'. An attractive, bespangled assistant would climb into an upright box. She'd wave cheerily at the audience before the door to the front would be shut and three blades inserted into the sides of the cabinet, dividing it into four separate pieces. Then each part – bar one; that was the key to the illusion – would be lifted down onto the stage. To the audience it looked as though the assistant had been sliced into four bits. After some patter and jokes and some other pretend distraction, the magician – usually his father; Uncle Barry was never that impressive at the magic part of the act – would conveniently forget which box should go on top of which, so puts them back in any old order. The front panels of each small box would then be opened to show that the assistant's body had been mismade. Feet at the top, torso underneath, legs in the third and at the bottom the smiling waving face and arms of the young woman. The magician tuts before restacking the boxes in the correct order and opening the box up. *Tadah*. The assistant is whole and normal once again.

This particular assistant, Hal remembered, looking at the oversized photograph hanging on the wall, was called Brenda. Bendable Brenda they used to call her. She would do all the tricks that required being able to squash oneself into tiny spaces. Tricks like the Mismade Girl. Luchewski wondered where Bendable Brenda was now. She'd be in her late sixties, he thought. Could be anywhere and doing anything. Thinking back, Luchewski remembered liking Bendable Brenda. She was always nice to him. Gave him lollipops. That sort of thing.

'Mr Luchewski. They'll see you now.' The receptionist gave one of those beams that receptionists acquire after years of pretending to smile. Luchewski fake-smiled back and pushed the door to the stairs open. There were more photographs on the wall above the handrail – smaller photographs of some of the other, less successful acts that Lenny Schinowitz had managed over the years. Bonnie 'Bad Boy' Englebert had done quite well in the early eighties with a couple of Saturday evening TV series, as had The Malicious Brothers. But none had really scaled the heights of Liddle and Moore. Liddle and Moore were still household names.

At the top of the stairs, Lenny's daughter stood holding the door to the office open.

'Hello, Becky. Long time no see.'

'Hi, Harry.' This beam was genuine. 'It *has* been a while.'

Becky Schinowitz was two years older than

Luchewski, with long curly dark hair and green eyes that could probably laser-cut images into glass. The business suit she was wearing was tight in all the right places and told the world that she was still managing to keep her incredible figure.

'You *still* not married?' Luchewski asked.

'Not yet. But don't worry, I'll invite you to the wedding when I've found the right girl.'

Becky Schinowitz was also the very first girl Luchewski had ever kissed. Ironic then that they both turned out to be gay.

Luchewski passed her and went into the office.

'Ah, Harry, my boy.' Behind his desk Lenny Schinowitz stood up to greet Luchewski. 'Good of you to come, my boy. Good of you to come.'

Luchewski shook the old man's hand and found it frighteningly cold. Lenny gave a nervous flash of a smile before sitting back down.

The other person in the room didn't even acknowledge Luchewski.

'Hello, Elizabeth,' he murmured to his sister who was sitting on a brightly coloured armchair with her legs crossed deliberately away from him.

'Harold.' Her eyes refused to meet his.

'Kids OK?'

'Fine. Lily?'

'Yeah. Great.' He hadn't spoken to his daughter for the last few days, so wasn't entirely certain himself.

Becky took up her position alongside her father.

'Well ...' Lenny started. 'This is nice. Just like old times.' The silence in the room nearly deafened everyone. 'Er ... Now –'

'What is this all about, Lenny?' Elizabeth interrupted.

Lenny sighed. 'Well ... er ...'

'It's all right, Dad. I'll tell them.'

'Tell us what?' Luchewski lowered himself down onto one of the stripy armchairs.

Becky gave both Luchewski and his sister a sharp yet concerned glance Then she began.

'As you are no doubt both aware, the first official biography of Liddle and Moore is being written – I think you've both seen the initial draft already, yes?'

Both Luchewski and his sister nodded. It was true, Hal had *seen* the initial draft. It had been sent to him a couple of months back. He just hadn't bothered to actually read it.

'And as far as I am aware there was nothing contentious in the text.'

Elizabeth shook her head, so Luchewski had to believe that was the case.

'However,' Becky started ominously, 'the biographer has now … well … stumbled across something.'

'Stumbled across something?'

She nodded. 'Yes. Stumbled across something. Something … big.'

For the first time Elizabeth turned to look at her younger brother.

'Big?' Luchewski asked.

'Oh, Jesus. Not Operation Yewtree?' His sister looked horrified.

Lenny leant forward. 'Oh no, no, no! Oh, Good God, no. Not *that*, Elizabeth my dear. Heaven forbid.'

'No. Not *that*.' Becky regained control from her father.

'Well, what then?'

Lenny and Becky both looked at each other.

'Do you remember Brenda Bennett?' Lenny's hand stroked his chin in a nervous way and Luchewski noticed for the first time the liver spots that covered the seventy-five-year-old's skin.

Elizabeth frowned. 'Brenda Bennett?'

'Bendable Brenda, we used to call her,' Becky clarified. 'Assistant during the 78/79 season.'

Luchewski thought back to the canvas in reception. Bendable Brenda in the Mismade Girl.

'I don't ... think ...' Elizabeth was racking her brain.

'Attractive girl. Very attractive.' Lenny would have licked his lips given the chance.

'What about her?'

'Brenda died a few months back.' Becky seemed to be reading it all from a sheet of paper. 'Stomach cancer. Sixty-seven years old. Her husband died the year before. She left behind one son. Patrick. He's thirty-six.'

'So?'

'Well, just before she died ... in the hours before she died, she confided something to Patrick. Told him something she'd held back all his life. Told him that his father ... wasn't his father.'

'Oh, God.'

'Said that back in the late seventies ...' Becky seemed reluctant to go on even though everyone had worked it all out already. 'Said that in the late seventies, she'd had an affair with Victor Liddle.'

'Oh, God.' Elizabeth pulled her legs up onto the chair and hugged them closer to her. 'No.'

'Dad.' Luchewski felt numb and a buzzing bee noise started up inside his head.

'She told Patrick that Victor Liddle was his real father.'

The room fell still as everyone tried to take it all in. Eventually, Luchewski broke the silence.

'What now?'

Becky sighed again. 'Patrick – Patrick Bayley is his

name – wants a DNA test.'

'Wants to check out his mother's story. See if she was right or not.' Lenny croaked. 'Can't blame him really. Only natural.'

Suddenly, Elizabeth's feet flew back down to the floor and she jumped up. 'No! This is rubbish. My father loved my mother. He bought her flowers every week. He gave her everything she wanted.' She wiped angry tears from her eyes. 'No. This is shit. Tell him he can fuck off. I'm having nothing to do with this. All he's after is money. They always are. Wants to get hold of Dad's money and ruin his reputation. Well, he can't. Tell him he can fuck off!'

She marched off across the room and slammed the door hard behind her as she left.

They all sat there for a moment afterwards, the buzzing in Luchewski's head finally subsiding.

'Harry?' Becky smiled warmly.

He ignored her and looked at Lenny. 'Lenny. You knew my father. Almost better than anyone, I'm sure. Do you think … do you *really* think …?'

Lenny shrugged. 'I honestly don't know, my boy. I honestly couldn't tell you. Sorry.'

Later, as he walked back to the car through the busy streets of Soho, the rain beginning to pick its way into the town, Luchewski felt even more isolated than he had earlier in the evening.

Typical.

It was starting to bloody rain. Pulling his collar up he turned around and walked away from the house, the bottle of wine and flowers gripped in his hands, and made his way back to the car. Last thing he needed was some nosy neighbour clocking his registration or even the colour and make, so he'd parked the car quite a long way away down a dirty-looking back street where the residents looked as though they couldn't be bothered.

The man was still in there with her. An oldish-looking guy who looked familiar. Perhaps he was off the telly? That was something he could do without. Somebody just turning up unexpectedly. Could interfere with his plans.

The old guy had been in there for over half an hour now and he was beginning to wonder if he'd actually get this thing done tonight like he'd planned. After she had phoned him and cried down the line all sad and *boo-hoo* devastated, he realised that tonight was probably as good a night as any to get it done. Even better if she actually invited him into the house. Seagrove never did that. He'd had to steal a spare key from her to get into the flat. Poor Alice.

It was the other phone call that worried him. He'd missed it, thankfully. But he knew he couldn't risk it. So, before setting out, he'd smashed the phone to pieces – it was only a cheap thing – and threw it onto the railway line. He was going to break it up anyway, but that weird missed call made him do it a few hours earlier than he'd intended.

He sat in the car and waited. The night was coming on fast and the rain was easing off. Give it another twenty minutes, he thought, and I'll go back and try again.

PART TWO

Made of Stone

Chapter Ten

Luchewski was feeling shaky. After Lenny Schinowitz's revelation the previous night he had driven home in a daze, not noticing a single thing about the journey until he pulled up on the forecourt of his house in Penge and wondered how he'd got there. He decided not to eat, instead hitting the bottle of ten-year-old Talisker Storm like a Catholic at an orgy.

His dad. His hero. The great Victor Liddle. The master magician. The faultless comedian. The loving father. The impeccable husband.

And now this.

It didn't tally. Just didn't add up. If Victor Liddle had faults they were minor. Unimportant petty things that fundamentally didn't matter. Not big things. Just little irritations.

But this? This was enormous. A massive crack in the character of a man who most of the country would have thought unimpeachable.

And the more Hal thought about it the worse it got. If Victor Liddle was capable of doing this the once, then he was capable of doing it a hundred times. Who knows how many half-siblings he might have floating around the place. Did he shag all of his assistants? That was more Uncle Barry's territory, wasn't it?

And all those tours. Numerous UK tours. The occasional European tour. Tours of the States and

Australia. All opportunities for him to bang as many groupies as he could handle. Jesus. It was a hundred cans of worms.

To distract himself, Luchewski had tried taking refuge in music. He had stumbled to the shelves bursting with CDs and systematically made his way along the spines, trying to find one that half-suited the moment. Perhaps something to take his mind off things. Unfortunately nothing seemed to help. Every CD was dismissed seconds into the first track and tossed aside like a small shiny frisbee. The Smiths' *Meat is Murder*. Gary Numan's *Replicas*. *High Violet* by The National. *The Stone Roses*. None of them were saying anything to him tonight.

Before crawling up the stairs to his bed, Luchewski made a phone call. It was horribly late or early depending on how you view these things, and at any other time he would have stopped himself from doing it. But tonight wasn't like any other night.

He let the phone ring until it went to answerphone before ending the call and trying again. Once more it went through to the message centre, so he cut it dead and redialled. This time the phone was answered.

'Hello? Yes? What is it?' The voice on the other end was urgent and Hal had a sudden spasm of guilt for scaring the old man.

'Barry? It's Hal.'

'Harry? What are you doing phoning this time of night? Is something wrong?' Barry was breathless, as if he'd had to run down the stairs of his incredibly big house in the Vale of Glamorgan to get to the phone.

'No. Nothing's wrong. Well, yes, something's wrong.' He steadied himself. Too much whisky was making him feel sick. 'Barry, can I ask you something?'

'Couldn't it wait till morning? Have you been

drinking?'

'Yes, I've been drinking. I've been drinking a lot. But don't worry about that now. Can I ask you something?'

Barry Moore, joint TV Personality of the Year 1979, gave a little huff.

'Can I?' Luchewski asked again.

'Yes, yes. Go on then.'

Too drunk to actually formulate a question, Luchewski pushed the phone closer to his ear and said: 'Brenda Bennett.'

'Who?'

'Brenda Bennett. Brenda the bendable Bennett. Bendy Brenda.'

'Oh.'

The way Barry Moore said 'oh' told Luchewski everything he needed to know.

'You knew all about it?'

'About what?'

'Don't lie. You knew all about it. About *them*. About their dirty little secret.'

'Look, Harry, don't –'

'Ah, look,' Luchewski spoke over the old man. 'I don't think I want to hear your lies just now. I'm not in the mood for them. Perhaps I'll call you back in a few days' time. Yes, that's what I'll do. I'll call you back in a few days' time when I'm not so fucking PISSED OFF WITH YOU!'

He slammed the phone down before ripping the wire out of the wall.

Andrew Cornish was running. Running faster than he'd done in years. His thin legs were pumping up and down and his feet slapping the pavement, making his cheap canvas plimsolls come apart at the place where he'd glued them back together only last week. He'd stupidly put his coat on. Why had he put his coat on? The sweat that was building up under his nasty non-breathable coat started running down his back and into the top of his trousers. Come to think of it, his trousers weren't helping too. They were too loose, too baggy. Chafing away at his legs. No, Andrew Cornish realised, he wasn't exactly dressed to be running.

And his lungs were struggling to take it. He'd been weak and unfit for too long to be able to run well. Not that he'd ever been able to run well. At school even the PE teachers had struggled not to laugh at him and once the laughs had worn thin, they spent the remaining years ignoring him and focused on the stupid fit boys whose brains were too dull to acknowledge pain. But *this* pain was almost unbearable. His chest felt like someone really fat had sat on it and his throat burned as if he'd been force fed sandpaper. If he didn't stop running soon he was going to be sick.

The people walking along Fairfield Road jumped out of his way when they saw him coming and a couple of cars had to brake suddenly as he passed across the roads down towards the cemetery.

Eventually, he turned down a small alleyway and stopped – his breathing heavy and difficult – and leaned up against the wall and threw up. Everything was blurred and dizzy and he felt like he was going to faint. Slowly, he straightened and looked around. He was safe. He was far enough away to be safe. The police wouldn't be coming after him now. Not here. Not this far away from it.

Seventeen Years Ago

The refectory at Longley Road was so much better than the canteen at her old school, Alice thought, pushing her tray a tiny bit further along. At her old school, the choice was rubbish. It was supposed to be healthy and well-balanced but everyone always chose the chips and sausages and beans so, in the end, the healthy options seemed to start disappearing. Lettuce at her old school was just something that rabbits hadn't bothered eating. Here there was a wide range of salady things to choose from. Coleslaw. Grated carrot in a balsamic vinegar dressing. Mexican bean salad. Couscous. Nutty rice. Alice asked for a big pile of couscous and a small dollop of coleslaw on the side. She looked down at Laurie Frasier's plate in front of her in the queue and saw that she'd gone for the chips and sausages and beans. She turned to see that Katie Thompson had also gone for the chips and sausages and beans.

'Not very healthy,' she said to them both.

'Tasty though,' Katie replied.

'Yeah, tasty,' Laurie agreed. 'Anyway, what's the point in being healthy? No need. We all die in the end.' She flicked her long dark hair back with her fingers. 'Doesn't really matter *when* we die, does it? We spend much more time dead than alive anyway. We spend millions and millions of years dead but only a few years alive. Yeah?'

'You're not very cheery, are you?'

'No. Not really.'

They paid for the food and made their way over to where Louisa had managed to find a spare table. Alice could see her tucking busily into her chips and sausages and beans.

'This school is shit,' Laurie moaned as they sat down.

'You off again? She off again?' Louisa asked them all through a mouthful of processed pig fat.

Alice nodded.

'I quite like it actually,' Katie pulled her tray out from under her plate. 'The teachers seem nice.'

'No they're not. They're full of shit. Especially that Lawson twat.'

'He seems nice enough to me.'

Laurie gave Katie a raised eyebrow look.

'The kids are OK actually,' Alice squeezed a vinegar sachet over part of her couscous. 'I thought they'd all be really horrible and scary. But they're not. They're all as scared as each other.'

'No one's more scared than that one.' Laurie jabbed her knife in the direction of a thin, pale-looking boy who was sitting at a table on his own. 'I've been watching him all morning. Looks as though he's going to shit his pants all the time.'

Alice recognised the boy from their tutor group. He sat on his own there too and could hardly answer when it came to his turn to announce his name to the rest of the class. What was his name? Alice thought. Devon. No. Cornwall or something. Something like that anyway. She watched him as he pushed and poked away at the food without actually putting anything into his mouth. His little dark eyes darting and dancing about as he nervously observed the rest of the refectory.

They ate mostly in silence, half-listening to the buzz of the voices. They polished off their main course and made slightly harder work of the stodgy custardy pudding thing – it seemed to offer up some resistance to the spoons – before shoving everything back onto the trays.

'That was horrible,' Laurie grinned at them. 'Not nice at all.'

They carried the trays back to the racks where they slid them onto the shelves.

'So, where have –'

SMASSSH!

Katie's tray slipped back out of the rack and onto the floor where the plate and cutlery shattered over the sticky parquet flooring. 'Oh no!'

'Wheyyyy!' A bunch of Year Nines cheered over in the corner.

'You all right?' It was another of the boys from their tutor group. Joshua something or other. Blond. Small-featured. Good smile. 'Let me help you.'

He squatted down alongside Katie and helped her to put the bits and pieces back onto the tray.

'Thanks. Sorry.'

'That's all right. Don't worry.' He pushed the tray firmly into the slot and turned to catch up with his two friends.

'Silly me,' Katie gushed at the other girls as they all made their way out of the refectory.

Chapter Eleven

'So how long have you both been married?' Luchewski asked the couple sat across the dining room table from him.

Josh Woodington turned to face his wife. 'What is it? Nine years now? Ten?'

'Ten!' His wife tutted. 'It was ten in August. Honestly, Inspector, you'd think he'd remember having just celebrated his tenth wedding anniversary, wouldn't you? The big cards and balloons with the number "10" on them that cluttered up the house for a week or two. Remember those, dear?'

Josh laughed. 'Katie's better at numbers than I am.'

'No, I'm just better at remembering the important things. Well, better at remembering *anything*.'

'That too.'

Hal smiled and looked around the room. It was neat but not completely bare like so many other people's houses. A large, fat armchair sat in the corner of the room with a standard lamp tucked away behind it. A whole load of cheap paperback novels sat on a row of recently dusted shelves. A modern dresser and a side table covered with polished framed photos of children.

'And you have two children?'

'Yes,' Katie answered. 'Zac and Sophie. Zac's ten and Sophie's six. They both go to the local primary school. They love it.'

'And you both work from home?'

'Well, *I* do.' Josh repositioned himself on his seat. 'IT. Remote remedial.'

'Hmm?'

'I … er … fix computer software problems. Remotely. Means I don't have to get dressed for work in the mornings. I can spend most of the morning in my pyjamas if I want.'

'Not if you're taking the kids to school, though.' His wife shook her head. 'I don't work, Inspector. Never have done. I stay home and wash, clean, cook, shop. The usual things. Take care of the children. Quite happy doing that, thank you very much.'

Singh shuffled in her seat.

Luchewski gave a slight cough to bring the inanities to an end. 'Mr and Mrs Woodington. I'm sure you know why we're here.'

The loving couple suddenly became serious. 'Yes. Alice,' said Katie. We saw it on the news last night. Dreadful thing. I couldn't believe it at first.'

'It said … it said she was murdered. That right?' Josh asked.

Luchewski nodded. 'She was.'

'I hope you don't mind me asking, but when was the last time either of you saw Alice Seagrove?' Singh had her notebook open.

'Saw her? Alice?' Katie turned to her husband. 'Not for years. Not since school I don't think.'

'No. Not since school.'

'Not once?'

'No. After school we went our separate ways. I remember her going off to university to do medicine. That's about it.'

Josh interrupted. 'Even at school you weren't that

close, were you?'

'Not really. No. We vaguely knew each other at primary school and in the first year at Longley Road we got quite friendly. But after Louisa disappeared … well … she didn't really want friends. Went in on herself a bit. Probably thought that if she made friends with someone they were likely to disappear too. I don't know.'

'There was no one she confided in? No one at all?'

'No. I think she might have talked to some of the boys as she got older. But she definitely didn't have any female friends to my knowledge. Not after Louisa.'

'Any boys in particular?' Luchewski asked.

'To be honest, Inspector, I can't remember.' Katie at least looked as though she was thinking hard. 'No. I can't help you, I'm afraid. Sorry.'

Luchewski tried not to sigh and decided to come at things differently. 'You were both there – at the disco – the night Louisa Gaudiano disappeared. Can you tell me what happened? I know it's a long time ago.'

'We've been through this with the police before.' Josh looked uncomfortable. 'Hundreds of times. Can't you just look back at the notes? Everything'll be there.' It was obvious from the man's expression that Hal was digging up terrible memories. It had probably taken these people years to deal with what had happened to Louisa Gaudiano, and here he was, asking them to dredge it all up again.

'Please.'

Katie Woodington clasped her hands together on the dining room table. 'There's not that much to tell. I met up with Alice on Collier's Wood High Street and we walked through the park to the hall. There was no one suspicious around as far as I could tell. At the disco, most other people were already there. You were there before me, weren't you?'

'I don't know. I think so. It was a long time ago.'

'I think you were. You were there with Conrad Phillips and Darren Westlake. Anyway, the DJ played all the usual music. The vicar man was there. And then, not long after we arrived, Louisa and Laurie – Laurie Frasier, she works on local news now, you might have seen her – they had an argument. I can't remember what it was about –'

'Money. It was about money. That's what it says in the police reports.'

'Was it? I can't remember exactly. I wasn't really listening to them. But they argued and Louisa was in tears and she ran out of the building.' She paused. 'And that was the last time I ever saw her. It was the last time anyone ever saw her.'

Josh pulled his chair closer to hers.

'Anything else that you can remember?'

'Not really. Alice went after her to see if she was OK but –'

Luchewski sat up. 'What?'

'Alice followed her. A few minutes later I think. I don't think she saw her because she came back quite quickly.'

'Alice went after her?' Luchewski gave Singh a nudge to tell her to put this in her notebook. 'But that wasn't in any of the statements you gave to the police.'

'Wasn't it? I suppose it's not impossible we just … forgot.'

'What? Alice too? She never mentioned it in her statement.'

'Funny …'

'And you're absolutely certain? You're not just remembering things wrong?'

'No. No. I definitely remember Alice going out

to check on her.'

Luchewski turned to the husband. 'Mr Woodington?'

Josh shook his head. 'No point asking me. I was too busy busting some sick moves on the dance floor. I didn't notice any of it.'

'So what are you thinking?' Singh asked as she climbed in the passenger seat of the TT.

'I find it weird that Alice Seagrove never mentioned that she went outside. Surely if one of your best friends had disappeared you would make sure that everyone knew you'd done all you possibly could, wouldn't you?'

'I suppose.'

'Of course you would.'

'So what do you think happened?'

Luchewski started up the engine and the car gave a satisfying roar. 'I think that Alice Seagrove saw something. Something she kept hidden for the rest of her short life. Something that eventually got her killed.'

Chapter Twelve

As the morning progressed, Luchewski's head got lighter but his thoughts got heavier. No matter what he did, his mind kept skip-repeating back to the meeting the previous evening. *Victor Liddle the philanderer*. Over and over again the words twisted about in his brain. *Philanderer*. Except that's not what the newspapers would call him. 'Philanderer' was such a quaint old-fashioned word that nobody nowadays would have a clue what it meant. They'd probably think it meant he collected stamps or rang church bells for a hobby. No, the papers would tell it like it was. *Love cheat. Serial shagger. Dirty old bastard. Deceived us all with his clean-cut public persona. His whole life was a lie*. That's what they'd say. In their eyes, if it sold copy, 'philanderer' wasn't too far short of 'pederast'. Only a few letters' difference. And the moral high ground was sometimes very easy to take.

By lunchtime, he and Singh had interviewed two others.

Darren Westlake was a foreman on a construction site in Orpington. Clothed in the classic Bob the Builder hat and oversized luminous jacket, he had led them to a Portakabin on the edge of the works and didn't even bother to offer them a cup of tea. Singh winced when she saw the girlie calendar hanging from the wall. Luchewski was just amazed that they still made them.

'New school. Seven million they're spending on it.' Westlake kept his coat on and rustled himself into the chair behind the desk, his hands tucked into his pockets. 'If you ask me council's mad. Perfectly good one the other side of the town. Spend a coupla million on that and it'd be as good as fucking new.' He didn't even look at Singh.

Luchewski asked all the same questions he had asked the Woodingtons, and the responses he got were all very similar, only answered with an arrogant air of disinterest.

No, he hadn't seen Alice Seagrove since school.

No, he never really talked to her at school – although he did fancy her a bit in later years. 'Always attracted to the more difficult ones, you know?'

No, he couldn't really remember very much about the night Louisa Gaudiano disappeared.

When Luchewski asked him if he could remember if Seagrove left the disco at any time in the evening, he laughed.

'God, Inspector. You don't ask much, do you? How am I meant to remember that? I can barely remember to wipe me own arse in the morning, never mind some shit that happened twenty years ago. You're asking the wrong person, I'm afraid.'

Conrad Phillips was quite the reverse. A quiet, nervous man helping out in the British Red Cross charity shop just off Eltham Hill, he escorted both Luchewski and Singh through the shop to the storeroom at the back.

'Between jobs at the moment,' he apologised, wiping his sweaty palms on his apron. 'Just doing this to keep in the habit.'

Around them were black bin bags full of other people's old tat. Dusty, crumpled old board games lined the floor and Luchewski wondered if *Liddle and Moore's Race to the Moon* was among them.

No, he corrected himself. *Not now. Don't start thinking*

about him now.

'How long have you ... worked here?' Singh asked trying to find the right word.

Phillips squinted in embarrassment. 'Four years. Well, three and a half. And a bit.' He laughed. 'Difficult to get much work nowadays. As an actor.'

Oh no, Luchewski thought. Not another actor.

Again, the answers to the questions were pretty similar, only more polite and full of detail. But it was when Singh asked if he could remember anyone chasing after Gaudiano that Conrad Phillips really got Luchewski's attention.

'Oh yes. Alice did.'

'Alice?'

'Yes. She went straight out after her.'

'Was she gone long?'

'Long enough.'

'How long?'

'Ten, fifteen minutes.'

'You're sure?'

'Of course I'm sure.'

'Why didn't you tell the police at the time?'

Phillips shook his head. 'I suppose because nobody asked me.'

As Singh and Luchewski made their way back through the shop, Phillips took up his position behind the till.

'I'll go back to my colouring now.' He picked up a felt tip pen and pulled the top off. Luchewski could see on the counter one of those adult colouring books with intricate pictures of wild, flowery gardens full of rich, fat orchids and long winding vines. Phillips was about a third of the way through this one. 'Got to have something to do,' he said. 'Lots of empty hours when you work in a charity shop.'

* * *

'Freddie,' Luchewski bellowed down his phone. 'Laurie Frasier. She's the last one on your list – God knows why she's the last one on your list. She should have been first. Forget the rest of them for now. Go and see her.'

'Why's that?' the gruff Yorkshireman grumbled back. 'We're halfway to ruddy Woolwich now.'

'Don't worry about that. You and Green turn around and head back to New Cross. And make sure you ask her about the argument she had with Gaudiano and also if anyone in the group tried to chase after her when she stormed off. OK?'

Burlock huffed. 'Whatever you say, Kemosabe.'

It was Baxter Perry's mum who opened the door.

'It's only me at the moment,' she said the second she saw them. 'John's out fishing and Baxter's still at work. Should be back soon. Come on in.'

The Perrys lived in a small terraced house on a long road lined either side with houses that looked just like theirs. Short, squat blocks made from brownish-red brick. Luchewski thought they might be a 1950s creation.

She led them through to the sitting room where a bulbous leather sofa dominated the room along with a sixty-inch television set. The television was off so the entire conversation that followed was reflected back at Luchewski in its large black screen.

'How long have you lived here?' Singh asked.

'For ever, I think! Sorry. Thirty-five years. We bought it just after we got married. Paid the mortgage off a few years back. It's worth half a million now. Can you imagine? Half a million.'

London house prices were always a fascination to Luchewski. His own house seemed to forever creep up in value to the extent that it was now worth more than double what he paid for it ten years ago. And that wasn't untypical. Buying a house in virtually any part of London thirty-five years ago would have made you a fortune by now. Even a tiny, squashed-in terrace like this was obviously still racking up the cash. You'd need to be a City banker to even consider living in it nowadays.

Mrs Perry was in her early sixties and plain and dumpy – just like her house. The spectacles that blew up her eyes like balloons were Olive-from-*On-The-Buses*-esque. Her hair was military helmet-rigid and her teeth grey and misshapen, like someone had pulled them out and put them back in all wrong.

'Can I get you both a tea? Or a coffee? It's not very good coffee, I'm afraid. Just some Asda own-brand stuff. I can't stand posh coffee. Can't taste anything. Have to dip a biscuit in to get any flavour from it.'

She shuffled off to the kitchen to boil the kettle.

'Half a million? Jesus.' Singh was looking around at the small room, which was in serious need of redecoration. 'London's a fucked-up place.'

'Where do you live again, Singh?'

'I moved.'

'Have you? I didn't know.'

'Well, after all the crap from earlier in the year, I thought I'd better move on. Wash my life clean. Start again.'

Luchewski nodded, not entirely convinced that the best way to progress from a messed-up relationship – a very, *very* messed-up relationship admittedly – was to wash yourself clean. He'd tried that after his divorce, and it hadn't gone entirely to plan. After the sense of liberation and the oddly satisfying trips to IKEA to furnish and to fill up his life with stuff, there had been a hollow feeling of alienation. Of isolation. That had sent him spiralling out into gay clubs and drink. The only consistent things at that time had been his work and his daughter. Not much more than a baby back then, the necessity for some degree of normality held him back from falling too far over the abyss. Now she was thirteen, and Lily was still a crutch to him. A wonderful, feisty slap in the face. He was suddenly overcome with a desperate need to talk to her. Just hearing her voice and the words she used, the snorts of derision and the tuts of disapproval, would take his mind off all the rubbish that really didn't matter. Yes, that's what he'd do sometime tonight. He would phone her and she would somehow, in her own magical way, make it all better. Put it all into perspective.

'So where have you moved to?'

'Kingston.'

'What? Jamaica?'

'Very funny.'

'That's a hell of a commute.'

She rolled her eyes at him. 'Yes. But the duty-free ...' she pretended to take a drag on a spliff, 'is out of this world.'

'Ha!'

The door seemed to burst open and Mrs Perry fell into the room with a heavy-looking tray. Singh leaned forward and moved some of the rubbish that was cluttering up the coffee table out of the way. The tray clattered onto the table and Mrs Perry stretched her back before sitting down on one of the armchairs.

'Not as young as I used to be. Even carrying a tray seems to take it out of me these days. Phew.'

Luchewski took a cup of tea brewed to a shade of off-black and dipped a bourbon biscuit into it as he asked the woman some questions.

'Did you know Alice Seagrove?'

'No. It was a big school. I can't remember everyone who went there?'

'Can you remember the time when Louisa Gaudiano disappeared?'

'Of course. It was terrible. Terrible. We went out looking, like lots of the other parents. We needed to. Just imagining what might have happened to her … well, you can't help thinking of your own, can you? Imagining what it would be like if that happened to your own child. Horrible. Gives me the shudders just to think of it. Only twelve. And they never did find her.'

'Did you know Louisa at all?'

'Never met her. Might have seen her a few times at Christmas concerts and that, but before she went missing I don't think I would have been able to pick her out from a group of girls from the school. Of course,' she lowered her voice, 'there were always rumours.'

'Rumours?'

'About the dad.'

'What about him?'

'Well …' She looked around the room to make sure no one was hiding behind the sofa and listening in. 'They reckoned he used to hit them. The children. Use his belt on them and stuff. I always wondered …' she checked the room again, 'if it was actually *him* that did her in. And that paedophile he killed was just a cover-up. Him trying to hide his tracks.'

'Who're "they"?'

'Hmmm?'

'You said *they* reckoned he used to hit them. Who're "they"?'

'Oh.' She looked a little taken aback. 'Oh, I dunno. Just people. Parents. Locals. You know. People.'

Singh looked at Luchewski over her cracked mug of undrinkable tea.

He steered the subject around a little. 'How did Baxter take it when Louisa disappeared?'

'Oh very badly. Like all the kids in his year, I'm certain. Had nightmares for a while.'

'Did he receive counselling?'

'Counselling? Not really. There was something that they did at school. Got them to talk it all through – that kind of rubbish – but nothing else. I think they all got over it in the end. Kids do, don't they? Resilient buggers they are.'

'What does Baxter do now?'

'Followed his father into the Post Office. John's retired now, of course, but Baxter's still there. Sometimes he's in the sorting office. Sometimes he's out on the rounds. Changes one week to the next.'

'He still lives at home with you?'

'Moved back a couple of years ago.' Hushed tones again. 'Lived with someone. Nearly got married. Didn't work out. Left him for a stuntman. Very messy.'

'Yes.'

'Still. I think he's all right here with us at the moment. His work keeps him occupied. Quite a physical job being a postman, you know. Actually quite dangerous too when you're delivering. Couple of months back a dog had a go at his hand as he pushed letters through a letterbox. Got hold of his fingers and wouldn't let go. Needed stitches.' She tutted. 'Some people don't know how vicious their dogs are. Idiots who can't control their animals. Should be locked up if you ask me.' She smiled. 'Another biscuit?'

The front door slammed shut and a young man in a hi-vis Royal Mail jacket came into the room, doing a double take as he spotted the two detectives dunking bourbons into their cups.

'Oh. Hello?'

'Baxter Perry?' Luchewski put his tea down on the coffee table and held out his hand.

'Yes? You're the police, aren't you?'

'Inspector Luchewski of the Metropolitan Police's Major Investigation Team. And this is Sergeant Singh.'

They all shook hands.

'Awful news about Alice. I assume that's why you're here.'

'That's right, Alice Seagrove. We'd like to talk to you. Ask a few questions.'

'Of course. Yes. I understand.' He looked at his mother who was watching them from her armchair. 'Mum?'

'Eh? What? Oh ...' she stood up with an effort. 'I'll ... er ... be in the kitchen if you need me. Leave you all to it.'

Baxter Perry was a warm young man. He sat back in the armchair that his mother had just vacated and answered the questions openly and expansively. Again there was little to add to what they already knew. He hadn't seen Alice since they were both much younger. He hadn't really had a great deal to do with her at school – perhaps the odd conversation in the dinner queue. Nothing much.

'I don't really understand why you've come here, to be honest.' He stole a chocolate digestive from the open tin on the coffee table. 'Her death hasn't got anything to do with school, has it? There must be a million other possibilities. Old boyfriends. Jealous wives. Whatever. Can't have anything to do with school, can it?'

'We like to consider all avenues,' Singh replied rather pompously. 'Don't like to rule anything out.'

'Unless you think there's some sort of connection to Louisa Gaudiano.' He looked from one to the other. 'That's it, isn't it? You think it's got something to do with Louisa's disappearance all those years ago.' He whistled to himself and sat further back in the chair. 'Can't be, can it?'

'Like I said, we consider all avenues.'

'That's the only reason to talk to people who went to school with her.'

'Where were you the night Louisa Gaudiano disappeared, Mr Perry? Can you remember?' Luchewski asked.

'Of course I can remember. Everyone can remember where they were that night. I was here. With Mum and Dad. We watched *The Bill* and some other stuff I've forgotten about. I think Mum made a lasagne. A real metropolis of fun, this place, when I was twelve, I can tell you.' He shifted forward and whispered not unlike the way his mother had done earlier. 'Still about as exciting nowadays, if I'm being honest. Can't wait to move out again. Do you know what it's like to live with your parents when you're nearly thirty?'

'Must be a bit … restrictive.'

'Too bloody right it is. They still wait up for me if I'm out late, y'know? I roll in a bit sheets-to-the-wind to find my mum sitting up in her nightgown, wagging her finger and tapping her watch. It's embarrassing.'

'So why not get your own place?'

'Will do soon. Just sticking some money away every month for a deposit. When Lisa left … when Lisa ran off with some tosser who likes to be set on fire for a living, she cleaned me out. Helped herself to all our savings and stripped the flat clean one afternoon with a little help from the removal men. I literally had the clothes I was standing up in. Her bloody Fall Guy idiot even made off with my Superdry gear and my Converse – which was a bit odd as he had much bigger feet than I did.'

'Much have been dreadful.'

Perry grinned. 'Well, in a way. In another way, it was cheap at the price. I'd've only gone and chucked her over myself sometime after that. And she would have been nuts enough to try and get her own back. So in a way, I got off lightly. I got the opportunity to start again.'

Luchewski could see Singh nodding vigorously out of the corner of his eye.

He couldn't believe it. He'd taken the long way around to his flat. Right the way around east London, he'd walked for hours, his stupid, broken shoes flapping about beneath him. Sore and sweaty, he decided he couldn't carry on like this for much longer and gave up. Nobody would be after him now. Surely.

So it was an awful wave of despair that hit him as he turned the corner and saw the two men in stiff, dull grey suits sitting on the wall outside the block of flats. In an instant he knew that they were there for him. Waiting to get him.

Blood rushing, heart thumping, he pulled his long dark coat around him and twisted off down a dirty side road, neither of the men noticing.

It was then he realised he could never go back home.

Chapter Thirteen

'She's not there.'

'Where?'

'Neither place. She's not at work – didn't phone in sick or anything – which is unusual for her 'cos she's always in work. Loves her job apparently. Never misses it. And she's not answering her doorbell. Even though her car is parked outside her house.'

Luchewski held the phone tighter to his ear.

'Anything suspicious?'

'Eh? No. Nothing looks suspicious.' Freddie Burlock answered. 'But I have a worrying feeling about it. Summat's not right.'

Hal rubbed the bridge of his nose with his fingers.

'Been around the back?'

'I may have a face that looks as though it's best suited to a moron, but I'm not a ruddy idiot, y'know.'

'No.'

Hal thought hard, his forehead creasing into a 'V'.

'What do you think?' Burlock sighed after a minute.

'Get an entry team. Straight away. Let me know what you find.'

'OK.'

An hour later, Hal's phone rang again.

'It's not good.'

'No,' Hal breathed out. 'I didn't think it was.'

The small house was well-furnished but oddly sparse, with a vase full of flowers taking centre stage on the dining room table. Luchewski knew nothing about flowers other than these were yellow and fluffy-looking. And fresh.

The flooring was hardwood – oak or something. Not original. A recent addition, given the way it was shining. And the walls were covered in black and white journalistic shots from the last sixty years. Hal recognised one of them as a picture he'd probably seen in a coffee-table book at some point – a gritty snap of a machine gun-carrying Viet Cong soldier wading through a paddy field. No pictures of family or of fondly recalled holidays. It was all strangely cold and uninviting.

Hal made his way up the stairs.

In the bedroom directly opposite the top of the stairs, a light glared. The whirr and flash of a forensics camera occasionally adding to the unearthly brightness of the room. Hal peered in through the doorway. White-suited forensics officers squatted over the bloody corpse on the floor near the radiator. One of them turned and looked at Hal before turning back to continue with the photography.

'Same as before?' Hal asked.

'Exactly the same,' John Good replied. 'Well, pretty much anyway. The only difference is this one's not in her pyjamas. Otherwise, a carbon copy. Hands are tied to the radiator pipes. Left leg seems to have been broken. Cause of death appears – at this stage – to have been strangulation. Some sort of post-trauma damage to the victim's torso judging by all the blood – although we've not touched anything yet, so I can't tell you if your man has graffitied the name of a long-dead pederast all over her. Not yet anyway. Give me another hour and I'll let you know.'

Luchewski went back downstairs, squeezing past another of Good's team dusting the banister for prints. In the kitchen, he found Burlock and Green staring out of the window that overlooked the garden. Hal just about managed to stifle a laugh at the way Burlock's beard stuck awkwardly out of the hood on his protective suit. Make it a blue suit instead of a white one and he'd look like fucking Papa Smurf, thought Luchewski.

'Wine,' Burlock pointed to the kitchen worktop where a single, drained wineglass sat, a tiny dribble of red at the bottom.

Luchewski nodded. 'So what?'

Green answered. 'No bottle.'

Hal looked around the room quickly. 'So what? Must be in recycling. Or she left it in another room.'

'We've checked all over, and in the recycling. There's nothing.' Burlock raised an eyebrow like it meant something.

'Probably in the bin then.'

'Nope. Checked there too. No empty nor half-empty bottle of wine to be found anywhere.'

'I don't understand. What are you getting at?'

Burlock gave his head a shake. 'There's no sign of forced entry. Whoever he is, she let him in. He took the wine bottle with him – and I reckon a glass that he used himself – because his prints were all over it. Probably because he brought it with him when he came over.'

Hal thought. 'Flowers,' he said eventually. 'There were flowers in the other room. Fresh ones. Do you think he bought those for her too? We need to find the wrapping they came in.'

'We're ahead of you on that one,' Burlock grinned.

Green shook his head. 'Again, nothing. He's taken it off with him. Her phone's disappeared too. Just like Alice

Seagrove's.'

'God, he's thorough,' Luchewski frowned.

'Aha!' Burlock seemed to bark and he raised his index finger in the air as if making a point. 'You would think so. But ...' He let the word hang in the air for a second or two. 'Not thorough enough!'

'What do you mean?'

'Well, at some point after the wine, they drank coffee. Only – after he'd murdered the poor girl – he *forgot* to take the mug off with him.' Burlock pointed to the opposite end of the worktop where two mugs with William Morris designs were pushed up against a vegetable steamer. 'If you look inside you'll see the milk hasn't curdled at all. That means they must have been made no earlier than last night. Any longer, there'd be lumps forming.' He puffed himself up. 'Could've made a cracking forensics specialist, me!'

Hal grinned. 'Freddie, you are a fucking genius.'

'Aye, well,' Burlock swaggered a little. 'Y'know. Yes. I am. It's true. I can't deny it.'

'Let's get them both printed as a matter of urgency. You,' he pointed, 'are a fucking genius!'

* * *

After all the noise and light of the day, the car ride home was a blessed relief. Hal deliberately didn't turn on the stereo and revelled in the darkness and the silence. He even took a few back roads to avoid the rush of the early evening traffic and the intrusive orange glare of the street lamps. His hangover had struggled to keep itself fixed inside his brain all day and had now mutated into a dull thud of a headache.

So when he walked through his front door and heard his daughter's voice coming from somewhere near the kitchen, his heart seemed to both sink and soar at the same time. He'd forgotten she was coming over this evening. Typical. In the sheer mess of the day, he'd forgotten she was coming over. All he really felt like doing at that moment was stuffing a sandwich down his neck along with three paracetamol before rolling into the warm fug of comfort that his bed sometimes allowed him.

But then again … there was probably too much crap rolling around his brain tonight to sleep properly. The two dead girls. All this rubbish about his dad. No, his mind would race for hours and hours. It's best Lily is here, he thought. Give me some distraction.

In the kitchen, Lily and Stevie were sitting around the dinner table, laughing at something. It was dark, and the two candles that lit up the room cast dancing flickers across the units. They both turned to look at him as he came in.

'Late again, Inspector,' Stevie tapped his watch in a jokey way. 'Becoming a bit of a habit, this tardiness, wouldn't you say?'

'Hi, Dad.' His daughter got up from the table and threw her arms around his waist.

'Hello, sweetheart.' He kissed the top of her head. 'Sorry, I got carried away at work. Big case, I'm afraid.' She smelled like flowers and sweets.

'That's all right. Don't worry. I understand.'

Hal cast a look over at Stevie that said 'See. *She* understands.'

Stevie ignored him and stuck a fork into something meaty-looking on his plate.

After dinner – which had, Stevie reminded Hal several times, been cooked by Stevie – they filled the machine up before crashing out in front of the big TV in the sitting room.

'Mum's coming to pick me up at seven. In the morning. Said she'd park down the end of the road again and that I should meet her there. At seven.' Jackie – Luchewski's ex-wife – did this sometimes. Whenever she had meetings out of town, she would practically dump Lily off in the middle of Penge, and later scoop her up somewhere nearby so that she didn't have to engage with the man she'd once called her husband. 'I don't know why she never wants to see you,' Lily added with a pinch of sadness in her voice.

Hal sighed and lowered the volume on the irritating, flashy game show that was currently trying to push his headache into migraine territory. 'Look, Lily,' he started, his voice soothing and warm, 'when you're young – which you still are, by the way, even though you like to think you're all grown-up and like Rita Ora or Jessie J or someone like that ...' She grinned at just how out of touch he was, but he didn't care. 'Even though you think you're all grown-up, you're not. Not really. Not yet. And when you're young, you still think that your parents are like superhuman. Like the Incredible Hulk or Wonder Woman or some rubbish like that. You don't always see their flaws and their cracks and their hopeless little ways. That comes when you're older. Sometimes a lot older.' Lenny Schinowitz jumped into Hal's head for a second. 'And as you get older, you come to realise that, actually, your parents were as messed up and useless as everyone else. They just managed to pull the wool over your eyes for a bit, that's all.'

Silence for a few seconds as the woman who'd just won ten thousand pounds grabbed the host around his stiffly coiffured hair and kissed him.

'It's OK, Dad,' Lily eventually replied. 'I'm already very well aware of just how dreadful my parents can be.'

She gave a wicked smile. 'It's obvious. I see it all the time. A useless pair of tossers, if you'll pardon my French.'

Stevie looked across the sofa and raised his eyebrows as if to say 'See. *She* understands.'

In the morning, Hal walked along the road with Lily, her schoolbag gripped tightly over her shoulder. The sun was slowly lighting the sky as they reached the end of Maple Road.

'Is everything all right with you and Stevie?' Lily asked. 'You didn't say much to each other last night. And he went back to his flat very late. Is everything OK?'

Hal pulled the long overcoat around himself. It was surprisingly cold this morning, he thought. Wintry, almost.

'Oh, nothing much to worry about, sweetheart. I think he's got a lot of work on with the teacher training. Y'know. That and thinking my job interferes with his free time a bit too much.'

'Didn't know what he was taking on with a copper, eh?'

Hal laughed. 'No. I don't think he did.'

The growl of traffic speeding through the amber lights on Penge High Street did its best to drown out their conversation, but Lily pointed to a silver Honda parked a hundred yards away on the opposite side of the road.

'There she is.'

'Yes.'

It was difficult for Luchewski to see properly.

'Your mum had her hair cut, has she?'

Lily looked questioningly at him. 'No. She's had it like that for a long time. Months now. Didn't you know?'

Months? It had been that long. They so rarely saw each

117

other nowadays and when they did it was always at a parents evening or some such thing. Always something to do with Lily. Never to do with them. They never asked each other how they were doing or what they were up to. Every solitary sentence was forcibly fixed on Lily. It was like they couldn't bring themselves to be civil or interested in the other person, so they pivoted themselves around the one thing – the one person – that they couldn't avoid being connected by.

They were both inconveniently stapled together by their daughter.

'It looks nice,' Hal said. 'Tell her it looks nice.'

'I will. See you soon, Dad.'

And with that, Lily skipped away.

Chapter Fourteen

Of course, nothing had ever been the same since the newspaper article. The newspaper article that revealed to the world that Detective Inspector Harry Luchewski of the Metropolitan Police Force was, in fact, gay. He had kept it all under wraps, carefully hidden away for years. Camouflaged amongst the alpha-males at Hartshorn. Concealed behind the drink and the job.

Ironically, in terms of his private life, being unavoidably outed in the press had been one of the greatest things ever to happen to him. He felt as though he'd stepped out into the open and could now just accept himself for what he truly was. It had been like having your leg caught in a rabbit snare, and then being released. Blissfully released. No, privately he was more at peace than he'd felt in many, many years.

But at work …

Work was a different matter altogether.

His colleagues at work seemed to fall into three distinct categories.

Firstly came the people who weren't remotely bothered by the fact that Luchewski was gay. He felt himself to be a good judge of character and so Singh, Burlock, Good, Woode and even Burlock's sergeant – Green – found themselves falling into this category. Corrie too. And a handful of others. Decent people who didn't care that Luchewski wasn't quite the witless hetero baboon that they'd previously assumed him to be. He was who he was, and that was that.

Next came the ones who tried their best to cover up the fact that Luchewski's sexuality was an issue. A number of the DCs and PCs that came and went through Hartshorn House. The ones who gave him quick, nervous glances when he wasn't looking, but who didn't look him in the eye when addressed. Desk sergeants and cleaners. One or two of the secretaries. All of them trying to cope and not managing very well.

But at least that lot were trying.

The last category didn't even bother. They smirked and sniggered and nudged and pointed out the freaky poof to anybody who asked. They would deny it, of course. Keep it all *just* under the radar. Ever so slightly below the surface. But it went on. Luchewski knew. He wasn't stupid. Thankfully the worst of them, Detective Inspector Andy Baldwin, was still off on 'gardening leave'. Would be off for another couple of weeks, apparently. Thank fuck. Hal was pleased not to have that idiot's face sniffing around the office for a bit. He'd already punched him a few months back and couldn't really be trusted not to do it again.

So walking into the office that morning he could sense the presence of all three groups. The friendly hellos and smiles; the twitchy glances; the nasty sneers. Could even sense them as he started his briefing.

'OK,' he started. 'Two young women. Dead. Both killed in exactly the same way. Strangled.' He pulled a couple of photographs out of an envelope and turned to pin them to the large board behind him. 'Both with the words 'BARTHOLOMEW KURTZ' cut into their torsos.' He stuck the large lurid photographs onto the board with a drawing pin. They showed Laurie Frasier's back, bloody streaks dribbling away from dark, deep cuts. Frasier had been slightly thinner than Seagrove so the last few letters of 'BARTHOLOMEW' had tapered away into a kind of smudge. 'Alice Seagrove and Laurie Frasier were at school together. They were also both with Louisa Gaudiano the evening she disappeared.' Luchewski looked around the room. His eyes landed on Woode, whose face was squinting towards the board and the photographs on it. 'We need to know why. Obviously. We need to find out what the hell is going on.'

'Sir,' a DC with especially red cheeks strained to raise his arm. 'Sir. Could it be a relative of Kurtz? Getting revenge, like. I mean, if the girls hadn't argued with Louisa Gaudiano that night she would never have left them, and she wouldn't have disappeared and – as a result – Kurtz wouldn't have been murdered himself. S'just an idea.'

Luchewski could tell that the constable had stumbled across this idea sometime in the early hours and was keen to spit it out at the first opportunity.

'No. Kurtz has no relatives. Not living anyway. His only relative was a spinster sister and she died eight years ago.'

'What about a friend, then? Someone he was close to.'

'When he was murdered,' Hal replied, 'the Force looked into acquaintances and connections. Anybody who might have known him or even just liked him. They found nobody. Not one person. No friends whatsoever. Bartholomew Kurtz was a very lonely old man. Besides, why wait so long to kill? Why not just do it straight away?'

'Could've been another nonce, sir.' This DC wasn't letting his amazing idea go without a fight.

A couple of youngsters snorted at the word 'nonce'

and Hal scowled hard at them.

'Doubt it. I don't think anybody else in this world gave enough of a shit about Kurtz to murder for him. Especially not another sex offender. They're not exactly known for their loyalty and camaraderie, are they?'

After the briefing, Woode came alongside Luchewski and pointed at one of the pictures stuck onto the board.

'This … this new girl. Frasier. She looks familiar.'

'She was a reporter. London News Channel. Called you a wanker a few months back. During the Granton case.'

'Did she?'

'Outside Danny Wiseman's flat. You tried to push her away, and she called you a wanker.'

'Ah,' Woode nodded his head. 'Of course, of course. Dear, oh dear. Dear, oh dear.' Luchewski wasn't sure if Woode was saying 'dear-oh-dear' because she'd got killed or because she'd called him a wanker. 'Poor girl.'

Big Issue spotted him again. He was shuffling along the pavement not twenty yards in front, teetering almost as much as Big Issue himself.

Big Issue blinked his eyes. He was already pissed so he couldn't trust himself entirely. But, no. It was definitely him again. Definitely. He was wearing the same long coat he had on yesterday … was it yesterday? Or was it a few days ago? Big Issue's life seemed to rub over the days like a scrubbing brush, and most of the time he had to think again and again to remember what day of the week it was. Anyway, it didn't matter. It might have been yesterday. It might have been last week. Who cares? But it was definitely him. And his coat was looking dirtier and more ragged than it had before.

Who was he? Who the fuck was he? He strained his

brain to try and remember. *Come on! Who was he?*

Big Issue tried speeding up. He pushed past some cold hard-faced women in grey suits and tried his best to catch up with him. But the man was too quick – so much younger than him – and within minutes he had twisted himself around a corner and slipped down into the underground station disappearing amongst the throbbing mass of humanity.

'Bollogs,' Big Issue mumbled to himself, the word not forming properly on his inebriated lips. 'Bollogs.'

The call came through about an hour later.

'Luchewski.'

'Hello, Harry.' It was John Good.

'The prints?' Luchewski went straight for the jugular.

'Yes. The prints. Had to call in a few favours to get them through so quickly for you, I hope you realise that.'

'Thanks.'

'Been up most of the night too, sorting out the Frasier scene. Bit knackered now, to be honest. Could do with a few hours under the duvet.' He yawned. 'Sorry.'

'Thanks, John. You know I love you, don't you?'

Good sniffed. 'Yes, yes. I'm sure you do.'

Hal screwed the phone closer to his ear. 'So?'

'So …' Good started. 'We got a number of crisp, clear prints on both mugs. On the one with the lipstick around the rim we found Laurie Frasier's prints. No surprise there. On the other …'

'Yes?'

'We found a perfect thumb and two reasonably decent and reliable fingerprints. Good enough to pin them down on a single person.'

'Well? Are they on file, these prints? Is it someone we know?'

'Oh yes. They're on file.' Good tried not to yawn again. 'You definitely know him.'

Luchewski was confused. It wasn't right. It just wasn't right. Everything about it seemed wrong. He knew it was wrong. He just bloody knew it. Why didn't anyone else feel it too? He looked around the office. Everyone else seemed to be bustling and energetic, fired up from this latest revelation. But Luchewski just couldn't believe it.

Woode was desperate to involve the ARVs. Again. 'Look, Harry,' he explained. 'If he's as dangerous as he seems, I don't want to risk any of my people. I'll get the armed boys to whip him out and they can take him to Brixton. You can interview him there.'

'But sir, I don't think-'

'No buts, Harry. This is *my* call. You and Sergeant Singh need to get yourselves over to Brixton. I've already let them know you're coming.' He waved him away with his hand. 'Go on. Off you go now.'

During the drive over to Brixton, Luchewski tried to sort it all out in his mind. Pulling it all together, trying to see how it all could work. But he couldn't. The route through this case came to a dead end with this recent piece of evidence. A big fat brick wall beyond which he couldn't see.

'What do you think, Singh?' he eventually asked her just outside Herne Hill. 'You think he's responsible?'

She squished up her face and wrinkled up her nose. 'I wouldn't have thought so...'

'No.'

'But ... his prints are all over the mug. He was clearly there the night Laurie Frasier was killed.' She sighed. 'Points to him being the murderer, I suppose –

but, then again …'

'You don't believe it any more than I do, do you?'

She shook her head. 'No. No, sir. I don't.'

He was cold and he was miserable. The thin clothes he was wearing weren't enough to keep the wind out. The chilly breeze blew straight through the worn fabrics and across the sore, risen scars that covered his limbs. He shivered and moaned. It was agony. His whole body was tense and ached with a dull, dull throb. The skin on his face was dry and tight.

He'd slept rough last night. For the first time ever, he'd slept rough. Throughout the day he'd walked and walked, never really knowing where he was going. Never really caring. So he kept on walking. Trying to forget.

It was probably about nine p.m. when he'd stopped walking, and his body suddenly felt like dropping. He was so tired – so incredibly tired. It was all he could do to keep his eyes open.

But he couldn't go back home. So instead he'd walked a little further – staggered, almost – until he came to an overgrown graveyard. He didn't know where he was, but the graveyard suddenly looked inviting, with its deep, straggly grass and stones and tombs behind which you could hide from the wind. He dragged himself over the wall and found himself a little nook behind a large, box-like Victorian monument.

That was last night. This morning he had picked himself with a massive crick in his neck after less than two hours' sleep and wandered off, not entirely sure where he should be going. He was stiff and his head hurt as he walked along brushing dead leaves out of his hair and from his dirty coat. He got the impression that people were staring at him.

Then that man started following him. The pisshead. Tried following him, anyway, but he was too fast for him and had slipped down into the Underground station before his stalker had time to catch up. Cornish had rammed the remnants of change from his pocket into the machine and bought the cheapest ticket he could. He slipped through the barrier and down the grey escalators into the tunnels below.

And now here he was – his third time around on the Circle Line. Staring at the floor any time anyone pregnant or elderly frowned at him for not giving up his seat.

He pulled his coat tightly around him again and leaned his head against the handrail. He'd never noticed it before but the Underground was surprisingly warm and snuggly. Soothing in a way. Cosy.

Then his eyes closed and he fell asleep.

Seventeen Years Ago

'Go on.'

'What?'

'Take it. Go on.'

'It's not drugs is it?'

'Fucking hell, it's a fag. Just a fag.'

'Where'd you get them? You didn't buy them, did you?' Katie sounded concerned. 'Only, shops can't sell you cigarettes unless you're like twenty or something.'

'Of course I didn't buy them. I nicked them off my grandad. He smokes loads – there are packets of them just lying around the house – and he's losing his marbles so he can't remember how many he's had. Go on, take it.' Laurie shoved it towards Katie again, who gave a small frown before taking it gingerly between her fingers.

'Oooh,' she now sounded surprised, 'it's lighter than I imagined. I thought it might be heavier.'

'Jesus,' Laurie muttered under her breath and Louisa and Alice laughed.

They all stood there for a few seconds, each of them with an unlit cigarette between their fingers, while Laurie tried fishing a match out of the packet of Swan Vestas she'd stolen from the kitchen drawer earlier that morning. 'You're meant to suck in when I light it. That's what they say. If you don't suck in, it won't light properly.'

She flicked the match against the sandpapery edge of the box a couple of times before the thing caught fire and then held it out to Louisa. Louisa leant forward, her eyes squinting as she watched the flame bob about at the end of the cigarette.

'Suck in.'

Louisa did so and the tip of the fag glowed bright. She immediately pulled it out of her mouth.

'Ugh. It's horrible.'

'Now you.' Laurie Frasier held the match up to Alice. Alice did the sucking-in thing and took the cigarette out of her mouth.

'It's not so bad,' she said before putting it back between her lips.

The match died and Laurie lit another one, bringing it up to her own fag. She took a drag on it and let it dangle coolly between her fingers. 'Yeah. I like it.'

'You've done it before!' Katie looked horrified.

'Yeah, loads. Loads of times.' Laurie took another drag, her eyes slightly watering from the smoke. 'I like it. Now it's your turn.' She fished another match out of the box.

'Er ... no. Don't worry.' Katie held the cigarette back to Laurie.

'You can have mine if you want,' Louisa offered hers to Katie.

'No. It's all right. I don't think I'll bother. It's too horrible.'

'I don't mind it,' Alice put hers back to her lips for another suck.

'Wussies!' Laurie laughed. 'You're both a couple of –

'Oi!'

'Oh fuck!'

The caretaker was marching across the playing field towards them, his shirt sleeves rolled up exposing the red-blue mess of his tattoos. 'Oi! What are you lot doing?'

'Quick!' Laurie threw the cigarette down on the grass and stamped down hard on it. Louisa and Alice followed suit.

'Mint! Have a mint, quickly.' Laurie fumbled with a packet of Polos, popping one into her mouth before handing them over to Alice.

'What the hell are you lot doing?' Mr Biggs came alongside them, his large face red. He grinned. 'Smoking, is it?'

'No, no,' Laurie replied. 'No we're not smoking. Just having a chat. You know. Just chatting.'

'S'funny then,' he snarled. 'The grass seems to be smoking.' He nodded down to the ground where smoke was lazily trailing upwards from the grass. 'S'funny that.' His face slithered into a smirk which only got bigger when he noticed the unlit cigarette in Katie's fingers. He pointed. 'And that's definitely a fag.'

'Oh,' Katie went a sort of beetroot colour.

'Oh, Katieee,' Laurie sighed.

'What year are you in? Who's your head of year?'

They all seemed to shuffle. 'Mr Lawson, sir,' Louisa mumbled.

'Right. Come on. Mr Lawson's office. Now!'

Chapter Fifteen

A pair of useless tossers.

That's how Lily had described himself and Jackie just the night before. A pair of useless tossers. The phrase bounced around his head as the desk sergeant led him and Singh to the interview room towards the rear of Brixton nick.

It was true, of course. He and Jackie *were* a pair of useless tossers. They could barely communicate with each other. Hated each other, almost. But once upon a time ... it had been different. It was, admittedly, a very, very long time ago when he was basically pretending to be someone else, but once upon a time there was something between them. A love of a sort.

Love.

A ridiculously short, stunted little word for something that causes such euphoria and such misery – sometimes at the same time. It could mean so much, but also so little. Luchewski loved his daughter. Full on *loved* his daughter. But Luchewski also loved steak and chips, and the smell of the tarmac after rainy days, and *It's A Wonderful Life* on Christmas Eve, and *Tigermilk* by Belle and Sebastian. He loved fresh clean sheets, and fast cars and being slightly pissed. The word *love* was bandied about too much, like it didn't really mean anything. Was it possible, he thought, to love – actually love – the big things and the tiny things in exactly the same way? Was there a *love* that

131

covered everything?

Bendable Brenda. He was struggling to shake the image of her body all squashed up in a box from his mind. Dead now. Squashed up in a different type of box. Rigor mortis putting paid to her flexible skills.

And her son. Patrick. Thirty-six years old. Four years younger than Luchewski. Four years younger!

Did he know? Luchewski asked himself. Did his father ever know about Patrick? Did he pay her off every month to keep her quiet? Buy her silence? Did he send the boy secretive presents on his birthday or a large cheque for Christmas? Did he buy him his first shoes or his first bike?

Did he know about him at all?

Did he ever visit him?

Did he care about him?

Did he love him?

Luchewski swallowed hard. *Did he love him?*

As he took up position behind the desk with the large, blocky-looking recorder on it, Luchewski came to a decision.

He needed to meet this Patrick.

'So?'

The man sat across the table from Luchewski and Singh raised his eyebrows. '*So* what?'

It was surprisingly cold in the interview room, like it hadn't been used recently and the management had decided to knock the heating off to cut back on the bills. Luchewski swore blind he could hear the hot water starting to burble through the pipes, as if somebody had just turned it back on again.

'What's going on? You need to tell us what's going on.'

Nino Gaudiano sighed. 'Look, all I know is that I'd just crawled into my bed after my nightshift only to suddenly find myself staring down the barrel of one of your lot's guns. Kicked in my door, they did.' He looked a tiny bit put out. 'Didn't have to do that. All they had to do was knock. I'd've let them in. Landlord'll probably throw me out now.'

Luchewski rubbed his nose and looked at the little red light glowing on the recorder next to him.

'You're certain you don't want your solicitor, Nino? You know, we can stop this interview right now and call them. Get them –'

'No. I don't want any solicitor.' He leaned back in his chair and folded his arms. 'Why would I want a solicitor? I've not done anything wrong. Anyway, solicitors didn't do me any good last time, did they?'

'Yes, but you did admit to everything,' Singh chipped in. 'Bit tricky for them to do *anything* in those sort of circumstances, isn't it?'

Nino smiled at Singh, and Luchewski noticed Singh give a wide smile back.

'*Last time*?' Hal asked. '*Last time*? You mean there's a *this time*?'

Nino looked confused. 'Sorry, Inspector, but I don't understand what you're saying.'

'Where were you the night before last, Nino?'

Nino sighed. 'I was at my work, wasn't I? Like every other night. I was at my work and then I –'

'You didn't clock in until nine. Your shift is meant to start at seven, but you didn't clock in until nine. Where did you go, Nino?'

A long silence as Nino Gaudiano stared at his feet. Only a slight buzzing noise from the recorder and the occasional clunk from the water pipes broke the peace.

'Shall I tell you where I think you were? Before you went to work.' Hal leaned in and rested his elbows on the desk. 'I think you went to see Laurie Frasier.' He let the name hang in the air for a second. 'You know. TV reporter. Went to school with Louisa.'

Nino looked back up and nodded. 'Did she tell you I'd been there? There's nothing wrong with two people meeting up, is there? No law against it or anything. Nothing that I know of anyway. Not yet.'

'What did you both talk about?'

Nino shook his head and gave Luchewski a violent look. 'What do *you* think?'

Luchewski threw the next question in just to see what would happen. 'Did you sleep with her?'

Nino leapt to his feet and slammed his fists down on the table. 'Fuckin' hell, NO! I did *not* sleep with her, for Christ's sake! Jesus!'

The uniformed officer who'd been sitting quietly in the corner of the room ran across and grabbed Gaudiano around the shoulders.

'For the record,' Luchewski spoke towards the big black box on the table, 'Mr Gaudiano has jumped out of his seat and slammed his hands on the table ...' He beckoned Nino to sit. 'He is now sitting back down on his chair ...'

Nino shrugged the bobby's hands from him and slowly eased himself back onto the seat. He glared hard at Luchewski as the uniform shuffled unconvinced back to his position in the corner.

'Shall we continue?'

'I wouldn't sleep with her,' Nino half-growled. 'She was a friend of my Louisa. I would *never* sleep with her.'

'I'm sorry, Nino. I just had to ask. If I hadn't, somebody else would have done further along the line.'

Luchewski gave a sad smile, and Nino responded accordingly, his shoulders relaxing. 'Sorry.'

'Look, all I did was go over there and talk to her. Ask Laurie. She'll tell you what we talked about. She'll even tell –'

'Nino. Laurie's dead.'

'Eh?'

'Laurie Frasier is dead.'

Nino looked as though his grandmother had just risen from the dead. 'No. No she's not. She can't be ... I was there. She was alive. The other night. We talked.' He glanced from Luchewski to Singh and back again. 'She can't be.'

Luchewski nodded. 'Somebody killed her. The night before last.'

Nino shook his head. 'No, no. This is rubbish. I don't know what kind of a game you're playing here, but that's rubbish. She's alive. I saw her ...'

'She was murdered by the same person who killed Alice.'

'No.' Another long silence as Nino stared back at his feet and tried to take it all in. 'It's not right. It can't be. She was young ...'

'Nino,' Hal's voice was soft. 'We have evidence that places you at the crime scene on the night of the murder. My Chief Inspector thinks it's an open-and-shut case. *You* killed Kurtz. *You* were released from prison recently. *You* knew both girls – true, a long time ago, but you knew both girls. *You* were in Laurie's house the night she was murdered. End of. As far as he's concerned you're the answer to all his prayers.' Luchewski took his voice down to a whisper. 'Thing is, none of this sits right with *me*. And I'm in charge of this case.' He stared Gaudiano in the eye. 'And I don't think you killed those girls.'

'Of course I didn't kill them. God, I'm not a ... I'm not a ...' It was then that Nino broke down and cried. His head fell forward into his hands and he sobbed hard, tears dripping off the end of his nose.

'Kurtz was one thing,' Luchewski pulled his chair so that he was sitting nearer Nino. 'Murdering two young women – that's another thing altogether. Not even in the heat of the moment.' Singh pushed a box of tissues across the table to Hal who pulled a few out and handed them to Nino. 'Just doesn't strike me as the sort of thing you would do. You're too much of a charmer, Nino. You love women too much.' Luchewski cast Singh a look. She suddenly flushed with embarrassment and her eyes flickered away. 'And women love you.'

'I didn't kill them. Poor girls. I didn't kill them.'

'I know, Nino. I know.'

'They were her friends. My Louisa's friends.'

'Yes.'

'Why would anyone want to kill them?'

'That's what I want to find out, Nino. I want to find out what this is all about. But first I need you to tell me what you were doing at Laurie Frasier's house.'

Gaudiano gave his nose an enormous blow and dropped the tissue onto the floor before reaching across and pulling a couple more out of the box. 'I needed to talk to her. See what she knew.'

'About what?'

'Alice's death. The police made a complete balls-up of Louisa's disappearance all those years ago, and to be honest, I don't have a great deal of faith in them. No offence.'

'None taken.'

The tip of Nino's nose was red from all the rubbing. 'I don't trust them to do their job properly.'

'So you thought you'd start your own little investigation? See if you can solve it before the police do?'

Gaudiano nodded. 'Couldn't do much worse, could I? Anyway, I owed it to her.'

Luchewski gave Singh a quick look. 'What do you mean?'

'*I* killed Kurtz. It was my fault. Nobody can argue with that. Nobody's *ever* argued with that. And if this sick bastard wrote Kurtz's name all over her ... well ...' Gaudiano looked a broken man. 'Even though I didn't kill her ... in a way, I'm involved. It might all be because of what I did with Kurtz. It might all be my fault. And that makes me feel like shit.'

Luchewski leaned back in his chair. It was a point he couldn't really argue with. In a sense, Nino was right. Whoever this killer was, he was deliberately bringing Kurtz back from the dead. Scratching him back into existence on the flesh of dead women. And Nino was at the very heart of the Bartholomew Kurtz case.

'How did you know where she lived?' Unable to reassure Nino, Luchewski came at things from a different angle. 'Have you kept in touch with her after all these years?'

Nino wiped the snot from the top of his lip and looked up. 'No.'

'So how did you know where she lived?'

Nino smiled a pathetic half-smile. 'If you know the right people and you ask the right questions, you get the right answers. Eventually.'

'What's that supposed to mean?'

'It means that I found out. That's all.'

Luchewski sighed and folded his arms. 'You know obstruction's a serious offence, Nino?'

'So I've heard.'

'So tell me how you found out her address. Who told you?'

Gaudiano shook his head. 'Trust me, Inspector. If I tell you who told me, it's not going to help your investigation. If anything, it'll only slow it down. You'll be chasing something that leads nowhere when you could be concentrating on better lines of enquiry. It'll just be a waste of time. Trust me.'

'*I'll* decide if something's worth chasing. Not you.'

Nino ignored him. 'The only thing that can come out of it is that someone just gets into trouble. Someone simply trying to help a fellow human being. A good Samaritan. That's all.'

'Who was it, Nino?'

Nino put his finger to his lips. 'Sealed, I'm afraid. And I don't give a shit if you throw the book at me. Fuck you all.'

'Perhaps you were followed.'

'What?'

Luchewski wiped some imaginary dust from the top of the table, his eyes deliberately avoiding Nino's. 'Strikes me as incredibly odd that the killer turns up straight after your visit. Quite a coincidence, don't you think? Perhaps he was following you. Waiting for you to lead him to Laurie Frasier's house. Waiting for you to show him exactly where she lived before strangling her to death.'

He looked quickly up at Gaudiano, whose face dropped like a cartoon anvil once more.

'I … I … no. No, surely. Oh, God, no … he didn't, did he? He couldn't have …' His eyes darted from Luchewski to Singh to Luchewski again. 'No, no. Please … you don't think … you don't think I led him there, do you? Oh, God.' His breathing became heavier and his eyes kept flashing between the two officers sitting in front of him. 'Oh, God. Oh, Jesus, God.'

Suddenly Nino jumped to his feet and doubled up, a waterfall of vomit spewing out of his mouth and splattering onto the concrete floor of the interview room. Pulse after pulse of the sick, retching itself out of his body. Then a comedic, momentary pause before a second cascade of orangey bile added itself to the puddle. Nino grabbed the corner of the table and steadied himself, spitting the final dregs of stringy puke onto the cold stone. He wiped his sleeve across his mouth and straightened himself up.

Luchewski smiled and tugged one of the tissues out of the box. 'You missed a bit,' he said.

Rebecca Defalco was a shit nurse. She knew that. All that 'concern' stuff that she was supposed to have in spades was somehow missing. If it had been there at the start of her career, it certainly wasn't there now. Nibbled away by year after year of struggling to pay bills and getting up far too early in the mornings. Corroded by the endless frigging bus rides and the simpering sniffles of the sick and wounded. The stupid broken bones, the lifeless livers of self-pitying alcoholics, the cancers and the heart diseases of the lazy and the thick.

She couldn't really give a fuck about the patients. They were all just an irritating hindrance to her life. She could do without them.

Rebecca Defalco was – she admitted to herself – definitely the shittest nurse she knew.

However, even though she cared next to nothing about the people she was supposed to look after and would happily and willingly ditch from her life the people she was supposed to work with, Defalco had a good eye. She knew people. Could understand them. Their little ways, their little thoughts. She could pick up on even the subtlest of things. Suppressed anger, gentle excitement, a flickering twitch of worry. She didn't give a shit about them, but she knew when these feelings were there in front of her. She could sniff them out.

Sitting squashed up against the jiggering, stuttering bus window – beads of condensation dribbling down the glass – Defalco thought about Dr Seagrove. She supposed she had been pleasant enough. Dead now, though, so it didn't really matter. All the other nurses had cooed and sniffed about it all. They all blew their noses and cluttered the coffee room up with their disgusting crumpled tissues caked with gunk and pretend tears. In truth, all the other nurses had cared as little about it as she had. They thought they did. Liked to make believe they did. But they didn't. Not really. They were all hypocrites. Lying, pathetic hypocrites.

At least she was honest to herself.

The bus juddered over a speed bump, almost sending her face slamming into the glass, and she wished the bus company would invest some money in decent buses. Not the usual old rustfucks that rattled their way along the Carshalton Road threatening to cough themselves to death at every zebra crossing.

Dr Seagrove. Alice. She'd liked to be called Alice. Defalco had no time for all that personal rubbish and had continued calling her 'Dr Seagrove'. The other nurses had loved it, of course. It was all 'Alice this' and 'Alice that'. 'This is Mr Thomas, Alice. He's broken his nose, Alice. Shall I take him over to X-ray, Alice?' Bunch of fuckwits. 'Oh look at me, I'm on first-name terms with a doctor!' Whoopdee-fucking-doo!

But even 'Alice' couldn't hide from Rebecca Defalco.

She had seen straight into her. She had seen the pain that lingered somewhere deep within her soul. Something tiny and intangible – the flicker in the eyes, the chewing of the lip – but something that was definitely there.

That had always been there. Since the first time she'd set her eyes on the doctor in the A&E department a year or two back. She couldn't pinpoint what it was exactly – she wasn't a fucking mind-reader – but it was there all right. A broken heart perhaps. Or a dead parent. Something like that.

What hadn't been there back then was the joy. The strange little peeps of joy that glittered through in odd moments. Rebecca Defalco had seen them. But only recently. Only in the last month or so. There'd been nothing like it before. It was a recent thing. Faraway looks and nervous grins. The twisting of the hair around the finger. The jolly, open little doodles on the paper towels. All of it evidence of a change. Hope and happiness. A fresh start. A new man? Must have been, she thought to herself.

And now she was dead. Lying on the slab in some coroner's office. Ready to be picked apart and sliced into. Bagged and tagged.

Life could be a cunt sometimes, Nurse Defalco thought as her hand reached into the bag for the packet of Maltesers.

Chapter Sixteen

'What is it you want …' Woode twisted one of his unlit smelly cigarillos around in his fingers. His office was as neat as a vicar's arse. Packed with stuff but neat. Everything had its own little place. The perfectly positioned photographs of Woode's wife and children; the awards and certificates that dotted the walls; the box files and folders that stood to attention on the dust-free shelves. It all smacked of order and control. Which, of course, was precisely what you wanted in a detective chief inspector. Order and control. It was something Luchewski knew he never had – could never have. His life was far too chaotic and messy for that. True, Stevie had given him a degree of stability he thought wasn't possible only a few months ago. Had calmed him down to an extent. But secretly Luchewski realised that order and control only had so much to offer him. Because of that, he'd hit his very own glass ceiling. He was never to going to rise through the ranks any more than he had done already. Wasn't going to be taking over Woode's office any day soon.

But that didn't really bother him.

Woode repositioned himself on his chair and continued to twist the cigarillo in his fingers. 'What is it you want? Exactly?'

'Twenty-four-hour protection.'

Woode sighed. 'Do you know how much that costs? Have you any idea how much of my budget that eats into?

How long do you want it for?'

'For as long as it takes.' Luchewski raised his eyebrows at the big man shuffling uncomfortably in his big chair.

'That's not the best answer to give, you know. It starts off as a day or two, then turns into weeks, before, four months down the line, I'm laying off a desk sergeant to balance the books.'

'It won't be that long.'

'So you say. What about we compromise and stick a couple of officers outside the house overnight, eh? He's killed the others at night. No reason to think he might start changing his MO now, is there?'

Luchewski sighed.

'And don't sigh, Harry. It's the best I can do in these fiscally challenged times. Anyway, there's no major reason to think he might go after this other girl, is there? It's just a hunch on your part.'

'With respect, sir,' by which Luchewski meant he didn't really have a great deal of respect, 'the four of them were best friends at school. Now three of them are dead. The very least we can do is – and I think it's a bit more than a hunch, sir – the least we can do is protect the last of them. Make sure he doesn't get to Katie Thompson ... I mean Katie Woodington.'

Woode popped the cigarillo between his lips and chewed on it. He couldn't light it inside, of course. He'd be breaking one of the very laws his job asked him to uphold. Besides which, it would only go and set the sprinklers off.

'Hasn't she got relatives she can stay with?'

'Probably. Her parents live quite near. But that's not the point. Wherever she is, I think she needs protection.'

Woode squinted at him. 'You've not talked about

it with them yet?'

'No. No, I haven't. No point in worrying them. We'd keep it quiet. Protect them without them knowing. If we can. Keep the house under surveillance. It's not as though she's got a job. And the husband works from home, so most of the time they're in the house. Should make it easy.'

The word 'surveillance' made Woode huff and shake his head a little bit more. Expense, thought Hal. Woode was always too aware of the expense.

'Surveillance is very expensive, Harry. You know that.'

'We could always move them to a safe house instead,' Luchewski said, a twisted grin on his face.

'Jesus Kid Jensen! Are you *trying* to bankrupt me?'

'No. Just *trying* to do my job.' He smiled. 'So?'

'So what?'

'Twenty-four-hour surveillance? Not too much to ask, is it?'

Woode frowned. 'Yes. It is. Twelve-hour. Seven to seven. It's the best I can do.'

Stevie was trying to write his essay. 'Consider the differences between Assessment *of* Learning and Assessment *for* Learning. Explain how both concepts can be applied in your own subject area.'

In nearly an hour he'd written a grand total of thirty-six words. Only another one thousand four hundred and sixty-four to go, he thought as he drained the last of the cold coffee from the mug on the kitchen table.

It didn't help that he seemed to be permanently pissed off with Luchewski at the moment. Everything the man seemed to do had the effect of winding him up until he felt like punching the wall or taking a knife to one of

Luchewski's expensive suits.

It was as though Stevie wasn't even there sometimes. Like Luchewski would prefer not to have him around. Take last night, for example. Lily was a lovely kid. A real sweetheart. He liked Lily, and he always thought that Lily liked him. He imagined himself a bit of a supercool stepdad. Perhaps they would both go up west shopping for clothes. They'd carry big, boxy bags filled with shoes and tops before crashing out in some over-expensive coffee shop where they'd sip hot chocolate and pull apart muffins while talking about boys. Stevie was good with kids – especially girls – and he liked to think that he was the sort of person kids would open up to.

But Luchewski …

Luchewski didn't help. It was as though he couldn't be bothered to try and join up these two people in his life. Stevie was over here and Lily was over there, and Luchewski was in the middle obscuring one from the other. It wasn't as if he was *actively* trying to hide one from the other, but indifference or distraction or something – something – stopped him from thinking about it, and stopped him from putting two and two together. Perhaps Luchewski was just stupid or something. Except he wasn't. So what was it? What was it about him that made him this way? So remote. So cold.

And friends …

Friends were another issue. Stevie had wanted to take Luchewski out to some of his usual haunts. Gay bars up east. Pubs and clubs around Vauxhall. Introduce him to some of his friends. Manic Mick and Nipple Ring Leslie. Curly Nichols and Willy 'Wendy' Craig. Gwen the dyke. Mad Marianne. DJ Spunk. Good guys and girls the lot of them. But Luchewski didn't want to bother. Didn't seem interested. Just wanted a warm dinner, a couple of whiskys, a quick fumble on the sofa and then start snoring – God, could he snore!

It wasn't as though it worked the other way around. Stevie had been clear he'd be happy – delighted even – to meet Luchewski's friends. But Luchewski just looked awkward and waved the whole idea away, before failing to answer any questions on University Challenge and knocking back the fifteen-year-old malt he loved so much.

It wasn't what Stevie imagined a relationship to be. Even though he and Luchewski were sort of together, he'd never felt so lonely in his whole life.

Stevie stood up and stretched. The tiniest glimmer of the Thames sparkled in the distance, and black, ominous clouds were starting to rumble into the sky. He was pleased to be here in his own flat tonight. He was too tired to deal with the long silences in front of the TV with Luchewski. Besides, he was in the middle of a case so only God only knows what time he'd be getting back home.

Stevie didn't even bother saving what he'd written. He just shoved the laptop lid down and wandered through to the sofa where some bloody rubbish on Sky Movies was awaiting him.

Luchewski was on his own tonight. Thank God. Stevie had some work for his teaching course that needed doing and didn't need Luchewski going on at him while he was trying to do it. So he'd stayed over at his scruffy little flat in Deptford, typing away until his fingers were raw, writing thousands and thousands of words on the best way to smack a stroppy kid in the head or kick some spotty tosser in the face or some such shit.

As soon as he'd got in through the front door, Luchewski had stripped himself naked and thrown himself into the shower. Full power and hot, radio blaring.

Afterwards he'd scrambled into some soft pyjama-type things and stuck a frozen pizza in the oven and poured himself a weirdly large glass of port. The CD collection beckoned, and he stroked his finger across the plastic spines, trying to pick out the one thing that he might tolerate listening to tonight. All of his music collection was on his iPod, and he could just as easily have stuck it into the dock and shuffled everything he had until he stumbled across a track that would tell him what he wanted to listen to.

But, no. He liked the way his finger clicked along the CD cases, his head tilted, quickly taking in the artist and title. One terrible, lonely day not that long ago, he had tried to put his music into alphabetical order. By artist, then album. It was almost alphabetical, even now. A few Ms had slipped in between the Ns, and the Elbow section was all over the place with the Eels section, but otherwise the system was more or less intact. Some of the CDs would be scratched and knackered, he realised. Some of them would be in the wrong case. Some of them could even be missing – lost under the sideboard in a stupid drunken stumble one hopeless night. But most would be OK.

He slid out a cracked case. Cocteau Twins. *Heaven or Las Vegas*.

As 'Cherry-Coloured Funk' kicked in, he took a huge bite of pizza and washed it down with the port. He loved this album: Elizabeth Fraser's vocals soaring and falling like leaves on a breeze, the melodic, soothing synths, and Simon Raymonde's bass picking its way calmingly along each song. Wonderful.

Luchewski threw himself back on the sofa and, by the time the player had reached *Iceblink Luck*, the pizza had gone and he desperately needed to refill his glass. No. Not *needed*. *Wanted* to refill his glass. He felt like he needed a degree of control, so he told himself he *wanted* to refill the glass.

Nino Gaudiano didn't bother going into work that evening. He'd phoned in sick. It wasn't a lie either. He wasn't just chucking a sickie. He really was sick. Sick to the bottom of his lower intestine with it all.

After he'd been released from the Brixton nick, a couple of uniforms had dropped him off back at the flat, neither of them really giving a toss about him. They didn't say anything for the entire journey and hadn't even seen him inside when they'd got there, just fucked off the moment he'd slammed the car door shut behind him. Useless doughnut-munching idiots.

They all were, though. Useless. Every single one of them. Useless then. Useless now. Not interested either. They weren't bothered about actually *solving* crimes. The only things they were bothered about were hitting targets. 'Targets' were society's latest waste of time and energy. He'd even had to set himself targets at work.

'We all have to set ourselves targets,' his line manager had said, playing with the wonky knot at the top of his tie. 'If we don't set ourselves targets, how can we ever truly know if we are improving as human beings? Eh?'

Nino had wanted to give the grinning git a bit of a slap, but instead had scribbled down on the form in front of him 'Empty waste paper bins a bit quicker'.

'Ah,' the ginger pillock had frowned. 'I'm afraid that's not good enough. You see, it's not SMART enough.' 'SMART' targets had quickly become the bane of Nino's life. Every target that was set had to be SMART – Specific; Measurable; Achievable; Realistic; Time-

Limited. 'That target. It's just not SMART.' Nino had sighed and wished his life away, but let the man continue. 'Let's go through it bit by bit. Now, is it Specific?'

'It's quite specific. I think everyone knows what a waste paper bin is. And emptying them a bit quicker … well, it seems obvious to me.'

'OK … What about Measurable? Is it Measurable?'

Nino shifted in his seat. 'What do you mean Measurable? All the bins are the same size, aren't they?'

The man snorted and Nino came momentarily close to ripping out the man's teeth with his bare fingers. 'No, no,' he snorted again, 'that's not what it means. Measurable means the action can be measured. You can keep count of the improvement.'

'Well, if I empty forty bins on a Monday and then empty forty-*one* bins on a Tuesday, does that count?'

'Yes, yes, that's it!' The line manager suddenly looked excited. 'That's it, exactly.'

'So it *is* Measurable then?'

'Yes. I suppose you're right. It is. But is it Achievable?'

'What? Emptying out forty-one bins on a Tuesday as opposed to forty?' Nino shook his head in despair. 'Course it is.'

The man scrunched up his face. 'Realistic?'

Nino grinned.

'OK,' the line manager rolled his pristine white sleeves further up his arms and popped the top of his pen. 'Let's bring in some percentages – percentages always look good – everyone's impressed by a percentage. What about we say you increase the number of bins emptied by … twenty per cent? Hmm? And shall we set a Christmas deadline date? So …' He scratched out the original target on the form and scribbled a new one down.

'There. What do you think?' He spun the piece of paper around and Nino read what he had written.

Empty 20% more waste bins by Christmas.

Even Nino, who wasn't the most literate of men, knew that the sentence made absolutely no sense whatsoever. Still, the frightening thought of arguing utter bollocks for a second longer with this twat of a man, made him want to bring the whole conversation to an end.

'That's fine,' he nodded.

Tonight though, he wasn't contributing to his extra 20%. The idea of having to work, after all he'd heard, made him want to vomit again.

Laurie Frasier. The sweet Laurie Frasier. Who pretended to be tough, but who was, in reality, as delicate as a butterfly on a daisy. He could see that the moment she opened the door to him. The world of journalism had built up a veneer of coldness around her. Tough, uncompromising Laurie Frasier.

But Nino knew women. Knew their flaws and their vulnerabilities. And she was vulnerable. Sad and lost. Lonely.

Who the hell would want to kill her?

They had talked for an hour or so before he'd slipped her his number and left. But the thought that someone else had come along after and … taken her life. Christ. If only he'd waited around a bit longer. Stayed later. She might still be alive.

He thought back to that evening. And thought hard.

And something tickled him …

She was nervous. That was it. Her eyes kept darting back and forth to the clock. As they talked, on her big fat sofa, her eyes kept ticking back and forth to the clock that was nailed above the doorway. Was she going out? He didn't get that impression. She wasn't in any sort of rush to get changed or put on make-up or anything like that. Was she expecting someone?

Ah.

Yes. That was it.

She was expecting someone.

Someone who was going to murder her …

Nino felt like throwing up again. The taste of the bile in his mouth had lingered all day, and he suddenly wanted to rinse a blob of Colgate around his teeth to be rid of it.

She was expecting her murderer. Was waiting for him to come. The killer hadn't followed him, like Luchewski had said. The killer was going there anyway. Nino had been a hindrance. Nothing more. Laurie had been expecting someone to come and Nino had been taking up her time, throwing back her coffee and trying to dredge up the distant past. And all the while, somebody had been waiting. Waiting outside? Waiting for him to leave?

Nino wiped the sweat from his face and slumped further back onto his patchy old sofa.

There was no point telling the police with their ridiculous lists and tickboxes. They wouldn't be able to get anywhere with this. He was going to swallow this down further and deal with it himself.

A flutter in his stomach and his heart made his face crack into a slight smile. Poor old Alice. Poor old Laurie. Yes. But their deaths were not in vain. Their lives weren't wasted.

By dying they were taking Nino one step closer to the person who took his beloved Louisa away from him.

Hal didn't really like texting. Hated the ambiguity of it all. Before he'd really understood all the little symbols and shortcuts he'd thought that LOL had meant Lots Of Love. That had led to an embarrassing situation with a friend from university whose mother had just died.

HOPE YOU ARE COPING he had texted, before adding *LOL* at the end. Needless to say, Luchewski had never heard back from them.

Still …

He found her name on his contacts thingamabob and started tapping away, his stupid thick drunk thumbs bollocking everything up now and then, and the crappy predictive text coming up with something totally nonsensical far too often.

BECKY, he texted. *WANT TO MEET THIS GUY. PATRICK. WANT TO SEE IF HE'S REAL. TELL HIM I WANT TO MEET HIM.* Because he was a bit pissed, Luchewski stuck a smiley face emoji on the end of his message.

Five minutes later he got a reply.

OK it said. *HE'S UP IN LONDON SOMETIME NEXT WEEK. WILL ARRANGE.*

A few moments later, a second message arrived.

ELIZABETH SPOKEN TO SOLICITOR. NOT HAPPY.

A sad-faced emoji was stuck on the end of that message.

Texting would have been no good with Uncle Barry. Uncle Barry had only just got to grips with television remotes and women being allowed to vote. Asking him to text would have been like asking him to land a space shuttle or perform open heart surgery or something. So Hal thought he'd better just bite the bullet and phone the old duffer. It was late, but Uncle Barry was renowned for staying up far too late and fizzling out in front of the box.

'Hello. What?'

'Barry. It's Harry.'

'Ah. Phoning me up to hurl abuse down the line again, eh?'

'No. Look. About the other night. I'm sorry. I'm really, *really* sorry. I shouldn't have spoken to you like that.'

'No, you shouldn't have.'

'I know. Only Lenny Schinowitz called a meeting –'

'Pah! Schinowitz still alive then? Still sucking his pound of flesh from all the Liddle and Moore repeats, eh?'

After Luchewski's parents had died in the car crash in Monte Carlo, Barry Moore had parted ways with the Schinowitzes, claiming years of mismanagement and questionable accounting had worn away his faith and trust in them. Nowadays, he was managed by a flash young media company that operated out of a Camden loft, probably filled with a bunch of hipsters tapping away on their Macs at those desks where you have to stand up.

Luchewski tried to pull the conversation back on track. 'Becky and Lenny called a meeting. It was about that biography that's coming out. The guy obviously stumbled across something to do with Dad and Bendable Brenda.'

Uncle Barry paused and sighed. 'Look, Harry … I don't know what they've told you but … they probably don't know what they're on about. Remember, I was there. I was always there. No one knew your dad like I did. Not even your mother.'

'So?' Luchewski asked quietly. 'What do I need to know? Tell me everything. Please. Tell me everything.'

Another sigh. 'I'd rather not do it down the phone, to be honest. I'd rather tell you to your face. I've never liked phones. Such a cold way of communicating. How can you understand what someone's trying to say when you can't even see their face?'

'There's always Skype,' Luchewski threw in mischievously.

'Eh?'

'Never mind.'

'Look, Harry. I'm up in London later in the week. This Channel 4 reality thing I'm doing. Having some meetings and doing a bit of filming. Looking a bit befuddled on the underground. Signing autographs for strangers. That sort of thing. What if I get Seymour – one of my PR people – to give you a call as soon as I'm in town and we'll meet up for lunch or dinner? Bring Lily along too if you'd like ... no, actually, perhaps not. Not in the circumstances. Better just be the two of us. This time.'

Luchewski nodded to himself and tried to stop his brain from imagining that Seymour had a *phat* beard and drank green tea out of jam jars.

'OK,' he said eventually. 'We'll talk properly later in the week.'

Chapter Seventeen

Luchewski felt oddly relieved as he strode into the office the next morning. Somehow he'd managed to sleep pretty well and when his alarm had beeped, he'd stretched and yawned before swinging his legs over the side of the bed and gently turning the alarm off. Even at that moment he realised he probably looked like some cheery-faced 1950s American advert for Kellogg's Frosties.

Good morning, honey! It's a beautiful day!

At the office, Singh gave him a massive smile before handing him a lukewarm plastic cup of coffee and the morning paper.

The *London Chronicle*.

Stevie had worked for the *London Chronicle*. Until recently, when his morals seemed to get the better of him and he'd decided that teaching was – for some reason – his career of choice.

Luchewski sat back on the chair in his office, took a sip of the tepid mocha and read the headline on the front page.

"MODERN LONDON: CITY OF DEPRAVITY"

Hal snorted and read on. The main thrust of the story was that crime in the capital was on the up and that pretty soon the whole city was going to turn on itself and implode. Or something like that.

The writer had honed in on three crimes in particular –

all of them having occurred in the last few days. The first of them, Luchewski was only too aware of. The murders of Alice Seagrove and Laurie Frasier. Luchewski felt the paper rather focussed on Frasier's death more than Seagrove's – journalists sticking together, even in death, he supposed.

The other two stories were new to Luchewski.

A woman in her late eighties had been attacked by a man as she took sixty quid out of a cash machine. He'd knocked her hard to the ground before running off with her bag and purse. Some stills of the CCTV footage showed blurry images of the incident. Two bodies – one tall and dark looking, the other stumpy and pale – tussling. A violent sweep of the arm. A stumble and a sprint. A sprawled, motionless, bloodied crumple on the ground.

The woman – Elsie Kenton – was currently in a coma. The man, still missing. Family and friends were – according to the article – pleading with members of the public to come forward and help catch the mugger. A reward of £5000 had been put up by a local businessman for any information leading to his arrest.

The other story being picked over by the *Chronicle* was about a flasher terrorising groups of young girls in South London parks. Dressed as a jogger, the man had approached a group of girls only the other evening. As he got closer, the girls noticed that the man was wearing a big rubber mask that, according to reports, was the image of Jeremy Clarkson.

Then he got his tackle out.

'If you have any information on any of these twisted, heinous crimes please contact the London Chronicle *office on ...'*

Cheeky buggers were using their office number like

Crimestoppers, when all they were really doing was fishing for the next little excerpts of the stories. Trying to be the first on the scene with their cameras and recorders. Cheeky sods.

Tap, tap, tap.

Luchewski looked up. Green was standing in the doorway flapping a sheet of pinkish paper.

'Laurie Frasier's phone records.'

Hal threw the newspaper down on his desk. 'Anything?' he asked. 'Numbers in common with Seagrove?'

Green nodded. 'One. Frasier phoned it a number of times last week. Twice the week before. Once last month.' He strode into the room and put the pink sheet on Luchewski's desk. 'This one.' He pointed. 'It's the number you tried the other day.'

Luchewski bit on his lower lip and thought. 'Any luck with Seagrove's network?'

'Unfortunately not. Any info other than the number was on the actual phone or SIM card itself. And he took that with him. Just like he took Frasier's phone.'

'Can we put a trace on it?'

'We've tried already. There's nothing. It's dead.'

'Dead?'

'Been destroyed. Crushed or smashed up. Easy enough to do.'

'It rang the other day though, didn't it?'

'Erm ...'

'Did Frasier make any calls to that number *after* we found Seagrove's body?'

Green picked the paper back up and squinted at it. 'Er ... yes.'

'Shit.' Luchewski slammed his hand down on the table. 'What time did we try phoning that number? Can

159

you remember? Was it before or after Frasier called it last?'

Green's eyes rolled up into his head to try and pull down the right information. 'We called at … just gone quarter past one. Probably not as late as twenty past. Say … seventeen or eighteen minutes past.'

Luchewski stared at Green. He was definitely OCD – no doubt – but now it looked as if he was also a fucking memory man to boot.

'According to this, Frasier phoned the number at one forty-six. So before. We definitely called it before. I'm 100% certain.'

'You're certain?'

'100%.'

Luchewski sighed, but didn't feel any better. What if by trying to phone the number they'd scared him off? What if Luchewski's stupid actions had made the killer break up the phone? Mightn't the techie guys have traced it by now if it was still going? Green could see the question forming behind Luchewski's eyes.

'He would have smashed it up anyway,' he said reassuringly. 'He's not an idiot. Two murders under his belt. Would've been madness not losing it. I bet he's got a whole case full of unregistered phones waiting to be used.'

Luchewski nodded. Green was probably right. Or at least Luchewski *hoped* Green was right.

Tap, tap, tap.

This time it was Woode who stood in the doorway doing his best to block out the light. He didn't look pleased. In fact, he looked worried.

'Inspector.' Woode's eyes took in Green but he didn't bother to acknowledge him.

'Sir. To what do I owe this pleasure?'

'Cut the crap, Harry.' He shifted his way into the office and stood awkwardly halfway between the window and Luchewski's desk. 'I've … I've just had a conversation with the Governor of Ashmoor Prison. A Mr Trevillick. He phoned me because …' He struggled to put the words together. 'He phoned me to let me know that … the case you're currently working on … He has some information – well, no. Not him, obviously. One of his inmates.'

Luchewski thought hard. Ashmoor Prison. The name was familiar to him.

Woode continued. 'Says that this particular inmate has information. About the school. The school the two women went to.'

'Longley Road Secondary,' Green chipped in.

'Yes. Yes.'

Luchewski suddenly felt his stomach drop. 'Who *precisely* is this inmate?'

Woode's face went pale. 'Have a guess.'

Seventeen years ago

Mr Biggs marched them across the playing field towards the main building. Lots of the other kids watched or pointed and laughed at them as the caretaker waved them on.

'Come on. Don't shuffle yer feet.'

'I've never been so embarrassed in all my life,' Katie moaned to herself, head bowed as they neared B block.

Longley Road Secondary was made up of a number of different buildings. Uncared-for Portakabins littered the edges of the school, and a new science block with shiny glass windows took up a prominent position next to the staff car park. But B block was the long, low Victorian building that dominated the site. None of the kids seemed to know why it was called B block. Alice had always supposed that when it was originally built it was named after a local businessman or explorer. Somebody with a surname beginning with the letter B.

'You! Stop dawdling!' Biggs shouted at Alice who had slipped slightly further behind.

Making their way up the first flight of stairs they could hear sniffing coming from around the corner. As they turned, Alice could see the sickly boy – Cornish – squatting on the floor in front of them, his face red, tears streaming down his cheeks.

Hearing their footsteps, he quickly pulled himself up, trying to wipethe snot dangling from his nose onto his blazer sleeve.

'You, boy. What's the matter?' Mr Biggs asked. Alice thought that the usual rasp in the caretaker's voice was slightly less abrasive than usual.

'Nothing, sir. S'nothing.'

Biggs looked the boy hard in the eye. 'Wait here until I've dealt with this lot. You hear me?'

Cornish nodded and Biggs continued down the corridor, four girls in tow, until he reached room B1:29. He knocked on the door and then pushed in roughly.

Lawson was sat behind his desk marking some work.

'Some girls here, sir. Say they're in your year. Caught them smoking on the far side of the playing fields.'

'Smoking?'

'Yes, sir. Go on. Get in, you lot.' The four girls sloped into the room, their bags banging into each other as they squeezed into the small space in front of Lawson's desk. 'If you'll excuse me, sir, I've got something else to attend to.'

'Yes. Of course, Mr Biggs. Of course.'

Biggs slammed the door loudly shut behind him.

Silence. Lawson slowly picked up the top of the Bic and pushed it back over the nib. Then a sigh.

'Oh dear, girls. This isn't good. It's not good at all. Smoking on school premises ... well, it's a good two weeks' detention. No lunch breaks for two weeks. Besides which, it's a really really stupid habit to start. Especially at your age. The occasional fag here and there to make yourself appear cool ... to make yourself look hard ... and before you know it, you're addicted and having to find five pounds every day to feed your awful habit.' He sat back in his chair and folded his arms, staring at them. 'Stupid. And I didn't think any of *you* were stupid.'

Silence again and the little red second hand on the clock above Lawson's whiteboard seemed to tick as loudly as a bomb.

Suddenly the teacher stood up out of his chair making the girls jump and walked over to the window. 'I tell you what I'll do,' he said turning to face them. 'Instead of all four of you doing detention for two weeks – which probably won't actually teach you anything – how about ... how about only *one* of you does the detention? Eh? What about that?'

The girls looked at each other.

'One of you does the time, and the others get away with it. What do you say?'

More silence.

Lawson perched himself on the edge of his desk. 'Yes,' he was smiling to himself. 'That will be much more character-building, I think. Now I don't honestly believe each of you brought your own cigarette into school today. They were brought in by one person – probably bought illegally in a shop by that one person.' He rolled his shirt sleeves further up his arms. 'Now, I either want that person to step forward and take the punishment coming ... or I want one of the others to tell me their name. Yes? Understand?'

They all nodded, Laurie more so than everyone else.

'So?' Lawson shuffled his bottom further onto his

desk. 'Step forward or be named.'

The clock ticked even louder as the girls all eyed each other. Alice felt like nudging Laurie forward, but Laurie wasn't budging – she twisted her hands nervously around each other, but wasn't budging. Why wasn't she budging? Surely she knew she should do the decent thing and admit it?

But Alice also didn't want to grass her up, so just stood there stuck in the thundering awkward silence of the situation, Lawson's eyes darting from one girl to the next.

Suddenly, Louisa stepped forward.

'It was me, sir,' she said gazing down at the wooden floor. 'I brought the cigarettes into school today.'

Laurie, Alice and Katie all glanced at each other.

'It was all my fault.'

Lawson folded his arms and sighed. 'Louisa. Oh, Louisa. I'm really disappointed by you. *Really* disappointed. I'd've thought you'd've had more sense.' He stood up and walked back around his desk. 'But clearly, no. I was mistaken.' He sat and pulled the top off his pen once again. Louisa kept staring at the floor. 'Two weeks detention. Starting right now.' He jabbed his pen towards the other three. 'You lot can go. You're dismissed. And I hope you remember this and learn your lesson.'

Alice, Laurie and Katie all shuffled – slightly dazed – out of the room leaving Louisa standing where she was. As the door clicked shut behind them, Alice gave Laurie the filthiest look ever.

'What?' Laurie growled. 'What's your problem?'

Chapter Nineteen

Singh hadn't been Luchewski's sergeant during the Arnold Richards case, so she knew only the bare bones of it all. Things she'd picked up from Luchewski himself, or stuff she'd read in the papers. So before they set off for the wilds of deepest darkest Surrey, Luchewski pulled the large file out of his cold metallic filing cabinet and handed it to her. During the journey she picked her way through it and filled in the blanks.

'So you couldn't pin these ones on him?' She wafted a document in the air as Luchewski changed gear. 'All these murders. You couldn't get him on any of them?'

Luchewski turned the fan up to try and de-steam the window. The rain was pelting the windscreen like hail and the wipers were moving so violently Luchewski worried they might shake themselves off the TT.

'No,' he eventually replied when a small patch of clear screen made driving at seventy miles an hour on the A3 a teensy weensy bit less dangerous. 'Insufficient evidence. Even forensics couldn't tie him into any of them. He's a clever cunning bugger.'

'Or perhaps he just didn't do them,' Singh added.

Luchewski gave Singh a stare. 'Oh, he killed them all right. I'd happily stake my testicles on it. And you know just how precious *they* are.'

Singh raised her eyebrows and went back to the notes.

It was true that Luchewski had a particular

distaste … no, 'distaste' was far too gentle a word for it – Luchewski had a particular *hatred* of Arnold Richards. Now in his sixty-fourth year and spending time at Her Majesty's pleasure, Richards had come to represent everything about the world that Luchewski loathed. A successful headmaster for most of his career – an establishment figure, in a way – Richards had been a pillar of the community. A member of numerous education and examination boards. A regular attender of his local church. A trusted and well-respected member of the locality. Upstanding. Decent.

But, hidden away …

A killer. A brutal and heartless murderer of young women. A torturer. A demon.

The hypocrisy of it all made Luchewski feel sick. And he knew precisely why it made him feel sick. Because, secretly, he knew that, in a way, he was not a great deal better than Arnold 'The Headmaster' Richards. Yes, there was a massive difference between hiding the fact that you were a serial killer and hiding the fact that you were gay. But nevertheless, to Luchewski, it pretty much amounted to the same thing. A deception. A pretence, a way of protecting yourself from yourself. A denial to the world. To one's self.

Richards had swallowed down his urges, only allowing them to bubble to the surface on rare, depraved occasions. Not unlike Luchewski. He had disguised his gayness under a cloak of heterosexual professionalism, only to surreptitiously sneak across London when the sun had gone down, to drink in gay clubs and pick up young, fit guys. Murder and sex. Were they not, more or less, the same thing? A selfishness? A need? A right?

But now they had both been outed. Richards in a court of law, Luchewski in the national press. So they were free to be who they wanted to be. Only people wouldn't generally allow it. The law of the land kept Richards tucked away from view. Stuck behind tall Victorian walls for the world to see. A blight. An embarrassment. Whilst Luchewski still had to endure the sneers and the mumbled snipes of the bigots in the Metropolitan Police. Neither of them fully allowed to be that which they needed to be. Both of them still confined and restricted.

'So these were the only two you could get him on?' Singh waved another sheet of paper in the area above the gearstick. 'Stacey Graham and Cassandra Shoneye.'

'Yep. Graham was a prostitute. Only eighteen years old.'

'Seventeen, according to this report.'

'Yeah. Heroin addict. Poor cow. Richards took her back to his garage, before raping and torturing her. Then a couple of days later he went out and kidnapped Shoneye. She was a bit older. He kept them both tied up before killing them both. Binmen found most of Graham in the wheelie bin.'

'Nice.'

'Hmm.'

Luchewski swerved just in time to avoid a middle-aged Day-Glo Lycra-clad cyclist, drenched to the skin, struggling up a small hill. 'What sort of idiot cycles on a day like this?'

'And he was a headmaster? Jesus. Incredible a sick bastard like him can rise up so high without anyone suspecting a thing. Especially in education. You'd think they'd be extra-cautious in education.'

'They probably are nowadays. Everyone's CRB checked. You can't move for records and data trails.'

'Do you think that's got something to do with him having information, sir? His connections with the schools and LEAs, I mean? You think he heard something about Longley Road Secondary? Or its staff?'

Luchewski shrugged.

Andrew Cornish hadn't slept so well in years, and he refused to move from his bed even though the day was slowly ebbing away and the sun was panning steadily across the pathetic, threadbare curtains. He yawned and pulled the sheets snuggly over his sore naked body. He felt as if he'd earned the right to spend the entire day in bed.

The last few days had been hell. Trying to sort out his mind. Trying to put everything in perspective. Trying to understand what it was that he'd just done. It had drained him mentally. But it was the physical exhaustion that had taken its toll more than the mental. Walking non-stop all over London. Sleeping in graveyards. Dozing on the Tube. His body was fit to slump, to the extent that, last night, he didn't care if the police arrested him. He didn't care if, when he walked up to his own front door and dug the key out from his pocket, they leapt out of unmarked cars and dragged him off to the cells. At least the police station would have a bed for him to sleep in. At least they would give him food. He wouldn't have to worry any more. Even if they sent him down for God knows how long, all his needs would be taken care of. He wouldn't have to struggle to stay alive any more. In fact, the prospect of prison had become quite appealing.

So he'd walked – legs as heavy as dumbbells – all the way back to his flat. Except, by the looks of things, there were no police lying in wait. As he pushed the front door shut behind him and scampered up the stairs to his flat, he still expected an angry buzzing on the doorbell to follow. Except it didn't. Just silence. So he slid his second key into the door and fell into the room.

Everything was exactly as he had left it. Old canvases stacked up in piles on the floor and new canvases leaning against the wall to dry. The lingering smells of gouache and his own blood. Unwashed plates, chipped coffee cups and broken dishes were trying to hide the sink from view. Mould speckled the walls. His unmade bed.

His unmade bed!

Within seconds he'd thrown all his clothes off and clambered in, the cold of the sheets barely registering. He'd thumped the pillow into submission, wrapped the duvet tightly around him, and closed his eyes. The hunger he was feeling was nothing compared to his exhaustion. He'd spent so long managing so well on very little food that, at that moment, it didn't really bother him that he hadn't eaten in days. All that mattered was sleep, and that came on very quickly.

When he eventually awoke, the sun was very definitely up. He couldn't have cared less what time it was, though. Time, as he liked to tell himself every now and then, was weakness. Spend your days worrying about time and what have you done? You've *wasted* your time *worrying* about time. You have even less of it than you did before you started worrying about it. It was one of those weird dichotomies of existence. Those who worried about ageing found themselves frittering away what little youth they had left.

He rolled over and stared at the canvases angled awkwardly against the wall.

Art.

His art.

His one true love. The only thing that had ever got him through the day. Creating art was his lifeblood. It fed his soul and his spirit and kept him hoping that one day – just

171

one day – people might accept him for who he was. He wasn't a friend or a lover or a son or a father. He wasn't a soldier or a doctor or a politician or a teacher.

But he was definitely an artist.

He tried lying there, staring at the ceiling for a few minutes, before restlessness kicked him out of the sheets. He was an artist, and an artist had to create. No two ways about it. It was an itch he just had to scratch.

'Tea, Inspector? Sergeant?'

The office was pristine. And far too large. It looked rather like a gentleman's club to Hal. A large portrait of a dull-looking man dominated the area above the impressive tiled fireplace, and a few of those old-fashioned leather sofas with what seemed like belly buttons regularly spaced across them sat huddled together in a couple of corners of the room. The mahogany desk on which Mr Trevillick was currently pouring the tea had the antique air of something that the Head of MI6 might have. Even the teaset conjured up images of Elizabeth Bennett and Mr Darcy. Luchewski subdued a chuckle when he saw Singh noisily dipping a malted milk up and down in hers.

'Ever since he awwived at Ashmoor, Mr Wichards has been an impeccable member of our community.' Trevillick spoke with a slight speech impediment which, in Luchewski's eyes, seemed to suit him. Apart from two large clumps of black hair around the ears, the governor was completely bald and the light from the crystal chandelier seemed to bounce off his billiard ball head. He wore thick spectacles that made his eyes bulbous, and a tweed suit that wouldn't have looked out of place on a Scottish laird. Sipping tea – saucer held daintily below the cup – Mr Trevillick came across like an ambassador rather than the governor of a prison full of violent criminals. 'He has played an active part in the wunning of the libwawy; he has organised a number of fund-waising concerts; he has even helped a fair few of the inmates to learn to wead and wite. He even cleans my office for me,' he waved his arm around the room, 'and does a pwetty good job of it, I must say.'

Luchewski found himself turning around to see, before coming to his senses. 'Did Mr Wich ... Richards say anything more to you about his reasons for asking me here?'

The governor put his tea down with a tinkle. 'No. Afwaid not. Just told me to let the Metwopolitan Police know that he had some information about the two murders. I'm sure he'd wed all about it in the papers – libwawy staff have access to all daily papers. Not just the *Sun* and the *Daily Miwwor*' He half-closed his eyes and smirked. 'That's what most of the pwisoners wead, I'm afwaid to say. But he was most insistent I call you. Specifically asked for *you*, Inspector. Said he would only talk to *you*. Said you would understand.'

Luchewski didn't say anything. He suddenly felt cold.

Trevillick leant back in his chair and interlinked his fingers. 'We've got one of our interview wooms weady for you. You can make yourselves comfortable in there and when you're weady, we can have Mr Wichards bwought up. That OK?'

'Actually, no.'

'I'm sowwy?'

Luchewski dumped his precious cup and saucer down with a worrying smack. 'To be honest, I think I'd rather see him on his own territory. In his own room. Is that possible?'

'Er ... well, it's a little unconventional but ...'

'And I'd like to see his room before he gets there. What I'm saying is that I want to be in his room when he arrives. I want him to think I've been casting my eye over all his stuff. I want to unnerve him.'

Singh looked across at Luchewski. Trevillick straightened up in his chair.

'I must say … that's a bit unneccesawy, don't you think? Like I said, Mr Wichards has been an exemplawy member of this community ever since he awwived.'

Of course he has, you silly old turd. Because he knows how to keep on the side of a stuck-up idiot like you. It was obvious that Trevillick would like Richards. Compared to the usual drug-fuelled thugs that populated the institution, Richards was a breath of fresh air. Educated, articulate, charming. *Everything a snob like you wets themselves over.* And Richards knew that. Knew exactly how to mislead and to deceive. For Christ's sake, he'd spent his entire career doing precisely that – fooling the educational hierarchy into believing he was a credit to them. After his arrest it had been rumoured that Richards had once turned down an OBE. Needless to say, no confirmation of such a thing ever appeared. All evidence seemed to miraculously 'disappear'.

'I would still like to do it, Mr Trevillick. Please. If it's not too much to ask.' *Besides*, thought Hal, *no one knows the fucker like I do*.

Liz hadn't been in to college the last two days and, for some reason, she wasn't bothering to return his texts. Stevie assumed that one of her kids must have been off school sick. Either that or her mother. Whatever it was, it was clearly taking up her time to the extent that she couldn't even be bothered replying to him. So, with no one to share lunch with, Stevie had skipped food and headed straight for the library.

The university library was a glassy, over bright building a hundred yards down the road from the Education Institute. Stevie beeped his card and the two waist-high barriers flipped inwards to let him pass. Glossy-leaved cheese plants lined the reception area, welcoming you in like a squadron of Triffids.

As he walked quietly through the General Reference section, he could see lots of earnest young things dotted across the tables, papers, books and iPads strewn all over the place.

Stevie made his way towards the stairs at the far end of the library and started climbing. He knew where he was headed. The Education section was on the first floor and, on the far left, tucked neatly between the Psychology shelves and a display on how to use the microfiche, was a long thin table that looked out over the street. Stevie had sat himself there a couple of weeks back and found that it was a place where he could really pull his thoughts together. The gentle distraction of the people walking along the street – sometimes strolling, sometimes hurrying – gave him a peculiar sense of ease, and he could slowly put ideas together and structure his essays.

He was pleased when he saw that the table was empty, so he unpacked his leather manbag and switched the laptop on. Down on the street a young couple were pottering along, hand in hand – he with a long grey raincoat, she with a Superdry windcheater. They looked a very odd pair. The guy was tall and borderline hipster – his beard was too weedy to be all-out Lumbersexual – and the girl was all labelled and dapper, like a trainee lawyer on her day off. But they were, without a doubt, clearly besotted with each other. As they wandered, they swung their arms together, and smiled and pointed and giggled.

Neither of them seemed to notice the other people having to walk around them.

Stevie hated them instantly.

As Word opened and the screen suddenly glowed white, Stevie turned away from the window and opened up the essay he had so miserably failed to start the previous evening.

Being a student at his age – nearly thirty – was weird. Having essays to write and micro-teaching sessions to prepare felt odd. Like he wasn't doing it properly. Wasn't a real, serious, actual student. It was like he was just pretending. All the younger students were legitimately there. Starting out. Embarking on their careers. Whilst he was there because he'd already bombed in one career.

As a journalist, he hadn't proved to be very good. He'd been too soft. Too eager to please. His stories always seemed, to Stevie, to read like the sort of thing you'd get in the *People's Friend*. Too gentle. Too cosy. Not knuckleduster-tough stories that won you Pulitzer Prizes. He hadn't had the gumption or the guts for that. No bullet dodging front-line stories for him. No heroin-pumped celebrity ambulance-chasing or serial killer-interviewing exclusives either.

No, it had been all lost lottery tickets and escaped dogs and humorous holiday coincidences. As a journalist, he'd sucked.

And now, here he was, the oldest queer in the class, trying to make deadlines and revise for tests. It felt strange. Scary, in a way. But it also felt right. The lectures had fuelled his mind, and there were some aspects of education that he really wanted to dig deeper into. The psychological and the sociological dimensions of standing in a classroom and sharing knowledge intrigued him and he started to wonder if, perhaps, going further with his studies might be an option. An MA or even a PhD. Yes, Steven Denyer, PhD had a certain ring about it. *Dr* Steven Denyer.

'Hello. Again.'

'Eh?' Stevie snapped out of his daydreaming and looked up.

The young guy from the pub was there. Hovering over the table. With another student that Stevie recognised from the course. Another guy.

'Oh. Hi.' Stevie suddenly felt flustered and he pulled the top of the laptop down for no particular reason.

'Busy?' the guy smiled and the name flashed quickly into Stevie's head. *Mike.*

'Just finishing off that essay for Dr Danborough.' Stevie grinned.

'Oh I haven't even started that yet,' said Mike. 'Have you?' He turned to the smaller, thinner young man standing next to him and Stevie was suddenly overcome with an inexplicable jealousy.

'Nah.' The thin boy looked utterly disinterested and glared out of the wide window at some youngsters kicking a football along the street.

Mike turned back to Stevie before pulling one of the chairs out from under the table. 'You found this little spot too, I see. I like it here. Best table in the whole library, if you ask me.' He dumped his bag on the floor and sat down. 'Don't mind if we join you, do you?' Stevie felt slightly annoyed when Thin Features also pulled out a chair and shuffled in alongside Mike.

'Not at all. Yeah, I like it here too. I like staring out of the window sometimes. Watching the people as they go past, you know.'

Mike nodded and pulled a large A4 pad out of his bag and onto the table. Thin Features did the same thing.

'Takes your mind off all the ridiculous deadlines.' Mike popped the top off a pen. 'Can get on top of you sometimes.' He started scribbling in the pad. 'Wouldn't you agree, Stevie?'

He's remembered my name. 'Er ... yes. Yes.' Stevie nervously pushed the laptop back open and the screen glowed back into life.

They all sat there in silence for a while – Mike and Thin Features writing stuff in their pads, Stevie typing the occasional line of gibberish on the Word document. After about twenty minutes – in which Stevie had added a further one hundred and forty-three words to his count – Thin Features stood up.

'Off for a slash.' He loped off down the aisle like an exhausted orang-utan.

Stevie peered over the top of his computer. 'Charmer.'

Mike laughed. 'Isn't he just?'

'Who is he?'

'Name's Tom.'

'Tom?'

'Yes. I've been trying to shake him off since the second week of term. Doesn't take the hint though. Just keeps following me around. Hasn't made any other friends.'

Stevie smiled. 'Well, here's your chance. Grab your stuff and run. Now. While he's having a "slash".'

Mike laughed again and Stevie's heart went *ba-da-boom*. 'It's tempting.'

You're tempting, Stevie thought.

Suddenly, as if he was reading Stevie's mind, Mike leant in towards the centre of the table. 'Look, Stevie. Before he gets back. We're having a party. Tonight. At my house. Would you like to come? It's only a few people.'

178

'Is cheery chops invited?'

'Of course not.'

'Good.' Stevie pretended to think about it. 'OK. Where?'

Mike ripped a sheet of the A4 paper off the pad and scribbled down the address before sliding it across the table towards Stevie. 'There. Come any time after about eight. Don't worry about bringing anything – Courtney, one of my housemates, works in an off-licence. She gets stuff dirt cheap. It might not be the best quality but at least it's cheap.'

Stevie peeled the paper from the table and looked quickly at it before folding it and slipping it into his pocket.

'And bring your friend, if you like. The one with the funny hat. If she's around.'

Stevie raised his eyebrows. 'Doubt it. She's not been around for a couple of days now. And she's not been texting me back.'

Mike gave an 'ah well' sort of shrug before turning to see Thin Features coming back to the table.

'Those bogs are the bollocks,' he said before slumping back in his chair.

Chapter Twenty

Luchewski sat on Arnold Richards' single bunk. The sheets and blankets were utilitarian grey and the bed itself was hard and unyielding. Thin strips of metal criss-crossed over the small window that, Luchewski noted, looked out over the exercise yard and the staff car park. The rain was spraying again and the glass in the window was smeared. It was, Luchewski thought, a grim view.

Good.

The wall facing the bed was covered in books. Three long, straining shelves tried to hold hundreds and hundreds of the things in position. But the shelf space had already been filled, and more books were piled in two toppling great towers on the floor next to the small MDF desk with the clunky-looking chair tucked under it.

Luchewski got up and pulled some of the books out from the top shelf and looked at them.

Geoffrey Chaucer – *Love Visions*

Alicen of Norwich – *Revelations of Divine Love*

Sir Gawain and the Green Knight

The Owl and the Nightingale / Cleanness / St. Erkenwald

Luchewski snorted, half-aware of his own ridiculous ignorance, and dumped them clumsily back on top of the other books on the shelf. Instead he picked up the first few books on one of the piles.

Emile Zola – *L'Assommoir* – in the original French

Ben Jonson – *The Complete Poems*
Lampedusa – *The Leopard*
Machado De Assis – *Epitaph of a Small Winner*

Hal sighed, none the wiser, and deliberately put them on top of the wrong pile.

He turned his attention to the desk. A portable Sony radio with its aerial sticking up sat against the wall and alongside that were several leather-bound notebooks and a small pot of pens. Luchewski took one of the notebooks and sat back down on the bed. Opening at a random page he started to read Richards' spidery handwriting.

"To think that I had committed these two terrible monstrous acts fills me with horror – and will continue to fill me with horror until my dying day.

It was as though I became possessed by some other being. Not me. Not me at all. Some demon that had corrupted my senses and filled my blood with desire and hatred. Until that point, I had always been a rational, intelligent man. A decent, hardworking, respected member of the establishment. Until that point, I had never once been in trouble with the police – not even a speeding ticket. Until that point, I had always considered violence the reserve of the impotent and cowardly, especially that perpetrated against women. So, considering empirical evidence, it seems unlikely that I, Arnold James Richards, would be capable of such barbarous acts.

And yet, it was most definitely me. Inexcusably, unavoidably me. No doubt about it. A fact as clear as an early morning on a summer's day.

I murdered Stacey Graham. I murdered Cassandra Shoneye.

How God can dare to look down on me with anything other than vengeful malice, I do not understand. I am not worthy of anything more. But God has shown me ways and has given me a chance. I look to God now – not for forgiveness, I can never truly be forgiven for what I have done – but for hope. Hope that I can somehow scrape together some slight, insignificant amends for my dreadful deeds. Hope that I can make life better for others."

Luchewski threw the notebook angrily onto the desk knocking over the radio. The whole thing smacked of appeasing the parole board. Richards meant none of it, he was certain. All that faux regret and faux remorse was designed to be found and read by those in charge. And no doubt some do-gooder would flash it about and say how it shows that Arnold Richards – brutal murderer of at least five women – had turned a corner. They'd say how it clearly demonstrated a new found sense of repentance and that, under the circumstances, Richards' sentence should be lessened or even quashed altogether.

Two MC Escher posters blu-tacked to the dirty off-white walls – black and white twisty stairs and that zig-zaggy aqueduct thing – added to the mindfuck feel of the cell, and Luchewski felt suddenly and irrationally angry that Richards was even allowed to have posters on his walls and notebooks in which to write a load of crap. The man should be kept in a bare cell with no warmth or windows whatsoever. He should be tied to the wall and fed Mars bars just once a day.

After all, that was exactly what he had done with Stacey Graham and Cassandra Shoneye – chained them to his garage wall before raping, torturing and killing them. If it was good enough for them, it was certainly good enough for him, and Luchewski secretly hoped that Richards had been subjected to a gang rape in the shower. Nothing too violent, of course. Just a bit of serial bottom violation. There were surely enough contenders in this place for such a thing.

'Sir.' Singh nodded at him from the doorway. The clop-clop from the landing outside told him that people were coming. Luchewski repositioned himself on the bed.

The footsteps slowed and then –

Arnold Richards stared hard at Singh as he turned into his cell, before frowning towards Luchewski.

'Detective Inspector Luchewski. A pleasure to see you again.'

Richards was dressed in the standard slate-coloured shirt and navy trousers of Ashmoor Prison. He looked older than Luchewski remembered, the lines on his face more pronounced than the last time Luchewski had seen him. His thick hair was now more white than grey and his usually neatly trimmed beard was poking out in clumps here and there. But underneath – below all the exterior crap which, Luchewski suspected, was just another ruse to fool the board of appeal – was the same old Arnold Richards. His eyes bright and watchful, his hands lithe and strong. He'd not put on any weight since the court case and he moved as smooth and snake-like as ever.

'Richards.' Luchewski deliberately refused to use the first name, and also to put the respectful 'Mr' in front of the second. 'Wish I could say the same.'

Richards eased himself into the cell and pulled the chair out from under the desk. Luchewski was delighted to note a slight sense of annoyance at the fact that he was sitting on the man's bunk.

'I see someone has been meddling about with my medieval literature section.' Luchewski peered up at the copy of *Sir Gawain and the Green Knight* that was half-hanging off the top shelf. 'Always good manners to put things back as you found them, Inspector.' Richards pointed to the two piles of books that sat on the floor. 'I've not sorted those yet, so it really doesn't matter all that much that you've rummaged through them. But I do take exception at having my personal thoughts read,' he redirected his index finger to the leather notebooks on the desk, 'and then summarily dismissed by a member of the constabulary who – in his clumsy, disrespectful way – tries to destroy the one piece of electrical equipment that I hold dear.' Richards leant over and righted the radio. 'Afraid in this place, not many people care for Radio 4 and the World Service. It's all Radio 1 and those awful stations where they play awful music in between the glut of awful adverts for awful car dealerships.' He lowered himself onto the chair and crossed his legs. 'Let's just say that the other prisoners and I don't have lovely late-night sing-songs together.'

Singh came into the room and stood, arms folded, in the doorway.

Richards nodded towards her. 'Your sergeant, I take it? Not the one you had during *my* case. Too much for him, was it? Left the police altogether, eh?'

'Nope.' Luchewski said no more. The fact was that his old sergeant had moved somewhere up north to be with his future wife and had transferred to one of the forces up there. Still, there was no need for Richards to know that. No need for Richards to know anything, in fact.

Richards sighed. 'So, Inspector. Tell me. Did you find anything interesting in my emotional outpourings there?' He scooped up the notebooks and straightened them into an ordered heap. 'Anything you can use against me?'

'No. There's nothing in there that can be used against you. Because there's nothing in them that's true. They're just a whole load of unpalatable lies.' Luchewski couldn't stop himself from sneering. 'Saying you regret all the terrible things you've done. What a load of fucking bollocks. The only thing you regret is not having the opportunity to kill more innocent women and girls.'

Richards smiled and brought his hands down to rest, fingers intertwined, in his lap. 'I remember now. You always expressed yourself in rather crude ways. Like your vocabulary didn't stretch beyond the coarse and the tasteless. Strange really. Considering your family background.'

Luchewski shifted his buttocks on the hard bed.

'Victor Liddle. That was your father, wasn't it? Liddle and Moore. *The Liddle and Moore Show*. Not that I ever watched anything like that. But you would think that having a rich and famous father might have had some bearing on your character, wouldn't you? You might think that the privileges that money can bring – even if it is *nouveau* money – would rub some taste and decency into one's skin. But no. Clearly not. He obviously didn't send you to the right school.'

Richards' eyes were focusing hard on Luchewski, trying to judge his reaction, trying to see the flashes of anger that he hoped he'd fired up. The inspector refused to give him that pleasure.

'Tell me all about Longley Road Secondary.'

'And as for "regrets" … we've all had them, haven't we. We've all had a few. But then again, too few to mention. Ha!' Richards laughed loudly at his own joke. 'Seriously, though … I'm sure even you – the seemingly unim*peachable* Detective Inspector Harold Luchewski – have had enormous regrets in your life. You know the sort of thing. Failed marriage. Homosexual encounters.' His eyes were staring even harder now. 'Unwanted daughter.'

Luchewski swallowed hard and Richards, spotting this, broke into a gigantic grin. 'Yes, even you, Inspector, have your weaknesses.'

Hal clenched his fists. He wanted to smash the living hell out of Richards and save the taxpayer the expense of having to keep this vile human being locked up for the next Christ knows how many years. He wanted to shove Richards' beloved radio right up his arse and rip out the pages of the notebooks and make him eat them until he choked. He wanted to pin him to the ground, sit on top of him and scream 'Don't you dare mention my daughter!' into his stupid beard.

But he didn't.

Instead he stared at Richards and repeated himself. 'Tell me about Longley Road Secondary. What information have you got that's so important you can only discuss it with me? Tell me, Richards, what made you drag me all the way out to this dump?'

Richards looked around his cell. 'I know. Not exactly The Savoy, is it? I've tried to cheer up my own personal space a little but –'

'Mr Richards. Sir.' It was Singh. 'Please tell us whatever it is you know.'

Richards half-twisted to see her. 'Ah. It speaks! I must say, Harry – you don't mind me calling you "Harry", do you? – I must say that the Met are coming on with their equal opportunities policy. First a homosexual inspector. Next an Indian sergeant. Remarkable. They'll be recruiting hermaphrodite opium addicts with three arms next.'

Luchewski became uncontrollably annoyed with Richards' baiting of Singh and, for the first time, he allowed his anger to spill out.

'Listen! Shut your face and tell us whatever it is you wanted to tell us or we'll just fuck off and leave you to rot in your own shit.'

Richards burst into a laugh, rocking backwards and forwards on his chair. 'That's more like it. That's the Detective Inspector Harry Luchewski we've all come to love and admire. Your father definitely sent you to the wrong school. Definitely. You spent too much time knocking about with boys from estates. Far too much time. And it could have been so different. It wasn't as if your family didn't have the means.'

After his outburst, Luchewski suddenly felt a whole load better. 'We're waiting, Richards. Tick tock. We're waiting.'

Richards stopped his laughing and sighed.

'You crack me up, Inspector. You really do.'

'Longley Road, sir.' Singh was unfazed by both Richards' racism and Luchewski's anger. 'Longley Road.'

'OK. OK. Shall I tell you exactly what I know about Longley Road?'

'Jesus, Richards, you like to draw things out, don't you?'

'Well …' He leant forward conspiratorially in his chair. 'Longley Road Secondary is an 11-18 co-educational school just outside Tooting in south London. Its Ofsted reports have, over the years, been little more than adequate. Not quite "unsatisfactory" but … unexceptional. It has approximately one thousand seven hundred pupils on its books and only five of its students have ever managed to get into Oxbridge. Its rugby team, though, had quite a run of wins in the early noughties – South London Schools Cup holders for four years consecutively, if I remember correctly – and the swim squad did once produce a not particularly successful Olympic diver. There was that unfortunate incident when the girl disappeared all those years back – which of course you know all about. It has had numerous headteachers over the years, a number of whom I knew particularly well through various educational boards and trusts – all of them rather drab and uninspiring, I'm afraid. Oh, except Jeremy Allin, who I always vaguely suspected of being into S&M and amyl nitrate.' He grinned again. 'You'd have got on well with him.'

Luchewski looked disinterestedly at his own fingernails. The whites were peeking out the tops and tiny clumps of dirt were caught under one or two of them. 'Anything else?'

Richards rolled his eyes around the room as if trying to search his brain for extra information. 'Er ... no. That's it.'

'So you brought us out here for no fucking reason. You brought us out here to waste fucking police time. You ignominious little shit.'

'I do love your style, Inspector. Or should I say your lack of it. I really do.'

Luchewski stood up. 'Come on, Sergeant. Let's go.' He walked towards the cell door but, as he passed the first of the Escher posters, Richards shouted.

'Stop!'

Luchewski found himself suddenly stopping and mentally kicked himself for doing so. He turned around slowly. 'What?'

Richards was now frowning. 'I'm sorry, Inspector ...'

Luchewski frowned along with him. 'What?'

'I got you here under false pretences.' He untwisted his legs and sat forward in his seat. 'Wrong of me, I know, but I didn't know if you would come otherwise. It was the only way I could guarantee your visit.'

Hal folded his arms and fixed his eyes on Richards. 'I don't understand. What shit are you talking now?'

Richards rubbed his hands over his arms as if he were

cold. He paused and then said, 'Caroline Merriman.'

'Caroline Merriman?'

Richards nodded. 'Yes. You know full well what I'm on about.'

Luchewski thought. And then it clicked.

'What about her?' he started warily. 'What about Caroline Merriman?'

Richards sat back in his chair, a slight look of relief on his face. 'Oh come now, Inspector Luchewski. You know only too well what I'm about to say. Why don't you just save me the job and say it for me? Eh?'

Hal took a step back into the room. 'OK. I'll tell you what you were about to say, shall I? I think you were about to say that you killed Caroline Merriman. Weren't you?'

'Was I?'

'Stop fucking about with me, Richards.'

Richards looked to the floor nodding sadly, and for a split second – just for the tiniest, most insignificant of nanoseconds – Luchewski felt a spasm of pity for him.

He quickly shook the feeling out of himself.

'Stop fucking about, Richards.'

'Yes.' Richards straightened up again. 'Yes. You're correct. I. Killed. Caroline. Merriman.'

Luchewski and Singh just stood there for a moment or two. 'You're confessing to the murder of Caroline Merriman? I don't understand. If this is just another of your bloody jokes …'

'No. It is not a joke. Just an old man desperate to make peace with the world.'

'OK then. What about all the others? What about Lisa Wilson? And Katie Wilson? What about Deborah Reed?' He squeezed his jaw tight. 'What about your little sister?'

Richards suddenly found the poison in his eyes again.

'I. Killed. Caroline. Merriman.'

'As far as I can remember you weren't even a suspect in the Caroline Merriman case. Your name probably came up after your arrest, but obviously not enough to bring charges. You lying, *Arnold*? You trying to fuck around with us just that little bit more?'

'You're a difficult man to persuade, *Harry*. Perhaps you should just learn to listen to others more. Might be good advice. Might do you some good to heed that advice now and again.'

'Oh, piss off.'

'Sir.' Singh had come alongside Luchewski and touched his elbow, her gesture telling him to keep it under control – that something more important than his own pride might be at stake at this very moment.

Luchewski sighed.

'You might want to give your lawyer a ring. I'll get the Met to send down someone who remembers something about the Merriman case to interview you. They'll take you down to the interview room and get all this down on tape before you change your mind and deny it all.'

'Too late for that anyway, sir.' Singh said as they left the cell. She was holding up the mobile phone that she'd somehow managed to smuggle past the gates. 'Got it all recorded anyway.'

'Sometimes I think I fucking love you, Singh.' The terrible weather had faded to nothing more than a dull grey sky as they drove back towards London. 'If I wasn't ...' he still struggled a little with the word, 'gay, I'd take you home and ravish you all night long.'

Singh squirmed in her seat. 'Er. Thank you, sir. Sounds ... lovely.'

They sat in silence for a short while and then, as soon

as Luchewski had enough of a run to leave the car in fifth gear, Singh asked the obvious question.

'So who was Caroline Merriman?'

Luchewski responded with something she hadn't expected to hear. 'I don't know.'

'What?'

'I don't know. Well, what I mean to say is, I don't know very much. Caroline Merriman was murdered a long time ago. Twenty-five, thirty years ago. Something like that. Way before I joined up. Raped and murdered. The killer was never found.'

'Where did it happen?'

'Somewhere near Wimbledon.'

Singh sat and stared out of the window. 'Wimbledon's quite near Collier's Wood, isn't it? You don't think Richards was the one who took Louisa Gaudiano, do you?'

Luchewski shook his head. 'As soon as Richards was arrested, South London AMIT allocated officers to go through every unsolved female murder and disappearance for the previous forty years. They found that the night Gaudiano disappeared, Richards was in Mexico ... or somewhere in South America ... anyway, on an educational exchange visit.' He shook his head again. 'No, Arnold Richards did not murder Louisa Gaudiano.'

'Those same AMIT officers also dismissed Richards as Caroline Merriman's murderer – a murder he's now admitting to. It's not impossible they got it wrong. Don't you think?'

'Pretty hard alibi to fake though, isn't it? Can't just nip across the Atlantic for a spot of murder before popping back for enchiladas and a tequila or two.'

'I suppose. Do you honestly think Richards murdered Merriman? And why is he owning up to it now? Why not three years ago when he was first arrested?'

'Singh,' he overtook a pale blue Nissan Micra, 'something you need to understand with Richards is that, even though his whole life before his arrest seemed to shout out order and reason and decency, in reality the man's always been a psychopath. Always. He just kept things hidden well. Incredibly well …'

Yeah, like you did, you hypocrite, Hal aimed a mental punch at himself. *Kept it all in and hidden away. Just like your father did before you.*

'There's not necessarily a reason why he's revealing this now. Just another cheery side of his sociopathy. Either that, or –'

'Or what, sir?'

'Or he stands to gain something from admitting to it.' He thought hard. What could he possibly aim to achieve by admitting to Caroline Merriman's murder? Was there anything? The more he thought about it, the more frustrated he became but also the more adamant he was that Richards was doing it for a reason. No, it wasn't just another cheery side of the man's sociopathy. It was something more.

Something much more.

PART THREE

I Am The Resurrection

Chapter Twenty-one

"Harold. Becky Schinowitz has been on to me. Says you've asked to meet this ... person – the one claiming to be ... well, you know. Look, Harold, I really don't think it's a good idea. The less we have to do with him the better. Let's face it, all he's really after is money. He's just made up these lies to try and get money out of us. Nothing else. Look, I know we've had our differences in the past ... but surely we have to stand together now. For Dad. For his memory. For all the people who grew up watching him on television. We owe it to them, you know. So please, whatever you do, don't meet up with him. If the newspapers get hold of this story they'll have a field day. We just need to bury it as quickly as possible. I hope you understand. Let's do it for the grandkids. For Lily and my two. Yes? Let's kill this horrible episode off as quickly as we can. I've spoken to my lawyer already. I know you'll see sense. Eventually. Bye."

As the phone message came to an end, Luchewski realised that he now *definitely* wanted to meet this Patrick. The fact that it was going to piss off his sister gave him the perfect incentive to do so.

Burlock and Green were watching the hipsters working in the café opposite. East London seemed to be spilling over with cafés serving alfalfa and wheatgrass on anything other than a plate.

'The thing is,' Burlock muttered, 'call me old-fashioned, but I rather like my food on a plate. A decent piece of porcelain or china, y'know. Something with a bit of a lip.' He waved his arm in the direction of Counter Culture. 'But those buggers – serving food on some lump of old wood or a tile from B&Q or the rotting carcass of a dead animal or whatever the new most-fangled thing is – those buggers are making life difficult for their customers.'

'How's that?' Green sometimes found it best to let Burlock have his little rants now and again. It was no good struggling against them, they would only come back and bite you in the end. But, then again, it was no good encouraging the rant. Burlock was easily stirred into a fervour, and Green liked an easy life. So, early on in their relationship, Green had come to realise that all he had to do was enable the conversation to occur. Say as little as possible and just tease the rant out of him.

Burlock pulled his too-small jacket tightly around his too-fat frame and prepared himself. 'Well, it's no good pushing your food around with your knife and fork if it's likely to drop off the end of whatever it's sitting on, is it now? You can't possibly eat anything that's too saucy or wet as it's all going to run off the sides and onto the table. Or your lap. Have a good look at these beardy types' trousers. See if they're covered in guacamole or summat.' He sat himself against the brick wall at the bottom of the steps. 'And as for the beards ...' Burlock stroked his own bedraggled fuzz. 'Not the beards of real men, are they?'

'How come?' *Tease it out*, thought Green.

'*This* is a real beard.' Burlock twisted some of it around his fingers and Green instantly wanted to go and run his hands under a tap. 'See the way it has been allowed to just grow the way that nature intended?

Unhindered. It gets the odd trim when a few of the hairs start to spring out, I'll admit. But *their* beards are shaped and sculpted like frigging ornamental hedges. I'll bet they're there every night, scissors in hand, tweaking and pinking away for hours. I'll bet they give their beards a good shampooing and conditioning each morning before putting curlers in and blow-drying the ruddy things.' Burlock tugged on some of his own facial hair and Green suddenly felt very sick. 'I'll have you know that not a single drop of aloe vera and jojoba conditioning oil has ever graced this little wonder. Not once. I'll give it the quick one-two with a towel after a shower but that's about it. Beauty regime complete.'

Green didn't particularly want to know about the things that Burlock did in the privacy of his own bathroom, so – believing the rant had run its course – he turned and looked back up at the front door of the house.

'He's obviously not in. Shall we leave it?'

Burlock pushed himself away from the brick wall and looked up too. He sighed. 'Dunno. Got a feeling about this one.' He clicked his teeth together for a few seconds, thinking. 'Tell you what, let's go get a coffee – from somewhere decent, I mean. Not that rip-off joint,' he nodded back towards Counter Culture. 'A latte will probably set you back a fiver in there, and you'll probably have to choose between the milk of a freshly lactating yak or some powdered macadamias. No, let's go to Starbucks – there's one just round the corner. You know where you are with a Starbucks. Let's go to Starbucks and then come back. See if he's in – or he's answering – then.'

'Is there any point me even being at yours tonight?' Stevie's voice was almost aggressive. 'Or are you going to be tied up in this case?'

Luchewski looked around the office. It had just gone four and nobody was showing any sign of going home yet. There was still far too much to do.

'I can't promise anything, I'm afraid.'

'No. I realise *that*.'

'Sorry. I'll try and make it up to you at the weekend. If we're making headway, that is.'

Stevie sighed. 'So, it's another night on my own finishing off assignments and watching old episodes of *Friends*, is it?'

'Looks like it. Really sorry, Stevie. You know what it's like.'

Stevie huffed before saying something that vaguely resembled a goodbye and cutting his boyfriend off.

Luchewski felt guilty. Not so much for the way his work intruded on their relationship – that was just a fact. Stevie had come into this situation way down the line and he was just going to have to put up with it. A policeman's lot, after all, was not a happy one. All those late nights and being called away at awkward moments – they were par for the course. Stevie would just need to realise that that was what he did, was what he had to do.

No, Luchewski felt guilty for something else. His silence. He hadn't discussed his possible half-brother dilemma with Stevie yet. In truth he hadn't discussed it with anyone, but there was a part of him that said he should at the very least have mentioned it to Stevie by now. They were, after all, a couple, and that was the sort of things couples did with each other. They opened up, they revealed their secrets and their worries. They talked things over. They resolved issues.

The problem was that Luchewski wasn't very good at that sort of thing at the best of times. The fact that an extra complication had been dumped into his usually very complicated life made matters even worse than usual, and he found himself with no great desire to un-bottle himself any time soon.

Josh Woodington uncorked a bottle of red wine and poured a glug into the bubbling mass of bolognese that he'd got going on the stove. It was a simple affair – an onion, two cloves of garlic, three mushrooms chopped infinitesimally small so that the kids wouldn't be able to detect them, a jar of Dolmio, a dash of Worcester sauce and now ... he tipped the bottle once again ... two glugs of wine. Thinking for a second, he tossed in a third for good measure.

The spaghetti itself was steaming away like an Icelandic geyser, and Josh remembered to turn the overhead fan on before the windows of the kitchen fogged up completely. The broccoli was in another pan, on standby.

He pulled two long thin glasses with brittle stems from the cupboard and split the rest of the wine slightly unevenly between the two. Fishing two packets of salt and vinegar crisps from another cupboard, he wandered through to the sitting room and handed his wife the glass with less wine and tossed the crisp packets to the kids.

'Thanks, Dad.'

Katie frowned up at him. 'What are you doing? They're going to have their dinner soon.'

'Chill yer boots, Katie,' he slumped down on the sofa next to his wife 'It's not the end of the world. It's only crisps.'

A rustle as the kids ripped open the bags.

'But it'll ruin their appetite. They won't eat their dinner properly.' She lowered the magazine she was reading onto her lap. 'They'll leave some of it.'

'Well, if they do, I'll stick it in a tub in the fridge and heat it up for my lunch tomorrow.'

She scowled at him. 'I think you've done it deliberately so that you get something decent to eat for your lunch tomorrow. Haven't you?'

'No. Of course I haven't.' He washed the wine into his mouth. 'I'm not clever enough to think of that.'

Josh looked at his two children. Zac was squatting on the floor playing some ridiculous Star Wars game on his Xbox – crackles of lightning shooting out from the character's hand, throwing a stormtrooper into the air. Sophie was brushing the mane on one of her My Little Pony things – the ones that weren't really ponies at all but teenage girls with massive eyes and rather snouty-looking faces. Both of them stuffing themselves with salt and vinegar crisps.

'I'm not entirely sure I believe you.' Katie picked up her magazine and whacked her husband on the legs with it.

'Mummy. What are you doing?' Sophie looked up half-disinterestedly from her dolls.

'I'm smacking Daddy for being so naughty.'

'Your Daddy's a very naughty boy see, Soph.' Josh gave the little girl a pretend sad face. 'And Mummy has to tell him off.'

'No you're not, Daddy. You're a good boy.' Sophie went back to her brushing.

'See. From the mouths of angels ...'

'Ha!'

'Anyway,' Josh sidled up nearer her, 'those children would much rather see us canoodling and being all lovey-dovey than watch you hit me with this week's copy of *Glamour*.' He leant over and gave her an overdramatic kiss on the forehead accompanied by a drawn-out sucking sound.

'Da-a-ad!' Zac was distracted from his game just long enough to get shot dead on the screen.

'Daddy!' Sophie dropped her horse/girl thing on the floor. 'Stop it!'

'Just giving my lovely wife a kiss,' he grinned, putting his arms around his wife's shoulders. 'Just showing her how much I love her. Don't mind me doing that, do you?' He leant in and gave her another smacker on the head.

Katie laughed.

'Ugh! Cut it out you two. It's disgusting!' Zac threw Sophie's half-eaten packet of crisps at them both.

'Yeah! Stop it. It's horrible.' Sophie stood straight up, her arms folded, a miserable frown stuck on her face. 'I don't like it.'

'Well, I do!' Josh said before doing it again.

'No!'

Katie and Josh giggled before Katie reached out to her daughter and pulled her to her breast.

'I don't like it,' Sophie mumbled sulkily.

'There, there, sweetheart. Daddy's just messing around.'

'Well, I don't like it.'

Josh gave Sophie a playful prod in the ribs.

'If *you* don't want to finish those crisps off ...' he suddenly dropped down onto the floor on his hands and knees. 'then I'm going to gobble them up.' He moved slowly, crouching, and crawled towards the armchair where the packet of crisps was teetering on the edge of a cushion.

'No!' Sophie squealed delightedly as Josh got nearer the crisps. She skipped off her mother's lap and ran around the coffee table arriving at the armchair just a second before her dad. She snatched the packet up and stuffed a handful of crisps into her mouth defiantly. 'They're mine!'

'Drat! So near and yet so far!'

Katie laughed again. Sophie giggled.

Zac shook his head, refusing to look away from his game for a second time for fear of falling into the Sarlacc's pit. 'Weird,' he said, punching the buttons. 'Just plain weird.'

Darren Westlake had skipped the last hour of work – they were awaiting the arrival of a new crane anyway, so there was nothing much doing while that was on its way. It had to have a police escort and was the size of a fucking Boeing 737, so it crept along the roads at about five miles per hour and probably wouldn't arrive until about four in the fucking morning. So he'd taken the opportunity to drive halfway across London to get himself some fresh supplies.

He'd phoned in his order in with the fat bird. She was usually pretty reliable – admittedly there had been that awkward incident a few months back when she was nearly rumbled – but that was smoothed over and since then there'd been no problems. He'd ordered some of the usual – for himself – and some of the other stuff that he knew he could sell on. Might as well make a bit of cash out of his situation, he told himself.

The sun was starting to lower itself past the raggedy London skyline as he waited on the bridge that went over the train lines. It was their usual meeting place. Quite near her work. But not that near. It wouldn't pay for her to be seen by her colleagues handing the stuff over to him. That wouldn't have done either of them any good. And he didn't want to hang about waiting for her outside that fucking graveyard. Even in broad daylight and with cars speeding past, it still gave him the creeps. Too much of a reminder about where exactly he was heading.

He felt the bundle of notes in his jacket pocket and watched the hazy orange sun slowly sink. This was his area. He'd been born and brought up here. His mum and dad had lived here for years until they'd upped sticks and moved down to the coast. He hadn't seen them in about six months – not since finding out. It was a tedious drive and then, when he'd get there, there was fuck all to do. There was only so much admiration you could give the sea. You could try staring at it all day, in awe of its magnitude. Gasping at its power. But in the end it was only just another fucking thing. Just one of a million fucking things. And none of them really mattered.

He'd told his ex all about it the other night. She'd been in tears, of course. Said she'd take care of him and they could move back in together. He could see the kids and she'd pack in her course to look after him. It was vaguely tempting. Vaguely.

He stood on tiptoe and tried to see the roof of his old house.

No. He couldn't. And he couldn't be arsed walking to see it. What good would it do? Like the sea, it was just … something. Something to mentally acknowledge and then ignore. Nothing to concern yourself with.

'Hello.'

He swung around quickly and nearly toppled over. It was her. Her arm was outstretched and her fingers clenched around the goodies.

'That'll be a hundred and fifty quid,' she said, a stupid great grin on her stupid fat face.

Luchewski was eating a pasty. Singh had popped out to

Greggs earlier in the afternoon and picked him up a corned beef one. He'd been so busy that he'd forgotten to eat it and so now, standing in front of the investigation board – pictures of dead women, dead paedophiles and missing schoolgirls filling his vision – he took big bites out of the cold pasty and scattered crumbs all over his suit and the cheap and nasty carpet tiles.

'I don't get it. Is he wooing them?'

'Wooing, sir?' Singh stood alongside him trying to avoid getting flakes of pastry on her.

'With Frasier, he took flowers. And wine. Is he wooing them?'

'But he hid in Seagrove's wardrobe. That's hardly the act of a keen-to-impress Lothario, is it?'

'No. And brutally murdering them isn't. What I mean is, is he winning them over by pretending to be romantically interested? He took their phones. They must have had his name and number stored in them. Certainly he and Frasier were close enough for him to bring wine and flowers.' They stared hard at the two murder scene pictures directly in front of them. 'Techies are working on their social media. Just in case.'

'What about Kurtz? Any leads that can come from there?' Singh brushed a stray pastry flake off her skirt.

'We've sent out a request for the names of the two boys he was convicted of abusing. Problem is, because they were under sixteen at the time, they were given total anonymity. Boy X and Boy Y. Even now, years later, it's not easy to get the names out of the system – their identities are still protected. It's going to take a lot of worming and squirming on our part to find out. If we can.'

Singh wandered over to the coffee machine, stuck some coins in and punched a few buttons before returning with two lukewarm and slightly rancid-tasting coffees for them both.

'Do you really believe he's going to go after Katie Woodington next? He can't exactly woo her, can he? She's already married with two kids.'

Luchewski winced. 'I hope not. Probably won't. Woode's put an overnight watch on the house. Seven to seven. Not what I asked for exactly but … there you go. Usual story.'

'OK, Soph. Six thirty. Bath time.'

'Aww. But Mummy I'm busy with my –'

'No buts, cheeky chops. Time for your bath.'

Sophie dropped the purple Furby onto the floor and it started making its awful noise again.

'OOOOOOhhhhhhHHHHaaaaaAAA. MEEEeeeAAA PLAY GAME. YOOOOWA PLAY GAME WITH MEEEEeeeAA?'

'Oh, fuck.' Josh muttered under his breath. 'Can you turn that off, Sophie love? It's making too much noise again.'

'Can't turn it off,' Zac said wandering back in from the kitchen with a glass of orange juice. 'Hasn't got an "Off" switch.'

'OOOOOOOOO. MEEEaaaa LIKE FRIEND. YOOOWWWAAA MY FRIEND. Mwwa mwwa mwwa. KISSY KISSY.'

It had been a Christmas present from Josh's parents. A brand new, state-of-the-art Furby. One that you could link to an app and play games with on the iPad. It probably cost Josh's parents a good fifty quid, he thought. The problem was that as soon as you put batteries in it, the fucking thing wouldn't shut up. It chuntered on and fucking on, asking to be fed, to play, to dance, to be stroked. If you put your finger in its mouth, it made weird sucking and chewing noises. If you shook it about, it went WOOOAH, WOOOAH like it was getting dizzy or something. If you tickled it, it sort of purred and groaned like it was about to ejaculate. And it kept having strange regenerations. One minute it would definitely be a bloke, and the next, after a bit of OoooOOooHhhhHHNoooOOO-ing it would suddenly acquire a squeaky female voice – 'WHHHEEEEEEEE' – and start grating on your ears again.

And it didn't have an 'Off' switch. No nice little black plastic switch under its arse for those times when you needed a bit of peace and quiet. Nothing. Josh had come close several times to 'accidentally' kicking it hard against the wall while no one was looking. But he hadn't quite had the heart to do it yet. Instead he was slowly biding his time, waiting for the batteries to eventually wear out and then to keep forgetting to buy some.

In fact, the only way that you could get the damned thing to go quiet was for it to 'go to sleep'. If you turned it on its side and left it alone long enough for it to start wondering where everyone had gone, it would give a drawn-out 'YAAWWWWWNNN' before wishing the room a goodnight and then snoring for about two minutes before falling asleep. Then you had to be extra vigilant not to touch it, otherwise it would give another yawn before going 'WAKEY WAKEY' like it was Billy frigging Cotton and starting its usual round of sycophantic begging.

'YAAWWWWWNNN,' it went as Sophie bent to pick it up again.

'No! Don't!' Josh shouted, startling his daughter. 'It's going to sleep! Don't disturb it! Dear God, no. Don't disturb it. Whatever you do.'

Zac came alongside and, bending over, threatened to poke it with his finger.

'Zac! Don't.'

Zac laughed and straightened up before taking a drink of orange juice and falling back onto an armchair. He scooped up the book he was currently reading and turned a page.

Katie was still standing in the doorway. 'Come on, Soph. Bath time.'

Sophie picked her way carefully around the sleeping Furby, being careful not to set it off again. 'Is it nice and hot, Mummy? You know I like it nice and hot.'

'Yes. It's nice and warm.'

Sophie stopped and looked up at her mother. 'Hot, Mummy. I didn't say warm. I said hot. There *is* a difference you know.'

Seventeen Years Ago

'OK. See you later.'

Louisa Gaudiano made her way back towards the building. It was lunchtime and everybody else was out in the yard. Lots of the boys were playing football. It was hot and the blazers had come off and ties were loosened. As Louisa got nearer the entrance, Alice could see Baxter Perry – who was in goal – stop the ball from bouncing into her. Louisa didn't seem to notice and pushed the door open, disappearing inside.

'Don't you feel guilty?' Katie asked.

Laurie didn't say anything.

'You should feel guilty. I know I would,' Katie continued. 'She took the blame. For you.'

'Well, I didn't ask her to, did I?' Laurie spat and started walking away. 'That was her choice. If she wants to be an idiot then that's her choice.'

'Well I think you should –'

'Don't, Katie,' Alice said softly. 'Let her be.'

'What?'

'Just leave her alone. She's feeling guilty.'

'But I think the whole school should know –'

'That's not going to help.'

'But Laurie needs to –'

'Oh, Katie. Just put a sock in it, will you?'

Katie stood open-mouthed as Alice ran to catch up with Laurie.

'What?' Laurie sniped over her shoulder.

'Ignore her. She doesn't mean any of it.'

'No. She's too fucking stupid to mean any of it.'

'Look. We all smoked the cigarettes. We're all to blame.'

'Little Miss Pigtails back there didn't smoke hers, did she? Perhaps that's why she's being so fucking up herself right now.'

'No. We're all to blame. Perhaps we should all go and see Lawson and do the detention together. What do you think?'

'What do I think?' She stabbed her finger back towards Katie who was looking a little lost on her own in the middle of the yard. 'I think that *she* should just fuck off and die.'

With that, Laurie whipped around and stormed off, leaving Alice just as bereft as Katie.

Chapter Twenty-two

It had been tempting to open up a second bottle of the red wine – after all, most of the first had managed to find itself in the bolognese – and it really was a particularly delicious bottle of Tesco's Finest, Josh thought.

But Katie had put the knackers on that idea.

'No. You'll only wake up at three and not be able to get back to sleep again. Then you'll drop off just before the kids have to get up and start snoring in that awful loud way you do when you're drunk.'

'I don't snore, do I?'

'You do when you're drunk.'

So, instead, Josh had made coffee and carried it through to the sitting room where his wife had just finished off her *Glamour* magazine. Zac had gone up to his room to make a start on his homework – some tedious nonsense about the role of women in the Second World War. Sophie was in the bath.

'Why don't you just forget work tomorrow?' Katie said, raising her eyebrows. 'We could go and see a film while the kids are at school. We haven't done that for ages.'

'Can I have some of those cheesy nachos?' Josh joked. 'The ones with the chillies on top? Please! Please!'

'OK. Yes, yes. You can. I'll allow it.'

'And a large Pepsi? Can I have a large Pepsi?'

'OK, OK. Whatever you want!'

Josh sighed. 'Anyway, no. I can't. Got to get that antivirus and spyware package ready for those people in Hastings. Has to be up and running by the weekend, they say.'

'Not even a couple of hours off in the morning?'

'Nope. Not even a couple of hours.'

Katie gave a frown. 'You work too hard, do you know that?'

'I know, I know. I'm the IT equivalent of Dermot O'Leary.'

'Ha!'

'Daddeeeeee!'

'Eh?'

'Which one was that?'

'Daddeeeeee!'

'Sophie.'

'DADDEEEEEEEEE!'

'Shit!'

Josh jumped up off the sofa, throwing his coffee cup to the floor, and ran through the door, down the corridor, through the kitchen and the utility area to the bathroom at the back of the house. He quickly twisted the handle on the bathroom door and threw himself in.

'What is it? What is it, Sophie? Are you all right? Christ! Are you all right?'

'Daddeeeee!' She was still sitting in the bath, water barely up to her belly button. Tears were dribbling down her face and she held her arms out for her father to pick her up.

Josh bent over and scooped her out of the water and pulled her close to him, squeezing her tight.

'Are you all right, Sophie? I thought something was wrong.'

Her little body jerked as she sobbed breathlessly, the

water running off her skin and onto the tiles and Josh's trousers.

'What is it, sweetie? What's wrong?'

Katie suddenly appeared in the doorway, closely followed by Zac.

'What's up, Dad?'

Josh ignored them and hugged his little girl tightly, comforting her with his swaying body and whispers in her ear.

'It's all right, sweetie. Daddy's here. Nothing's going to happen. I'm here now.' Katie leant over and stroked Sophie's hair softly.

After a few seconds, Sophie's breath came back under control, and Josh reached over and wrapped a towel around her. 'That's better. Can't have you getting cold now, can we?' He patted her dry. 'What was it, Sophie? What scared you?'

Sophie pushed herself away from her father a few inches and pointed towards the window. Her breathing suddenly started stuttering again as she said, 'The man.'

'What?'

'The ... the man. Outside.'

Josh, Katie and Zac all looked towards the large frosted pane of glass, black now with the onset of an autumn evening.

'A man?'

Sophie nodded. 'There was a man ... outside ... in the ... in the window.'

Josh's stomach dropped about a mile. 'Christ!'

He lowered Sophie to the floor and turned towards the back door.

'Dad?' Zac's voice sounded uncertain.

'No!' Katie grabbed Josh by the arm and pulled him back to her. 'Don't go out there! It's him.'

'What?'

'Who is it? Mum? Dad? What's happening?'

Sophie started crying again and Zac absentmindedly went into the bathroom and put his arm around her.

'If there's someone out there, I need to see.'

'No! Don't! It's him. Don't go out there. It's dangerous.'

'But –'

'No. It's him. I know it is. It's the one who ...' she stopped herself from saying it, suddenly aware of just how frightened she was making her own children. 'It's him, I'm telling you,' she whispered.

Josh relaxed his grip on the door handle and looked at his family. His family who were always happy and laughing and joking. And now here they were – suddenly confused and scared witless. And there was nothing he could really do about it.

'Call the police,' Katie said kneeling on the bathroom floor and throwing her arms around her children. 'Call that one who came here the other day. Get his card, lock the back door and call him. Now!'

Luchewski was just about to open the coroner's report on the death of Laurie Frasier when his mobile rang. It was a number the phone didn't recognise.

'Luchewski.'

'Mr Luchewski, my name's Josh Woodington. You came to speak to me and my wife the other day.'

The voice was rushed and nervous, and Luchewski found himself standing up from his desk and walking out of his office, clicking his fingers towards Singh. 'I remember.'

'Well, there's a man in my garden.'

'What?'

'A man. In my garden. Right now. My daughter saw him.'

'Shit.'

Singh got up and came alongside him, her face screwed up with questions.

'He was looking in through the window ... the bathroom window.'

Luchewski looked at his watch. 7:03.

'One minute, Mr Woodington.' Luchewski pulled the phone away from his ear and covered the receiver. 'Singh – the two officers stationed outside the Woodingtons. Get hold of them. Tell them to go to the house and ring the doorbell three times.'

'Sir.' Singh whipped around and started punching numbers into the cream-coloured phone on her desk.

'Mr Woodington. Stay indoors, whatever you do. Do not go outside. There are two officers parked directly outside your house – we put them there for your safety. My sergeant is calling them now to tell them to come into the house with you. They will ring the doorbell three times. OK? When you hear the doorbell ring three times, you know it's them. They'll take care of everything after that. Until we get there at least.'

'OK,' Josh replied, not sounding completely convinced. 'Three times?'

'Yes.'

Singh chattered on the phone before putting it back down. 'They're not even there yet.'

'What?'

'Road closures have slowed them down. They're about half a mile away.'

'For fuck's sake.' Luchewski didn't care if Woodington heard him. 'Mr Woodington, keep all doors locked and keep your family in the one room – the sitting

217

room, perhaps. Don't leave that room until you've heard the officers ring the doorbell three times, you understand? They're on their way right now. They shouldn't be long. Keep your family calm and distract your children. Try not to give them nightmares.'

'It's a bit too bloody late for that.'

Luchewski listened as the family all bustled through to the sitting room, followed by the slam of the sitting room door.

'OK, now just sit there. The two officers are literally just around the corner from you. When they arrive they'll –'

'Sssssssssshhh!'

'What?'

'Sssssh. Be quiet, all of you.' Luchewski realised that Woodington was talking to his wife and kids. The phone went silent for a moment, except for the sniffing and sobbing of a child. The little girl, thought Hal. The six-year-old. Sophie. He thought of his own daughter at six. Tiny, frail, easily scared.

'What is it?'

More silence and then, 'Oh God!'

'Mr Woodington, sir. What is it? Please. What –'

'Someone's trying the back door. They're trying to get in. Oh my God!'

'Mr Woodington, stay calm please.' Lots of sobbing now. 'Please. Just stay –'

'They're still there. They're trying to open the door!'

Suddenly, a loud shrill ring. Followed by another. Then another.

'Those are my officers. Let them in and hand this phone to them straight away.'

A shuffle and a rustle and then …

'Hello? Sir?'

'Who is this?'

'Detective Constable Williams, sir. I'm here with –'

'He's in the garden. He was there a few seconds ago.'

'Who's in the –'

'Our suspect! He's in the fucking garden! Right now! Go get him and if he runs off give chase.'

'Oh.'

Another rustle. Luchewski listened as the second officer mumbled his introductions to the family and tried to soothe them with promises of more officers on their way.

Luchewski felt completely impotent. He was miles away from where it was all happening and he desperately wanted to be right there, hunting down this sick bastard, reassuring the kids. But all he could do was listen in on his phone. Singh stood with her arms folded, watching him listen in.

The voices muttered and mumbled until another person came back into the room and took the phone off whoever was holding it.

'He's gone. Must've heard the doorbell and scarpered, sir.' It was DC Williams. 'No sign of him.'

Luchewski shook his head. 'OK. Seal it all off. Everything from the back door to the back gate – don't let anyone go anywhere near it. It's a crime scene. Keep it secure.' He looked over at Singh who immediately picked up the phone once again. 'We'll be over as soon as we possibly can.'

Chapter Twenty-three

Before they left for the Woodingtons' house, Hal had taken the moral high ground with Woode.

'If we'd had twenty-four-hour eyes on both back and front, we'd have probably got him by now.'

'Assuming he hadn't spotted the eyes to the rear of the property,' Woode returned.

Hal squirmed at what a weak argument that was, and it was obvious from Woode's reaction down the phone line that he was only too aware of it himself.

'OK, OK,' Woode relented. 'You've made your point. So, what is it you want now?'

'One of the safe houses. I want it opened. And twenty-four-hour live-in security. Until we've caught this tosser. I don't want that family at risk any more if I can help it.'

'Done. I'll give family liaison a call too.'

By the time they got there, the whole house was lit up like the Eurovision Song Contest. All the neighbours were out in force, standing in their front gardens watching all the comings and goings, half of them secretly desperate to see a body bag or two being carried out. Meanwhile, forensics were ferrying their clever little boxes in through the front door and down the corridor to the rear of the house.

Luchewski and Singh flashed their cards and ducked under the cordon before walking through the front door and into the sitting room.

The Woodingtons looked like they were about to go on holiday and were just waiting for the taxi to take them to the airport. They all had their coats on and two large suitcases sat on the floor before them. The only things that gave away the fact that they weren't actually going on holiday were the looks on the parents' faces and the way the children were sitting either side of their mother, hugging her tightly. The young girl was sniffing like she'd been trying to stop herself from crying.

Two female officers stood up as Luchewski and Singh came into the room. Family liaison. One of them had a big A3 sketch pad and had clearly been trying to calm the daughter down by drawing pictures of animals. The colouring pencils on the sofa looked untouched to Hal.

'Mr and Mrs Woodington.' He gave the children a smile. 'Zac. Sophie. Have my officers explained everything?'

It was Zac who spoke first. 'They said we're going to go to a different house.'

'For a few days.' Sophie clung even tighter to her mother. 'That's what they said. Only for a few days ... we'll be coming back home though, Mummy? Won't we?'

Katie kissed the top of the girl's head. 'Of course we will. It's only for a few days.'

'Why do we have to go away? Who was that man?' Zac frowned firstly at his father and then at Luchewski.

Luchewski looked at Josh Woodington who seemed to be staring into the distance like he hadn't heard his son.

'He's just someone we need to find,' Hal said delicately. 'Somebody we need to talk to.'

'What was he doing here? I don't understand what he was doing here. And why was he trying to get in? Through the back door as well?'

'Like I said, we'd like to find him so that we can speak to him. Then we'll know.'

'Don't worry about the man, Zac,' Katie put her arm around the boy. 'The police will take care of everything. We've nothing to worry about now, do we, Inspector?' She glared hard at him, threateningly.

'Yes. Yes. You're safe.' He didn't sound entirely convincing and Katie Woodington's face seemed to suddenly contort with a kind of bitterness.

'Everything is going to be completely fine now.' Singh went around to the sofa and knelt down before the children. 'I give you my promise that whoever this man is, we will catch him very very quickly and we will lock him away so that you never have to worry about it all again. You understand? Now, the house we are going to take you all to tonight is a secret house that no one knows about.'

The boy seemed to straighten up. 'Like Grimmauld Place in Harry Potter.'

'Yes. A bit like that.' Singh gave a warm smile and the children relaxed their grips on their mother. 'Very like that, actually. The only people who can see it are the police and anybody else we *allow* to see it. Not just anybody, mind you. We don't just let anybody in. You are a very lucky family because you are actually going to *stay* in it for a few days.'

'Are we allowed?' the girl asked.

'Yes. You're allowed. All the police had a big vote and they agreed that you're allowed.'

Katie gave Singh an appreciative nod and Luchewski felt like a clumsy overgrown twat compared to his sergeant, so he coughed an excuse and went back out into the corridor and down the hallway towards the back door.

Luchewski was disappointed to find the Senior Forensics Officer wasn't John Good.

'Not Dr Good's night to be on call,' the man with the shiny tan and decent bone structure said under his little white hood. 'Mine. Unfortunately.'

'Anything yet?' Luchewski stabbed his finger in the direction of the back door.

'Steady on. We've only just got here. Haven't even properly unpacked everything yet. It takes time this gathering evidence lark, you know?'

Luchewski felt his skin prickle. 'But is there anything obvious? He spent time looking through the bathroom window. You might want to start there.'

The man stopped unravelling the whatever-it-was he was unravelling and looked Luchewski hard in the face. For a split second, Hal was reminded of the cold stare that Katie Woodington had given him not a minute before.

'Inspector, I've been in this job for fifteen years now. I'm sure I know what I'm doing. So please, if you don't mind, just let me get on with it and I'll feed back any findings the moment I have them. Yes?'

Luchewski calmed himself down. 'OK. Sorry.'

'That's all right. You're understandably keen to get on. As am I.'

'Yes. Sorry. I'll leave you to it.'

'Thank you.'

Luchewski turned to leave, feeling slightly chastened.

'Oh. Actually there is something I suppose. Need to take a cast of it, of course.'

'What?' He looked back over his shoulder.

'A footprint. In the flower patch. When he was looking through the bathroom window, he left a footprint. Only the one. But absolutely perfect. Every last detail as clear as crystal.'

The Woodingtons only had a few minutes to wait before

the unmarked cars arrived to take them to the safe house. Two large officers carried the suitcases to the boot and Luchewski and Singh followed everyone out to the street.

Before getting into the front passenger seat, Josh Woodington nodded back to the house.

'Tell them to be careful with the house, won't you? It's the only one we've got.'

Luchewski smiled. 'Don't worry, sir. We will. Forensics will do their bit and then they'll straighten everything up for you. Probably be gone by morning. You won't even know they've been. Best house cleaning service this side of the river, they are.'

Josh tried a grin but the worry on his face stopped it from fully developing.

You could hear the party three streets away and Stevie suddenly felt like turning around and going straight back home. What did he think he was doing? He was too old to be going to student house parties. He was going to look *so* out of place. Everyone else was going to be at least six years younger than him. No, what he should do is stop, go back home and drink the two bottles of wine – one red, one white – that he was currently carrying. Knock himself out and tell himself not to be so bloody stupid. Tell himself to grow up.

But he didn't. He kept on walking until he found himself having to step around a bent-over, heaving boy spilling his stomach all over the weeds that littered the tiny front garden. As he passed, the boy looked up, spew covering his chin. Stevie could see it was Thin Features from the library.

'All right,' he gargled before continuing his chunder.

'Hmm.' Stevie gave him a wide berth, skipping lightly over the puddle of sick and pressing the doorbell. Nobody came, so he pressed it and held it for ten seconds. Under the constant thump of the music, he could hear its piercing screech.

Twenty seconds or so later the door opened and somebody Stevie had never seen before looked him drunkenly up and down.

'Mike?' Stevie said, holding up the two bottles of wine. 'Mike said –'

'Nice to meet you, Mike,' the boy opened the door wide and beckoned Stevie in.

'No, no, I'm not –'

'Anyone armed with alcohol is welcome here! Come on in.'

Stevie stepped in and the boy took the wine off him. 'Let me relieve you of those.'

A couple were sat on the stairs, their tongues wrapped around each other. 'Do you know Jordan and Sienna? No? Well, that's Jordan and Sienna.' Stevie gave a little wave at them but they didn't even come up for air. 'They're always breaking up and getting back together. Does my fucking brain in. Oi! You two!' They didn't stop snogging but opened their eyes slightly and squinted at the boy like they were conjoined twins attached by the lips. 'Try not to leave stains on the curtains again, OK?' They closed their lids and went back to focusing on their tonsil gymnastics.

The boy poked his head around the sitting room and Stevie noticed the enormous tunnels he had in each of his earlobes. 'Everyone!' Stevie came alongside and peered around. Inside were sat eight people – five guys and three girls – knocking back shots of something or other and passing a doobie around. 'This is Mike.'

'No, I'm –'

'Hi, Mike,' some of them nodded.

'Wow. What a coincidence!' One of the girls – a thin

thing with glasses far too big for her – slurred. 'Mike lives in this house. A different Mike. Not you, of course' She giggled to herself. 'You don't live here ...' Her face scrunched quizzically. 'Do you?'

Stevie shook his head.

'Come on,' the boy nudged him. 'Follow me. They're just a bunch of fucking stoners. The real action's down here.' He took a few steps towards the door at the end of the corridor and pushed. The music was coming from inside and, as the door opened, it suddenly exploded.

It was the dining room. Or sort of a dining room. The dining table had been pushed up under the window and a long green sofa faced it on the opposite wall. A large TV – which was on, soundlessly showing some old Jeremy Irons movie on ITV4 – dominated a corner of the room, and a doorway led to some steps down into the bright light of the kitchen. About a dozen people were standing about holding plastic wine or pint glasses filled with different-coloured liquids. Some were squatting on the sofa or its arms. One or two, on the floor.

The boy and Stevie stepped into the room and through to the kitchen.

'Couple of decent bottles of wine courtesy of our friend Mike here,' the boy said holding them up so that the two people busying themselves around the kitchen could see. 'Better than that battery acid shit you brought back, Courtney. Fucking horrible that is.' He slammed them down on the work surface.

'Careful, Gez.' The young guy fishing pizza out of the oven with William Morris oven gloves gave Gez a look.

'Yeah, Gez. That 'battery acid' cost me, you know. I didn't see you contributing to this little beauty either.' A slight girl with a shaven head was busy pouring bottles of rum into a large silver tureen. 'Need a couple more sliced oranges in there. And some vodka.'

'Pass me that knife, will you.' The boy with the pizza looked around and Stevie could see that it was Mike. Mike smiled and pulled off the oven gloves. 'Oh, you came then.'

'You know each other?' Gez smiled.

'Yes. We're on the same course.' Stevie felt the words to be clumsy and infantile and stupid, spilling out of his mouth like that. Like trying to hold too many marbles in there at any one moment.

'Are you now?' Stevie caught Gez raising his eyebrows at the girl who promptly stopped what she was doing, wiped her hand on her Blondie T-shirt and gripped Stevie's hand tightly before shaking it.

'I'm Courtney. Nice to meet you ... er ...'

'Mike,' said Gez.

'Stevie,' said Mike.

'Yeah, Stevie,' said Stevie.

'Oh,' said Gez, looking confused.

Stevie smiled at Mike and Mike smiled right back. *Oh God*, thought Stevie. *What am I doing here?*

'Would you like a drink?' said Courtney. 'I'm trying out a new invention. I call it the Clapham Brainfuck.'

'Oh?' Stevie grinned. 'What's in it?'

'Dunno yet. I'll tell you when I'm finished.'

Brian Lawson had just got back from a run and had started the shower going. He unzipped his tracksuit top and tugged down his jogging bottoms – no pants underneath, of course – and yanked off his socks before climbing in. The water was lukewarm and thin and it took a minute or two before the boiler woke itself up and kicked into action. Lawson pumped the top of the shower gel bottle up and down and smeared the creamy, lathery stuff all over him, working up a good froth. He'd been sweating, and he wanted to wash all the sweat and grit off his body.

If only it was as easy to wash the mind, he thought as he let the water stream down all over his face. Cleaning one's mind was an infinitely more difficult act. He'd spent most of his adult life trying to do so, and had so far failed. No matter how many times he had tried, no matter how hard he had attempted to cleanse his mind, thoughts and ideas and feelings and urges and needs kept returning. Over and over again. Over and bloody over again, to the extent that they had altered and changed beyond recognition. Became kinked.

He turned the shower off and grabbed the large burgundy towel, patting himself down and tying the thing around his waist.

Tonight had been a waste of time. He'd left it far too late. There was nobody around. Nobody. In the end he'd given up looking and came straight home. There were reports he needed to write before the middle of next week anyway, so perhaps he should just concentrate on getting those finished. They were, after all, hanging over his head like the proverbial sword of Damocles.

Yes, that's what I'll do, he thought as he made his way across the landing to his bedroom. I'll finish those reports for Year 10. Take my mind off things. Distract myself.

Keep my desires at bay.

Luchewski had driven Singh back to Hartshorn House to pick up her car from the station car park. It had gone ten thirty and most of the lights in the building appeared to be off. It was only the strip of windows on the third floor glaring hard into the darkness that told you that night officers were still on duty.

Singh got out of the TT and headed for her Peugeot.

'Singh,' Hal called after her and in the dimness of the badly lit car park, his voice seemed to take on a foghorn type quality.

Singh turned around. 'Sir?'

'Do you think …' he struggled to say the words. 'Do you think he would have killed them all? If he'd managed to get in. Do you think he would have killed those kids?'

Singh seemed to shudder and Luchewski didn't believe that it had anything to do with the coldness of the evening. 'I don't know. If it meant getting to Mrs Woodington … possibly. I don't know.'

'What is it she knows that makes him want to kill her? Or, at least, what is it he *thinks* she knows that makes him want to silence her?'

A long pause.

'The name of the person who killed Louisa Gaudiano?' she replied.

Luchewski nodded sadly. 'Yes.'

'You think *our* killer is the same person who killed Louisa Gaudiano?'

He shrugged. 'Maybe. Or maybe they're just protecting someone.'

Nino's line manager was called Lee Duvall. He'd done a few management courses and thought he was an embryonic Alan Sugar. He loved to wag his finger around and point and tell everyone what to do, how to improve. He was in charge of setting the dreaded SMART targets that Nino had come to hate so very, very much.

It was about a quarter to eleven and Lee had called a staff meeting in the estates canteen. 'Canteen' was far too generous a word for the poky room that had a table with four chairs around it, a fridge with a light that never worked and a kettle that made as much noise as an ocean liner when it started to boil.

Nino was sat on one of the chairs sipping his lukewarm tea along with two more of the night cleaners – Dave and Shirley.

'Now then,' Lee started, standing over them with his perpetual clipboard. 'I've been looking at figures.' Lee loved figures. Nothing gave him greater pleasure than to look at some numbers and pretend he knew exactly what they meant and what they told him. Nino pictured him curled up on the sofa at home with a book of refuse collection statistics, masturbating furiously. 'I've been looking at figures and I've –'

'You said that already.' Shirley chipped in, her mouth full of custard cream.

'What?'

'You said that already. "I've been looking at figures". No need to say it again. We heard you the first time.'

'That's roight,' added Dave, a craggy red-nosed Brummie who probably should have retired years ago but, due to not having taken out a personal pension, found himself having to work way beyond his useful years. 'Yow did say that. We all 'eared yer. Didn't we, Neen?'

Nino nodded. Both Dave and Shirley hated Lee Duvall almost as much as he did, and both took great delight in winding him up at any possible opportunity.

'Well, look, don't worry about that. What I'm saying is –'

'If you repeat yourself, it slows everything down, doesn't it? Keeps us away from cleaning for longer, doesn't it? I mean, we could all be cleaning and getting the offices ready for tomorrow. Instead you've got us in here so that you can keep repeating yourself at us.'

'That's roight, Shirl. Slows us down. Oi could be well

231

through Floor Eight by now if Oi wasn't here trying to drink this kipper tie.'

Lee Duvall coughed. 'Well, of course. It's good that you're thinking of the Company like this. Keen to get on and get to work, and so on. Keen to get this workplace sorted so that in the morning, when the workers return, the Company can drive itself on to greater heights. No, it's good that you think like that. The problem is –'

'I'd've cleared out the recycling boxes on Four by now,' Shirley continued, pretending not to have heard him. 'They'd be empty. And the plastic water cups would have been replenished.'

'And Oi noticed earlier that one of the Henrys on *this* floor needs its bag changing.' Dave turned to Nino. 'Didn't Oi tell you that one of the Henrys on this floor needed its bag changing, Neen? Said when yow came in, didn't Oi?''

'You did, Dave. You did.' Dave had done nothing of the sort, but Nino always found it amusing to play along whenever the two of them started to stress Lee out. 'When I came in, you distinctly said to me, you said, "Neen. One of the Henrys on this floor needs its bag changing." I distinctly remember you saying so.'

Duvall shook his head. 'Look. Just *sshhh* now, guys. There're a few things I want to say. Firstly, the targets you all set with me earlier this year are not really being met.'

'And how are we meant to meet targets when, at every chance you get, you drag us in here for a bollocking, *Mr* Duvall?' Shirley glared at Duvall who, like a frightened rabbit, fixed his eyes back on his clipboard.

'The targets are not being met. The number of bins being emptied has not increased. If anything, the numbers have fallen. Several times this week I've had complaints from the managers that some of the bins – especially those on Floors Eleven and Twelve – are only being emptied twice a week. At most. I'm sure that I don't have to remind you that all bins have to be emptied every evening, or else we are contravening the Company's own Health and Safety policy.'

Nino looked down and played with his polystyrene cup.

'Not to mention it's disgusting. Stick a half-finished sub in a bin on a warm Monday, then come Friday you've got a whole raft of problems. The stink. The flies. Not nice. Not nice at all. It's a real health hazard, I can tell you.'

'I like your shoes, Mr Duvall.' Shirley mumbled.

'Eh?'

'Your shoes. I like them.'

Lee Duvall looked momentarily befuddled again and it took a few seconds for him to carry on where he'd left off.

'Anyway … where was I? That's right. Also … window grime. Some major issues down on Three with window grime. And on Five and Six. Incorrect usage of the Windolene, I'm afraid. Too much used elsewhere, I reckon, and not enough left for Three, Five and Six. Everyone needs to be more sparing with its usage.'

Nino could feel his blood starting to stir. 'Usage'. What sort of a prick actually used the word 'usage'?

It suddenly felt wrong him being there. Stuck in this job, in this room, being lectured at by an overgrown boy scout with boils. Nino had bigger things that he needed to be doing. More important things. Two girls were dead and one – his daughter – was missing. He'd spent time in prison because of it all. And now he found himself picking over the tossed away shit of heartless,

233

bloodsucking insurance agents. Wiping down their dirt and hoovering up their crap. He had rolled up into a ball and was keeping his head tucked tightly in. And it felt wrong.

'... not helped, of course, by the poor sickness records of you all in recent weeks.' Duvall peered up briefly from his clipboard.

'Oi couldn't help it,' Dave moaned. 'It were coming outta me like nah tomorrow. Nothing was stopping it. I tried some of that stuff that blocks yer up but –'

'OK! Thank you, Dave!' Duvall waved his hand in front of him. 'That's quite enough.' He looked over at Nino. 'What about you, Nino? That "sickness" bug,' – he made air apostrophes with his fingers – 'that you allegedly picked up the other night. Fancied a night off, did you?'

Nino grabbed the polystyrene cup and tossed it roughly into the bin that was sat alongside the fridge. 'No. I didn't.'

'Only, you seemed to make a rather dramatic recovery in my opinion.' Duvall sneered at Nino. 'Nothing wrong with you when you came back into work, was there? And sickness bugs usually take a few days to get over.'

'Perhaps he should just have taken more time off, eh?' Shirley leant forward in her seat. 'Perhaps he should have just taken a week off and then come back to work, is that what you're saying? That it's better to take longer off?'

'No, no, of course I'm –'

'Only that's what it sounds like to me.'

'No. I'm just –'

I'm just wasting my time, Nino thought. *All of this. Just a waste of time.*

Suddenly, without warning, Nino stood up, pushing his chair back behind him.

'Er … Nino?' Duvall seemed to back away, but Nino walked straight past him.

'I'm going. I've had enough.'

'You can't do that!'

'I can do what I fucking well want.'

'Not on the Company's time, you can't!' Duvall tried puffing out his chest.

'I'm not on the Company's time. I quit. I've had enough.'

'But …' Lee Duvall seemed to skip about. 'But you have to work your notice … it's not right. You can't just leave like this. Think of the Company …'

'Fuck the Company,' Nino said as he opened the door. 'I'm off. Cheerio.'

He slammed the door behind him and walked down the corridor towards the lift. Hitting the button on the wall he suddenly realised he was grinning.

It was strange, he thought. But he felt better than he had done in years.

The two guys with beards and aprons had started to clear away. Collecting the glasses and empty bottles of wine, blowing out the candles and wiping the tables down. It was almost eleven and they were trying to drop the heavy-handed hint that eleven o'clock was, in fact, closing time. One of them yawned and glanced over at him to see if he was catching on yet.

Andrew Cornish sat in the window of the café, cradling his eighth coffee and watching the house directly across the road. His head was light – a combination of stress, exhaustion and too much caffeine, no doubt – and the horrible stark glow of the orange streetlights was tearing away at his retinas. He'd been sat there since four o'clock, only ever getting up to make use of the unisex bathroom tucked towards the rear of the shop.

At first the two guys who seemed to run the place were delighted to see him. Organic lattes at four pounds fifty were never going to be to everyone's taste, so they had welcomed him into the empty coffee house with open arms. As the afternoon wore on and more people had flitted into and out of *Counter Culture* – words frosted on its wide glass windows – the proprietors seemed to forget about him – only truly reminded he was there when he waved his hand in the air and ordered another £4.50 latte.

'Would you like to order food?' one of them had asked around about the time of the fourth or fifth coffee. 'We have a very good falafel and couscous bake on the go.' Cornish had said 'no', and the man went back to pulling corks out of the tops of bottles of pesticide-free Merlot and flapping around the loving couples who all seemed to gravitate to the darkest corners of the place.

By the time of his seventh latte, the beardy guys were starting to get a bit fed up of him and Cornish's money had run out. So he had to dig into the pocket of his long black coat and pull out the purse. He'd avoided even looking at it so far – it was too harsh a reminder – but the time had come to use it. The thought of it made him feel slightly sick, but he clicked it open anyway.

The day had started off so well too. Three new canvases created. Two of them new *Preludes to Suicide* – the freshly opened wounds on his arms, burning with the flow of his blood and the need to create. Squatting over the square stretched frames, he allowed the blood to run down the length of his forearm, off the tips of his fingers and *drip, drip, drip* onto the canvas. It always amazed him the way the blood came out and sat there in perfect little globules. The meniscus – or whatever it was called – holding it all intact. Come at them with a wooden skewer, though, and *pop*, out it all flows, like a balloon or a bubble. Then Andrew would guide the blood, make it move over the white skin. This way. That way. Over in loops or with the regularity of a straight line. Sometimes he would lay the skewer flat against the frame and drag the blood until it dropped off its edge, flicking onto the already badly stained carpet.

Pain had always been his way of coping. Ever since those awful days in his childhood when ... but he stopped himself from thinking about it. He'd put a nail in that particular coffin and – even if some of the nails had to sometimes be knocked back into place through his own body – that coffin was well and truly buried.

After he had made the two *Preludes*, Andrew looked over at the last blank canvas that he owned. His wounds had dried up now, and were cold and aching. He didn't want to add to them. The pain that leaked out when he made those cuts had softened now, so he put the razor blade back on the shelf near the window. But the empty canvas called to him. And he knew he had to paint something completely different. Something he had never painted before.

The sky.

Sleeping rough, he had woken to see the crimson bleed of the sky slowly change into a light, then dark, blue billboard. Lying in the wetness of the dew – and practically unable to move due to the stiffness – he had watched it happen. As the darkness of the night disappeared, the red dawn spread itself over the sky before slowly developing into the blueness. The warm and hopeful blueness. The blueness of a new day.

After rubbing TCP into his arms, Andrew grabbed the busted up old toolbox that he had always used to store his paints in and clicked the lock open. Half-used tubes of reds and blacks were foremost, but beneath them lay unopened, unsqueezed tubes of yellows and greens and blues. Lots and lots of blues. Andrew fished them out along with some equally unused whites and a couple of the ends of red. The brushes he took from the jam jar half-filled with filthy water had to be washed thoroughly with some Fairy Liquid to get rid of the slime in their bristles. He flicked them dry over the sink and wiped them on a tea towel before putting the canvas onto the easel that usually stood empty in the corner of the room.

This was a painting that he needed to think about. The *Preludes* were all about feeling and pain. They were a way of screaming that made no noise but stamped themselves into view for the world – eventually – to see. But this painting ... the sky. It was something that required him to think. To remember and recreate. The hopeful blue. It was something he didn't usually deal with. His life was ruled by the blacks and reds. The depths of despair. But this ... warmth ... was something else.

He squirted some of the whites and blues onto a plastic pallet. A small blob of red. He chose his thickest Daler Rowney and stuck it bang in the middle of the darkest blue, swirling it around until it started to nudge into the splodge of white. He teased some more of the blues into the white until he reached a colour that he felt was right. Then he started painting. Straight sweeps across the canvas. Left to right. Top to bottom, like reading a book. As the paint faded on the brush, he replenished it, loading the bristles with thick glistening gouache.

After a few minutes he stood back and admired his work. It wasn't quite right. It was too regular. Too uniform. So the small blob of red came into play. It wasn't right to keep the whole thing blue. That was unreasonable. Unrealistic. He needed to make some sort of reference to the moment when it all changed from the black of night to the blue of day. And the redness – just the end, this dying glint of the redness – was it.

He dabbed the brush into the red, spiralling it slightly into the white/blue mix. Then he tapped it gently onto the picture. Just a touch. Not too much. Just enough so that the point of transition could be acknowledged. The top left hand corner. He smeared it imperceptibly. Delicately, like a surgeon.

That was it.

He twisted his head from side to side. It was beautiful. So unlike any of his other work. He put down the pallet and the brush, not caring if it messed up the carpet even more, and went to sit on the edge of his bed.

It was perfect. A perfect vision. A spiritual vision. This was the painting he had always been striving to create.

It was an epiphany.

Then the harsh buzz of his doorbell had slapped him back to earth, and his heart banged hard in his chest.

It buzzed again. Then again. Andrew lay back on the bed and stared at the ceiling, praying for it to stop. Then it buzzed one last time. He sighed and tried to calm down, staying on his bed for a good half an hour, revelling in the silence.

It was just as he was about to sit up that the doorbell buzzed yet again, a shrill ringing filling his small room.

'No!' he had said to himself. 'Please, no.'

Buzz.

Slowly, he swung himself off the bed and padded softly across the room to his door. He opened it and scurried like a spider down the staircase to the hallway. Keeping his distance, he stared at the frosted glass of the front door and could see a large man standing the other side of it. A second man – looking as though he was holding a coffee – came alongside and one of them pressed the bell again. Andrew could hear the screech coming from his room somewhere up the stairs behind him. He squinted and could make out … suits.

They wore suits.

It was the police again.

The police hadn't given up on him just yet.

His stomach dive-bombed and he crouched on the stairs sobbing. Eventually the two men turned and faded from the door.

He went back upstairs to his room and wept on the bed for an hour.

The police were still coming to get him.

Suddenly the room seemed to choke him. If he stayed where he was, the room was going to choke him. His heart raced and he straightened up, his face red with the sting of tears. He slipped his broken-up shoes onto his feet, grabbed his long black coat and marched out of the room, down the stairs and out of the front door.

The brightness of the afternoon made him wince and it took him a few seconds to adjust to the light. But nobody was there waiting for him. No police. Nobody.

But they were going to come back, he just knew it.

So he ran across the road to the coffee shop that he'd never been in before, took up a table near the window and ordered a £4.50 organic latte. From there he could watch. Watch and wait. See them when they did return and see how many of them were there to arrest him. He imagined the two officers in suits, and a couple of police cars with some uniformed officers in tow. They were trying to catch him *in situ*, weren't they? They hadn't got themselves a search warrant just yet because they were trying to catch him at home. Well, he was going to take some control. He was going to sit there and watch them be disappointed one more time.

Only they didn't come back. He'd sat there knocking back caffeine after caffeine like an addict and they hadn't bothered coming back. His mood was falling by the hour. He was tired. He wanted to go home.

But he couldn't.

'Ahem ...' One of the hipsters tapped the face of his watch. 'I'm really sorry, sir. It's eleven o'clock and we shut at eleven. So ... er ...' He kind of nodded towards the door.

'Yes. Of course. I'm sorry.'

'No. no. No need to be sorry. It's just ...'

Andrew Cornish stood up and swayed a little.

'You all right, sir?' The hipster tried to look concerned. 'You feel OK?'

'I'm fine. Yes. Thanks. Goodnight.'

'Goodnight, sir.'

The hipster followed him to the door and, after Cornish stepped out into the cold night air, locked it tight behind him.

He felt lost. As lost and lonely as he did when he was eight years old. He stood there for a few minutes, not doing anything, until the lights in Counter Culture flickered to a blackness.

He was foolish to think that he could just carry on as he had done before. His actions two ... three days ago now, was it? –he couldn't remember – it felt like years. His actions on that fateful day had changed everything. Nothing was ever going to be the same again.

What an idiot he had been to think that by changing his art, by taking a new direction with his work, he could make things different. So, *so* stupid.

He forced himself across the road, fished out his key, stuck it into the lock and let himself back in. Behind one of the doors, someone was playing music far too loud for that time of night. He went back up the stairs and into his room. He grabbed a small rucksack, put a few clothes in the bottom. A toothbrush and some toothpaste. Bottle of tap water.

They weren't here waiting for him now, but they were coming back – he could sense it. They would be back tomorrow. But they were never going to find him here. This time, he was going. And going for good. This time he really was never going to return.

Before he left, Cornish took the drying blue picture from the easel, propped it against the wall and put his foot through it.

'I didn't think your friend was invited.'

'Friend? What friend?'

'The one in the library today. You said he wasn't going to be invited. But I passed him spewing his ring outside.'

'Oh, him. I know. Couldn't shake him off, I'm afraid. Overheard me on the phone to Courtney and ended up just inviting himself. To be honest, I think he was well away before he got here. He barely sniffed the vodka we gave him and he was off.' Mike took a sip of his Clapham Brainfuck. 'I hope nobody's let him back in.'

They were sat on the stairs next to each other. The couple who had previously occupied the stairs had clearly found somewhere better to suck each other's faces. Music still pounded from the dining room and the occasional uncontrollable giggle squealed its way out of the sitting room.

'I always find these things so repetitive,' Mike said, his elbows resting against his knees. 'It's like a merry-go-round. The music, the drink, the pills and the dope. And then the lazy, drunken, pseudo-intellectual conversations with people you've never met before and are unlikely ever to meet again. And then the restless night and the ruined day that follows it. Pretend regret. A sore head. Exhaustion.' He took another glug of the Brainfuck. 'And yet, it happens again. As soon as we've forgotten about how awful we felt, we're back pouring drink down our necks and talking rubbish and throwing up yet again. Just a merry-go-round. Round and round we go.'

'We forget,' Stevie said, his own head light and buzzing. He was on his third Brainfuck and could kind of see why Courtney christened it so. 'Humans are pretty stupid creatures at the best of times. We fill our lives up with so much stuff and so many thoughts that we forget all the really bad stuff. We just remember how good it felt at the time to be pissed or high. The crap just gets tossed aside.'

They sat there for a while just listening to the jeers and boos coming from the dining room when some Ed Sheeran started playing, and a crashing sound from the sitting room.

'Would you like to see my room?' Mike eventually asked, his face animated.

'Er …'

'Come on.' Mike stood up and turned to go up the stairs. 'It's nothing special. Just a room. Come on.'

Stevie stood up and followed. *Fuck*, he thought. *Oh fuck. What am I fucking doing?*

Mike's room was practical, neat and oddly adorable. The black and white checked curtains were pulled closed, and the double bed with the old-fashioned looking patchwork quilt was precisely made. A desk ran along one side of the wall and a Macbook and a tall, bent-double reading lamp were glowing away gently upon it. Clothes were hooked over a rail that sat in front of the window, and six or seven pairs of shoes were lined up on the floor beneath. On the wall over the bed hung a large picture of the New York skyline at night.

'My humble abode,' Mike said before sitting down on the edge of the bed. Stevie looked around again and saw that there was no chair except for the one tucked under the desk, so he strode across the room and pulled it out, spinning it around and straddling it – Stevie thought – a bit like that classic shot of Christine Keeler.

'Nice room.'

'Looks out over the front though, so it's sometimes difficult to get to sleep at night. What with the pubs kicking out and the street lamp just outside my window there.'

Stevie instinctively turned around and saw the crass orange glow through the black and white curtains.

'I see.'

Mike didn't say anything. He just stared at Stevie. After a few moments the silence became unbearable and Stevie picked a book off the desk for something to do.

'What's this? *Catch-22*. Haven't read that. Always meant to but –'

'You didn't come here tonight to discuss *Catch-22*, Stevie.' Mike grinned.

'Didn't I?' Stevie replied, instantly thinking what a stupid thing that was to say.

'No.' Mike patted the bed beside him. 'You came here to see me.'

Stevie swallowed hard. It was true, he said to himself. He *had* come here to see Mike. Why else would he go to a house party full of drunken and drugged-up nineteen-year-olds? He couldn't deny it.

'Why don't you come and sit next to me?'

'I'm … er … I'm not sure.'

'Why not? You're not in a relationship, are you?'

He wasn't too sure himself. Was he? Was what he and Luchewski had *a relationship*? He thought it was, but sometimes he had his doubts. Luchewski was so stand-offish at times that the barriers seemed impossible to scale. Perhaps they were little more than fuck buddies who occasionally had dinner or watched TV together. Perhaps Stevie had always got the wrong end of the stick. But you wouldn't introduce your daughter to your fuck buddy, would you? Surely even Luchewski wasn't *that* screwed up?

It was true that Luchewski was one of the oddest gay men he had ever met. He was, quite simply, oddly gay. He didn't seem to do many – or any – of the things that most gay men Stevie knew did. Wasn't exactly embracing of the culture or the community. Stevie had always put that down to the fact that Luchewski had only recently come out. Been outed. By Stevie himself. He'd assumed that Luchewski was simply taking his time to adjust. To accept what he was.

But perhaps he wasn't. Perhaps he would always be this oddball with a world-famous dad and a job that took up far too much of his time. Perhaps he would never completely accept being gay and continue to try and live his life in a sort of half-light, constantly losing lovers like leaves from a tree.

'You're not, are you?' Mike asked again, his eyebrows raised.

'I … er …'

Mike patted the bed again. 'Come here. Come sit next to me. I won't bite. Not unless you want me to, of course.'

Stevie's fingers gripped tightly to the chair. 'I … er … I don't know if I should.'

Mike leaned back on his arms for a few seconds, thinking. 'OK then.' He threw himself upright and took the three steps to where Stevie sat, before bending towards him and kissing him full on the lips.

The bed was a tight squeeze. There wasn't enough room for all four of them and Josh found himself sort of squished against the wall and the radiator which was – thankfully – off.

The kids had eventually dropped off to sleep. It had taken them hours, of course. They were in a new house, in a new bed crammed between their parents. Oh and not to forget the fact that a strange man had tried to break into their own house only a few hours earlier with the intention of killing them all. In fact, Josh was surprised that they had managed to fall asleep *at all* tonight.

Katie had also managed to nod off. Josh watched as she breathed, her body turned towards Sophie, a protective arm covering her daughter.

No, Josh was the only one awake. He stared at the dull grey ceiling and thought. Couldn't stop thinking. He was going to be absolutely bloody knackered in the morning, that was for sure.

He felt so hopeless. So useless. Somebody had tried to attack his family tonight, and there was nothing he could do to protect them. All he managed to do was call the police and get them to deal with it. It was wrong of Katie to stop him going into the garden. It was *his* garden. He had every right to be in it. The man didn't. Josh should have gone into the garden and – at the very least – scared him off.

But he didn't.

Instead they had all hidden in the sitting room, waiting for the police to rescue them.

It made Josh feel like shit.

Who was the man, anyway? Why did he want to kill them? Was it even him? Couldn't it have been somebody else? A passing thief just chancing his arm? Some local kids just messing around?

Still, it made him feel like shit.

The problem was that that wasn't the only thing to make him feel like shit right now. He'd been working on a package of first-class ICT security for a company in Hastings. They were paying him a handsome sum to put everything together and to get it all up and running as seamlessly as possible. And they wanted the first level of security – essential password protection, initial firewall, anti-Trojan and spyware installation – in place by tomorrow evening. At the latest.

The thing was that, in the rush to get away from their house, Josh –obviously – hadn't even thought about it, and it was only now in the dead dark silence of the night that it crept into his mind.

He shook his head. How awful it would be if as well as scaring Josh out of his own house, the man ruined one of the biggest contracts he'd had in a long while. A double whammy of violation. A spit-roast of humiliation – fucked over in two different ways. It made Josh feel sick.

Everything he needed was back at the house. In the spare bedroom which doubled as his study was a hard drive containing all the files he'd been working on. Stuck on one of the shelves with all the other hard drives and passports he'd been using in recent months. There were loads of them. Dozens and dozens. If he could get the right one along with one of his laptops he could do the work here in the safe house and get it all ready for the required time. That would show the bastard who'd tried to hunt him down. Fuck him, the fucking psychopath. Josh could feel in control again. Protecting his family. Taking care of them.

Unfortunately, just asking one of the coppers who was assigned to the safe house to go and get it wasn't going to be good enough. The drives all looked the sodding same and chances were they'd come back with the wrong one. Only *he* knew which one he needed. Only *he* knew the urgency with which it was needed.

There was nothing else for it. He was going to have to go back to the house and get it himself.

Chapter Twenty-four

The man who had taken Louisa Gaudiano all those years ago was driving across south London. The roads were virtually empty at this time of the morning – only night workers returning home and those people unfortunate to have to start their jobs at an unreasonably early hour zoomed along the tarmac. The occasional milk float and police car added to the sparse flow of morning traffic. The sun was only just registering on the horizon and the air outside was cold and still. He tried turning up the heating but all it did was shoot an icy wind at his face, so he quickly knocked it off again.

He kept his speed just over the legal limit and made his way out of London towards the green fields and unexciting hills of Surrey, as the radio – tuned as it always was to Absolute 80s – blasted out ABC's *Poison Arrow*. He half-sang along to it, hardly able to remember any of the words.

As he got closer and closer to where the faltering sprawl of London gave way to the rest of the world, he thought about everything he'd read about in the papers and seen on the news over the last few days. Those two women. Dead. The women who had been at school the same time as Gaudiano. The ones who had been with her the night she 'disappeared'. Both of them murdered.

It was a worry. The killer was dredging things up too much. Getting the cops thinking about the wrong things.

Things that he'd hoped had been long buried and forgotten about. He'd managed to get away with it for so long that he'd almost forgotten it had happened himself. It was like a strange and slightly unformed dream that he'd once had. Was it real? Did he really do that? Or had he just imagined it all – a sort of feverish hallucination? Sometimes he wasn't too sure.

But then, at other times, he knew it had been as real as the blood that ran through his veins. No, there was no getting away from it. It always came back to haunt him in the end.

The road swept down a twisting hill, digging deep into a long, furrowed valley. Little pockets of houses seemed to clump here and there, and a stream ran alongside the road, trickling down towards the large open lakes that he loved so much.

Of course it was a massive worry that the police were having to think about things they hadn't thought about in a long, long while. That was obviously going to be a worry for him. But there was something else that added to this unsettling situation. Something else that gave the whole resurfacing of the 'incident' an extra dimension of instability.

He knew who the killer was. Or at least *strongly* suspected. He shook his head to himself in the car. No. No, that wasn't right. He *knew*. Definitely knew.

Suddenly a car shot out from the left and he had to slam down hard on his brakes. The van skidded and stalled as he gripped the wheel tight to stop himself from veering off into the verge. The big box of gear in the rear of the van banged up against the back of his seat and one of the rods came off its moorings, the fat end bouncing against one of the boxes.

'Fucking cunt!' he screamed as the car sped off into

the distance, seemingly unaware of what had just occurred. 'Fucking shit driver! Look where you're fucking going!'

He stopped and caught his breath. There was no other traffic around. He shook himself back together before slowly and deliberately restarting the engine.

'Fucking idiot,' he mumbled, letting the handbrake off and continuing along the long twisty road.

Before driving over to Hartshorn, DI Freddie Burlock decided to renegotiate the awful roads towards east London. Buses and cars clogged up the lanes and made any progress annoyingly slow. At one point it took him nearly twenty minutes to cover the hundred and fifty yards to the junction he needed and he looked enviously on as people on foot strode past, and cyclists sliced in and out of the cars as if showing off.

After what seemed like an eternity stuck behind a school bus where the kids on the back seat were laughing and taking pictures of him on their phones – Burlock pretending to be angry and flicking the 'V's at them – he managed to get to where he was going. He parked the car illegally with the two near side wheels mounting the pavement and locked it behind himself.

The front door of the large Victorian building in which Andrew Cornish lived was black with ornate frosted side windows. The paint was slightly bubbled and peeling away, revealing the colour it had been painted previously – a dullish red. A dusty light fitting dangled uselessly in the alcove of the door.

Burlock pressed the bell for flat number four and waited. A minute later he did it again.

Burlock considered himself the most down-to-earth guy that he'd ever known. He particularly enjoyed conjuring up the image of someone whose mantra was 'what you see is what you get'. He was straight down the line and called a spade a spade and all those other daft sayings that you could use to knock the pretentious stuffing out of a poncing *poseur*. Even the word *poseur* gave him a chill, He, of course, meant poser. Not *poseur*. Poser. That was it.

Burlock didn't believe in the supernatural. Didn't go in for ghosts or spirits or zombies or whatever. That was – in his opinion – all bollocks. The reserve of the mad and the bad. People who banged on about vampires or relatives who acted as guardian angels were either desperate, deranged or just out to squeeze cash from the desperate and deranged. Burlock just didn't hold with it.

But something Burlock *did* believe in was gut instinct. That unmistakable feeling that something was right or wrong. He didn't think there was anything otherworldly about it. Just the accumulation of a lifetime's worth of common sense and experience. Empirical data. Taking everything that had gone before and using it to extrapolate an understanding of what was going ahead.

And there was something bugging him about this Andrew Cornish boy. He couldn't pin it down, but the fact that he hadn't answered his door on three occasions now played on Burlock's mind a little. It wasn't quite the way he had felt before finding Laurie Frasier's body the other day – it wasn't like that. But there was something, an indefinable something that pricked at his very mind.

They didn't have a great deal of information on him. His address; the fact that he'd been claiming benefits for the last eight years. A short stint at art college before being kicked out at the end of his second year. His parents' address – if they couldn't get hold of him soon, they'd have to start trying the parents.

That was about it. Not much. They didn't even have a photograph of him.

Burlock hit another of the bells. He held it for a long time. Eventually the door edged open and a small hairy face peered out.

'Yeah? What?' The eyes were squinting against the daylight and it was obvious to Burlock that the doorbell had just woken them up. 'What you ringing my bell for this early?'

Burlock flashed the man his ID card and suddenly the eyes sprang wide open.

'Trying to knock Mr Cornish up. Flat four. He's not answering though. Thought p'raps you could just let me in so I could go up and see if he's there.'

'Oh,' the man looked incredibly relieved. 'Oh, I see. Who was it again?'

'Cornish. Mr Andrew Cornish.'

The man frowned and gave his head a little shake. 'Never heard of him. In number four, you say? Don't know if I've ever seen him.' The man pulled the door wider and beckoned Burlock in. 'Not sure.'

Burlock stepped into the hallway and the man pushed the door shut behind him. Burlock could see that he was right about the young man – his pyjamas were ruffled and looked dirty. 'YOU'RE ON MY TO DO LIST', the pyjama top boasted, but if anybody was actually on this one's to do list, Burlock thought, they were surely well below 'having a decent wash' and 'getting some remedial dentistry work'.

'You still need me?' the man yawned.

'No. That's fine. Thank you.'

The man seemed to stumble back into his room, allowing the door to click gently to, leaving Burlock alone.

He looked around for flat number four and soon realised it was up the stairs. The stairs creaked noisily underfoot and at the top, just on the left, was a door with a '4' on it.

It was open.

Burlock pushed it softly open. 'Mr Cornish. It's the police, sir. Are you in?'

The room was quite wide and long and smelt of paint. In the corner sat a single bed – unmade – the sheets and duvet rather grubby and creased. Next to the door was a halogen oven, a toaster and a kettle. Burlock felt the side of the kettle with his hand. Stone cold.

The things that really caught his eye though were the strange wooden things stacked up against the walls under the window. There were several of these stacks, some bigger than others, and some looked as though they were on the point of tipping themselves over.

Burlock went over to one of the teetering towers and lifted the top level off. It was a picture. A painting. And a bloody awful painting it was too in Burlock opinion. Just a brown swirl and some brown drips, as if the person who painted it couldn't be bothered opening up a different pot of paint. There was nothing to see – no discernible shape – and definitely no colour. Burlock tutted and lifted up another one. It was exactly the same. In fact, the only picture that looked any good – a bluish canvas of the sky, or was it the sea? – was the one propped up against the wall. And that had a ruddy great rip in it.

Burlock turned the two pictures in his hands over. On the back of the first was scrawled in pencil *Prelude to Suicide Number 12*, and on the back of the second was written *Prelude to Suicide Number 11*.

'Oh shit,' Burlock moaned to himself. 'Oh bloody shit.'

***

'What is that?' Luchewski pointed at the stains on the carpet. 'Is that blood?' He turned to look at Burlock. 'Freddie, why haven't you sealed this off? This is a crime scene.'

Burlock chuckled and shook his head. 'Course it's not.'

'But if that's blood ...'

'He paints with it. Go on, look at his paintings. Terrible bloody things, they are.'

Luchewski picked one up. 'This is blood?' he pointed at the canvas. 'He paints with blood?' The inspector frowned. 'Whose?'

'His own. Bunch of razorblades on the mantelpiece there. Cuts himself and paints with it. "Prelude to Suicide".' Burlock let the last phrase hang heavy in the air between them.

'You think he's got anything to do with the Seagrove and Frasier murders?'

Burlock walked over to a shelf where he picked up a small paper wallet full of photographs. He pulled one out and held it up to Luchewski.

'At some point he was experimenting with photography. Namely taking pictures of himself. Lots and lots of them.'

Luchewski came closer and looked at the picture that Burlock held up. It was of a thin, gaunt man. A *very* thin, *very* gaunt man with short stubby hair and a wrinkled brow.

Burlock took out another one and showed it to Luchewski. This time the selfie showed the unsmiling man wearing a long black coat, standing on a bridge near a river. It had been taken at such an angle that you could see almost the entire length of the man's body. The coat looked too big on it, like a child wearing the coat of a dead, fat uncle.

'Do you honestly think that *that* is capable of murder?'

Luchewski raised his eyebrows. 'No.'

'It's a wonder he has the strength to get himself up off the loo in the morning, never mind hold down a fit young woman and strangle her.'

'So what are we doing here, then?'

Burlock winced. 'I dunno. I honestly don't think he's got anything to do with any of this. But ...' his voice trailed off.

'But what?'

Burlock gave a short sigh. 'I think he's unwell.'

'He paints with his own blood, I'm pretty certain he's unwell.'

'You saw the paintings. "Prelude to Suicide." He's not here. Where is he? Something's wrong with this one. He may have information, I dunno. But I want to find him.'

'Is this your fatherly side speaking, Freddie?'

'Aye. Might be. Anyroad, I think we should put out a missing persons on him. Get the locals to keep an eye out.' He flicked one of the photographs back and forth. 'I really need to find him.'

'OK,' Luchewski nodded and shoved his hands deep into his trouser pockets. 'I agree. Let's get people looking for him.'

'Besides which ...'

'What?'

Burlock pointed at the face on the photo. 'I recognise him. I don't know why ... but there's something about him I recognise. It'll come to me, I'm sure ... but I'm sure I know him.'

* * *

'Why, Josh?'

'Because we need the money, that's why. The contract specified getting things in place by tonight.'

'Perhaps they'll be able to give you an extension. I mean, I think you've got a valid enough reason for not delivering on time.'

Josh grimaced. 'They've already given me an extension. I had to practically beg to get it moved to today.' He took a bite out of his toast. 'I have to get it done today. I have to.'

Katie gave an almost imperceptible nod of the head. 'Well, perhaps the police can go back to the house and get the stuff for you. I don't see why you have to go. They can get it –'

'They won't know what it is I need. They won't have a clue.'

'But the kids.' Her voice lowered to a whisper. 'They're scared. They need their dad around them right now. They won't want you going back to the house.'

'We won't tell them then. We'll tell them I'm going over to your parents for something or other.' He threw the crust back onto his plate. 'But I need to get it done today. Don't worry. It's not like I'll be there on my own. One of the officers outside can run me over. I'll be in and out of the house in five minutes.'

Katie looked through the doorway to the sitting room where the kids were playing on the Wii with their new-found friend PC Andersen. Zac was cheering as Sophie wobbled the little remote thingy up and down, and PC Andersen – on her knees in front of the TV – threw her own controller down on the floor in mock disgust. Thank God for her, thought Katie. She's doing her best to keep their minds off things.

'OK. But don't be long. Please, don't be long.'

He jumped up from his chair. 'I won't. I promise I'll be quick.'

Nino was going to try a different tack. Everything he'd done so far had got him nowhere – had only really managed to get him into trouble, in fact. He still couldn't get over the idea that Laurie Frasier's killer had been waiting for him to leave her house. To think he had been so close made him both shiver and kick himself at the same time. He could have caught him. Could have stopped him before Laurie was killed. He clenched his fist tight, digging the nails into the palm of his hand. To top it all, he'd just walked out on the only job he was ever going to get after spending so much time in prison. Money was going to be tight, but he couldn't bring himself to think about that at the moment. There was so much more he needed to deal with before he could think about that.

The door opened.

'Hello?' The woman smiled the smile of someone who was about to say 'no' to some special door-to-door offer or free uPVC windows quotes.

'Oh. Hello. I hope you don't mind … you might have no idea what I'm on about, but I'm looking for a Mrs Jean Smith. She used to live at this address, I think.'

The woman's face fell. 'Yes. She did. She was my mother.'

'Oh.'

'I'm afraid she died four years ago.'

'I'm sorry.' They both stared at each other in silence for a few seconds. 'My name's Nino Gaudiano. Your mother gave evidence at the inquest into my daughter's disappearance. She was the last person to see her alive.'

The woman gasped. 'Mr Gaudiano. Yes, I know. Of

course.' She pulled the door wide open. 'Please, come in. I have something that I need to give to you.'

'The footprint in the garden matched the smudge in Seagrove's wardrobe all right. Same tread, same size. Eight or possibly an eight and a half.'

'Make?'

'That's the thing,' John Good rustled some paper down the other end of the phone. 'It's not on our database. It must be some obscure foreign make that we've not picked up on yet.'

'Any idea where it's from? Any other markings on the tread? Words, numbers, that sort of thing?'

'None. The tread's quite distinctive, and judging by the depth of the sole left in the flowerbed in the Woodingtons' garden, it's pretty heavy-duty. A serious walker's or hiker's boot. Tough.'

'Can you chase it up? See if you can find where it's come from? If it's unusual we might be able to trace an address.'

'I'll get my boy Spound onto it right away. He can wade through hikers' forums and boot manufacturers' websites. He'll enjoy that.'

Luchewski smiled to himself. 'Good. Anything else your colleague found at the Woodingtons' place?'

'No. No prints. A slight smudge on the outside of the bathroom window where we think he peered in. Perhaps a fibre or two from the back door handle – he clearly had gloves on. We've sent them off for analysis, but I wouldn't get too excited if I were you.'

'No.'

Suddenly John Good's voice changed from a professional tone to something a bit lighter. Less formal. 'You still up for a meal sometime next week? You and

Stevie? Margaret's keen to meet him. As am I, of course,' he added as an afterthought. 'Friday next week any good for the pair of you?'

Luchewski winced a little. 'Er …'

'Don't worry. No rush. I know you're busy at the moment. We all are. Talk to Stevie. It might be he doesn't want to meet a boring couple of old farts like me and Margaret. Couldn't blame him. But I'll pencil in next Friday, and if you can't do it then just let me know. OK?'

'Yes. Great.' Hal tried to sound pleased but wasn't entirely sure he'd pulled it off.

Constable Neil Dixon wasn't exactly chatty. In fact he hadn't said anything ever since they drove up the hill from the safe house and turned right at the lights in Sidcup.

'Busy bloody road, this,' he had said before disappearing into his own thoughts and practically ignoring Josh for the rest of the journey. Josh muttered a few inane pleasantries in the hope of getting the man up and running again, but nothing had worked. So he just sat there and stared out of the window, looking at the people walking past and wondering if any of them could be the person who tried to break into his house the previous night.

As the car eventually rolled into the streets surrounding his estate, everything looked normal. An old woman carrying shopping. A dog walker he recognised who never picked up the messes his dogs left behind. Two young girls pushing buggies with two fat faced children screaming their guts up. The Royal Mail van parked awkwardly on the corner. The *beep, beep, beep* of a reversing delivery lorry. It all looked normal.

Rounding the corner onto the estate, everything looked peaceful. There was nothing to show that the police had the whole street lit up like Blackpool only the previous night. There was no flapping yellow police cordon, which Josh was sort of expecting. No armed guard. No forensics. It was all the same as it had ever been. Still. Peaceful. Home.

Dixon pulled up right outside the house and killed the engine.

Josh popped his belt. 'I won't be long. Couple of minutes at the most.'

Dixon grunted and watched as Josh nervously trotted up the path to the front door, fished about for his key and let himself in.

The room smelled of mothballs. It took him back to when he was a kid. Nobody had mothballs these days, did they? Could you even buy them any more? He hadn't seen any around for years – although, he did realise that for many of those years he'd been incarcerated at Her Majesty's pleasure. But this house *definitely* smelled of mothballs.

He supped his tea from the overly delicate porcelain that the woman seemed to have dug out specially and took extra care to put the cup back down on the equally delicate saucer.

Anne Smith was in her late fifties. She'd already told him how, being the only child, she inherited the house from her mother. And since the break-up of her marriage just a couple of years back, she'd taken on the house as her own.

'Most of the furniture is hers though,' she said over her shoulder as she rifled through an ornate 1950s writing desk. 'My mother's. After the divorce, I got rid of most of my stuff – couldn't bear to have it any more. It was all contaminated by … him. So I just kept the house as it was. It's old-fashioned, I know. But I like it.'

'No, no. It's nice,' Nino replied, even though a reply wasn't needed. 'I like it too.'

'Help yourself to another Rich Tea if you'd like.'

'Thank you.' Nino leaned across the coffee table and scooped one up, before dunking it daintily into the fragile cup.

'Here it is. I knew it was in here somewhere.' She turned and came back towards the sofas, an envelope in her hand. She sat and handed the envelope over to Nino. 'Before she died, she told me that if you should ever come, I should give you this.'

Nino took it and looked at the front of the envelope. *Mr Gaudiano*, it said in flowery script.

'I think, in a way, she knew you'd come. One day.'

He threw the remainder of the Rich Tea into his mouth and slid his index finger under the corner of the envelope, before ripping the top as gently as he'd been with his porcelain cup seconds earlier. He teased the paper inside out and opened it up.

'I've no idea what it says,' Anne Smith said, leaning forward on the other sofa. 'She never told me what she put in it. Told me never to open it. It was just for you.'

Nino straightened the paper out and started reading.

"Dear Mr Gaudiano,

It has been a long time, I realise, since your beloved daughter Louisa disappeared, but I know that the confusion, the pain, the terrible sense of frustration and loss – none of this – will have lessened over the years. If anything, they may even have grown – spread and expanded, like the cancer that now eats me up. I too have a daughter – you know this by now – and the thought that she might have vanished at such a young and beautiful age fills me with a dreadful despair, so God only knows just how you have managed to cope all this time.

Mr Gaudiano, I am dying. Have been doing so for the last couple of years. It started in my breasts – the indignity of a double mastectomy, I'm afraid – but soon after spread to my lungs and now – alas – my stomach. The doctors have given me a matter of weeks and it is with the last of my strength that I write this letter to you.

But before I tell you what I know, I need to explain. I need to set the scene.

The evening Louisa disappeared, I had been shopping. I had locked up the florists at a little after seven and then went to the nearby Tesco to pick up a few bits and pieces. – don't ask me what they were. My memory certainly doesn't stretch that far! – It was as I was walking home that I saw Louisa. She looked as if she had been crying. It was only a quick, fleeting thing. I was here and she was there and we passed each other in a flash. But she was definitely crying. And it was definitely her.

You know all this, of course. You heard all this in those terrible days after.

What you didn't hear about was the guilt. My overwhelming sense of guilt. What if I'd stopped and talked to her? Asked her if she was all right? Walked her home? If I'd done those things, surely she'd still be alive today. If I'd just done those few simple things, she might well be caring for her own children now."

Nino took a breath, swallowed, and carried on reading.

"In much the same way as you have suffered since that fateful day, so have I. Every day I think about those split seconds, those moments when everything could have been

so very, very different. When everybody's lives could have been so very, very different.

I gave up the florist's soon after. My mind couldn't really cope with the detail needed to run a business. I passed it on to Anne – my only daughter. I tried travelling. Spent weeks and months in strange and foreign lands. Egypt. Morocco. Japan. Australia. Indonesia. But that didn't help. I tried distracting myself with a wide variety of different hobbies. Photography. Painting. Creative writing. Swimming. Again, it offered no relief. I even tried drinking myself into the grave before I realised that actually it wasn't doing me any good. All I could ever think about was the little girl whose life I could have saved.

And then, the inevitable cancer made an appearance. I tell you, when it does, it makes you sit up and take notice. When your life is at risk, it's incredible what a spur that can be. My days were numbered – despite what the doctors said in those early days, I knew my days were numbered. And when I knew that, it jolted me into action.

I couldn't save Louisa. It was far too late for that. But perhaps there was something else I could do. My mind leapt back to June 1999. The day we all found ourselves having to change. What if there was something I'd missed? What if, all these years, my mind had been hiding something away? Something that could help bring – I hate this word but I'm going to use it anyway – "closure" to the situation. Closure to you, Mr Gaudiano.

I don't know why I hadn't thought of it earlier. Too busy wading through the depths of despair to piece together this possible solution. Too busy trying to fool myself into believing I could find a way to cope. But when I thought about it, it was so incredibly obvious.

Hypnotism.

I've never really believed in hypnotism – but I was dying. Why not try it? Why not open yourself up to things that may be rubbish in the hope that they may not be?

So I booked a series of sessions with someone who claimed to be very good. Five sessions. Fifty pounds a time. The first session was a virtual disaster. He couldn't get me to go under and I left the building vowing never to go back.

Only, I did. Thank goodness. The second time, I actually went under – quite an odd experience from what I can remember. Nothing of any interest came out of that session though.

But during the third, fourth and fifth sessions ...

Slowly, over the weeks, my memory dragged the few tiny scraps of information from somewhere inside my mind and put them together to make a whole. Afterwards, I thought about going to the police. But the information I had was so insubstantial – so insignificant in a way – and had been gleaned in such an unscientific manner, that I thought they would just laugh me out of the station.

So I decided to leave it all to you.

Mr Gaudiano, there was someone else there that evening. Someone I recognised but couldn't name. It may be that they had nothing whatsoever to do with your daughter's disappearance. In some ways, I hope they didn't.

But I saw their face and I saw their car."

Nino read on. Quicker and quicker, his mind tripping him up and missing out words so that he had to go back and reread everything at least twice. When, eventually he got to the end, he lowered the sheet, not really looking at anything.

'Anything useful?' Anne Smith asked.

Nino seemed to snap out of his thoughts. 'Oh, yes.' He nodded. 'Very. Thank you.'

Did the safe house have Wi-Fi? Shit. He couldn't be sure. He hadn't even turned his phone on last night, so he didn't know. He couldn't risk it, so he pulled down one of the long cardboard boxes that sat on the top shelf and dug out a decent length of Ethernet cable. He threw that onto the chair in the corner of the room along with the two hard drives and one of his spare laptops. Now, was there anything else that he needed to take with him? He racked his brain to try and think of what else he needed.

And then he picked up on the smell. The smell of something wrong. Something out of place. Josh knew this room intimately – he spent most of his working day in there. He knew precisely how the room should smell.

But there was something different.

He turned to look towards the door and a fist slammed hard into his face.

Seventeen years ago

'There's a disco. Next Tuesday,' Louisa lay back on her bed, the Spice Girls CD playing out of the tiny stereo thing that took up most of the even tinier bedside table. 'In the youth club at the church. Shall we go?'

Alice took a gulp of the orange squash that Louisa's mum had given her. The room was small and smelt slightly of damp and part of the wallpaper was beginning to peel away in the top corner where there was a nasty brown stain. Louisa had put some posters over her bed. Five. A1. A large Spice Girls one dominated the wall nearest the window.

The half-term holidays were always so pointless. Just one week. You couldn't do anything in one week. At least with Christmas and Easter you got two weeks off. That felt like a decent break from school. And as for the summer holidays ... Alice *lived* for the summer holidays, where you had so much time to fill it became almost impossible, and you could just squander time like it didn't matter. But half-terms? Before they had started they had come to an end. What was the point in that?

'Why not,' Alice replied repositioning her bottom on the edge of the bed.

'We'd better let Laurie and Katie know. That's if they want to come.' She went quiet.

'Look, Lou,' Alice put her empty glass down on the

carpet. 'The thing with the fags. You didn't have to take the blame. We should all have had detention.'

Louisa shrugged. 'Doesn't matter.'

'But it does. Laurie feels guilty for letting you take the blame, I think. That's why she's been angry ever since. And Katie's been treating her like she's some sort of ... monster.' She sighed. 'We were all guilty so perhaps we should *all* have done it.'

'But what's the point? It's better one of us does it, isn't it?'

'But why you?'

Louisa smiled. 'Me this time. Somebody else the next.'

Chapter Twenty-five

'I'll drive.'

'If you like.' Luchewski was rather relieved. He'd already had to fight his way through the Blackwall Tunnel twice that morning, so he turned away from where his car was parked to the space where Singh's Peugeot sat. She unlocked it and he crouched into the passenger seat, pulling the lever and pushing the seat back to accommodate his long legs. Singh slammed the door shut behind her and turned the ignition.

Luchewski's TT always ran so quietly that, sometimes, he wasn't even sure if he'd started the engine. He'd have to give the accelerator a little pressure to hear it rev up. But Singh's car was a lot older and a lot more run-in than his. It roared to life and the gearbox kind of scrunched as she slipped it into first.

'Which safe house were taken to?' she asked as the yellow barrier swooped open and let them out onto the main road.

'The one just outside Sidcup. The place with the funny name. Pratt's Bottom or Pratt's End or whatever it is.'

The safe house was, Hal tried to remember, one of a number of similar buildings teetering on the edge of rough common land. A horrible, white 1950s block of brick with a tiny weed-ridden front garden. It was down a long sweeping road that came away from Sidcup town centre, past a large garage and a few hopeless shops. Boggy fields and scrappy grassland surrounded the house and no one – not even the disinterested neighbours – would ever suspect that the house was one of a number owned and shared by the local police forces to hide people away. It was usually women and children, temporarily housed to keep them away from violent partners. Or supergrasses, giving away all their terrible and prosecutable secrets.

It was not usually used to keep an entire family out of the way of a serial killer.

Luchewski's mind jumped back to the previous day's meeting with Arnold Richards. What was he up to? Why had he dragged them out to Surrey to reveal that he had murdered Caroline Merriman? What had he to gain from admitting to it? No matter how he looked at it, he couldn't see any reason for Richards admitting to the murder. Richards wasn't the sort to try and make peace with the world. If Richards could drag it all down with him as he fell, he would willingly have done so. The man was poison. He did nothing out of a sense of propriety. Everything he ever did was to satisfy some sort of a need or a desire within himself.

So what the hell was he playing at?

Guilt was a terrible thing. It could swallow you whole and spit you out, bones bleached and dried. Or it could nibble away slowly, like a sort of lethargic piranha, working its way little by little through your righteousness and morality. Either way, if you didn't stamp it out – squeeze it until it died – it would get you in the end.

Stevie struggled to stand upright on the tube. He held on particularly tight to the yellow handrail and as the train jerked right then left and all the other bodies around him jerked right then left in time, he desperately felt the need to throw up. The two poor Indian guys in black suits right next to him glared worryingly and tried to stretch themselves slightly further away from this pale, sickly looking young man.

He heaved once but managed to hold onto the contents of his stomach. The train lurched to a stop, the doors hissed open and several of the people around him stepped out onto the platform at Chancery Lane. Stevie noticed one or two step off the train only to get back on in the adjoining carriage. Despite wanting to spew all over the place, he smiled to himself, oddly pleased that he was having such an effect on people this morning.

The doors beeped before sliding themselves shut and the tube moved off once again.

Aside from feeling sick and carrying one of the heaviest hangovers ever experienced by a single human being, Stevie was feeling guilty. Guilty for the way he had behaved last night.

He had gone to the party knowing full well what was going to happen. He could try to deny it to himself, pretend that he had been naïve and foolish – an innocent abroad. He could tell himself that he had gone to make new friends, have a laugh, sing some songs, smoke some dope. But he didn't. He had gone to the party because Mike had invited him.

More precisely, he had gone to the party to have sex with Mike.

He was sweating now. The alcohol forcing its way out of his body through the pores of his skin. He guessed that he was smelling of vodka and rum. Reeked of it, more than likely. He was probably giving off fumes and knocking the tube load of Japanese tourists out with them. He held on tighter than ever and prayed for the train to reach Queensway.

When Mike had kissed him he wasn't really shocked.

He knew it was coming. He'd been expecting it all evening. The whole evening had basically been a preamble to that moment. He had both expected it and wanted it.

So he surprised himself when, after Mike's lips had pulled away from his own, he shook his head.

'I can't.'

'What?' Mike looked amused.

'I can't. It's not right.'

Mike gestured around his room. 'Who's going to know? There's nobody else here. It can be our little secret.' He raised his eyebrows. 'I won't tell if you won't.' He leaned in to kiss Stevie on the lips again, but Stevie stuck his hand out to hold Mike back.

'No. I'm not going to do this.'

Mike straightened. 'Why not? It's the reason you came here tonight, wasn't it? You can't deny that.'

Stevie struggled to find the right words.

'I've seen you looking at me across the lecture theatre, and across the refectory. Today in the library, I know you went there to see me.'

Stevie thought, frowned and shook his head again. 'Er ... no, I didn't actually.'

'Oh, come on. Of course you did. You went there knowing where I usually sit and waited for me to turn up. Admit it.'

Stevie half-laughed to himself. 'No. I didn't.'

Mike turned and sat back down on the bed. 'OK, lie to yourself as much as you want. But I know it's the truth. You've become obsessed with me. You can't stop thinking about me. I've started to intrude on your every waking thought. You know it's true.'

Stevie gave a sort of a snort. *Was he kidding? He didn't look as if he was kidding.*

272

Mike's face was deadly serious. He ran his hand arrogantly through his hair and stared at the wall. 'You're only human. Anyway, even if you refuse me now, it won't be long before you change your mind.' His eyes focused on Stevie, and for the first time Stevie noticed just how cold and superior they were. Not the dazzlingly blue, attractive eyes he had seen winking across the room at him just days before. This time they were like ice. 'You see, I always get what I want. In the end.'

Stevie found himself smiling. 'You're actually quite a prick, aren't you?'

'What?'

'You heard.' He stood up from his chair and walked out of the room, down the stairs and out the front door, stepping over the comatose body of Thin Features before striding away towards home.

That was last night. The major problem was that when he *did* get home he downed half a bottle of vodka to try and knock the memory of the whole incident out of his head. So now he felt like shit.

And he still felt guilty. He hadn't gone ahead with it, but just the idea that he had *wanted* to ... it gave him the shivers.

It was true, Luchewski could be almost as much of a prick as Mike. But Luchewski was fucked up. *Properly* fucked up. He'd spent most of his adult life pretending to be straight when he was gay. His parents died in a car crash moments after arguing with him. He had a daughter to worry about. His job was stressful and draining and took up any spare time that he had. And he'd been unceremoniously outed in the press – Stevie's fault, admittedly. Luchewski had a *right* to behave like a prick sometimes.

What Luchewski didn't need was a partner – a

boyfriend – who was tempted to stray whenever the stresses and strains of their relationship got too much. His life was insecure enough. He needed someone who would be there for him. Not necessarily a 'little housewife' type – Stevie could never be the little housewife type – but somebody who took all the crap on board and knew both how to react and how *not* to react.

Overnight, Stevie had come to realise that if he wanted to make it work with Luchewski – and in his heart he believed he really did – then it meant not demanding too much from him. Take it on the chin sometimes. Push back at others. Choose your battles carefully and sensitively. Support, don't demolish. Give space but also be close. Try to love but don't always expect it in return – it'll come when it's ready.

Compromise, essentially.

Stevie had never been in a serious relationship before and perhaps he was still struggling to get used to the idea of compromise. But Luchewski – Harry – was one of the good guys, there was never any doubt about that, and Stevie knew that if he was ever really going to make a go of it with anyone, he'd be hard pushed to find someone more fundamentally decent and caring than him.

The time to calm down and take things slowly had finally arrived in Stevie's life.

He knew it was going to be tricky – there was no doubt about that – but he was more than willing to try.

Anyway, he was pleased he'd decided not to go into college today. He needed the day off to recover and to sort his head out. A little bit of retail therapy was required, so he'd armed himself with one of the credit cards that still had a tiny bit of leeway on it and headed up west.

As the tube pulled onto Queensway, Stevie suddenly

felt a whole lot better. He stepped off the train, went up the escalator and walked out into the sunshine where he was promptly sick all over a passer-by's shoes.

Luchewski's phone rang with the embarrassing ringtone that he never got around to changing. He fished it out of his jacket pocket and squinted at the screen. Woode.

'Sir?'

'We've a man down, Harry,' his voice sounded urgent.

'What?'

'Outside the Woodingtons' house. One of the constables based at the safe house. I've tried contacting the female officer at the safe house, but there's no answer.'

Luchewski looked at Singh as she negotiated the lights. 'That's where we're headed now.'

'I know. I've got the local force heading there too. How far away are you?'

Luchewski slapped the dashboard and pointed ahead of them. Singh took the hint and sped up. 'Not far. Just a minute away.' Behind them Luchewski could hear the distant wail of police sirens.

'What was he doing at the Woodingtons? Is he dead?'

'Yes. Strangled. Found sitting in the car by a neighbour.'

'Fuck!'

Singh drove even faster, overtaking the Honda Jazz that seemed to be taking its time and whizzing in and out of the rest of the traffic. Luchewski found himself mentally acknowledging what a good driver she was. Towards the bottom of the hill, Luchewski could see the small crop of dull, ugly houses at the end of which the safe house sat.

'We're almost there, sir. I'll call you soon.' He

switched the phone off and shoved it quickly back into his jacket pocket.

Singh raced past the large garage and the boarded-up shops, past the smattering of cars and vans parked along the edge of the road – a blue Picasso, a silver Fiesta, a red van, a green Clio – until she came to the last of the houses and screeched into place right outside the front door. As she killed the engine, Luchewski hopped out. Back up the hill two police cars with lights flashing were catching them up.

Hal sprinted up the path and in through the wide open front door. The house felt cool compared to the warmth outside and he wondered how long the front door had been left open for. He peered around the door into the sitting room and found the body of a youngish woman lying on the floor in front of the television, blood slowly seeping from her head. PC Andersen.

'Fuck!'

Singh came up behind him. 'Oh, God.'

A small thump from upstairs.

Hal pushed past Singh and took the stairs three at a time. At the top were three doors. The one on the right was open and he could see a white bathroom suite. Suddenly the door in front of him opened and a young boy looked out. The name shot straight into Luchewski's usually hopeless-with-names mind. Zac. Behind him the face of a confused little girl appeared. Sophie.

'What's going –'

A noise from behind the door on the left. Without thinking, Luchewski shoved the boy back roughly into his room making him fall over backwards, slamming the door shut behind him before turning and forcing his way through the door on the left.

A man. Next to a bed. Squatting over a woman. A rope

or some sort of cord in his hands. The man looked up. Luchewski's heart leapt into his mouth. The head was completely covered by a black balaclava.

'Nooooooo!' the man yelled, jumping up towards Luchewski and knocking him off balance. The two of them tumbled out onto the small landing, each of them flailing useless punches at each other.

Face, thought Hal. *Must see the face*. He tried to reach up to grab the balaclava off the man's head but the man thumped his hand out of the way, twisting and writhing until the two of them were rolling down the stairs, gouging and kicking and hitting, and taking chunks of wallpaper with them. Singh leapt out of the way as they came to rest in the hallway.

Luchewski smashed his fist hard into the side of the man's chest, winding him momentarily. Seeing his advantage, Luchewski tried to pull himself out from under the man's weight. But the man was too quick. He rolled so that Luchewski was under him and slammed his fist into Luchewski's jaw. Hal's face burnt with the pain and, instinctively he brought his knee up into the man's groin. The man creased up, pushing his weight up from the floor and swung another punch at Luchewski's face. The blow caught him on the cheek.

As the man straightened, Singh threw a fist, but he easily knocked it away before pushing her to the floor and disappearing through the sitting room door.

Hal scrambled up, blood pouring out of his nose and mouth. 'Upstairs! Get upstairs!' he shouted at Singh before racing after the man.

By the time Luchewski had got through the open French windows, the man was throwing open the back gate and sprinting through it. Hal followed, flinging the gate wide as he went.

The land behind the house was a flat expanse of untended countryside. Tufts of spiky grasses littered the uneven, wet ground and, as Luchewski chased after the man, he nearly broke – or at the very least twisted – his ankle on boggy clump after boggy clump. Soon his shoes were covered in thick mud and the ends of his trouser legs were soaked through.

The man was at least thirty yards ahead of him. Where he was heading, Luchewski couldn't tell. But he was obviously younger and fitter than Hal was, and the gap seemed to be increasing. Hal put on an extra spurt and the blood pounded in his ears.

Eventually, the man seemed to stop. Luchewski squinted to see why. A barbed wire fence ran for as far as the eye could see in both directions. The man picked himself slowly over the two long strands of wire, gently easing his legs over before racing off again. The slowness of the climb brought the gap between the two men down to about fifteen yards and Luchewski realised what he had to do. If he wanted to have any chance of catching this man, he was going to have to try and clear the fence in one go.

As he approached the razor-sharp wire, he sped up. Two yards from the fence he jumped as high and as hard as he could possibly manage. He brought his legs up to his body…

…but not tightly enough. The sharp barbs caught the part of his right leg a few inches above the ankle and the momentum of his body made him pivot awkwardly, slamming his chest and head into the mud the other side.

For a moment or two he was stunned. Where was he? What was he doing? But quickly he shook the feeling off and, ripping his caught leg from the wire fence, picked himself up and started running again.

Only this time, the pain in his shin took his breath away, and he found it almost impossible to put any weight on his leg. He tried to shoo it away, but the body knows when it is beaten, and it screamed at him to stop. Pleaded with him to stop. Begged him not to carry on.

The man was just a dot now, tearing up the slight incline on the left to where the outskirts of Sidcup started or ended depending on your view of it.

Luchewski stopped. He reached into his jacket pocket for his phone. He needed to tell Singh to tell the woodentops who were arriving at the house that they needed to get searching the back streets of Sidcup. But his phone wasn't there. He hobbled back to the fence and checked the ground, assuming it had fallen out of his pocket when the barbed wire fence had decided to make a grab for him. But it wasn't.

It must have slipped out in the house.

'For fuck's sake!' He spat angrily and kicked a wooden post. Half a second later, as the pain swirled up his ankle through the bottom half of his leg, he wished he hadn't.

'Jesus Kid Jensen! Look at the state of you.'

'I know. This suit cost me twelve hundred quid, you know.' Luchewski kicked his still bleeding leg out, and Woode could see the long, muddy slash in the fabric from the bottom of his trousers to the knee. 'One of Henry Herbert's best, this is. Or *was*, should I say?'

'Sit still,' the female paramedic dabbing something purple at his swollen cheek frowned. 'Stop jabbering on.'

Luchewski raised his eyebrows at Woode who raised his in return.

Luchewski was sat on the wall outside the safe house. *Huh*, he thought. *That's a misnomer if ever there was one.*

Safe house. Two ambulances had already rushed away from the house, sirens blaring. Police and forensics were currently picking their way over the inside of the house and the fields beyond, led by Singh.

'The wife? She all right?' Woode asked.

'Thankfully, yes. A couple of minutes later and ...' He paused for effect. 'She'll have a sore throat for a few days, but nothing worse than that. Grandparents have taken the kids off. Best really.'

'The PC?'

'Again, she'll live. Slight concussion they think. Bit of blood loss.' Hal winced as the purple stuff hit a nice, open fresh bit of his flesh.

'Oh, shush. Don't be a baby.' The paramedic tutted.

This time Woode was the first to raise his eyebrows.

Hal continued. 'The husband went back to the house to get something for his work. That's what the wife says.' Both Luchewski and Woode exchanged meaningful glances. 'He's hasn't turned up yet, has he?'

Woode shook his head. 'No. He wasn't found at the house. And he's not here.'

'So where the fuck is he then?'

'Language, please!' The woman with the silicon gloves on gave him a disapproving stare.

Woode ignored her. 'What about you? You all right? You know,' he sighed and nodded towards Luchewski's leg, 'you don't have to go in for all this heroic stuff. You can leave all that to the S.O. boys. That's their job.'

Luchewski laughed. 'Trust me, you can shove all the "heroic stuff".' He avoided the gaze of the paramedic who, quite frankly, was beginning to get on his tits. 'I'd rather spend the rest of my life not even thinking about the "heroic stuff". It was only a case of wrong place, wrong time as far as I'm concerned.'

'He needs stitches.'

'What?'

'He needs stitches.' The paramedic put the purple liquid back in her big box of goodies.

'So she says,' Luchewski moaned. 'It'll be all right, I'm sure. Stick a plaster on it.'

'It needs stitches.' She pulled her gloves off one by one. 'That gash is too wide to heal on its own. You're going to need at least four or five stitches.'

'Rubbish!'

'I'm the expert here. You need to get it stitched up.'

'If the lady says you need stitches then you'd better get them.' Woode seemed to nod in agreement.

'Not you, too, sir.'

'Don't want it to go all septic and drop off now, do you?'

Luchewski spotted an ally somewhere behind them and waved.

'Singh. Singh. Tell them I don't need to have stitches, will you?'

She came over and looked down at his leg. 'Ooooo. You need stitches, sir. That's still bleeding. Look.'

Luchewski gave a mock shrug. 'Thanks a lot, Singh!'

'You did ask, sir.'

'No, I didn't. I told you to tell them that I didn't need stitches. I didn't consult you for your medical expertise now, did I?'

Woode shuffled forward. 'I'll run you into hospital.' He looked down at Luchewski's bleeding leg again. 'On second thoughts, somebody else can run you in. I don't fancy getting any of that all over my upholstery.'

'Thank you, sir. Your concern is duly noted.' Luchewski smiled at Woode who smiled back.

'I'll take you, sir.' Singh said. 'I'll just get this lot here sorted and then I'll drive you in.'

Woode's phone suddenly rang and Luchewski was delighted to find out that Woode's ringtone was *Livin' On A Prayer* – almost as embarrassing as his own.

'What? ... when? ...' Woode's face crumpled. 'OK ... OK.'

He shut his phone down with his large, fat fingers.

'Woodington's been found.'

'Where?'

'Couple of miles from here.' He pointed in some general nondescript direction. 'In a layby.'

'Dead?'

'Surprisingly not. Stabbed half to death but still hanging on.'

'Get them to take him to St George's.' Luchewski hopped off the wall and winced.

'Why St George's?'

'It's where I got the paramedics to take Mrs Woodington and the PC. It's also where Singh is going to take me in a minute to get me all sewn up. I might be able to have a nose about while I'm there. Interview a few more staff about junior doctor Alice Seagrove. That sort of thing.'

'Don't overdo it, Harry.'

'Don't worry, sir. I don't intend to.'

Twenty minutes later, Luchewski climbed back into Singh's passenger seat. He let it back a couple of extra inches to be on the safe side, before Singh headed back up the hill towards the lights in Sidcup, past the same smattering of parked cars – a blue Picasso, a silver Fiesta, a green Clio. With a little less urgency this time they passed the boarded-up shops and the large garage, Luchewski thinking deeply all the way.

Chapter Twenty-six

He couldn't believe it. He just could not fucking believe it.

For some reason he'd drifted back to the graveyard where he'd managed to scrape a tiny bit of sleep a few nights ago. This time, though, he found that his mind raced too much and he ended up not sleeping at all. Instead, he watched the sun come up reluctantly into the new day before picking himself and his small rucksack up and moving off towards the centre of the city.

It was as if none of this was happening to him. He forgot to eat and barely drank from the taps that occasionally stuck out of walls. His head was light and he felt like he was drunk or off his face on something.

The morning workers passed him like the ants he always believed them to be. Only this time, they gave him a particularly wide berth, like he was clearly a carrier of some awful tropical disease, or a suicide bomber.

Suicide ...

The word kept filling his mind.

Suicide ...

It would all be so easy.

By late morning, his legs had carried him about as far as they were going to be able to carry him and he slumped in a doorway just off Shaftesbury Avenue. It smelled of piss and rotting bins and, for a few minutes, he found himself sliding off to sleep, his head resting on his rucksack, oblivious to the passers-by.

'Oi! Yeh cun'!'

Cornish woke with a start. His leg hurt suddenly and, as he looked up, he could see the wide, mad eyes of a red-faced, unshaven man with very few teeth and a filthy blue sleeping bag wrapped about his shoulders.

The man kicked Andrew Cornish's leg once again.

'Da's it. Way up, yeh cun'. Tha's mah fuggin patch, pal.' He gesticulated around from under the sleeping bag. 'Evrah fugger roun' here knoos da.'

'What?' He rubbed his eyes and the man kicked him even harder in the stomach. The wind shot out of his chest and he curled up in pain.

'Nay fuggin respect. Nay one's gah nay fuggin respect dees days.' The man suddenly spotted the rucksack on the ground. 'Wha's in da ba'? Wha yeh go in da ba'?'

Cornish grabbed the bag and held it close to him. 'Nothing. There's nothing in there.'

'Nay look la' nuthin te meh, pal.' He licked his lips. 'Wha's in da ba'?'

'Nothing!'

The man straightened and looked firstly over his left shoulder then over his right before coming back to rest his eyes on Cornish. 'Givvas da ba'.'

'No. I won't. Leave me alone.'

The eyes went wider, the head tilted at an aggressive angle. 'I sed givvas da ba, yeh cun'.' The sleeping bag fell to the ground and the man pulled something out of one of the pockets in his tattered tracksuit bottoms. 'Or ah'll cut yeh.'

Cornish noticed the short, stubby blade that protruded out of the man's hand.

Suicide …

The word was still there like background noise in his

mind. Floating like something that needed anchoring down.

It could be so simple ...

'Go on, then.'

'Wha?'

'Cut me. Kill me. Go on. Do it. Who gives a shit any more? I don't care. Just fucking do it.'

The man looked confused.

'Go on! Just fucking do it!'

The man looked nervously over his shoulders again before pausing and then kicking out with his left foot, catching Cornish under the chin. Cornish's head jerked back hard, hitting the steel door behind it with some force. The man leant forward and pulled the rucksack away.

'Ah meh be a feef,' he whispered. 'Bah ah ain' a fuggin psycho.'

He swept up his sleeping bag with his other arm and ran off quickly.

That was at least an hour ago, but his head still throbbed and pounded as much as it did then. With any luck, he thought to himself, he had internal bleeding – his brain was haemorrhaging – and he'd drop down dead any second now. That would bring an end to these feelings of hopelessness that he always seemed to have these days.

The same sense of hopelessness that he felt as an eight-year old. The same all-consuming black despair that smothered him in his bed at night, when the monsters from the day came out to haunt him. The same sense of desperation that was put there – manufactured, in a way – by Kurtz.

He couldn't believe it. He just could not fucking believe it.

He really had had enough.

He hurt all over. But he really didn't care.

He forced his legs to carry him slowly west. Slowly. So slowly.

After all, there were some pretty bridges in the west.

Big Issue pulled himself up off the ground just outside Foyles bookshop. The people who went up and down Charing Cross Road, he found, were more often than not, book lovers. And book lovers generally speaking had a bit of disposable income and were pretty liberal. Taking up a spot on Charing Cross Road could earn you about twenty quid on a good day. Admittedly you also had the people who thought that giving money to a beggar would just encourage drug abuse and addiction, so would instead hand over a lukewarm cheese pasty from Greggs. Still, even that was pretty good if you were particularly hungry. Saved you wasting your own money on food. You had more to spend on cider and cheap vodka then.

The boy looked in a daze, like a fucking zombie or something. He was shuffling slowly along, not really caring where he was going. And his eye was black and swollen. Somebody had given him a good smack by the looks of it. He was in a total state. His long black coat was ripped and muddy and his hair was greasy and clogged in clumps. Every time he saw him, the boy looked worse.

Big Issue kept his distance. He hadn't had anything significant to drink yet – just a couple of cans of Breaker lager to take the edge off things – and he was torn between following and paying a visit to the off-license to swap some of his hard-begged coins for something wet and strong.

The boy wasn't well, that was clear, and for the first time in many years Big Issue made a decision not based

on personal gratification – an altruistic decision almost –
and kept on trailing behind Andrew Cornish, making sure
the boy didn't spot him.

'Do me a favour, will you, Singh.'

'Sir?'

He handed her his house keys as the rest of the other
A&E patients watched the large TV screen showing a
programme about dodgy builders. The sound was turned
off so nobody really had a clue what was going on – each
of them providing their own soundtrack in their own
heads.

'Go pick up some fresh clothes for me, will you?' He
gestured to his trousers and filthy shoes. 'I can't go about
like this. I look like something out of *Last of the Summer
Wine*. Bit of string holding my trousers up and I'd fit right
in. And pick up some shoes too. Trainers or something.
You'll have to rummage through my wardrobe. Just get
some stuff. Oh and no peeking at my large stash of porn,
OK?' He smiled. 'Pretend you can't see it.'

'Er …'

'That's a joke, Singh. Don't worry.'

'Sir.'

She went off and left him sitting watching the people
watching the programme.

Half an hour later and he was lying on a bed, torn
trouser leg cut completely off, having a young female
doctor poke at the gash with her finger.

'Just some butterfly stitches, I think. It's nothing too
serious. I'll clean it up and put some on.'

'Butterfly stitches?' Luchewski asked.

'A couple of strong plasters. Not real stitches.'

Luchewski sighed. 'I told them it wouldn't
need stitches. They wouldn't listen to me. I said it

only needed a plaster.'

'How recently have you had a tetanus boost?'

'Er ...' He really didn't have a clue.

'I'll give you one. Just to be safe.'

She took a bottle of antiseptic liquid and a few swabs and dabbed at the wound.

'So, you're investigating Alice's death. Any idea who did it yet?'

'No. But we'll get there soon. It won't be long.' Hal wasn't entirely sure if he had just lied. 'How well did you know her?'

'Not at all. She came in, did her job and went home again. She never really integrated with us other junior doctors, or any of the senior ones for that. Never came with us on nights out or anything. A bit of a loner, if you ask me. She'd never have made consultant like that. People skills have to stretch to colleagues as well as patients if you want to make consultant. Not sure if she even wanted to specialise. She never talked about it. Happy just doing what she was doing, I suppose. Nothing wrong in that.'

She took a small sliver of mesh, pulled a backing off and, squeezing Luchewski's leg, patted it in place. Then she repeated the process.

'There. Done. Book an Outpatients appointment for two weeks' time and, with a bit of luck, it'll soon be as good as new.'

Luchewski was pleased to see a significant police presence in the reception area and outside, in the hospital car park. Somewhere in the building two members of the Woodington family were being checked out. Well, Mrs Woodington was probably just having some salve rubbed into her neck but her husband was actually fighting for his life.

Standing just outside the revolving door entrance, an old couple passed him and scowled at the way he was dressed – a pair of trousers with the best part of a leg missing. He smiled politely back and got two vague tuts as replies. *Hurry up, Singh,* thought Hal as his phone started to buzz in his pocket.

'Hello, hero!' It was Corrie. 'Heard all about your Bruce Willis in *Die Hard 2* impersonation. What a hunk, Harry! Wrestling with a killer like that. Could make a girl swoon.'

'Yes, yes. Very good. Ha. Ha,' he said dryly.

'Oh yes, could win a woman's heart, that.'

'What about me being –'

'A bender? We'd work something out!'

This time he really did laugh.

'What news, Corrie?'

'We've had the names of the two kids Bartholomew Kurtz abused in the mid-nineties. Obviously we've been told that in any public record we need to keep referring to them as Boy A and Boy B. But Boy A was a James Linard. Nine years old when Kurtz started grooming and then abusing him. No online stuff for Kurtz. Just plain old-fashioned one-to-one chats in the park before inviting him back to his place to see his non-existent new puppies.'

'Linard?' It was a name Luchewski had never heard.

'Yeah. Parents moved down to Brighton after it all came out. Trying to get away from it all. Unfortunately Linard topped himself when he was eighteen. Tied his dressing gown cord to the curtain rail. Two years ago, parents sold everything they owned and upped sticks to China. Been teaching English there ever since. We've run checks on visas and they haven't left China once in those two years.'

'What about Boy B? What was his name.'
'Boy B was Andrew Cornish. Single mum, went –'
'What was that?'
'Eh?'
'His name? What was it?'
'Cornish. Andrew Cornish. Why?'

Burlock had all of Cornish's photographs spread over his desk. They were all selfies except for one or two shots of buildings or bridges. In most of the pictures, Cornish was unsmiling. And thin. Horrendously thin. Like a brittle stick of rock.

'Come here, Green!' Burlock called out of his wide open office door.

Green sauntered across from his desk which he'd been polishing up with some wet wipes.

'Sir?'

'Why do I recognise him? I can't put my finger on it. There's some reason why I recognise this bugger. Any idea?'

Green came alongside the desk and tilted his head to get a good look.

'You ever arrest him?'

Burlock shook his head vigorously. 'No. It's not that. It's something more recent than that.'

'Perhaps he shops where ... hold on.' He reluctantly picked up one of the shots and twisted it about. 'Wait a minute.' He walked back through the door into the large communal office.

Burlock, still sitting behind his desk, shouted after him, 'What yer doing, Green?' He rolled his eyes. 'What's he up to now?'

Detective Sergeant Robbie Green did have an incredibly good memory, even if he said so himself. He could recall the most minor of details sometimes. Working his way through the old discarded papers in the coffee area though was anathema to him – they were all crumpled and half-open with little doodles all over. It gave his brain a slight tickle and he struggled to resist the urge to dig out another wet wipe for his fingers. Thankfully he quickly managed to find the paper he was looking for, and holding it between index finger and thumb he carried it back to Burlock's desk.

'What's that?'

'Newspaper.'

'I can see that. Why've you brought it in here?'

Green lowered it gently onto the photographs on the desk. Another little tickle in his mind.

'Page three.'

Burlock pulled the paper back into some semblance of shape before turning to page three.

Some stills from some CCTV footage. An old woman at a cashpoint. A man in a long black coat. A struggle. One badly injured octogenarian.

'That's him.' Burlock stabbed the paper and half rose from his chair. 'That's Cornish.'

'He's the one who mugged that old woman. The one that's in a coma.'

Burlock looked up at Green and gave a tight, curt nod of appreciation. There was no doubt about it. Green was a funny bugger. But he was good. Frighteningly good.

Suddenly the phone on Burlock's desk started bleeping. Burlock scooped up the receiver and answered, his heart racing.

'Yes?'

'Freddie. It's me.'

'Harry.'

'Look, I've got some info on Cornish for you.'

'S'funny,' Burlock replied. 'I've got some for you too.'

Thankfully Singh didn't take that long. She handed him the two plastic bags of clothes she'd taken from his wardrobe and he snatched them off her almost hungrily.

'I wasn't sure what you wanted exactly, so I stuck a load of different stuff in there. There're a couple of pairs of shoes too.'

'Cheers, Singh. You're a star.'

He went into the nearest disabled toilet, locked the door and changed. The ruined trousers he rammed into the bin. Everything else he'd been wearing that morning – even the mud-clogged shoes – he pushed into one of the plastic bags. In the end he decided to wear the jeans and plain white T-shirt along with the cotton navy blue summer blazer. At one point, there was a bang on the door.

'Hurry up!' someone wailed. 'I'm busting!'

'Hold your horses!' Hal shouted back.

'But I'm busting!'

'I'm nearly done. Jesus.'

As Luchewski came out of the disabled toilets, two full plastic bags in hand, a young man in a wheelchair frowned hard at him.

'You shouldn't even be in there!'

Some passers-by were looking.

'It's all right, kid. I'm out of there now.'

'That's not the point. I'm going to –'

Luchewski pulled out his ID card and flashed it at the boy. 'It's all right. Don't worry. I'm on official business.'

It baffled the kid long enough for Luchewski to get away.

After dumping the bag in the back of Singh's car,

Luchewski made his way up to the top of the building where the Secure Ward was located. The Secure Ward was tucked away from the main part of the hospital – hidden at the top of some stairs and around a few corners, it was where patients deemed to be dangerous were usually taken for treatment. The security there was extra-tight – several coded doors to pass through, shatterproof glass, nothing remotely sharp or pointy to grab a hold of. Staff who worked there were trained in self-defence and had undergone courses in counselling and crisis management.

Today though it was harbouring a married couple under police protection. Just outside the main entrance to the Secure Ward sat two uniformed police officers, one of them busy reading the *Sun*. As Luchewski approached them, the one with the newspaper threw it under his chair and they both stood up.

'Sir.'

'They both here?'

'Mr Woodington has just come out of surgery, about twenty minutes ago. They wheeled him in. Mrs Woodington's been discharged and she's in there with him.' The one who hadn't been reading the *Sun* pointed his finger over his shoulder towards the Secure Ward. 'Doctor's in there too.'

The officer pushed a button to the left of the door before giving a thumbs up to the camera with the little blinking red light. The door buzzed and Luchewski pushed his way in.

He entered a short, surprisingly dark corridor which ended at a wide window overlooking the dirty, cluttered streets of south London. On his left was a nurse's station with two nurses and a doctor pointing at a clipboard.

Luchewski dug out his ID for the second time in five

minutes, and one of the nurses nodded and shoved a large hardback notebook towards him.

'Sign in, please.' She didn't smile.

Luchewski took the pen that was chained to the front desk and put his signature just below the shaky scrawl of Katie Woodington.

'How is he?' Luchewski directed the question to the doctor who was trying to stick an extra sheet of paper underneath the spring on the clipboard.

'Lost a lot of blood. Tiny bit of internal bleeding – we can easily keep that under control, though. We'll keep him under for a few days and monitor his vitals. He was very lucky actually.'

Lucky? Thought Hal. *Being kidnapped by a nutjob, then driven halfway across London by said nutjob before getting stabbed Christ knows how many times and dumped in a lay by? Not my definition of lucky.*

'Some of the knife wounds were very close to organs. One came within about three millimetres of his liver. That's a pretty close call.'

'Is she …?'

'Yes. She's in his room.'

'Can I …?'

'Second door on the left.'

'Thanks.'

Luchewski walked off, his newish trainers squeaking on the sterile polished tiles.

Katie Woodington didn't look up as he closed the door respectfully and quietly behind him. Her husband was strapped to large flashing machines that seemed to *phut* and *hiss* and *click*, and a VDU glowed like a particularly green TV against the far wall. Katie was sat on a chair at the side of the bed, his right hand sandwiched gently between hers. Luchewski came alongside and softly touched her on the shoulder. She didn't flinch or react in any way. It was as if she wasn't really there. It was as if she were trying to tune into whatever land her husband was currently floating around – trying to fly in it herself.

'Can we talk?' Luchewski asked eventually.

She nodded, lowered her husband's hand and stood up. 'Thank you.'

'What for?'

'You saved my life. And my kids' lives.' Her neck looked red and ever so slightly swollen, like someone had put a badly inflated water ring around it. Her eyes suddenly filled with tears. 'While he was doing it … strangling me … all I could think of was the kids. I prayed they wouldn't hear. That they'd just carry on playing quietly in their room and that they wouldn't see what was happening.' A tear rolled down one cheek. 'And that he wouldn't … hurt them.'

One of the very few things that wasn't strapped down in the coffee area was a half-empty box of tissues. Luchewski leant over, pulled one out and pathetically handed it across to her. She took it off him but didn't wipe her eyes.

'I've never worked, Inspector. I've put all my efforts into my family. Some people think that's madness in this day and age. That a woman should go out to work if she can. But I've always found that attitude as bigoted and as sexist as the one which says that all women should stay at home and look after her husband. Isn't it down to every woman … every person to decide what is best for them? Society or rules or fashionable ideas shouldn't affect that, should it? Everyone should be able to have the choice.'

Luchewski was pleased that Singh wasn't with him at that moment.

'So my family are everything to me. I couldn't bear it

if anything happened to them. Zac and Sophie.' A second tear rolled out of the other eye and down the other cheek. 'So it was lucky you came when you did. Thank you.'

Luchewski shrugged.

'No problem. Did he say anything to you? Did you recognise his voice? Tell me what happened.'

She heaved a sigh and her eyes went all far away. 'The kids were in that second bedroom. They were pulling all the old board games out of the cupboard and looking through them. They love games. They never last very long at home though. Pieces always go missing or someone stands on something important and breaks it. It usually ends in tears, I'm afraid.' She focused. 'I was in the main bedroom trying to put the few clothes we'd taken into the drawers and wardrobes – just trying to make it a bit more homely. It's not a very nice place, that safe house, you know. Too cold. There's been too much fear in that house. It's like it's seeped into the walls. You can almost smell it. I was bent over one of the drawers when a hand – a gloved hand – came around my face and covered my mouth. I was petrified. He pulled me close to him and held me tight.' Her eyes started filling up again.

'What happened then?'

'He said … he said "Hello, Katie. It's been a long time".'

Hal leaned forward. '"It's been a long time"?'

'Yes.'

'And he said "Katie"?'

'Yes.'

'Did you recognise his voice?'

She twisted the tissue over in her fingers and flicked a pointy tip against her thumb. 'I don't know. There was something familiar about it, but … I couldn't pin it down.'

'If he said "it's been a long time", it kind of suggests

that it's someone who knew you at some point. A "long time" could, of course, mean anything. But let's think about school. Someone you were at school with.' Hal felt like a hypnotist. 'The person I fought and chased this morning was not an old man by any means. He was far too strong and moved far too quickly. So let's just assume – and I might be wrong but I don't think I am – let's just assume that you went to school with him. Could that voice have belonged to anyone you went to school with? Anyone at all?'

She thought hard, or at least *looked* as though she was thinking hard. 'I … don't know. He had a man's voice. Not a boy's voice. I don't know how to join them up.'

Luchewski pulled a face. 'No. I suppose. I understand. So,' he continued, 'what happened after that?'

'He turned me around so that he could see me.'

'What could *you* see?'

'His eyes. I could see his eyes. They were blue.'

'Dark blue? Light blue? Bluey-green? Greeny-blue? What?'

She stared into the distance again, trying to recall. 'Just blue. My mind was on the children. I didn't think about grading the blueness of his eyes, to be honest, Inspector. It wasn't top of my list at that point. But they were definitely blue.'

'OK. Then?'

'Then he threw me backwards to the floor and put that thing around me. He slipped it around quickly. I barely had time to take a breath. He pulled tight. Then he asked me a strange question.'

Luchewski straightened up. 'A question? What question?'

'He said, "What did Alice Seagrove tell you about the night Louisa disappeared?".'

'Is that *exactly* what he said? Word perfect?'

'I'm not sure. But it was something along those lines.'

'Try and remember if you can.'

'Like I said, Inspector, my mind wasn't totally on the ball.' She gave him a fierce look and Luchewski suddenly realised that beneath the soft, motherly exterior lay a tough survivor that would kill to protect her own. His admiration for her seemed to slip up a couple of notches. That well-hidden survival instinct was probably the thing that kept her clinging to life in the moments before Luchewski found her. Hal nodded appreciatively and the trust between was re-established.

'What did he mean by that, do you think?'

'I honestly couldn't tell you.'

'*Did* Alice Seagrove ever tell you anything about Louisa Gaudiano's disappearance? What did she see when she went outside to look for her? Did she say?'

'No. She never said anything. When she came back into the disco she might have said something along the lines of "she's gone home". But that would have been all.'

'You see, I think she saw something or someone when she went to look for Louisa,' Luchewski's voice dropped a semitone for some reason. 'She saw something and now, years later, she was killed because of the thing – or person – she saw.'

'But why wouldn't she just say what she'd seen? Tell the police?'

Luchewski sat right back on the extremely uncomfortable sofa and stared at the ceiling. It was smooth and white and seemed to exaggerate the horrendously harsh strip lighting that ran along its centre. 'She might have been scared. Everyone goes on about how, after Gaudiano ... Louisa,' he quickly corrected himself, 'disappeared, Alice changed. She became insular.

Went in on herself. Everybody attributes that to the stress of not knowing what had happened to her friend. But what if it wasn't? What if it was because she knew what had happened to Louisa, but she could never bring herself to talk about it? Out of fear.'

'So why is he coming after the rest of us?'

'Because he thinks she told you all the truth.'

'But why now? Why not back then?'

'Perhaps ...' he thought. 'Perhaps he needed to become a man to do what he had to do. He needed to be stronger.'

'He left it a long time though, don't you think? All those years.'

Luchewski knew precisely what she meant. 'Yes. All those years in which one of you might spill the beans. No. It's not that.'

'What then?'

Hal puffed out his cheeks, blowing them up in frustration, before letting the air go – flapping his lips as it went. 'I wish I knew. It seems like it should be obvious but ... I don't know.'

They both sat there in silence for five minutes, neither of them even looking at the other. A nurse came in and cluttered two institutional cups and saucers filled with a suspiciously brown liquid onto the coffee table in front of them.

'Thought you might want these,' she said before turning specifically to Katie Woodington. 'I've put an extra sugar in yours. Thought you might need it.'

The nurse went out and the two of them resumed their vow of silence. Until –

'Oh!'

'What?' Luchewski asked, delighted that the noise now allowed him to shuffle forward in his seat and take one of the cups.

'He didn't say "disappeared". It's just come to me.'

'I'm sorry?'

'When he said "What did Alice Seagrove tell you about the night Louisa disappeared?" He didn't say "disappeared".'

'What did he say?'

Her eyes filled with tears again. 'He didn't say "disappeared". He said "died".'

Seventeen years ago

'You look nice.'

'Do I? Thanks. So do you.'

The two girls stood on the pavement, the final dregs of rush hour traffic fading away. Katie was wearing a long floral summer dress – a neat clash of blues and reds and greens and yellows. She clutched her tiny leather purse tightly and ran her hand through her freshly washed hair.

Alice looked down at her own comparatively dull jeans and white cheesecloth top. She'd dabbed a bit of her mum's blusher on, but nothing as much as Katie. Katie was full-on made up. Eyeliner. Lipstick. The whole thing. Alice felt naked in comparison.

'Shall we go through the park? No point calling on Lou. She's making her way there on her own.'

Alice nodded. 'Hope it's not too loud. I hate it when discos are too loud.'

'Oh I know. Some of the ones at primary school were terrible, weren't they? I think Mrs Tripp went deaf trying to run them. My mum says she's retiring this year.'

They walked through the gates and made their way slowly along the wide, sweeping path past impressive beds of tulips and marigolds. The lawns were kept short and stubby and, aside from the occasional scuffed patch of earth, the whole park was covered in a rich and lush green. Lots of rainy days – and now the sun – had brought all the plants and trees out from their winter shells, exploding into the glorious warmth of early summer.

The wind had also died and it was almost beginning to feel stuffy.

'Do you think there'll be many people there?' Katie asked, her eyes fixed on Alice.

'You mean, Josh Woodington?' Alice laughed. 'He might be.'

Katie gave her head a tiny shake as if dismissing a silly idea. 'No. I don't care if he's there or not. I really don't.' Her voice suggested otherwise. 'I'm not interested in him.'

'You are!'

'I'm not!'

'Yes you are. We all know it.'

Katie stared down at her feet and they both marched on.

'Is it that obvious?' she muttered.

'Yes.'

They came out the other end of the park onto a peaceful residential street where a car was having some difficulty trying to park.

'Do you think he knows?'

'He's a boy. Boys are the stupidest things ever. They don't notice anything.'

'Oh.'

'But,' Alice continued sensing the disappointment in her friend's voice, 'I'm sure he will. Soon.'

'Oh. Nice.'

The disco was already underway by the sound of the thumping coming from the church hall. A couple of other kids from school were hanging about outside drinking cans of Pepsi and Tango and trying to look as if they were bored, kicking their feet at the moss on the stumpy little wall.

'Y'all right,' one of the boys said.

'Hi,' Alice and Katie chirruped as one.

'Shit in there,' one of the others ones said. 'Loada shit.'

'Is it?'

'Yeah. Shit.'

'Oh dear,' Katie said popping open her purse and getting the entrance fee together.

'Yes. Shame.' Alice dug her hand deep into her pocket and fished out a two-pound coin.

Chapter Twenty-seven

He was angry with himself. So frigging angry. He felt like punching the wall hard and breaking one of his knuckles on purpose. He deserved it. He bloody deserved it. All the pain. He'd earned it.

He hadn't finished the job. He'd been too slow. That copper had come in and ruined it. Katie Thompson was still alive. She was still alive! He'd made everything ten times worse now! If he'd left alone, there was a chance that whatever Seagrove had told Thompson would have remained unspoken. In all these years, she'd obviously not said anything to the police. If he'd left alone, she might have continued to keep it all to herself. But now that he'd tried to kill her … and she was still alive …

He'd as good as pushed her into the hands of the police. Anything she knew was now going to come out.

He felt sick. It was all his own fault. He'd probably gone and ruined everything now. What an idiot!

He'd taken out some of his annoyance on Josh Woodington, of course. He'd stabbed him over and over again in the back of the van – he was going to have to clean that up before anyone at work noticed the mess – before tossing him dead out onto the road.

Out in the Kent countryside he'd changed out of his bloody clothes and into clean ones before driving back home and showering.

Lying on his bed and staring at the ceiling he tried to

plan his next move. Thompson was going to have to wait. Perhaps she didn't have any information at all, in which case it would all be all right. He tried to make himself believe that was the case, and soon he'd persuaded himself that he should not deviate from his original course of action. Put Thompson aside, he thought, and carry on regardless.

It was time to move on from the girls.

Luchewski left Katie Woodington once again holding her husband's hand accompanied by the sound of the machines beeping and hissing and puffing in a bid to keep him alive. Looking at her through the glass of the door, Hal knew that no matter how hungry or tired she was going to feel, there was no way that she was going to leave his side until he eventually opened his eyes. A weird pang of jealousy washed across his spine and he wondered if anyone would do the same for him should he ever find himself in a similar position. That was quickly followed by a pang of guilt. Perhaps Stevie would. Perhaps he was the sort that would do that. But it wasn't right for Luchewski to just assume that Stevie wouldn't. That wasn't giving him – or their relationship – a chance. Hal needed to be fairer to the poor kid.

The two coppers on the door stood up when he exited, one of them sort of half saluting, the other shuffling his feet.

Luchewski made his way slowly down the stairs to the main floors of the hospital. So Louisa Gaudiano was dead. Apparently. No surprise, of course, but odd after all this time to have a case he was so intimately involved with from the outset refreshed with this extra nugget of possibility. Everyone had always assumed she was dead – not the parents, perhaps, but then they were allowed their little slice of hope. Even the officers who'd investigated at the time basically assumed that it was a case of murder. If Katie Woodington knew anything about Gaudiano's murder, she was doing a damned good job of hiding it. Luchewski felt himself to be a decent – if not perfect – judge of character, and he believed everything she said. She was an honest and reliable witness.

Unlike this one, he thought as a short round woman dressed in the washed-out green of the nursing staff came out from one door, looked nervously around her before stumping off down the corridor.

Nurse Defalco.

Shifty. Up to something. Luchewski hung back on the stairs. She hadn't spotted him and there was no one else all along the corridor. She moved like a little bobbing apple, stopping every few steps and spinning to see if anyone else was there. Luchewski had never seen a more suspicious looking person in his entire career. If she was trying to get away with something she was doing a pretty bad job of it.

Suddenly, Defalco stopped dead beside a door and hurriedly punched a code onto a keypad next to it. She pushed the door and disappeared inside.

Luchewski came down the bottom of the steps and crept silently along, which was difficult given the way his new trainers were squeaking on the floor. As he got nearer to the door he could see the sign above it.

PHARMACEUTICAL STORES 2.
NO ENTRY EXCEPT FOR STAFF WITH LEVEL 3+
STATUS.

He continued past the door and waited.

After a minute, the door opened slowly and Defalco

stepped back into the corridor, something white clutched in her left hand. As the door pulled itself to, she looked up and saw Luchewski standing directly in front of her.

'Jesus!' She brought her left hand up to her palpitating chest and whatever she was holding rattled. 'You scared the shit out of me.' She craned her head forward. 'Oh it's you. What happened to your face?'

Luchewski instinctively touched one of the large red bulbous bruises that made his face look even more oddly shaped than usual.

'Ate a peanut. I'm allergic to them.'

Defalco seemed to squash her whole face up in disbelief. 'Really?'

'Yeah. What have you got in your hand?' Luchewski asked, pointing.

She gulped. Hal could not get over just how transparent this woman was.

'Some ... medicines. I had to come up and get 'em for a patient.'

'But this is just a pharmaceutical storeroom. Surely you would have to go through the pharmacy itself. They'd administer whatever it is you'd need, wouldn't they? And they're on a different floor, I think. Second floor, is it?'

She nodded. 'Yeah. Second floor.'

'So? What are you doing?'

'They'd run out of the right stuff ... so I had to come and collect it.'

Hal stabbed his finger towards the sign above the door. 'Do you have Level 3+ status, then? And before you answer, remember it's easy for me to check.'

She swallowed again. 'No. I don't.'

'So do you have *written permission* from someone with Level 3+ status to collect these medicines?'

'No.'

Luchewski folded his arms and felt like a headmaster ticking off a young child who'd just been caught urinating in the playground. 'What's going on then?'

Her eyes darted desperately around the corridor in the hope that they would alight on something that might just get her out of this particular sticky wicket. They found nothing.

Hal sighed. 'I think you are stealing those, aren't you? Give them here. Let me see what they are.'

She reached out and handed the pills over. Two long white tubes. On the first, Hal read 'Diamorphine'. On the second 'MXL'.

'What's MXL?' he asked, giving the bottle a shake.

'It's a type of morphine. Like a painkiller.'

'I know what morphine is. And diamorphine. I also know that they are opiates. Like heroin. You a drug addict, Defalco?'

'Me?' She looked horrified. 'No fucking way.'

'So why are you stealing them? You a pusher?'

'No way.' This time she didn't look quite so horrified. 'I give 'em to people. People who need 'em.'

'You *give* them to people, eh? You mean you sell them to people. That makes you a pusher.'

'No I don't.' She was looking nervous now. 'I give 'em to people who need 'em.'

'Yeah, smack addicts.'

'No. I give em to people with cancer and shit. Sometimes they don't get as many as they need – cuts and that. So I get some extra and give it to 'em.'

Luchewski smirked. 'Look at you. A right little Florence Nightingale and Robin Hood rolled into one. Putting your job at risk for the benefit of others. How magnanimous!'

'Eh?'

'What a lot of bullshit! Come with me.'

He'd been spotted just off Regent's Street. One of the selfies Cornish had taken had been distributed to all the cars in and around central London and one of them had phoned in a sighting of someone looking not unlike Cornish making their way down one of the side exits on the western half of Regent's Street.

As soon as he had heard that, Burlock hopped into his car and sped in towards the centre of town – although 'sped' was perhaps not the right word to use. For the second time in one day. Burlock found himself cursing the stuttering traffic of London. Too many cars, too many pedestrians. Stop. Start. Stop. Start. At one point the temperature gauge on the dashboard looked certain to nudge into the big nasty splodge of red, so he pulled over to let the engine cool – much to the annoyance of the cyclists whose lane he blocked.

Singh and Luchewski sat on one side of the table while Defalco – face red from all the sobbing she'd done – sat the other. On top of the table, exactly halfway between them, sat the two accusatory bottles of morphine that Defalco had been stealing.

'We had a similar case not that long back, didn't we, Singh? That kid doing some part-time hours in a pharmacy in Balham. Helped himself to the happy pills. How long did he get again?'

'Oh, eleven years wasn't it?'

'Eleven years. Body clock would have finished ticking in eleven years, wouldn't you think, Miss. Defalco?'

Of course, there wasn't a kid from Balham who had stolen from a pharmacy. And even if there were, he'd probably have gone down for two years at most. But that didn't matter. What mattered was that Luchewski and Singh gave Defalco a bloody good scare.

'Last I heard of him,' Singh added, 'he'd tried to cut his own wrists.'

Defalco gave a little whimper.

'Poor bastard. Only took some Diazepam. Could've just gone to his own doctor, feigned depression and got some on prescription. That would have been the sensible way around it. Unfortunately he stole it instead. Very foolish.'

'I ... I ... I was only ...' she stumbled in between the blubs. 'I was only ... trying to help others.'

Lying cow, thought Hal. *You lying bloody cow.*

'What are we going to do with you, Rebecca?' Luchewski gently shook his head. 'What on earth are we going to do with you?'

She shrugged, her eyes staring down at the floor.

'Tell you what. Let's see if we can't come to some arrangement, shall we? What do you think, sergeant?'

'I don't see why not,' Singh replied, giving Luchewski a slight wink. 'Be nice to find a comfortable way through this.'

Defalco raised her head a touch. 'What do you want? Money?'

Jesus fucking wept, thought Hal.

'No. We do not want money.'

'What do you want then? You're not a couple of perverts are you?'

Singh could not contain her shocked delight at this and spat out a short, sharp laugh.

'Does Sergeant Singh *look* like a pervert to you? Do *I* look like a pervert? On second thoughts, don't answer that.'

Defalco stared at Hal like she was debating the issue

so Luchewski pulled things quickly back on track.

'What we want is the truth.'

'The truth?'

'Yes. The last time we talked to you, you failed to tell us everything you knew about Dr Seagrove.'

'I don't unders –'

'You lied to us, Rebecca.'

She went quiet.

'You were holding something back. What was it? Tell us and we'll see what we can do for you. Otherwise …'

'Blackmail?'

'Your choice, Miss Defalco.'

She sat in her chair looking not unlike a partially deflating balloon, the corners of her mouth almost trying to pull her face downwards.

'S'nothing much. Didn't think it was important, that's all.'

'What?'

She rubbed one of her nostrils with the back of her hand, and then rubbed that on the leg of her trousers, slipping it back and forth to get all the snot off. Singh winced.

'She changed.'

'What does that mean?'

'Dr Seagrove changed. Over the last few months.'

'In what way?'

'Well … before she was all miserable. Didn't even smile. To be honest, I always assumed she was a stuck-up miserable bitch with a real attitude problem. But I think, really, she was just sad.'

'And then what happened?'

'Dunno. Fella I think. She cheered up a bit. Got a bit nicer. You could see it happening.'

'When did this change start?' Luchewski strummed his

fingers on the table top. Defalco watched them and gave another little gulp.

'Two, three months back. Summat like that. I noticed it. I don't know if anybody else did. She didn't like to have big discussions or nothing. Just kept her head down. But she definitely changed. I'm good at spotting that sort of thing.'

The room went quiet. Outside the clang and buzz of the hospital carried on.

'And that's it, is it? I'd hate to think you were still lying. Seems a tiny thing not to tell us.'

'Well, like I said, I didn't think it was that important.'

'Hmm.'

Silence again.

'What do you think, sir?' Singh asked without moving her gaze from Defalco. 'You think she deserves a chance?'

'Not sure.'

'Oh, go on,' Nurse Defalco begged. 'I told you what I know. Please.'

Luchewski gave his forehead a rub to make it clear that he was tired with it all. Then he made her wait another twenty seconds.

'OK.'

'Oh, thank you. Thank you.' The relief was as obvious as a green top hat.

Luchewski sat forward and pushed the two bottles of morphine towards her.

'What's this?' she asked a note of confusion in her voice.

'I want you to take these.'

'But –'

'Take them. Do with them what you will. It's up to you.'

'Can't you –'

'No. I want you to take them. You decide what to do with them. It's your choice.'

She stared at the bottles before slowly picking them both up in one hand.

'OK. OK then. I will.'

It had taken Nino a bit of persuading.

'Look, Gaudiano,' the voice down the phone had growled. 'When I said I'd help you, I thought it would be a one-off. Or a two-off. This is turning into a fucking nightmare. I'm accessing files all over the fucking place. If any of my superiors poke their noses into this, they're going to see my prints all over it.'

'One more thing. That's all I'm asking,' Nino said, his voice warm, calm and sympathetic even though he wanted to shout at the man and tell him to get the fucking info he required and not be such a cowardly twat. 'I think I'm really close. I've got a good tip-off.'

'Yeah, well, don't do anything fucking stupid, OK. It's not just you that would end up in the shit.'

'I promise. No one is ever going to know about your involvement.'

'Good.' The man relaxed a little. 'What is it you're after?'

Nino told him and just under two hours later, his phone rang.

'Write this down,' he said, so Nino wrote it down. 'Now leave me alone. Don't call again.' The phone went dead.

Two hours after that, Nino was ringing the doorbell at the address he'd just been given.

He rang it three times and after the third ring the door creaked open and a rotund middle-aged woman in glasses

314

poked her head around the door.

'Mr Gaudiano?'

'Yes.'

She looked momentarily baffled. 'What are you doing here?'

'Can I come in? We need to speak.'

A flicker of a thought and then she opened the door wide and beckoned him in. 'Yes. Come in.'

They went into the sitting room where a large leather sofa sat facing a very large TV set. The semi-finals of the snooker were on and every time a ball hit another ball the soundbar on the floor under the TV made it sound like someone outside was kicking a bin.

'I'll go get some tea. You sit here and watch the snooker – I'll turn the sound down – and I'll go get us some tea.' She seemed nervous.

Nino sat down on the nasty leather sofa and waited. Was this it? Was he right? Had the far reaches of Jean Smith's subconscious stumbled upon the truth? If so, he should be calling the police right now, not sitting here. He ought to be getting Luchewski to mobilise his forces, ripping the place apart with their bare hands. Not sitting here watching the snooker and waiting for some tea.

He found that his heart was racing under his shirt and he absentmindedly patted his chest to calm it down. The problem was that he couldn't completely believe it himself. All the years he'd spent in prison for murdering Kurtz – who he now admitted to himself was innocent – had pulled him away from the reality of the situation to the extent that he wasn't sure what to believe and what not to believe. Time had created a gap, and it was difficult to fill with the truth.

The minutes dragged by and on the television Shaun Murphy was leading Barry Hawkins by six frames to two.

Nino gave it another minute before standing up and walking through the door that led to the kitchen.

'Hello?' he called as he stepped into the brightly tiled kitchen with the sun streaming through the window. He squished his eyes together to adjust to the brightness and found himself looking down on the floor.

A hole.

A large square hole.

Suddenly he felt somebody hit him solidly in the back with something hard and all the wind shot out of his lungs and his legs buckled forward. He tried to straighten, but a second blow sent him tumbling towards the floor. Towards the hole.

Not a hole, he realised as his head slapped the edge of it and his whole body fell into the cold air, smashing into the hard concrete beyond. Not a hole.

A cellar.

He twisted himself around, his back screeching out in pain, and tried to look back up.

'WHAT ARE YOU DOING?' he shouted, his chest hurting. 'WHAT HAVE YOU DONE WITH HER?'

The woman peered down at him, her eyes cold and stupid-looking behind her thick-framed glasses, before pushing the heavy trapdoor back into position and shutting out all the light.

Seventeen years ago

There weren't as many people from school as Alice had thought there were going to be. Josh Woodington, Conrad Phillips and Darren Westlake were messing about on the dance floor. There were some others sitting in groups or huddled in corners or handing over twenty pence pieces at the refreshment stall. Otherwise it was mostly kids from other schools that she didn't recognise.

Mr Zippy, the DJ, was a fat middle-aged man with a T-shirt that hardly managed to cover his belly button. He was purple in the face and seemed to be struggling to get the unimpressive light display to work properly.

The local vicar seemed to be wandering around the hall, dog collar and woollen jacket in place, embarrassingly tapping his thigh along to the beat. He was acting like a sort of nonchalant policeman, keeping an eye on everything.

Alice and Katie gravitated towards a couple of chairs blocking the emergency exit.

'Not *that* loud, thank God,' Alice shouted.

'What?' Katie replied.

'I said, it's not *that* loud.'

'Yes it's a good crowd.'

Katie's gaze kept skipping towards where Josh Woodington and his friends were having a jumping-up-as-high-as-you-possibly-can competition, nearly knocking a couple of younger kids over. The vicar went over to them and said something. The three boys looked sorry, nodded their heads and reined in their overly exuberant dancing.

Suddenly, a loud female voice contended with the blare of Eiffel 65.

'I said I didn't need your help. I could have just gone back home.'

Everyone turned to see Laurie Frasier marching into the hall. Some distance behind her, Louisa Gaudiano was fiddling with the strap on a small handbag.

'What's up?' Alice asked.

'Oh. Nothing. I'm just being treated like rubbish again, that's all.'

Louisa caught up with them all. 'No you're not. Don't be stupid.'

'What's going on?' Katie momentarily diverted her attention from Josh.

'Forgot my money, didn't I? Left it in the house.'

'It doesn't matter,' Louisa found another chair and pulled it nearer to her.

'Of course it matters. I said I'd go back and get it. It's only a ten-minute walk. But Little Miss ... Little Miss ...' she hissed, 'Little Miss Helpful here thought she'd sort me out.'

'I was only trying to help, honestly.' She rolled her eyes at the other two. 'You'd think I was trying to steal her shoes. All I did was pay for her to get in.'

'Like I said, I don't need your help.'

'But Laurie, she –'

'I don't mind walking back home. It's not that far.'

They all went quiet for a few minutes and watched

the boys on the dance floor start their idiotic pogoing once again. The song changed to ... *Baby One More Time* by Britney Spears and Katie had a go at singing along – trying to look impressive and sultry.

Laurie spotted her. 'Fucking hell, Katie. What are you doing?'

'Hmm?'

'All that ...' She mimicked the pouting and the soft shaking of the head. 'You look retarded.'

'That's not very –'

'It's very hot in here,' Alice chipped in before they all pissed each other off even more. 'Why don't we get something to drink.'

'Yes. It is a bit –'

'Not me. No money.' Laurie was in a foul mood. 'Too fucking poor.'

'I wish you'd stop swearing,' Katie admonished.

'And I wish you'd stop grinning like a prozzie on her night off.'

'Well, I –'

'Whoa!' Alice held the palms of her hands out. 'Let's calm down. I'll go buy us all some drinks.'

'Don't buy me one.'

Louisa shook her head. 'Please, Laurie. Don't be stupid.'

Laurie seemed to rise up like a dragon about to attack. 'Don't be ...? Fucking hell, that's rich coming from you. Doing the detention for us. How stupid is that? But then, you love it, don't you? You love being the centre of attention.'

'What?'

'Nothing better than to make everyone think what a marvellous person you must be, is there? Making everyone else feels like a load of shit so that you can act all angelic and pretend to be some sort of fucking wonder. When you're dead they'll probably turn you into some sort of fucking saint. Saint Louisa the Fucking Twat. That's what they'll call you when you're dead.'

'No. Stop it.' Louisa's face fell.

'Anyway, what did you do that detention for? We should all have done it. Do you fancy Mr Lawson or what? Shag him every lunch hour, did you?'

'No. No, I didn't. Why are you being so mean?'

'Touch you up, did he? I've seen him looking at you. He's a perv and you fucking love it.'

'He's not!' A tear ran down her face. 'He never did anything. He's just nice. I don't understand why you're being so mean.'

'Because I'm sick to death of you and the way you think you're better than everyone else.'

More tears now, and Alice could do nothing but watch this terrible spectacle being played out in the corner of the room. 'I don't.'

'You do. You think you're better than everyone else.'

'No I don't! We haven't ...' she cried hard and struggled to catch her breath. 'We ... haven't got ... much ... money. My dad hasn't ... even got ... a job.'

'Well, boo hoo. Pardon me for not fucking crying.'

'Laurie!' Alice reached out to touch Louisa on the arm, but she stood up before Alice could get there and walked steadily out of the hall, her head in her hands.

Katie slammed her handbag down on the nearby table. 'Now look what you've done!'

'Oh shut up!'

The music carried on playing and everybody else seemed oblivious to the incident. The three of them sat in silence for a couple of songs, each of them weighing up what had just happened.

Eventually Katie gently took her handbag and placed it back on her lap. 'What was all that about?'

Laurie flared up again. 'Oh, don't you start going on. Sitting there trying to get him to ask you to dance. In fact ...' She stood up and walked across to the dance floor, pushing aggressively past some Year Eights, and grabbed Josh Woodington by the arm. She pulled him towards the chairs where Alice and Katie sat and stabbed a finger at Katie.

'She likes you. She wants you to kiss her.'

Josh looked nervous and confused and Katie blushed.

'Ask her to dance, will you? She's driving me fucking nuts.'

Josh looked embarrassed, and managed to pull his arm out of Laurie's grip. He smiled politely at Katie before turning back and heading to his mates who were once again being told off by the religious policeman.

'See,' Laurie sat down. 'He's not interested. Get over it.'

Alice suddenly found her legs straightening.

'What you up to?' Laurie's voice was cold and uncompromising. Like her eyes.

'Just need some fresh air. Just going to get some fresh air.' To the sound of *Boom Boom Boom Boom* by the Vengaboys, she walked slowly out of the village hall and into the warm air of a June evening.

Chapter Twenty-eight

'What's this?' Luchewski took the large, thick envelope from Singh.

'Dr Seagrove's social media. Everything she ever posted or tweeted. I got the techies to print it off and bring it straight here. Thought it might be best if we were going to be here for any amount of time.'

'Good thinking.'

'Thanks.'

'You looked at it yet?'

'No. Only arrived just before our meeting with the nurse from hell.' She poked the side of the envelope. 'Doesn't actually look all that much to me. She was on Facebook for ten years, Twitter for seven. Not much for that time. Not exactly prolific.'

Luchewski had a Facebook account and would, every so often, have a bit of a look at what other people were saying. He very rarely posted anything, so anything more than an entry once every four weeks was prolific to him.

He handed the envelope back to Singh.

'Hold onto it a minute. I just want to chase up John Good.' He pulled out his phone and called up the correct number. After a few seconds, Good answered.

'Inspector L. How are you?'

'The boots? Any joy?'

'Most certainly. New company in Auckland. Only been going five or six months. Walking boots for the serious amateur.'

'Any international orders?'

'My boy's on the phone to them right this minute. Give us a couple and I'll get straight back to you.'

'OK.'

He cut the call and took the envelope back from Singh.

'Come on. Let's have a look at this stuff.'

It was pitch-black. Nino couldn't see a thing. The trapdoor that had been dropped back into position up above him had blocked out all the light. And it was cold. Very cold.

Nino twisted himself onto his side. His back was badly bruised, he knew, but nothing else seemed damaged. He wriggled his fingers and toes, bent his legs and arms and concluded that he'd managed to fall into the cellar without breaking anything.

He sat up, his back against the wall, and caught his breath.

He'd really done it now. He should have just called the police and shown them the note from Jean Smith. He should have left it to them. The problem was that he'd always been an interfering bastard. He wanted to be the one to find the person who'd taken his daughter. And now, here he was, sitting in that person's basement. Probably to be left to starve to death. Or worse.

His phone!

He dug into his pocket and took out his phone. He brushed his finger across its screen and it lit up. It still worked.

Unfortunately the little bars in the top left-hand corner showed no reception. He scrolled through his contacts list regardless and tried to make a phone call to the one person who he thought could help him most right now.

He pressed the 'Call' button and waited.

No signal.

He tried a second time.

No signal.

It was useless. He could probably have got a signal in the room above him, but down here, tucked away in this hidden room, it was impossible.

He composed a text to Luchewski and tried to send that, but after a few moments the phone gave up and merely gave him the option of 'Resend? Y/N?'

The glow from the phone lit up the room. It was about twelve feet by seven and the ceiling above his head would be more than a foot away from his outstretched arm if he stood up. The walls were bare concrete and the floor was slightly uneven, like somebody had tried to put down some screed and done a really bad job of it.

There was nothing else in the room.

Back when these houses were built, Nino thought to himself, this was probably used as a storeroom and a cold room. Somewhere to keep the weekly meat fresh. God knows what it's been used for since.

Footsteps above him. Voices too. A man and a woman. Arguing.

He was in a hole. *Literally* in a hole. Trapped like a rat with no means of escape. All they needed to do was open up the hatch, poke a shotgun down here and he'd be dead within seconds. It wouldn't be difficult for them. They'd probably enjoy it.

Nino stood up and tapped the walls with his knuckles, hoping to find something hollow. Something that he might be able to use. A gap. An old air duct. Anything. Instead the walls just responded with a constant dull thud each time.

He scoured the floor looking for some discarded little

thing that might possibly be adapted as a weapon. But he found nothing.

It was no good. This was how it was going to end. With him knowing who took his Louisa, and nobody else having a clue. He punched the wall in frustration and two of his knuckles started to bleed.

Seventeen years ago

Alice looked up and down the road. There was no sign of Louisa anywhere. Alice thought she might just have been sitting outside on the wall, straightening herself out before coming back in. But, no. It looked as if she had headed home.

Alice set off, thinking she might just catch up with her before she got too far. As she walked she thought how vicious Laurie could be sometimes. Heartless and cruel. Not caring who she upsets. Sometimes she would just trample all over anyone who annoyed her. Alice imagined her growing up to be a politician or on the telly – like Jerry Springer. Something tough and cold like that.

She turned the corner and passed an old woman carrying two Tesco carrier bags.

The evening was still warm, and Alice could feel the heat that had built up in the old stones during the day. It seemed to throb out of the walls.

Another corner and then ...

A car. Blue. A blue Vauxhall. She knew it was a Vauxhall because her Uncle Simon had a Vauxhall, and she recognised the shape. Astra, she thought. It had stopped in the middle of the road. There was no other traffic around. Just this one car sitting with its engine running and the driver's door wide open.

The driver was opening the passenger door for

somebody. Somebody small. Alice stared hard and saw that it was Louisa. She looked like she'd been crying. And now she looked scared.

Alice opened her mouth to call out to her, but just before she did, the passenger door slammed shut and the man who had shut it walked around to the driver's door. He looked over at Alice and scowled.

She knew his face. She saw his face every morning. It was a face she never liked. A face she never trusted. It was a face that knew exactly where she lived. A face that knew her parents. A face that knew exactly who she was.

He smiled an awful smile at Alice, and a shiver ran along her back.

Then the man squatted and climbed into the car, pulling the door closed behind him. The engine revved and the car moved away slowly – a bit like a hearse, thought Alice. Just like a hearse.

She stood rooted to the spot. She was scared, just like Louisa looked. Something was wrong. Something wasn't right. But she was scared. More scared than ever.

As the car turned the corner in the distance, Alice noticed something else.

There was somebody else in the car. Sitting on the rear seats. Another small person.

Another child.

Chapter Twenty-nine

Luchewski and Singh were back in the room where they had recently had their little 'discussion' with Nurse Defalco. Singh had pulled all the printouts of Alice Seagrove's social media out onto the table and they sat alongside one another, Luchewski leaning his elbow on the table and resting his cheek against his fist.

'If Defalco can be trusted – which, let's face it, is dubious – then perhaps we'd better just rule it down to the last few months. Concentrate on those for now.'

'OK.' Singh rifled through the paper and skimmed a hefty pile off the top. Then she took the Twitter feeds and did exactly the same thing. There wasn't a great deal left.

'Facebook or Twitter, sir?' She held both reams of paper up.

'You choose, Singh.'

'OK then. I'll take Twitter. There's less of it.'

The room went quiet as they both read through the posts, turning the occasional sheet over.

'Nice shot of her dinner here,' Singh pointed. '"Faggots and peas. Mmm. Haven't had that in years."'

'Haven't you?'

'No, that's what she says.'

'Oh.   Did   she   have   many friends … followers … whatevers, on these things?'

'No. A handful. Most of them abroad. Nobody of any interest to us. She seemed like quite a lonely person,

329

didn't she?'

'Mmm.'

They waded through the innocuous and inane posts. Moans about television programmes. Moans about senior managers at the hospital. Shared videos of puppies and pandas. Shared images of inspirational poetry. All dull, uneventful, impersonal milestones in a far too brief life.

'Hold on …' Luchewski sat up. 'What's this?'

'What?' Singh looked over.

'It's a deleted post. From July 30th. Why would she delete this?'

'What's it say?'

'"Met an old friend from school today." Then she's put one of those emoji things. A big smiley face.'

'And she deleted it?'

'Yes.'

'Perhaps he told her to. Saw it and told her to take it down.'

'Hmm.' Luchewski sat back in his chair and thought. 'July 30th. Thursday. I wonder if she was working that day?'

Suddenly Luchewski shot out of his chair and marched out of the door.

'Wait for me, sir!'

He strode along the corridor and down a flight of steps towards the office of the Human Resource manager. Singh ran to catch up.

Luchewski gave a polite tap on the glass of the door before opening it anyway. The middle-aged woman who was sat behind her desk almost jumped to see them both, and the glasses that were perched on the top of her forehead slipped quickly back down onto her nose.

'Yes. Can I help?'

Luchewski introduced himself and Singh and

explained what they needed.

'I'm afraid you need a warrant to access our information. Everything's confidential.'

'No, I don't,' Hal grimaced. 'I need a warrant if you refuse to let me see. As this is a murder investigation and the information I request is on a person believed to have been murdered, then any warrant I apply for will be pretty much automatically granted. So, please … let's not waste any time here. All I want to know is if Dr Seagrove was working on June 30th and, if so, in what department.'

The woman gave a little huff as if to have the last word on the matter, but then swivelled back to her computer and called up the hospital work records. Luchewski and Singh came up slowly behind her and peeped over each of her shoulders.

'There. Yes, she was. A twelve-hour shift. Nine a.m. to nine p.m.'

'Where?'

'Accident and Emergency.'

'Thank you. I now need access to the names of everyone admitted to A&E on that day. Can you give me those?'

The woman tutted. 'You'll need to speak to the Chief Registrar. And you'll *definitely* need a warrant for those records.'

They left the office and walked what felt like a quarter of a mile to the Chief Registrar's office at the far end of the hospital.

Before they got there, Luchewski's phone rang, and a passing nurse gave him a filthy look and tapped an 'ALL PHONES TO BE TURNED OFF' sign. Hal gave a soporific nod and answered it anyway.

'Harry, it's John.'

'Anything? UK orders?'

'Yes. Couple of individuals – one in the Outer Hebrides, another in West Yorkshire. But more substantial is the order by B.Y.H. Workwear.'

'B.Y.H. Workwear?'

'Yes. Based in Southampton. Ordered two hundred and fifty pairs of this particular boot in a variety of sizes. Delivery was about three months ago. B.Y.H. supply specialist clothing to a number of organisations. Mountain rescue. The Coastguard. Royal Mail. A couple of police forces. That kind of thing.'

'OK. Send us what you've got and we'll get to checking it.'

'Roger that. Over and out.'

In Luchewski's opinion, the Chief Registrar didn't look well. A man in his late fifties with a face that was craggy and grey, he moved like somebody twenty years older than himself and gave little oohs and ahhs every time he shifted more than half an inch in any direction. Bizarre, thought Luchewski, to think that the man was a doctor.

'Must I?' the registrar asked. 'Only, patient admittance data is highly classified. We can't just let anyone go and have a butcher's at it, you know? If we did we'd be sued left, right and centre.'

'But we're the police,' Singh said.

'Yes, I realise that,' the man replied with an extra 'ooh'. 'But supposing I let you look at it, and then you went after a particular person and then that particular person turns out to be innocent. If it comes out that we've just thrown his medical records at you, then we'll be up the creek. As will you, Inspector.'

'Nothing's going to happen, Mr …?'

'Turner. *Doctor* Paul Turner.'

'Dr Turner. I promise you. If casting my eye over a list

of patients results in something, I'll get a warrant issued as soon as possible and nobody will suspect a thing.'

Dr Turner was on his own in his office. He picked up a pencil and started tapping his front teeth with the end of it, his mind ticking away, trying to put things together.

Turning to his PC, he wiggled the mouse and the screen came to life. He punched in his password and accessed a long Excel page full of names and dates. Singh could see him applying some sort of filter to the data.

'Now, if you'll excuse me,' he stood up from his desk, yawned and stretched, 'I need to pop to the loo. If at least one of you could keep an eye on my computer here – make sure nobody accesses anything they shouldn't while I'm away, that would be very kind.' He gave a wink before walking past them and opening the door. 'I'll be about two minutes.' He went out into the corridor and closed the door behind him.

'Come on.' Luchewski grabbed the man's chair and sat down in front of the PC. Singh squatted alongside him.

'Lot of people for a Thursday,' Luchewski said. 'Jesus. These A&E departments really are overworked. The next time a bunch of junior doctors decide to go on strike, remind me not to moan on about it too much.'

He scrolled down the list of names. It was all in alphabetical order with the reason for admittance in the column next to the surname.

'Ha!' Luchewski laughed when his eye caught an entry which told the reader that Chris Eagleton had to pay a visit to the emergency department as he had somehow managed to get one of his testicles stuck in his Dyson. 'Painful.'

He kept on scrolling. Past the 'F's, 'G's, 'H's … past the 'L's, 'M's, 'N's'…

Then he got to 'P'.

Both he and Singh saw the name at exactly the same time. Singh pointed and Luchewski just mumbled, 'Yeah. I know.'

He read the reason for admittance next to the name and the treatment provided and Hal found himself rubbing his own damaged leg in response.

Six stitches required to back of right hand. Dog attack.

What was it Good had said just a few minutes ago?

'*B.Y.H. supply specialist clothing to a number of organisations. Mountain rescue. The Coastguard. Royal Mail ...*'

Royal Mail.

Luchewski stood up and nearly toppled the chair over.

'You think it's him, sir?'

Luchewski didn't answer. His mind was at least a thousand miles away, tying things together and seeing if they worked.

'Sir?'

He snapped out of it. 'Sorry, Singh? What? Oh, yes. Yes, it's him. I'm sure.'

'Do you want me to get a team out to the house?'

'Yes. Call them. Tell them to meet us there. It's only around the corner from here. We can be on the scene in about four minutes. Three even. Say we'll meet them there.'

The Chief Registrar poked his head around the door.

'Anything?'

'Oh, yes,' Luchewski said pulling the door wider. 'Lots.'

'Oh,' replied the registrar. 'I was worried there might be.'

PART FOUR

Bye Bye Badman

Chapter Thirty

Nino had an idea. It was desperate and needed a moment of extraordinary good fortune to work, but at least it was something. If it didn't work – which it was likely not to – then he really would be dead. Strange, he thought, how everything comes down to this eye of a needle. This tiny gap of luck through which he now had to pass to live out the rest of his life. An almost insignificant chance. But he had to take it. There was absolutely nothing else to do.

He stroked his finger across his phone and it lit up the cellar again. The voices above had stopped. They clearly calmed down and were discussing the best way to dispose of him. The phone only had eight percent charge left, and he kicked the wall in anger at his own stupidity for not charging it more. Still, eight percent was enough.

Nino went back to his messages and opened up the one that he'd recently written to Luchewski.

'Resend? Y/N?'

He clicked it one more time, then a couple of seconds later the phone buzzed.

'Message not sent. Resend? Y/N?'

The battery bar in the corner dropped to seven percent.

He stood up and got himself ready. Positioning his thumb over the 'Yes' button on his phone he started shouting.

'HEY, YOU FUCKS! YOU BUNCH OF STUPID FUCKING CUNTS! YOU EVIL BASTARDS! HERE I

AM, DOWN HERE! YOU'VE FORGOTTEN ALL ABOUT ME, AIN'T YER! WELL I'M GOING NOWHERE! ABSOLUTELY NO-FUCKING-WHERE!'

It didn't matter what he shouted. All he wanted to do was get their attention. Get them back to the trapdoor.

Get them to open it.

'HERE I AM, YOU STUPID UGLY PAIR OF TWATS! WHY DON'T YOU COME OVER AND LOOK DOWN HERE AND SEE THE REDS OF MY FUCKING EYES, YOU FUCKING BASTARDS! GIVE ME A LADDER AND –'

Footsteps above. And voices. He refreshed his phone again and got himself ready, standing directly below where the middle of the trapdoor was.

'THAT'S IT, YOU THICK AS SHIT PAIR OF –'

The trapdoor pulled up and a man's face filled the gap. It took a couple of seconds for Nino's eyes to adapt to the light but it was a face he recognised. A face that he hadn't seen in years. It was older – much older – cracked and leathery, and the hair was thinner and wispier than it used to be. But he would recognise him anywhere.

The man obviously recognised Nino too.

'Hello, Nino,' he said, an oddly appreciative smile playing across his lips. 'It's been a long time.' The man threw the trapdoor all the way open and Nino seized his chance. He lifted his arm as close to the opening and pressed the 'Yes' button on his phone.

'What are you doing?' The man looked puzzled.

A second or so and the phone buzzed. Fuck! It still hadn't sent it. He clicked it again.

'What is it? What are you doing?' Slightly more nervous this time.

Buzz.

Fuck!

338

He tried one more time.

'You forgot to take this off me, you fucking idiot! When your wife pushed me down here she forgot to take my phone! I've been phoning loads of fucking people!' He stood on tiptoe, stretching – painfully stretching – up, desperately trying to catch a signal. 'Loads of fucking people!'

The man reached forward and snatched the phone out of Nino's hand before throwing it hard somewhere in the kitchen behind him. There was a loud crash and the man turned angrily back to Nino.

'You liar! You can't get a signal down there! I've lined it so nobody can!' He was red in the face and bared his teeth as he talked. He steadied himself on the floor of the kitchen, taking a deep breath, trying to calm himself down after his violent action. Nino thought once again how old the man looked. Tired.

The man grinned. 'Still looking for Louisa, eh? Still trying to be the big hero dad and save your little girl?' There was poison in his voice. 'Well ...' he raised his eyebrows, 'now you've found her.'

'What?'

'You found your little Louisa.' The man pointed to the ground at the back of the cellar, where the screed looked especially uneven. 'After I was finished with her, I buried her in the corner. Just there.'

'No ...'

'Nice to think of you both being reunited. In death.' The man smirked. 'Die well, Nino. Die quick.'

He stood up and flung the trapdoor back into position. It banged hard and heavy into place and Nino was plunged into a blackness darker and more unyielding than any he had ever experienced before.

As Luchewski and Singh walked up the path to the front door, two things happened. Firstly a couple of police cars seemed to screech into the remaining parking spaces on the street. Secondly, the phone in Luchewski's jacket pocket beeped.

Not now, thought Hal. *Not right now*.

Singh rang the doorbell. Luchewski turned to the officers in the cars behind and gave them the signal to wait.

Singh rang it again and soon after an oldish man with thinning hair opened the door and looked around at them.

'Yes?'

'Mr Perry? I'm Detective Inspector Luchewski from the Metropolitan Police Force. I spoke to your wife the other day. Is Baxter in?'

The man shook his head. Rather too nervously, thought Hal. 'No. No, he's not. Gone out.'

'Can we come in, please?'

'What for?'

'It's best if we talk inside. Can we come in, please?'

'Er …' The man was scanning the floor, trying to find a reason not to let them in. 'Er … yes. OK.'

They walked through the hallway and into the sitting room with the massive television. On the screen, the snooker was playing. The sound seemed especially loud, to Hal, and he suddenly found himself thinking back to earlier in the week when he'd argued with Stevie about the fucking snooker. Snooker! Of all things. It wasn't even about what to have for supper or where to go on holiday or some other pathetic thing. It had been about the fucking snooker. Jesus!

Hal remembered he had a lot of making up to do.

'My … er … wife is in the kitchen. Tidying up. She … er … just knocked something over. You wait here and I'll ... get her to get you some tea.' He walked through the other door and into the kitchen.

Luchewski frowned. Something didn't feel right.

He reached into his pocket and pulled out his phone.

'One new message.'

He opened it up. It was from a number he didn't recognise.

Trapped in John Perry's kitchen cellar. He took L. Need help. NG.

Luchewski froze.

NG.

Nino Gaudiano.

John Perry ... he took L.

'What is it?' Singh asked.

Luchewski's mind skittered across the facts. John Perry takes Louisa Gaudiano. Years later his son Baxter kills Louisa's friends. *What did Alice Seagrove tell you about the night Louisa died?* Baxter had asked Katie Woodington. Was he protecting his father?

Yes. That was it. Baxter Perry was protecting his father.

Luchewski pointed towards the front door. 'Tell them to get in here, right away.'

'Right.' Singh almost sprinted out of the room.

Hal took three long strides to the kitchen door and threw it open. John Perry was filling the kettle and his wife was on her hands and knees with a dustpan and brush, scooping up the odds and ends of something smashed.

They both turned as he walked into the room.

'NINO!' Luchewski shouted, and as he shouted Mrs Perry dropped the dustpan and brush and started crying. John Perry stood perfectly still, the tap still running. 'NINO! WHERE ARE YOU?' He looked at Mrs Perry.

'Where is he?' Behind him in the sitting room, Luchewski could hear the scuffle of the police officers as they entered the house, and through the window he spotted a couple of them coming in through the garden gate.

Mrs Perry glanced downwards, and Luchewski looked at roughly where her gaze fell. It was well disguised. In the linoleum flooring – a busy intermingling pattern of flowers and vines and grapes – he could just about make out a large square outline, and on one side of the square, a small dip. The dip was a handle. The outline was a hatch.

'I ... can explain,' John Perry whined, seemingly unaware that the kettle was now overfilling in his hands. 'I can explain.'

'Don't you move, either of you. You're both under arrest.'

Luchewski dropped to his knees and slid his hand into the dip. He pulled upwards and found himself struggling – the hatch was heavier than he imagined. He gave it an extra yank and then pushed it until its momentum tipped it over and slammed onto the floor the other side. Cold air seemed to hit him and there was no light in the room beneath.

'I can explain ...' the man repeated.

'Be quiet. You'll explain all right.'

The officers spilled into the kitchen, Singh somewhere amongst them.

'Nino?' Luchewski called into the dark, but all he could hear was a quiet sobbing from somewhere below.

Brian Lawson was feeling hornier than he had done in days. It was something that seemed to come in waves. For weeks sometimes he could go without a solitary carnal thought – as if his body wasn't that bothered or even up to it. Nowadays, though, he was permanently horny. He sometimes wondered if it was somehow connected to the phases of the moon. Perhaps he was just some sort of libidinous werewolf. Yes. He rather liked that idea.

He'd tried to relieve the stress in lots of different ways, but the more he tried, the hornier he seemed to become. It was a strange spiral that he couldn't shake himself out of. And as he got older, the more perverted he became.

The one thing that gave him any degree of satisfaction or relief these days was the jogging. He wasn't a great runner by any means, but the only running he really needed to do was running away. As long as he was fast and nimble enough to get away afterwards, that was all that mattered. He didn't care about keeping fit. That wasn't the point. The point was merely relief.

As soon as he got back from the school, he changed into his running gear – no underwear, of course – and dug one of the masks out from the bottom drawer.

'So, where is he?'

The Perrys had both been taken away – separately – to different police stations in South London, and now the officers were stripping the house apart like locusts.

An ambulance had come for Nino and whisked him off to be checked out. He looked physically OK to Luchewski. But he couldn't bring himself to stop crying. As he passed Hal in the sitting room, he had indicated the kitchen.

'She's down there. He told me he buried her down there.'

Luchewski had nodded and reached out, squeezing the poor man's shoulder.

'OK, Nino. Thank you, Nino.'

Over an hour had passed since Nino's discovery and

there was still no sign of Baxter Perry.

Luchewski was strolling up and down the pavement outside the Perry's house. Singh flicked through pages of her notebook and approached him.

'So?'

'Not at work. Called in sick today.'

'Sick? Ha! I should fucking coco.'

'He's got a Royal Mail van out – sometimes staff take them home overnight if they're using them the following morning. They've given us the registration and we've put a call out on ANPR. If he's using it, we'll get him pretty quickly. Oh and there's another thing we've discovered.'

'What's that?'

'He's in trouble at work. It's all yet to be confirmed but it's thought that he's been accessing the resident databases unofficially.'

'Resident databases?'

'Tells you where people live. They're only available to certain postal staff. He's not one.'

So that was how he got people's addresses. That's how he knew where they all lived.

Luchewski suddenly found himself starting to feel worried again. 'He's not been to work. Security at the hospital is extra-tight. And we don't know where he is.' He folded his arms and sighed. 'He's got a list of addresses of people he believes need to be killed. So what's he up to now … who's he after now?'

Big Issue didn't know what the fuck the kid thought he was doing. He weaved in and out of the crowds like he didn't even notice they were there. He crossed roads, ignoring any traffic and got fingers and shouts of abuse for doing so.

He must have been so off his fucking face on

something that he didn't know what was going on.

Big Issue had been like that at times. During his smack years, he'd lose weeks or months at a time. He would start off in one place at one time and then end up in a completely different place on the other side of the city days later. Now he'd shaken that shit off he could view it from a distance. It had controlled him. Led him astray. It wasn't good.

Now he was in a better place.

It was his decision to live on the streets. It was his decision to stay on the booze. It was also his decision not to take anything stronger. He was in charge of his own life – it might not look like it to outsiders, but he was. No one told him what to do or where to go. No one ruled his day or forced him to do this, that or the other. It was all his own choice.

Much like following the kid had been his own choice. He didn't have to do it, but he chose to do it. And it made him feel strong.

A part of him wanted to run up to the kid, grab him and give him a good shake. Ask him what the fuck he thought he was playing at. Splash a load of water over his face and get him to wake up. It was tempting. The sooner he sorted him out, the sooner he could chill. Living on the streets was a selfish business. You didn't really have time for others. You had to put yourself first.

But for some reason, Big Issue just kept following. Following and waiting. Watching from a distance.

'They found it.' Singh dropped her phone away from her ear.

'Where?'

'Streatham Park area.'

They both climbed into Singh's Peugeot and before

Luchewski had time to strap his belt on, Singh had revved off. Behind them John Good climbed out of his white van and gave them a slightly bemused wave.

'Any sign of him?'

'Perry? No. But he can't be far away.'

It took them fifteen minutes to get to Hillbury Road. As they turned onto the expensive-looking red-bricked Victorian terrace, they could see the police officers that had found the Royal Mail van waving passers-by away from it.

'Anyone we know live around here?' Luchewski asked.

'I don't believe so,' Singh replied as they both got out and walked towards the van.

'Well spotted,' Luchewski acknowledged the two officers that were swanning around like a couple of recently promoted puffer fish. 'Any idea how long it's been here?'

'Old woman in the house behind thinks it's been here about half an hour now,' said the one with eyes that looked like dots in the middle of his face and lips that had no curve to them whatsoever. 'Half an hour to forty minutes. Mind you, I think she's got a wig on so I'm not sure how trustworthy her judgement is.'

Luchewski stood in the middle of the road and spun around slowly. 'What's he doing here, Singh? Why's he come here?'

Singh shrugged.

The officer with the raisin eyes spoke up once again, just as another police car pulled into view. 'P'raps he's gone for a run.'

'Eh?'

'On the common. Sometimes people park here instead of the using the proper car park. I've seen it before. Just depends what route they wanna take.'

Luchewski frowned. 'What do you mean?'

'On the common. It's only the other side of these houses.'

Tooting Bec Common. Luchewski ran up to the end of the street and stared out over a long, flat grassland with numerous clumps of trees and paths cutting over and criss-crossing the land.

Tooting Bec fucking Common.

He raced back to the van. 'He's on the common. I don't know why, but I swear to God he's on the common.' He took Singh aside. 'Get this place surrounded. I want every officer we can spare somewhere on the periphery of this green in the next ten minutes. If he's in there, I don't want him getting out. And get someone round to the proper car park and run a check on all the plates there.'

'OK, sir.' Singh was dialling already. 'What about you, sir? What are you going to do?'

'I'm going for a leisurely stroll in the park, Singh.'

He didn't know anything about trees, but this one was perfect – whatever it was. The branches were long and spindly and, even though it was nudging into autumn, the leaves were thick and heavy, dragging the branches down until they nearly brushed against the ground. Of course, he'd scouted it out before. As soon as he'd started following him and understood precisely what it was he did for fun – the dirty bastard – Baxter Perry had found this place.

The tree was also quite near to the path – he'd seen him running along this way a couple of times as it was clearly halfway between two of the dirty bastard's regular hunting grounds. The playground and the outdoor swimming pool.

It was like a cave under the branches. The earth was knotty with roots and a couple of discarded Coke cans and crisp packets proved that it wasn't a completely unknown place to hide, but he hoped that today it would be sufficient for the job in hand. It wasn't like he needed that much time.

He wasn't going to be able to pull off any of the fancy Bartholomew Kurtz stuff he'd done on Seagrove and Frasier. No ankle-breaking. No carving into the back. No. He'd had to become much more practical and resourceful as he'd progressed. He'd had to kill Josh Woodington in a practical manner, so now he was going to do them all in a practical manner. No pissing about. Just crack on and get it done.

He pulled the long knife out of its sheath and wiped Woodington's blood from its length while he waited.

Brian Lawson loved the sensation of the jogging bottoms against his penis. With no underwear, he could make himself hard in no time just by running a little bit faster than he walked. And nobody suspected a thing. There he was bounding past them with a semi and everyone ignored him. He'd tried jogging with one of those buzzing cock rings on once, but the sensation was too delicate to feel. So he tended to just go commando underneath.

He'd driven across to Tooting Bec Common. He hadn't had a great deal of success there recently, but that was a good thing. No one would suspect him and there wouldn't be dodgy photofit posters up on the railings warning about the local flasher. He held the mask squashed up in his hand and started to jog. Slowly. Letting the friction start to get to work on his penis.

There were some afternoon dog walkers around. Some

blokes, one or two women. No hotties though. Not that he would get off by revealing himself to just any woman. They had to be young. The younger the better. And if they were in uniform …

The paths were long and straight and he took the route towards the playground. School was well finished by now and he hoped that some teenagers would be loitering about near the swings. Swigging Red Bull and downing entire packets of Haribo.

Lawson suddenly felt himself stiffening even more, so he sped up to maximise the sensation.

The common was a vast, empty looking place with paths that crossed this way and that way over the green. Trees lined the paths and the occasional cyclist or jogger rushed past the occasional dog walker. Luchewski pulled his jacket closer to him and marched on. He'd not seen him yet, and he began to worry that he'd got the wrong end of the stick. That somewhere in the houses behind him, Baxter Perry was busy carving BARTHOLOMEW KURTZ into some poor fucker's torso.

'Come on, you bastard. Where are you?'

His phone rang and he answered it.

'What?'

'Checked out the cars in the car park, sir.'

'And?'

'One of them belongs to Brian Lawson. The Deputy Head at Longley Road.'

'Lawson? Oh, Jesus.' Luchewski stopped and looked all around him. 'What's Lawson doing here?' He could see no one that looked like Baxter Perry or Brian Lawson.

'Running, sir?'

'Running?'

'Popular place to jog.'

'You think he's here to kill Lawson?'

Singh said nothing.

'He's worried those girls said something to their teacher. That's it, isn't it? He's worried that Seagrove told Lawson.'

'But Lawson would have told the police if she had, surely?'

'He's taking no risks, Singh. He's not sane. He's doing his best to cover it all up. Protecting his father.' The sky was darkening above. 'Is this common completely surrounded by coppers yet?'

'Not yet. Going to need a bit more time.'

'Shit. If he gets out, Singh ...'

'Yes, sir. I know, sir. I'm trying to organise it, sir.'

'Good. Call me when it's happened.'

The playground was a no-go. A couple of burly dads were pushing their daughters on the swings, and the last thing he needed was a couple of young fathers handy with their fists on his case. So he'd run around the outskirts of the playground and started making his way along the path towards the lido.

But he didn't need to go all that far to find exactly what he wanted.

About a hundred yards away, sitting on the grass on the side of the path, he could spot three schoolgirls. They were sprawled out, smoking. From where he was, Lawson estimated them to be about fourteen. Perfect. This was going to be today's bit of fun.

Still jogging slowly, he opened up the rubber mask and pulled it down over his head. His breathing became loud inside the thick rubber and he seemed to start sweating straight away.

There was no one else nearby and, as his penis

bounced up and down within his tracksuit, he licked his lips in anticipation.

Shanice, Nikki and Mercedes were having a sneaky last couple of fags before they headed to their respective homes. School had been a bitch today – an almost impossible maths mock – and they needed to chill before finding themselves having to deflect the inevitable criticism from their families.

'See, my dad, he ain't no intellectual. He don't help me with nothing when I ask him,' Shanice admitted, blowing out a lungful of smoke.

'Mine's just mental,' replied Mercedes. 'Always barking on about me doing good and that, but he don't help at all.'

'All dads are fucking useless,' Nikki agreed. 'Hello, what's this?'

A man with a weird-shaped head was jogging awkwardly towards them.

'What's wrong with him?'

Suddenly, he stopped about twenty yards away and pulled the top of his trousers down over his genitals.

'Ahhhhaaahhaaaaa,' Shanice laughed.

'Fucking 'ell, look at 'im!' Nikki spat her cigarette out onto the grass and rolled about laughing. 'What a fucking perv!'

'That's the funniest thing I've ever seen! Jesus fucking Christ!' Mercedes wiggled her little finger. 'My fucking hamster's got a bigger knob than yours.'

'Your hamster shits bigger things than that,' Shanice agreed. 'What a tiny cock! It's a wonder you can find it to slip into your pants in the morning, mate!'

'I'm gonna get a shot of that.' Mercedes pulled her phone out and took a picture. 'That's the funniest thing

I've ever seen.'

Lawson tried tugging himself, but the girls laughed even harder.

'Oh my God! You can't tell where his fingers end and his knob begins! What a loser.'

'Oi! Loser! Want me to blow you, eh?' Shanice stood up. 'Betcha never put that anywhere near a woman before, have you?' She took a few steps towards him and the other two girls stood up behind her. 'Betcha still a fucking virgin, aincha?'

Lawson felt his penis softening in his hand.

Shanice took a few more steps. Lawson didn't know if he should just run off or not. He hadn't come yet – wasn't anywhere near coming – but he couldn't just leave it like this, could he? He needed relief. He must get relief.

The three girls edged forward a little more.

'How about all three of us help you to pop … your … CHERRY!'

Shanice jumped and hit Lawson square in the chest. His hand let go of his genitals and he fell over backwards and hit the grass the other side of the path. Suddenly a foot in a school shoe slammed into the side of his head, and another one kicked him in the testicles.

'Nice mask, by the way, loser!'

One of the girls ripped the mask off the top of his head, taking a few hairs with it.

Shanice punched Lawson twice in succession – once in the eye and once on the side of his nose, breaking it instantly.

'Get off!' Lawson cried out. 'Get off me!'

'Take that, you fucking perv.' Nikki stamped on his nuts again. 'Oughta fucking lock people like you up. Trying to scare the shit out of innocent girls like us. Take that!' She gave his bollocks an extra kick.

*** *

'What's going on?' Luchewski muttered to himself. Some people seemed to be writhing about and fighting on the grass. 'What the …'

He ran along the path to where it was happening. As he got nearer he could see that three girls were kicking a man in running gear on the ground.

'Hey! Hey!' he called out and the three girls pulled away from the man. 'What the hell's going on?'

'Fucking perv, ain't he.'

'Shaking his bits in front of us.' One of the girls held up the mask. 'Wore this.'

'What?'

'He's a fucking flasher, man. Came up out of nowhere and started banging his pathetic toadstool right in front of us.' The largest of the three puffed herself up with pride. 'Got a mint pasting off us, though. Teach 'im to mess wi' us.'

Luchewski struggled to get his breath back and looked down at the battered jogger on the ground, instantly recognising him. 'Lawson?'

The man either moaned by way of a response, or just because he was in terrible pain.

'What the fuck is going on?'

'Like I said –' the larger girl started.

'Yeah, I know. I know.' Luchewski got his phone out again. 'Singh. You might want to get some officers in here. And some paramedics. I've found Lawson.'

'Is he OK?'

Luchewski stood over him. 'Let's just say, I think he might be giving up his favourite hobby soon enough.'

'Eh?'

Luchewski tucked his phone away again.

The smallest of the two girls stared at Hal. 'Hey, man.

You're beaten up too.' Luchewski's hand instinctively went up to his face, and he suddenly remembered how sore it was. The girl frowned. 'You ain't no fucking perv too, are ya?'

'No. I'm police.'

'Yeah, yeah. That's what they all say, I'm definite.'

Suddenly, out of the corner of his eye, Luchewski saw a figure dash out from under a tree and start running away in the opposite direction.

Perry.

'Shit.'

Behind him Luchewski could hear one of the girls scream, 'See! I said he was a perv too!'

Hal hit the stony path as hard as he could, the pain in his leg barely registering. He was not going to let this bastard get away from him again. Not like this morning. This time he was going to catch him.

Perry glanced nervously over his shoulder, saw Luchewski gaining on him and quickened his pace. Hal's legs pumped even harder and he just about managed to maintain the same distance between them.

Dog walkers and genuine joggers moved out of their way as the two men raced their way towards the main road on the south of the common. Perry leapt over a fallen tree trunk and continued sprinting as fast as before. Hal jumped it too, landing expertly on its other side, a spasm of pride pushing him on.

They sped on, nearing the closed lido. As they got closer to it, Luchewski had the terrible sense that he was falling behind. Not much. Just enough to start making a difference.

'Fuck!' he spat and tried to pull more power out of his legs.

But it wasn't working. Perry was a lot younger and a

354

lot faster than him, and the gap slowly started to widen.

'Fuck, fuck, fuck!'

He was going to lose him again.

'Fuck!'

Then something weird happened.

Perry stopped running. He brought himself to a standstill, put his hands on his hips, tried to catch his breath and then turned around to face Luchewski who was still powering towards him.

Luchewski slowed down, coming to a stop about thirty feet from Perry.

Luchewski's heart raced and he had difficulty speaking. 'Give yourself … up, Baxter … it's … no good now. Just … give yourself up.'

Baxter Perry said nothing, just stood there looking at Luchewski under the darkening sky of an autumn afternoon.

'We've already taken … your mum and dad into custody. There's no point protecting him now.'

'Ha!' Perry laughed. 'Protect him? Why would I protect him?'

'Your father killed Louisa Gaudiano seventeen years ago. You've been protecting him ever since. All these murders … Alice Seagrove … Laurie Frasier … you did it to protect him.'

'No! You've got it all wrong. I didn't kill them to protect him.' Perry looked angry. 'I was scared of him all my life. He would beat me … lock me in the cellar. Anything I ever did to protect him was done out of fear. Fear of what he might do if he thought he was suspected. Of course, I knew he killed her. Always knew. And *he* knew *I* knew – for Christ's sake, he took her right in front of me. So no one could ever find out … otherwise I was dead.'

'So you kept it hidden all these years to protect yourself? You killed all the others to protect yourself? What sort of an excuse is that?' Luchewski was suddenly aware that Singh was standing nearby.

'No. That's not the reason I killed the others.'

'What then?'

Perry squeezed his hands into fists. 'Bartholomew Kurtz.'

Luchewski shook his head. 'What?'

Behind Perry, Luchewski could see a number of uniformed officers making their way towards him. The common had been sealed. There was no escape for Baxter Perry now. He was totally surrounded.

'Bartholomew Kurtz,' Perry repeated, and Hal thought that he could detect tears. 'I killed them for Bartholomew Kurtz.'

Hal shrugged. 'I don't understand.' He cast his eyes across at Singh before facing Perry again. 'You need to explain what –'

'Bartholomew Kurtz was the only man who ever had any time for me. My father ... well ... never even wanted me – that's what he always said. Hated the very sight of me. No one at school ever paid me any attention. The only person who did was Bartholomew Kurtz. He liked me. Asked me about my day. Laughed and joked with me. Made me feel special. When he died, that was taken away from me. The one person who seemed to care was gone.'

Luchewski couldn't believe what he was hearing. 'He was a paedophile, Baxter. He was just grooming you. That's what they do. He was just waiting for his moment to –'

'No, no, no! You really don't understand. He cared for me. Was going to look after me. That's what he said.'

Luchewski looked at Singh again and Singh gave her

head a tiny shake.

Perry's shoulders seemed to slump a little as he told the story. He was aware of the officers coming up behind him – but it didn't seem to bother him. It was as if all he really wanted to do now was tell his story. Get it all out in the open. And what more open place was there than Tooting Bec Common.

'So when I had to go to the hospital and get my stitches ... when I met up with Alice over coffee in the hospital canteen ... when she told me that on the night Louisa died she'd seen her getting into a car ... when she said that the car belonged to a postman that delivered letters to her house and that she was scared of him, I realised.'

'Realised what?' Luchewski took a few steps towards Perry.

'I could never have told the police about my father. I was far too near to him. He would have killed me just as easily as he killed Louisa. Taken me down with him. But *she* could have. *They* could have. If Alice or one of the others had spoken out, Bartholomew Kurtz would still be alive today. They'd have taken my father away – my mother too, she's as much to blame – but Kurtz would still be alive. I blame them all – Alice, Laurie, Katie, Josh Woodington – I blame them all for his death. If they'd just said something ... just something ...'

'What about Brian Lawson? Where does he fit in? Why were you lying in wait for him?'

'He was their tutor. He should have been aware that something was wrong with Alice. Should have picked up on it and teased it all out of her. But he didn't. He just spent all his time ticking the right boxes to move up the ladder at the school and lusting after the sixth formers. He's as much to blame as anyone else.'

'No,' Luchewski said. 'Your father was the one to blame. Nobody else. You were a child. You were scared. Alice was a child. She was scared too. Anyway, I don't think she ever told anyone. She buried it as deeply as you did.' He thought for a moment. 'Wait. The night Louisa disappeared … Kurtz was seen hanging around, like he was waiting for someone. That was you, wasn't it?'

Perry nodded. 'But my father came after me. Drove round the streets until he found me.' He sighed. 'Then he found her. She got in the car because I was there.' Luchewski could see a tear running down the young man's face. 'She wouldn't have got in if I wasn't there …'

The police stood all around Baxter Perry.

'Look … it's going to be OK, Baxter. Let's just bring it all to an end right now. No need to do anything stupid. Let's call it a day, yeah?'

Baxter reached down and pulled out a long knife.

'Baxter. Please.'

'Don't worry,' Perry said before throwing the knife down hard into the ground so that it stuck out of the dry earth. 'I've had enough. I'm tired of living my life like this.' He put his wrists together and made a motion to one of the policemen nearest him. 'Take me in. Please.'

Chapter Thirty-one

He'd been seen headed towards Chelsea. Reports were coming in that he was currently somewhere around Pimlico, but heading towards the river. Burlock – who'd spent most of the afternoon *trying* to drive around central London roads, squeaked the car into first and pulled off the pavement, shoving his way into the angry mid-rush hour traffic. No driver in the middle of London liked any other driver in the middle of London at any time of the day, but all drivers could be positively violent between the hours of four and six. It was like some sort of tarmac-based *Lord of the Flies*, with brash bully boys overpowering and cutting up the more sensitive and delicate of road users. Luckily, Burlock didn't give a shit about what most people thought of him, so he pushed on as hard and as fast as he could possibly manage.

Where was he going? What was he up to? Burlock had a bad feeling about it all. Cornish didn't strike him as the sort of person to mug old ladies. He wasn't that way inclined. Perhaps the Kurtz abuse had left more anger inside him than anyone suspected. Burlock didn't believe so.

The sky was turning dark now. Black clouds were trying to stuff up the sky, and evening was coming on fast. The air was warm, and it felt like a storm was on its way. Burlock nudged his way over into a feeder lane and joined another queue heading down past Victoria Station.

An image flashed into his head. A picture of Cornish on a bridge. A selfie. One of the ones covering his desk at this very minute. The boy was making his way across London – very slowly, true – but he was heading somewhere.

The bridge.

'Bugger!' There was only one reason that Burlock could think of for Andrew Cornish to be heading towards a bridge in his current frame of mind. And it wasn't to take another selfie.

Burlock thought hard. He half recognised the bridge in the photo. Which one was it? He wished he'd brought the bloody thing with him, instead he strained his memory. Chelsea, was it? Chelsea Bridge? The bridges in this part of London all looked similar. Perhaps it was Albert Bridge? He wasn't sure. Couldn't remember.

Yes. Albert Bridge. It must have been. Albert Bridge. Albert Bridge was fresher-looking, more attractive, than Chelsea Bridge. Wasn't it?

As the traffic sluggishly worked its way towards Sloane Square, Burlock had to make a flash decision. Chelsea Bridge was down one road, and Albert Bridge down another. He could actually just go straight to Chelsea Bridge and then along the embankment to Albert Bridge afterwards. But that would take ages at this time. It was a notoriously slow road.

The junctions were coming up soon and he needed to choose.

The photo? Albert Bridge?

Burlock ignored the turning for Chelsea Bridge and made the decision to head straight down the King's Road.

Thankfully the boy was moving so sodding slowly that Big Issue had enough time to nip into an off-license and pick up a half-bottle of Vladivar. That kept him going. It seemed to be taking the kid forever to get to wherever he was trying to get to and Big Issue was wondering if he shouldn't either just run up to him and ask him what the fuck he thought he was doing, or just leave him to his own devices and just get fucked off his brain down some alley or other.

But two things kept him moving. Firstly, he hadn't been in this part of London for a very long time. The houses were all posh and clean, and the gardens all trimmed and richly green. It was strange because he normally knocked about the same, tourist-covered streets – begging and drinking, occasionally sleeping – every day of his life. But now, here he was, stretching himself out of his comfort zone. And he rather liked it.

The second reason he kept following Cornish was that he remembered Cornish's little secret. About Bartholomew Kurtz. Many years ago, Andrew Cornish had made him promise not to tell anyone. And he hadn't. After that, he'd tried to keep an eye on Cornish.

And that was more or less what he was doing right now. Keeping an eye on him.

Only he wished the boy would hurry up. His legs were aching and he wanted to just sit down for a bit.

And perhaps eat a pasty.

But he didn't look as if he was stopping. In fact, it looked as if Cornish was heading south of the river – now Big Issue hadn't been over *there* for a while. A few years at least. And before that, not since Longley Road. Which was, what, fourteen … fifteen years ago now? He shook his head. It was hard to remember sometimes.

Traffic was virtually at a standstill as the boy shuffled onwards, the bridge at the end of the road looming up into the early evening sky.

Burlock was getting nearer and nearer. What he was going to do when he got there, he wasn't entirely sure. He'd already called in and arranged for a band of woodentops to go straight to Chelsea Bridge in case he'd gone and picked the wrong one to hurry to. Whichever bridge it was, Burlock knew that no good was going to come of it if there was nobody there to stop it happening. He just prayed that it hadn't happened already.

At last the traffic flowed on a bit more and he turned onto the bridge itself. The lights on the struts and supports had literally just flickered on when he noticed something halfway along, on the opposite side of the road.

A young man in a long coat, pulling himself up onto the side of the bridge, standing on its edge.

'Shit!' Burlock screeched the car to a stop, opened the door and rushed out.

'Fuck!' Big Issue almost dropped the Vladivar from his lips when he saw the boy climb onto the side of the bridge. 'Fuck!'

All fucking day long he'd been following him – keeping an eye on him, watching over him like a sort of pissed-up guardian angel. All day long he'd kept his fucking distance, waiting and watching, letting him swerve all over the roads and pavements. And all day long he'd been heading for this fucking bridge.

To fucking throw himself in.

Fuck!

He walked on quicker – the sores inside his ill-fitting boots swelling up like balloons – past the pedestrians who had either not noticed or chosen to ignore the suicidal nutter on the bridge, and looked up to see a do-gooder jumping out of his car and rushing over to Cornish.

* * *

'Andrew!' Burlock barked above the low rumble of cars and buses. 'Andrew! Come down from there. Please. This is no answer to anything.'

The boy stood with his feet on the very end of the large riveted iron girder, his hands holding onto the thick , slanted wires either side of him. Hearing his name he looked around, puzzled.

'Please, Andrew! Come down.'

'Who are you?'

Burlock could see that the boy's face was puffy, bruised and split. Something nasty had happened to it. Perhaps he was concussed. Perhaps he didn't know what he was doing.

Burlock didn't want to say he was from the police. 'I'm here to help. Let's talk. I know people who can help you sort out whatever it is –'

'I don't need help!' the boy screamed back over the wind that whipped across the bridge. 'I don't want help!' Then in a softer voice, 'I just want to stop it all.'

'Stopping everything isn't the answer. For God's sake, you're still very young. You've got everything to live for. What about your art?'

Small crowds of people were gathering on either side of the spectacle.

Cornish frowned. 'Who are you? Who sent you to get me?'

Burlock ignored the question and clutched at a straw. 'If there's anything to live for, it's your art. Surely? You can't just leave it here. Imagine what you could become. With time. Imagine everything you could possibly achieve. In time.'

'You don't understand … I killed an old woman.'

'You didn't kill her. She's in a coma and the doctors

363

hope she'll be out of it in a few days' time.'

His head swivelled back to Burlock. 'I don't understand. Who are you?'

'ANDREW CORNISH!'

Both Burlock and Cornish looked around to their left. A homeless guy with a scraggly beard, two mad eyes, clothes that hadn't seen the inside of a laundrette in months and an almost empty bottle of cheap vodka pushed his way past the small cluster of rubberneckers and got closer to the centre of the action.

'ANDREW CORNISH!'

Burlock squared up to the drunk. 'I'm sorry, sir. You need to go back. This is a police matter. I know you're trying to help but –'

'Police? You're the bloody police?' Cornish seemed to sway in the breeze.

'ANDREW CORNISH!' the man roared again, completely oblivious to Burlock. 'THAT'S YOUR NAME, ISN'T IT?'

'Sir, you need …'

Cornish looked the old wino up and down.

'DO YOU REMEMBER ME? DO YOU REMEMBER ME AT LONGLEY ROAD?'

Cornish squinted, the fading light making it difficult for him to focus, and gripped tighter onto the thick wires.

'DO YOU REMEMBER ME?'

Burlock took a small step back. There was something here that he wasn't too sure of, and he didn't quite know how to react.

'Mr …' Cornish looked doubtful. 'Mr Biggs?'

'YES!' He stopped shouting. 'I was the caretaker at Longley Road. You remember?'

Cornish seemed to half turn on the girder. 'Yes … yes …' His eyes filled. 'Of course I remember.'

The drunk staggered forward a little more, and Burlock let him. 'You remember.' He nodded. 'Good. You remember.' He sort of grinned and his brown and blackened teeth were momentarily revealed. 'It's been a long time. A very long time.' His eyes became serious. 'You remember that time I found you crying? On the stairs? Then I took you back to my little storeroom down near the boiler? Do you remember that?'

'Yes. I do, sir. I remember it well.'

'And you told me all about Kurtz and the court case and how you didn't think you would ever make friends with anyone again? How you couldn't trust people. You remember?'

Cornish nodded.

What the bloody nora is going on? thought Burlock.

'And I made us tea and we ate those horrible biscuits …'

'And we talked all afternoon,' Cornish took up the story, the tears trickling along his cheeks. 'I missed all my lessons. But I didn't care.'

'No. It didn't matter.'

Burlock suddenly spotted a warmth and a strength in the eyes of the drifter that didn't seem to belong there. He'd dismissed him as a sodden old tramp, but that was clearly wrong. There was something more to him than that. Something infinitely more … solid. He was like a scruffy uncle who just happened to drink too much at the Christmas party.

'We had lots of talks in the end, didn't we?'

Cornish had spun completely around and was now staring down at Biggs and Burlock.

'Yes … we … yes … we did.' He was crying. Hard. So hard he could barely catch his breath.

'We talked about everything, didn't we? We talked

about school, and we talked about politics and we talked about art. Art more than anything.' Biggs tilted his head as if trying to recall something. 'You were very good at art, weren't you? Brilliant, in fact.'

Cornish nodded, the words too difficult to express.

Burlock folded his arms. He felt quite redundant.

'An incredible artist. Unbelievable.' He stepped closer to the handrail. 'Are you still doing your art? I hope you are.'

Cornish jerked his head up and down.

'Good. Good. I'm pleased you're still doing it.' Suddenly Biggs held his hand out to Cornish. 'Come on. Come down.'

Cornish didn't take it. Instead he summoned up the voice to ask Biggs, 'What about you, sir? What are you doing these days?'

Biggs smiled revealing his hopeless teeth once again and looked himself up and down. 'Just ... taking tiny steps towards being a better person. Tiny little steps.'

He extended his hand an inch or two further and Cornish released one of his before grabbing onto it.

'That's better.' The wino's voice was soothing. 'We still haven't finished our little chats, Cornish. Still got a few more to have, eh?'

Andrew Cornish nodded, his face sore with tears, and jumped down from the girder onto the pavement.

The small crowd clapped and cheered, and a bemused Burlock led them both safely across the traffic into the back of his battered old Honda.

Chapter Thirty-two

Baxter Perry had been open about everything. He'd come to realise that, now it was all over, there was no need to hold back. He began by telling them all about his childhood – his hidden, abusive childhood. Beaten by his parents. Days spent locked in his room or in the cellar. Withheld food. Broken toys. All the little tortures liable to turn you into a psychopath.

The night Louisa disappeared, John Perry had found Baxter walking around the streets. Baxter had been heading for Bartholomew Kurtz's place, but never got there. His dad was angry and forced him into the back of the car. It was then that Louisa walked by, crying.

'He could be charming when he wanted to,' Baxter had explained in the cell in Croydon. 'And he was charming then. When he asked her if he could give her a lift home, she said no. But then she saw me, and he asked again. 'It's only around the corner', she said. But for some reason he managed to persuade her to get in. When she was in the car, he said that she could come around to our house first. To sort herself out.'

He wiped his nose and rustled a little in his all-in-one orange suit.

'What happened then?' Luchewski asked.

'In the kitchen, my mum made tea and we all ate biscuits. And then ...' He stopped. 'And then my dad seemed to suddenly become angry – like he was *trying* to make himself angry – and he told me to go up to my room and stay there. He was looking at Louisa. And she looked scared. Petrified.'

'Where was your mother while this was going on?' Singh leaned forward.

'Oh, she was there. She's as bad as he is. An evil cow. Evil. She didn't care about Louisa. As long as her husband was happy she didn't give a shit. She helped him with … it.'

'So, you went upstairs. Then what?'

'At one point I heard a scream. I put the radio on to block it out. Tried to deny what was happening. After an hour, I went back downstairs. Louisa wasn't there any more. But Mum and Dad …' He paused again. 'John and Sheila were cleaning up the kitchen. Scrubbing the floor and throwing everything down into the cellar. I assumed that was where he'd dumped her.

'Then they sat me down. Said I wasn't to say anything about Louisa coming to the house. No matter who asked. Said I was to keep it all quiet, otherwise they'd kill me too.'

'What did you say?'

'I didn't say anything. I was petrified. Then they tried being nice to me. Said I could have a PlayStation if I wanted one.'

'Did they get you one?'

Baxter nodded and stared down at his feet.

After a short break, he told them about his meeting with Alice. How she recognised him when he came in after the Alsatian had torn his fingers to shreds and he needed stitches. How they'd met up for lunch in the hospital refectory. How she'd opened up to him.

'It was like she needed to tell someone. Like all those years, she'd wanted to say what she'd seen that night.

Like it had been eating away at her.' He sighed. 'Ironic that *I* was the one she told.'

He told Luchewski and Singh how, during another visit, he'd stolen a spare key from her. How he'd found her address on the database at his work. How he told her not to even mention his name on social media as he didn't agree with it and, anyway, it could be bad for his career.

How he killed her.

'I didn't enjoy it. But I was angry. Angry for Mr Kurtz. And angry at my dad for putting me in that position.'

'So you cut her up.'

'Yes. I cut her up.'

Laurie Frasier was easy to trace – he didn't need the address database to find out where she lived. He simply had to follow her home from the studio one day. Then he 'accidentally' bumped into her when she was out shopping.

'We got talking and I told her if she was ever worried about anything, to give me a call. She was easy to flirt with.' A flicker across his eyes, and suddenly Luchewski didn't take quite so much pity on him.

For the Woodingtons and Lawson, he used the system at work – and got caught. 'I was in the shit, then. Likely to lose my job. This was before I ... killed Alice. All of a sudden, I had an extra reason not to care.'

'What about the safe house?'

'After I strangled the copper in the car – that was unintentional, by the way, sorry – I put Woodington in the back of the van and told him that if he told me where his wife was, I wouldn't harm his kids. I'd leave them alone.'

His voice had become matter of fact, and Luchewski became aware that the man he was talking to – regardless of his awful upbringing and the dreadful position his own parents had put him in – was a stone-cold killer. A murderer prepared to destroy a family for his own twisted sense of justice.

'Naturally, he told me where she was. Before I stabbed him who knows how many times and dumped his dead body on the side of the road.'

'You didn't kill him,' Luchewski said. 'He's still alive. Badly injured. But he'll survive.'

Baxter looked up at Hal, before turning to look at Singh.

'Oh,' he said, and Luchewski was horrified – but not completely surprised – to pick up on the sense of disappointment in his tone.

It was after ten when Singh drove Luchewski back to Hartshorn House. They were both knackered and neither of them said a word for the entire thirty minutes they were trapped in the car. As they pulled into the car park, Luchewski was amazed to see that the lights on the top floor of the building were still wide awake and blazing.

Singh parked the car next to Hal's TT and they both made their way silently up the stairs.

As they pushed into the large open plan office, Luchewski and Singh were hit by a wall of noise and action. There were still a great many DCs and officers milling about the place. Some were laughing near the coffee machine. Others were reading reports or writing reports or scrunching up reports and throwing them into the over spilling bins that littered the place.

At Singh's desk, Freddie Burlock was scribbling in pen on the back of a large manila envelope. Luchewski and Singh idled across.

Burlock looked up at them. 'Sorry, Priti, love. I'll be away from your desk now. Just needed a nice clear space to write this bloody nonsense up. My desk is covered in photographs still.'

At that moment, Sergeant Green came up to Burlock and slid another sheet of paper onto the desk. 'Don't forget this one too, sir. And we need three copies of the one you've just put in that envelope.' He picked the envelope up and took out the folded up paper that was inside.

'Jesus Nelly. Bloody paper bollocks. You love all this stuff, don't you, Green?'

'Eventful afternoon, Freddie?' Luchewski asked, and Burlock just raised his eyebrows in response.

'You've a visitor, by the way – or B.T.W. as the youngsters say nowadays. Well, text or Tweet, I suppose. Not "say".' He pointed across the room to a tired looking man sitting on a swivel chair.

'What's he doing here?'

'Discharged himself. Got one of the constables to drive him over. Wants to give a statement. Said he wanted to give it directly to you.'

Nino Gaudiano jerked his head in acknowledgement, and Luchewski jerked his back.

'What, now? But it's fucking late.'

'That's what the man said.'

Suddenly, a cluster of Major Investigation officers bundled down the steps at the other end of the office.

'What's that?' Singh asked.

But before anyone gave her an answer, they could all see.

In the middle, flanked either side by two officers in grey suits, hands cuffed tightly together, was John Perry.

'Wait. What's *he* doing here?' Luchewski scowled.

'Being interviewed in one of the rooms upstairs,'

Burlock replied. 'Must be taking him off to a proper station for the night.'

The small crowd with Perry at its centre came down the end of the steps and made its way through the middle of the room. As it did so, it started to get closer to the desk where Nino Gaudiano was sitting.

Blood suddenly rushed through Luchewski's head. 'Wait. No.' He started to walk towards the crowd.

As Perry was marched through the office, the officers had to skirt around a couple of chairs, edging them even closer to Gaudiano.

Luchewski watched as Nino's hand crept up to the desk and took something from it.

As Perry passed Gaudiano, he smirked. A wide stupid, smug smirk.

'Nino! No! Put it –'

It happened in the splittest of seconds. Nino leapt to his feet and swung his arm in a wide, violent arc at Perry's head. It made contact and Perry slumped to the floor taking down the officers either side of him. Another of the policemen shoved Nino hard in the chest and he toppled over his chair and onto the floor beyond.

'FUCK!'

One of the officers scrambled to his feet, the other one crawled onto his knees and sat over – as Luchewski could now see – the twitching body of John Perry.

'WE NEED AN AMBULANCE!' the officer shouted. 'GET A FUCKING AMBULANCE!'

Luchewski pushed his way into the area. Jutting out of one of Perry's eyeballs was the last inch or two of a biro. Blood was spraying down his cheek.

'SOMEONE CALL FOR A FUCKING AMBULANCE!' the kneeling officer screamed again, but in less than a minute it became clear that no ambulance was necessary.

The twitching suddenly stopped and everyone in the office just stood there, stunned and silent.

The interview rooms at Hartshorn were never really any good. The AMIT team always tended to make use of the rooms over at Lewisham or Croydon, and the ones at Hartshorn were only ever used in an emergency. It had been an especially busy day in South London, with an above average number of people taken in for questioning, so John Perry had been transported to Hartshorn out of desperation.

It was Nino Gaudiano who now sat in the same room where Perry had been interviewed not an hour before. There was no need for a lock on the door. He didn't resist arrest. So Luchewski gave a small tap on the door and let himself in.

Nino was sat on one of the rickety chairs that needed to be chucked. He didn't look happy. Didn't look sad. It was as if his mind were a thousand miles away, replaying something over and over again.

'Nino.' Luchewski closed the door behind him and pulled up one of the more solid looking chairs. 'Your solicitor's on his way. I don't give a toss if you want him or not, he's on his way.'

The chair scraped on the linoleum and he sat down.

For about two minutes, they both sat there, not saying anything, each of them in their own dazed little world. It was Luchewski who eventually broke the silence.

'They read you your rights, didn't they?'

Nino looked up and nodded. 'Yeah. They did.'

'Right. Good.'

'Not that I care all that much.'

'No. I suppose not,' Hal agreed. 'But you'll be going

away for a long time again. You do know that, don't you?'

'Yes. I know. Only this time …' he gave a sort of half-hearted smile. 'Only this time, I'll be going to prison for killing the right man.'

Luchewski sighed, thinking back to the very first time he had met Nino Gaudiano, sitting on another wonky chair in Kurtz's dining room. It was a scene he'd re-enacted a million times in his mind. His dreams had been filled with that picture for years and years.

And for some reason something had never sat right.

In the middle of the night sometimes he would wake up and play it all through, second by second. Word by word. Until, years later, an idea had formed. He couldn't be certain, of course. But he'd weighed it all up and juggled the facts around and tried to see if he was being ridiculous. But he kept coming back to the same idea.

And now was the time to try it out. Test it. See if he was correct.

'Nino,' he started. 'I know.'

Gaudiano looked at him through confused eyes. 'Know what?'

'What happened at Kurtz's house. The truth.'

Nino shook his head. 'I don't understand … What are you on about?' But his eyes looked scared.

'You know what I'm on about.'

'No, I don't.'

'Yes, you do.'

Luchewski pulled his chair closer. This wasn't a formal interview. He probably shouldn't even be in here now, talking to a murder suspect like this. Woode would probably have his nuts for ankle socks if he knew.

Luchewski didn't care though. He felt it owed it to Nino for not having caught the right man sooner.

'"My fingerprints are all over it." That's what you said when I found you sitting in Kurtz's house. It was about the torture equipment. "My fingers are all over it." That's a really funny thing to say, don't you think?'

'I don't know what you're on about. I thought it was all obvious. I killed Kurtz. For Christ's sake, I was convicted for it. That's all there is to it. Nothing more.' But his eyes still betrayed him.

'Nino.' His voice slipped into a whisper. 'There are no microphones in this room – you are not being recorded. And I swear to God that I will never tell anyone the truth – there's no point. No point in ruining another life. I think everybody's suffered enough, don't you? I simply want you to know that I know. And that you're not carrying the weight of that knowledge alone. OK?'

Nino rubbed his wet eyes. 'But if you know, then others can work it out too.'

'How can they? Only you, me and Colgan were in that room at that point. There's no actual physical proof – or at least none that was discovered and used in the court case – to link him to the crime. That case is over. They've closed the book on it. No need to reopen it.'

'I was right to do it though, wasn't I?' Tears were welling in his eyes now. 'I was right to take the blame. He's done well for himself. Medals for bravery. He rescued some kids, you know? If he'd taken the blame – if he'd gone to prison – they'd be dead now, wouldn't they? Those kids. He wouldn't have been there to save them.'

Luchewski nodded.

Angelo Gaudiano. Son of Nino. Helicopter pilot. War hero. Sixteen years old when he tortured and killed Bartholomew Kurtz, desperately trying to find out what had happened to his twelve-year-old sister.

'Yes,' Luchewski gave a small smile. 'Yes. They

would have died without Angelo. He's a brave man.'

'So I'm pleased I took the blame.' A single tear ran down Nino's cheek. 'It was the right thing to do. My Louisa couldn't be saved, but those kids could.'

Luchewski thought about his own daughter, Lily. How perfect and strong and amazing she was. How he'd easily kill anyone who tried to hurt her. Nino Gaudiano was not a monster. Angelo Gaudiano was not a monster. They were just despairing men who dealt with a terrible situation the only way they thought they could.

'Please ... Inspector. Don't tell anyone. Don't tell his mother.'

Luchewski grinned his warmest grin. 'Nino. We take this secret to the grave with us. You, me, Angelo. No one else will ever find out.'

'Thank you.' Nino smiled. 'Thank you.'

Luchewski stood up, stowing his chair under the table. 'There's one other thing.' He spoke at a normal volume again. 'The person who was helping you ... getting the addresses, all that.' He raised his eyebrows.

Nino shook his head. 'I made a promise. I'm grateful that you'll never reveal ... about Angelo. But I made a promise.'

Luchewski nodded. 'Not even as part of a plea bargain? Might help.'

Nino closed his eyes. 'Sorry, Inspector. No plea bargains. Nothing. This time I go to prison a happy, guilty man.'

EPILOGUE

Love Spreads

Nurse Rebecca Defalco finished her shift as usual, stuffing her uniform into her locker and grabbing her bag. Looking up at the top shelf of the locker, she could see the two bottles of morphine that that stupid copper had handed back to her.

He was such a gullible, trusting fucker thinking she would just go and put them back in the stores. She'd sat and cried in front of him and he'd swallowed it all. She'd done exactly the same thing when Dr Seagrove had caught her stealing pills a couple of months back. Defalco had wept and said how difficult she was finding everything at work – played the stress card – and Seagrove had turned a blind eye, telling her not to do it again. It had helped that Seagrove was in a surprisingly good mood at the time. Obviously smitten with the fella who probably eventually did her in. Poor cow.

But Defalco was better than all those stupid fuckers. She was more clever and cunning than any of them knew.

Screw you, copper, she thought as she scooped the two bottles off the shelf and pushed them deeply into her bag. That one with the prostate cancer – What was his name? Westlake. That was it – paid well for the morphine. She assumed he sold most of them on, just keeping a few aside for himself. Not that she cared. He could do what he liked with them. Shove them up his arse for all she cared. As long as he kept paying.

It was a shame he was dying, though. He was a nice easy earner for her. When he did eventually die, she'd have to find someone else to sell to.

She shut the metal locker and made her way towards the lift.

It had been a long, tiring day and she sighed when she thought that she still had an annoyingly tricky bus journey to contend with. All those mums with pushchairs and old people who kept farting without knowing they were doing it – sardine tins packed with shit. That's all buses were. Sardine tins.

She came out of the lift and walked out of the building into the cold evening air. It was weirdly dark as she crossed the hospital car park, over the zebra crossing and out onto the main road.

'Miss Defalco?'

She turned. A car had suddenly pulled up alongside her, so she stopped walking.

'What?'

The driver got out, followed by the passenger. The two men wore shiny suits and Defalco's stomach seemed to drop.

'Police.' A flash of a card. 'Could we take a look inside your bag and your coat, please?'

'Why?'

The other spoke this time. 'We have reason to believe you have stolen property on your person.'

'What?' She wanted to run, but she knew she couldn't. 'Ridiculous. That's just ridiculous. How dare you –'

'Your bag, Miss Defalco.'

Defalco stood there unable to move.

'Your bag, please.'

Slowly she handed it over. The man unclipped it and rummaged about.

'Are these yours?' he asked pulling out one of the plastic bottles of morphine.

'Er ...'

'There's no name on them. Are they yours?'

She felt like a tonne of lead rooted to the spot.

Balls!

'Miss Defalco, I'm placing you under arrest. You may ...'

But she heard nothing else. The other officer opened the back door of the car and waved her in. She bent and crawled into the back seat, numb. Someone else clicked her seatbelt into position and she found herself staring at the back of her hands, thinking how much older they would look the next time she saw freedom.

Before Stevie crawled into bed, his phone buzzed and lit up the bedroom. He picked it up off the bedside table and read the message. It was from Liz.

"HEY STEVIE. HRU? SORRY HAVEN'T GOT BACK TO U. REALLY BAD NEWS HERE. MY EX HAS BEEN DIAGNOSED WITH PROSTATE CANCER – TURNS OUT HE'S DYING. WANTS TO SPEND TIME WITH THE KIDS SO WE'VE BEEN LOOKING FOR SOMEWHERE TO LIVE. LIFE IS SHIT. DARREN'S ONLY GOT THREE OR FOUR MONTHS LEFT TO LIVE – GIVING HIS NOTICE IN AT WORK THIS WEEK. THEN WE CAN BE TOGETHER. GOT TO GIVE UP THE COURSE, I'M AFRAID – YOU UNDERSTAND. CAN'T DO ANY OF THAT WITH THIS SHIT GOING ON. THANK YOU FOR BEING A GOOD LAUGH. WORK HARD. HOPE YOU COP OFF WITH THAT CUTE GUY. L.X"

Shit, thought Stevie. Shit a brick. Life was cruel sometimes. You could just tick along, oblivious to anything and then – bang – everything turns upside down. Her kids were only young. *Shit.*

He took the phone across to the sitting room. It made you think, all that stuff. Death and misery and loss and pain. Made you realise that life was such an unbearably short thing. One minute you're born, the next …

And Harry dealt with that on a daily basis. It was his bread and butter. Fuck. It was hardly surprising he found it hard to connect sometimes. All that crap swilling around his mind, poisoning his system. Stevie suddenly felt even more determined to do the right thing.

Settling himself onto the sofa, he started tapping in a reply.

"Sorry to hear that. Hope u and D make the most of the time he has left and that the kids can come to terms with it. No chance of me copping off with cute guy tho – I'm already happily taken. Call me if you need to chat. Tonnes of love. Xxxx"

Within hours, Forensics had ripped up the flooring in the Perrys' cellar. Under a layer of cement had been found three small, female bodies, two of which – a pair of thirteen-year-old twins last seen at a nature reserve in Sussex in 2005 – would remain without names for weeks.

But the third – the smallest body of all – was much quicker to be identified.

Over the next few days, officers compared its DNA with that willingly given by Nino Gaudiano.

It was a perfect match.

'OK, Shanice, love,' the female officer gave her a sympathetic look. 'Are you sure you want to do this? You don't have to. As you're under sixteen you can have an adult with you as you –'

'No, no. S'cool.' Shanice chewed her gum and shoved her hands deep inside her pockets. 'I'm cool with it.'

The officer pushed a button on the wall and spoke into a small box. 'OK. Show them in.'

Behind the two-way glass, six men wearing exactly the

same things – including large rubbery Jeremy Clarkson masks – shuffled along in a line.

'OK.'

They all stopped and turned to face Shanice and the officer.

'Would you like them to remove their masks?'

Shanice nodded.

The officer pushed the button again. 'Please remove your masks.'

They all did so.

'Number four.'

'You sure?'

'Yeah. Number four. No question. Hundred per cent.'

'I can get them to turn to the side so you can see their profiles if you like.'

'No need. Number four.'

The officer nodded to the other officer in the room who scribbled something down on a form.

'Smallest knob in the world.'

'Hmm?'

'Number four. He's got the smallest knob in the world.'

The female officer smiled. 'Do you want me to ask them all to get them out? See if you can recognise any of them?'

Shanice seemed to think seriously for a few seconds. 'Nah. Better not.'

'I was only joking.'

'Oh, I see. Right. Yeah. Nice one.'

Later on in the morning, Brian Lawson found himself standing in an identity parade twice more.

'Number four,' Nikki had said, half-yawning.

'Deffo four,' Mercedes pointed an hour later. 'Dirty fucking perv. Tiny todger though.'

The other officer in the room filled in the forms, lined them up nicely, wrapped a paper clip around the top left-hand corner and passed them over to his boss.

Andrew Cornish felt strangely refreshed. They'd given him fresh clothes at the station – no belts with sharp edges as he was deemed to be at risk of suicide – and he'd had a really good scrub in the surprisingly clean-looking shower cubicle.

The bed was a bit hard, but he rather liked that. It pushed back and held him tightly in place as he slept.

The doctor had treated the cuts on his face, wiping them clean before holding them all together with long white strips of sticky plaster.

And they fed him. Porridge – the irony of it tickled him – in the morning, bacon sandwiches at lunch, and cottage pie and peas for dinner. Even though, to any other person, the food tasted bland and insipid, to Cornish it was like nectar from the gods. He'd spent so many years forgetting – or being unable to afford – to eat, that he'd lost the whole wonderful concept of food. But this place was like a hotel, and he felt like tiny pieces of jigsaw were slowly being allowed to shift back into place. One by one.

It was just after he'd finished the cottage pie that one of the policemen at the station flipped back the little window in the door and said: 'You gorra visitor.'

In the interview room, Mr Biggs was almost as freshly washed as he was. He wore the same clothes as he'd been wearing the previous evening when he'd held out his hand and helped Cornish down from Albert Bridge, but they looked as if they had had a bit of a dunk in a sink full of water. Even his beard had been trimmed.

'Cornish.' There was only the vaguest smell of alcohol on his breath. 'How are you?'

Cornish shrugged his shoulders and sighed. 'Better. Thank you.'

'Good. Good. So ...' Biggs rested his arms on the table between them. 'Tell me about your art. What sort of things are you into these days? What sort of work are you creating? Tell me.'

Cornish thought about his *Prelude* series, but decided not to say anything about them. Instead he talked about the sky pictures he was imagining painting. He talked about the way clouds scud across the enormous blues of the morning, and of the way the rich reds of dusk can obliterate the sky before slowly easing into darkness. And as he talked, he found himself becoming excited. Keen to get started on them.

He found himself becoming hopeful.

Biggs smiled small, tight smiles and nodded with the sense of a man who knew nothing about art but who could see the love of it in another person. Cornish talked for ages, his hands and badly cut arms waving, gesticulating, trying to make himself clear. And Biggs continued to listen.

After a while, Cornish seemed to tire himself out, and a quietness fell between them. It wasn't awkward. Or difficult. It just felt like something that was there, and didn't need explaining.

'You know what I did, I suppose?' Cornish eventually whispered. 'You know why they arrested me.'

Biggs nodded. 'You mugged an old woman.'

Cornish winced. 'Yes. I'm not proud. I just felt desperate. I didn't have much money ... and now ... I don't know what I can do to make it right.'

Biggs scratched at his crispy beard. 'Well, I suppose you're halfway there being in here.' It was odd, he hadn't felt this sober in days. And now, he was speaking clearly and coherently. 'Part of making up for it is to be punished. From what I gather, you'll stay here for the weekend, then be taken for a court hearing, and after that they'll hold you in a real prison until your court case.'

Cornish nodded.

'And it's unlikely you'll get off – you'll spend some time in prison. So, you're halfway there already.'

'Yes. But it doesn't feel like enough.'

'No. Well, what you also need to do is apologise.'

'Apologise?'

'Write the family a letter. Explain everything – don't try to justify it. Just … explain. They may just tear it up. Even so, you have to try. For them. For you.'

Cornish smiled at Biggs, and Biggs grinned right back.

'Thank you, Mr Biggs.'

'You're welcome,' said Big Issue.

As Big Issue walked from the police station right next to Victoria, he made a sudden decision. Instead of turning back towards the tourist-filled centre of the city, he walked south and west, back over the streets where, just the day before, he'd followed Andrew Cornish.

The traffic was thinner than it had been previously, and the rain was holding off. As he walked, he played with the half full bottle of gin that he'd bought earlier in the day, twisting the top open and closed in his coat pocket. He could feel it sloshing about as he marched on.

Coming out onto Chelsea Embankment, he pulled the bottle out and launched it over the wall and into the muddy Thames. Perhaps he'd try to give it a miss for a bit. All it did was smudge the day for him. It wasn't doing him any good.

He found himself thinking about his own life since leaving the unit. After Iraq in 1990, it was all he could do to walk away with his body in one piece and his sanity barely intact. Nowadays he'd be offered PTSD counselling. But back then ... it was different back then. He was left all alone.

That led to the struggle. The struggle to hold down a job. The struggle to keep his relationship going. The struggle with drink. The struggle with drugs. The struggle. Always the fucking struggle. Non-stop fucking struggling.

Well, he was sick of struggling.

He passed Chelsea Bridge and found himself strolling up onto the bridge where he'd followed Cornish yesterday. As he got exactly halfway across, he stood against the edge and looked upwards.

The sky was wide and open. In the middle of London you could never see the sky. The buildings dominated the skyline, and were all squashed in like tins and cereal boxes. But here, on this bridge, you were as far away from buildings as you could ever get in this sprawling mess of a city, and the sky opened up like an umbrella above you.

It wasn't a sunny day, by any means. The clouds were puffed up and gloomy. But Big Issue could kind of see what Cornish had meant. It was like a different world above the superstructures, the glass-fronted office blocks and the long, slow rolling river. A separate world, always moving, always changing. Evolving. Managing itself. Natural.

He gripped onto the railing and sighed.

He knew where he was going. It had been a long time since he had seen his son. Perhaps nearly three years. And Clapham wasn't even all that far away. It saddened him to think he hadn't tried earlier.

He could remember the address, despite the ravages that the alcohol had had on his brain. He could remember it exactly. All he hoped was that his son would be pleased to see him. It was true he hadn't been a good father, but there was always time to learn.

Wasn't there?

He breathed in the evening air and carried on, over the bridge into the wild lands of South London.

Katie had almost fallen asleep, slumped over onto the scratchy blankets that the hospital used, when Josh stirred for the first time. Some machine he was attached to seemed to give an extra beep and she lifted her head – sight all blurry – and looked at him.

One of his eyes pulled itself stickily open, joined a minute or so later by the second one.

'Hello,' she said as his bloodshot eyes adjusted and tried to focus on her.

'Hey ...' His voice was hoarse and hardly audible. 'Hey.'

'How'd you feel?' She felt like crying, but all she could summon up were inanities. 'You hungry?'

Without moving his head from the pillow, he looked around the room. 'The kids? Are they OK? You?' He anxiously tried to sit up, but a spasm of pain, made him fall back onto the bed.

'Ssssh. It's all right, Josh,' said Katie. 'The kids are fine. I'm fine. It's all over. There's nothing more to worry about. They caught him.'

He stared hard at her neck. 'Your throat ... what ...?'

'It's nothing.' She pulled the silk scarf she'd been given by one of the doctors over the long red mark that encircled her neck. 'Don't worry. It's nothing.'

Josh swallowed and Katie reached up and poured a small dribble of water into a plastic tumbler on the bedside table. She stood over him and tilted it so that a thin stream trickled into his dry mouth.

'I'm sorry,' he said between sips.

'What?'

'He said ... I had to tell him ... if I told him where you were ... the kids would be safe...' Suddenly his body jerked and he cried, his mouth twisted into a strained diagonal. 'He ... said ... that he wouldn't touch them ... if I gave him you ... I'm ... I'm sorry.'

'Hey, hey, hey.' Katie put the cup down and stroked her husband's hair. 'It's all right. I understand.' She kissed the top of his head.

'I didn't ... know what to do.'

'You did the right thing ... OK? You did the right thing. You protected our kids, and that's all that matters. Nothing else matters. Nothing.'

Josh's hand fought its way out of the bedsheets and reached out for hers. She took his hand and squeezed it.

'I love you, Katie.'

'I love you too, you daft sod.' They both grinned. 'Now hurry up and get better. Zac and Sophie want to see their daddy again.'

Luchewski had his own suspicions. So, he called Corrie up and asked her to run a check on the name that was floating around his mind. She didn't need to.

'I know him well,' she said 'Works with the Enfield bunch.'

'You know him?' Luchewski asked, amazed.

'Of course. We HOLMES databasers – if that's a word – need to stick together. He is a bit of a miserable bugger, mind you.'

HOLMES. Of course. Now it all makes sense.

Luchewski put in a call to the AMIT North team and told them he was on his way and that he needed to speak to a particular member of the team.

Just before he unlocked the doors to his black TT, Luchewski's phone buzzed, so he pulled it out and read the message. It was from Becky Schinowitz.

"Harry. Patrick Bayley is in town tomorrow night. Has booked a table for three – bring Elizabeth or a friend or somebody – at Sketch on Mayfair for 7:30. Says he would love to meet up. Let me know if you'll agree to meet and I'll let him know. Becks."

Sketch, thought Hal. *Not cheap*. He'd never eaten there before but he'd heard and read fantastic things about it.

He immediately sent a reply and within seconds Becky had responded with a swift: *"OK. Good luck. Becks."*

In Enfield, Luchewski introduced himself to the desk sergeant.

'Ah, yes, Inspector. We've cleared an interview room for you so that –'

'That won't be necessary,' Hal cut him off. 'All I want is a quick five minutes with him. If you could go and tell him I'm here, I'll just wait outside on the steps. Thanks.'

Luchewski stood, leaning against the blue handrail in the centre of the outside steps and watched the slow line of traffic inching its way past, most of it probably heading towards the M25. It seemed to Luchewski that London was becoming increasingly clogged up. Too many cars and too few roads, he thought as the automatic door behind him swished open.

He turned.

An elderly man with a walking stick stumped out through the door and towards the top of the steps.

'Yes?' he barked. 'What is it? What do you want? I'm a busy man you –' He stopped talking and jutted his head forward a little, trying to get a closer look at Luchewski. 'You,' he said eventually, jabbing his finger towards Luchewski. 'You.'

The years had not been too kind to Unlucky Jim Colgan. He stooped awkwardly, his eyesight was clearly no longer up to the mark and not a single hair was left gracing his head. The face was wrinkled like a decomposing prune – the result of a life spent constantly being a miserable bastard – and his lips were thin and cracked.

'Hello again, Mr Colgan. It's been a few years.'

Colgan straightened up. 'I suppose I oughta call you "sir" now? Been making your way up the ladder.' He nodded his head back towards the station. 'Been reading about you in the papers.' He had a face like bees were fucking inside his nostrils and he couldn't get them out.

'Harry's fine. Just call me Harry.'

'Tch!'

Luchewski ignored him. 'So, you're AMIT North's HOLMES whizz, eh?' He didn't mean for it to sound patronising, but it definitely did.

'HOLMES *2*,' Colgan corrected him. 'We use HOLMES *2*. I'd've thought a supercop like you would know that.'

They stood staring at one another, neither of them making any move nearer to the other.

Colgan continued, keen to put things into context. 'Retired a few years back. Got sick of the force. But a load of crap happened as soon as I gave it all up. House burnt down – the third house of mine to burn down, believe it or not – girlfriend found a new bloke, got waylaid with fucking gout, lost my car in a drunken bet. Load of crap happened. So I asked if there were any roles I could do – just to get away from the shit luck I always had. Get me out of the hostel I was in. They said I could train. As a civvy. Help them with the databases. And you know what? Turns out I'm fucking brilliant with them.' A slight flicker of a smile on his thin lips, and then it was gone.

'So I hear,' Luchewski said. 'So I hear.'

'Whaddya mean?'

'A good friend of mine speaks very highly of your abilities to pull information out of the system. A good *mutual* friend.'

Colgan suddenly looked shifty. 'A friend?'

'Yes. You remember. Nino Gaudiano. You arrested him once.'

The man's shoulders dropped a little. 'He's fucking told you, hasn't he?' He shook his head. 'He told me he'd keep it all quiet.'

'No, he didn't tell me, Jimmy. In fact, I wasn't completely certain. It was just a bit of a guess, to be honest.'

'A guess!'

'Hmm.' Luchewski walked a few steps closer. 'Lucky that, eh?'

'Yeah. Really fucking lucky.'

'It wasn't right, was it? Nino being locked away for all those years like that. All he was doing was trying to find out where his daughter was. Mitigating circumstances and all that. It just went a bit far, that's all. Ended up with Kurtz on the slab. And to think you were the one to bring him in.'

'What are you saying?'

'It wasn't exactly the big heroic arrest you wanted, was it? Not exactly preventing the next 9/11, eh? In fact, it all felt a bit shitty. Poor bastard trying to find his kid. Going down for twenty-odd years. Didn't feel right.'

392

Colgan visibly gulped.

'So when he did get out, and you – unbelievably – found yourself in a position to help him ... well, you tell me. Was it *him* that contacted *you* first, or the other way round?'

Colgan seemed to be leaning even harder on his stick. 'I ... I contacted him. I found out where he was staying ... some horrible little flat. And I went round. Said if there was anything I could do ... to help. If he ever needed any help ...'

'So you fed him addresses? Told him where these people were now living? Misused police data?'

'Yes ... it felt like the right thing to do. He just wanted to find his daughter.'

They both stood there glaring at the bus that didn't seem to be moving, neither of them saying anything. Behind them, somebody came out through the swishing door and made their way between them, down to the street below.

'What happens now?' Colgan asked, his face more pale than it was five minutes before. 'You'll report me. I'll be arrested. What happens then?'

'Who said anything about reporting you?' Luchewski muttered.

'What?'

'This is quickly turning into the week of secrets ... I said, who said anything about reporting you?'

'But ...' Colgan looked confused, 'You must. You're my superior. You have to report me.'

'No. I don't. It doesn't do me or you any good to report this. Let's just call this an informal warning – between the pair of us, best not get HR involved – and move on, eh?'

'I don't –'

'You go back to doing what you do so brilliantly, and I'll go back to doing what they pay me for. OK?' Luchewski went down the first step. 'But ...' He lowered his voice once again. 'Should *I* require a little extra insight sometimes – in much the same way Nino did – I know I can count on you. Can't I?' He gave Colgan a little wink.

'Oh, I see.' Colgan stretched himself up to his full five feet eight inches once again. 'Blackmail, is it? You're holding it above my head so I can be your internal snitch, is that it?'

Luchewski deliberately put a puzzled look on his face. 'Blackmail's a bit of a strong word. Let's just say that if this was an MOT, it'd be described as an advisory.'

Colgan looked oddly furious for a minute before releasing all the anger in one huge sigh and saying, 'OK, then.'

'Good.' Luchewski turned and made his way down the steps. 'Take care of yourself, Jimmy. Take good care.'

Whatever it was, it smelled delicious.

'It's just a few vegetarian enchiladas.' Stevie was standing over the cooker, oven gloves on. 'It's a Jamie Oliver recipe.' He pointed a gloved hand towards the iPad which was leaning precariously against the tiling. 'Forgot the feta cheese, so it's cheddar all the way, I'm afraid.'

Stevie spun around and saw Luchewski standing in the doorway holding the flowers and champagne.

'These are for you.'

'Oh ...' He removed the oven gloves and went up to Luchewski. 'They're lovely. Thank you.' Stevie took the flowers and champagne from Hal and immediately set about trying to find a big enough vase. 'What are we celebrating?'

'I dunno. Me not being a twat for ten minutes.'

'Ha! Sounds good.'

Luchewski took his jacket off and threw it onto one of the stools sitting alongside the breakfast bar. 'No. Seriously though. I'm sorry if half the time I behave like a prick. I forget you're not a copper. I forget sometimes that there's a life outside of the bloody job. I don't mean –'

'No. Don't. I understand.' He opened yet another cupboard. 'Do you actually own any vases?'

'Er … no. Probably not.'

'Ah well.' Stevie stood the flowers up in the sink and half-filled it. 'Please. Don't apologise. I was an arsehole the other night. I mean, your job's your job. It's a massive part of you. It's wrong of me to expect you to just cut out that bit of your world just because it doesn't involve me. I'm sorry. I can be very selfish at times.'

Luchewski rolled his sleeves up and threw his arms around Stevie.

'You're not selfish. You're just you. And I'm so pleased I met you.' Luchewski bent his head and kissed Stevie full on the lips. 'You're a breath of fresh air in my stale, repetitive, dead-body strewn life.'

Stevie reached up and pulled Hal towards him again, and they violently kissed – lips and tongues clashing together – for well over a minute.

Afterwards, they stood holding each other – head resting on head – both of them feeling the warmth of the other's body.

'Hope you don't mind, but I arranged to go shopping with Lily tomorrow. Into town.' Stevie looked towards Luchewski. 'Thought it would be nice. Bit of a bonding session.'

'Ah …' Hal sighed.

Stevie loosened his grip. 'You don't like the idea?'

'No. No. I love the idea. She likes you almost as much as I do. It's just …'

'What?'

'I've already arranged something. For the two of us.'

'Oh, yes?' Stevie hugged Luchewski tightly again.

'Hmm. You see, there are two other men in my life …'

Grip loosened again. 'I'm sorry?'

Luchewski pulled Stevie closer. 'Yes. Two other men. One of whom I've not even met yet.'

'Huh?'

'But I think it's time you met them both. Tomorrow. That OK?'

Seymour wasn't *quite* as much of a hipster as Luchewski had imagined. He was short and squat with a day's worth of stubble around his chin and a week's worth of stubble on his cheeks. It looked as if he was slowly trying to grow himself a couple of Rhodes Boyson lamb chops.

'Sorry,' he held his hand out flat towards Luchewski and Stevie. 'No one can speak to Mr Moore at the moment. We're busy filming. If you could stand out of the way …'

'But –'

'If you could stand *out* of the way.'

'Harry!'

Seymour's head jerked back to where Barry Moore was currently dragging a silver Samsonite suitcase on wheels across the arrivals area in Terminal Three. A camera crew were walking backwards in front of him, nearly tripping over other people's luggage. A producer with a clipboard frowned at Seymour, and Seymour shrugged his shoulders.

'Look. Enough of this bollocks for a minute.' Moore shoved the extendable handle back into the suitcase and left it where it stood. 'I'm going for lunch.'

Moore made his way over to Luchewski, Stevie and Seymour. As he did, a number of people pointed and muttered amongst themselves, recognising the TV personality. Even after all these years, Barry Moore had to contend with passers-by doing double takes and asking for autographs. He was, without a doubt, a part of British television history.

'Harry! Good to see you.'

Seymour raised his eyebrows at Moore who frowned and growled at him. 'Harry,' he explained. 'Vic's son.'

'Vic?' Seymour asked.

'Victor. Victor Liddle.'

'Who? Oh. Your old partner.'

Moore gave his head a despondent little shake and mumbled under his breath, 'Fucking hell.'

Luchewski couldn't stop himself from grinning. 'Looking good, Barry.'

Moore narrowed his eyes. 'That's because I'm covered in fucking make-up. Underneath I'm like something out of *The Creeping Flesh*.'

His eyes fell upon Stevie. Luchewski noticed and reached up to squeeze Stevie on the shoulder. 'Barry, this is Stevie. Stevie, this is Barry.'

'Lovely to meet you, Stevie.' Moore leaned in and gave Stevie a surprisingly warm hug. 'I would say I've heard lovely things about you, but this bugger never says anything about anyone.' Luchewski and Stevie smiled at each other. 'Always plays his cards close to his chest.' And then, in a hissy comic whisper, 'Not exactly a big talker.'

'Oh I know that, Mr Moore.'

'Barry. Call me Barry.'

Stevie gave Moore a wink. 'Barry. I'm working on the

talking thing, though. He's a tough nut to crack, but I'm working on it.'

'Good. I bloody hope you do. Now,' he looked towards Seymour who fidgeted on his phone, *'we're* off for some lunch. Tell that lot,' he stabbed his finger at the film crew who looked a bit confused about what was going on, 'that we can carry on where we left off in … about an hour and a half, OK? And don't expect any continuity because I intend to be completely pissed by then.'

'Erm …'

'Come on. Let's eat. Not you though, Seymour. This is a private party. Better just pop into M&S and grab yourself a sarnie. Okey dokey?'

'So what scenes are you supposed to be filming today?' Luchewski asked taking a large gulp from his frighteningly bulbous glass of Merlot.

'Arriving back from a trip to New York.'

'I didn't know you'd just been to New York.'

'I haven't,' Moore replied, poking his buttermilk fried half chicken with his fork. 'Not due to go to New York for months. They just want to "can" it beforehand for some reason – just in case I die, probably.' He shovelled some of the food into his mouth. 'It's all a load of bollocks, TV nowadays. It's a bloody farce. You can't trust anything you see on the box. It's all lies.'

'Not like when you were on it, then?'

Moore stopped chewing and gave Luchewski an indignant look. 'I am *still* on it, I'll have you know. Well, I will be when this bloody series airs next year.'

'You know what I mean, Barry,' Hal smiled at Stevie. 'Back in the day.'

'Mmm. It's all CGI and bluescreen now. All deception

and trickery.'

Luchewski couldn't stop himself from snorting. 'Wait a minute ... you and Dad spent most of your careers deceiving and tricking people with your magic. Half the time you were misleading the public. How's that any different?'

'It was different because, back then, it all came down to the skill of the person in front of the camera. These days it's just done by wizards with computers whose faces you don't ever see. Back when we were hitting ratings highs, everything depended on our skills as magicians ... well, your dad's skills anyway.' He looked up from his plate at Stevie. 'His dad was a fantastic magician. Really accomplished. I was rubbish. I used to just fall over and pull funny faces in the hope that people wouldn't notice just how shite I was.'

Stevie took a sip of his white wine. 'I've watched lots of your programmes –'

'Forced you to watch them, has he? Stood over you with a pointy stick while you endured them, has he?'

'No, no. I enjoy them. They're really funny.'

'It's all right, Stevie. You don't have to say that for my sake.'

'No, no. Honestly. I do. I think they're brilliant. Classics.'

Moore stared at Luchewski. 'I like this one, Harry. Don't let this one get away. He's good for an old man's ego.'

Some people at a nearby table were staring. They were clearly debating if the person currently stuffing their face with chicken really was Barry Moore. Was it? Could it be? No, it couldn't be. Could it?

Moore spotted them and gave a friendly wave.

'What about you and ...' Luchewski struggled for the

name but didn't need to.

'Finished. Kaput. Over and out.'

'Oh. She seemed nice.'

'She *seemed* nice. Bloody wasn't, in truth. Money-grabbing cow. Kept wanting this and that. Didn't let up. So in the end I chucked her.'

'I thought she was going to be wife number four.'

'Balls to that! I've had enough of women.' He looked at Stevie. 'Not that I'm going ... turning ... oh, you know.'

'Queer?' Stevie finished.

'Mmm.'

'Excuse me ...' A man was suddenly standing next to their table. 'I'm sorry, but my friends and I ... you *are* Barry Moore, aren't you?'

'I am. Yes.' Moore 's hand shot up like the pro he was and he shook the man's hand before he even had time to proffer it up himself. 'Hello.'

'Oh. Wow. I can't believe it. I'm a huge fan of yours. I loved your programmes. When I was growing up.'

'Really? That's brilliant.' If it was meant to be sarcastic, it certainly didn't sound it. Moore was such a seasoned pro. Slick and practised.

'Yes, yes. I can't believe it. My colleagues at work aren't going to believe I've met the actual Barry Moore ... actually ...' he dug his phone out of his pocket and Moore gave Luchewski a quick 'here we bloody go' glance, 'I wonder if I could take a selfie with you ... in fact,' he smiled at Luchewski, 'I wonder if you could ...?'

'Of course.' Luchewski gave a silent sigh and took the man's phone from him. The man leaned his head close to Moore's and grinned. You could see all his teeth. Moore's smile was more measured, but still pleasant and warm. Luchewski snapped the shot and handed the man his phone back.

After a few more exchanges and shakes of hands, the man went back to his table to show his friends the pictures of him and Moore before pasting them all over his social media.

'That's another thing nowadays. Everyone wants a sodding selfie. Back in the old days I'd have to carry pens around with me for autographs. Not these days. These days you have to grin like a baboon to make someone happy. Hurts your cheeks after a while.' He gave them a little rub.

They all went back to their food and wine and eventually Luchewski brought up the subject.

'So, Barry,' he said finally putting his knife and fork down together on his plate. 'Tell me about Bendable Brenda.'

On the way over to Heathrow in the car, Luchewski had told Stevie all about his possible half-brother, and Stevie had been sympathetic and supportive. So when Luchewski mentioned Bendable Brenda, he wasn't surprised.

'Bendable Brenda?' Moore sat back in his chair and made a start on his second double whisky. '*Beddable* Brenda I used to call her.' He laughed to himself. 'Not that I ever did, mind. Would have done given half the chance. But I didn't.'

'But Dad …?'

Moore cleared his throat. 'Strong stuff, this whisky.'

'Dad?'

'Once.' He spat it out like an orange pip. 'Just … the once. It was on tour. Up north, I think. He'd been drinking. We all had.' He rubbed his squidgy nose with the palm of his hand. 'The next day, he told me what had happened. He was devastated. Saying how he'd betrayed your mother and how he couldn't even bring himself to look in the mirror ever again. He said he'd betrayed the trust of his kids. That he didn't deserve them. It was awful. We cancelled two shows while I straightened him out. He was broken.'

'Then what?' Luchewski was staring hard and listening to every slight intake of breath. 'What happened then?'

'I did what I thought was the best thing to do at the time. I got rid of her.'

'You sacked her?'

'Yes. I did it without Victor's knowledge. I didn't tell him. Thought we could just pack up the Mismade Girl act and move on. When he found out he hit the fucking roof. He kept saying how it wasn't her fault. That she shouldn't have to suffer because of his stupid actions.' He ran his fingers around the rim of the almost empty glass. 'Almost split us up, it did. You have to remember, Harry, that your father was the most honourable man I ever knew. It took a lot for the thing to happen in the first place, and it took a damned sight more for him to live with it afterwards.'

'But you fired her.'

'Paid her off well. More than well, in fact. You see, I didn't want this … incident to split us up. We were too good. Too much on a roll. The whole world was ours for the taking … But,' he suddenly looked sad, 'then again, more importantly … I didn't want it to come between Victor and Mary. They were so strong together. And she was a good woman, your mother. It would have been disastrous for everyone if this one, tiny mistake had come out. Disastrous.'

'A tiny mistake!' Luchewski wanted to cry. 'She had a child by him. Did you know that? She had his child.'

Moore dusted some crumbs off his side of the table.

'Yes,' he said. 'I know.'

Luchewski was taken aback. 'You knew?'

Moore nodded. 'Yes.'

'Well ... does that mean ... did my father know? Did he have a secret family that my mother never knew about?'

Stevie reached his hand across the table and gave Luchewski's a squeeze. Luchewski suddenly felt calmed. Centred. Like it didn't matter what Moore would say. Hal looked up at Stevie and Stevie's eyes told him that he was there for him. That he wasn't going away and that – whatever the outcome of all this – Stevie was going to help Luchewski through it.

Luchewski's chest burst in ... could it be? ... a sensation that had rarely bothered him in his whole life.

Love?

'No.' Moore shook his head. 'Victor didn't know.'

'But you did. So you didn't tell him. You never told him.'

'Thought it best. He had you and Elizabeth. He doted on you. Loved you both more than anything.' Moore's eyes appeared tired. 'So I kept it all hidden.'

'What about the boy? Didn't he have a right to a father?'

'He got one in the end. She married someone. Bayley, his name was. A good man from what I heard.'

'Hold on ... what? You kept in touch with her?'

'Of course I did. I made sure that neither she nor the boy went without. I took good care of them.'

Luchewski didn't know what to say. All those years, Uncle Barry had been paying money to a woman to keep her from tearing Luchewski's family apart. Was that good? Was that bad? He didn't know. Couldn't think. It was all so ... strange. Unreal.

'You see, Harry,' Moore looked Hal straight in the eyes and for probably only the second time ever, there was nothing between them both. No jokes. No quips. No stupid remarks. Nothing. 'You see, you ... your mother ... Elizabeth ... the rest of the world. You weren't the only people to love Victor Liddle.'

Stevie squeezed even tighter, and Luchewski just nodded.

'Mr Moore.'

They all jumped.

'What?'

Seymour was standing over their table, tapping his watch. 'We really must get on. The crew are keen to finish the filming before the light starts to fade.'

Moore sighed loud and heavy and lots of people in the Rhubarb restaurant turned to see.

'For fucking hell's sake!' Moore took the napkin from his lap and threw it onto his plate. 'You see what I mean, Harry. Stevie. Modern television is a tonne of putrid old shit.' He stood up and pointed to the table. 'Stick this on expenses, would you, Seymour. I'm sure Channel Four can afford it.'

They both decided to wait outside *Sketch*. The air was surprisingly warm and the evening seemed particularly slow to arrive – the sun was holding onto the sky more than it should have done for an October evening – so they decided to wait.

'Haven't you got homework to do, Mr Denyer?' Luchewski ribbed. 'Essays to write or something? Lessons to prepare?'

'Not tonight, Inspector. You see, I'm a bit busy meeting the in-laws.'

'Lucky sod.'

'Yeah. Right.'

Luchewski suddenly threw his arm around Stevie's shoulders and pulled him tightly, kissing his head.

'What was that for?' Stevie grinned.

'Oh, you know ... don't know really.'

A man in a short dark jacket passed them both and goggled. 'Poofs,' he muttered and continued, head down.

Luchewski released his arm from Stevie and turned angrily to the man. 'What did you just –' But before he could finish, Stevie had placed his finger across Luchewski's lips and shook his head.

'What?' Luchewski asked, puzzled.

'Ssh. Don't let it tread all over your life.'

'What do you mean?'

'Some people are filled to the top with poison. It swishes around them, making them bitter and hateful. They don't really want it, so every now and then they try to offload it onto others. Shift it.' Stevie looked so serious that Luchewski found himself just listening. 'You've only just come out, so all of this is new to you. Every time someone calls you a poof or a batty boy or whatever they think is most hurtful or funny, you're going to want to teach them a lesson. Give them a kicking. Try to teach them the error of their ways. Only, you won't. Smashing someone in the face is a nice way of relieving stress, but beyond that it's futile. They won't change their opinion of you – other than realising that you've a mean left hook or your boots have steel toecaps. They'll just carry on believing whatever they've been taught to believe and you'll have just wasted time and energy on them. The only way you can get rid of vile opinions is to do all the right things like educate the young, promote different lifestyles – stuff like that – and then let time do its magic. Hopefully over time the world changes, people's views change, everyone gets on better. *Everything* gets better. What I'm saying is, you rarely get anywhere by shouting back. It just degenerates. Two brick walls smashing into one another. It hardly ever works.'

Luchewski grinned as Stevie removed his index finger from his lips. 'You're quite a hippy at heart, aren't you?'

Stevie laughed. 'Sometimes. At other times I like nothing better than to bring my knee up into the bollocks of a homophobic Nazi with dubious taste in footwear.'

The wine from lunch and the rum from the early afternoon visit to the Wetherspoons on Whitehall still had a bit of a hold on them, and Luchewski suddenly felt the need for more alcohol to maintain his current high.

And to steady his nerves.

Just then, a Rolls-Royce Silver Cloud pulled up outside the white Georgian façade of the restaurant.

'Fancy,' Stevie said, revealing once again that he had absolutely no understanding of cars.

The man driving the Rolls wore a peaked cap, while in the back sat another man. Luchewski momentarily wondered why they weren't sitting up front together. And then it dawned on him.

'Chauffeur, look.'

'What?'

'He's the chauffeur.'

'Oh, yeah.'

The chauffeur – a thin man in his fifties – hopped out from the driving seat, ran around the car and opened the door for the passenger in the back. Luchewski immediately felt the need for both him and Stevie to move out of the way so that the man could get past them to the restaurant.

'Mr Luchewski?'

'What?' Luchewski was taken unawares. 'Hmm?'

'Harry Luchewski?' The man getting out of the car, straightened and offered his hand to Hal.

Luchewski looked him in the face, and knew right away.

The eyes, the fall of the hair, the slope of the shoulders, the point of the chin. Even the tone of the voice. Everything reminded him of his father. It was weird. Confusing. Alien.

Patrick Bayley was definitely his half-brother.

'Harry? I'm Patrick.'

'Er …' Luchewski tried to pull himself together and eventually reached his hand out to shake Bayley's. 'Good … good to meet you, Patrick.'

'I'll be parked somewhere nearby, sir,' the chauffeur interrupted. 'Call me when you need me.'

'Yes. Thank you, Wilson.'

The chauffeur closed the door, went back to the driver's seat and restarted the sixty-year-old engine before zooming off.

Stevie noticed the resemblance too and gave Hal an open-mouthed stare.

'Hope you've not been waiting too long. You could have just waited inside if you'd wanted. I've booked a table.' Patrick Bayley was dressed beautifully in a light silk suit. His shoes were clearly handmade and the smell that accompanied him was certainly not cheap. He was shorter than Hal, but his hair was much thicker, and he had an aura of confidence which was almost as strong as his aftershave.

'No. We thought we'd wait outside for you,' Stevie replied. 'As it's such a nice evening.'

'Yes.'

Bayley and Luchewski took each other in for a few seconds.

'It's really good to meet you at last, Harry.' Bayley smiled. 'Ever since my mother told me the truth I've wanted to meet you.' He waved his arm. 'Your sister not with you?'

'No,' Luchewski beamed. 'No. In fact she'd kill me if she knew I was here right now. You see, she seems to think that you're only after her money.' He looked Bayley up and down, deliberately taking in the rich clothes, as if to make the point. 'Thinks you're out to take her for whatever you can get.'

'God, I'm not after your money,' Bayley frowned. 'Nothing could be further from the truth. My company – I'm in imports and exports – made a clear profit of two hundred and twenty million last year. Of which I pay myself five per cent ...' He let the statement ring for a moment 'So, no offence to your sister – and I really don't mean to brag – but I think I'm well enough off already.'

Luchewski laughed. 'Yes. I think you are.'

'The reason I wanted to meet you was ... well ... I thought it was right for you to know that you have another sibling. Well, *half*-sibling. I don't have any brothers or sisters. The only uncles, aunts and cousins I have are in Canada. There's no one in the UK. I just thought that ... well, we should all know about each other. Have some degree of contact.'

'You told the Schinowitzes that you wanted a DNA test to prove we had the same father.'

Bayley shook his head violently. 'No. I just said that to see if I could force a meeting. I don't care if some scientific test says I'm your brother or not. I already know it. And the last thing I want is to discredit your father ... our father. God forbid. I know he wasn't a bad man. I know he didn't know anything about me. But if we can all get on together – you, me and Elizabeth – if we can acknowledge each other's existence, then I think our lives could be richer for it.'

Stevie seemed to be nodding next to Luchewski.

'This is Stevie, by the way. My boyfriend.'

Bayley didn't bat an eyelid. 'Nice to meet you, Stevie,' he shook Stevie's hand. 'Really nice to meet you.'

An awkward silence.

'Patrick,' Hal finally started. 'Can I just say ...' he looked directly at Bayley. 'Can I just say that you look ... well ... you look just like my dad.' Suddenly, upon saying the word 'dad', Luchewski found himself welling up. 'You look just like my dad ... and there is no doubt in my mind that you are ... his ... son.' A tear appeared out of the corner of one eye and zig-zagged down his cheek. 'You are ... my brother. I have no doubt about it. You're ... my brother.'

Stevie threw his arm around Luchewski's waist and hugged him tight. Supporting him.

Bayley's eyes went wet too. 'Thank you,' he croaked. 'Thank you. It means a lot to hear you say that ... it really does. After all this time. Thank you.'

It was like a dam had burst. A terrible, stressful pent-up dam of anxiety and emotion. And now it was all out there and free and unleashed.

Bayley came closer and all of them stood there on the pavement in a massive three-way embrace, pedestrians walking around, wondering what was going on.

When eventually they all released each other – tears, snot and sniffles galore – Bayley wiped his nose with a spotless handkerchief, pulled his long coat tightly around himself, coughed and spoke.

'I don't know about either of you, but I'm starving. Shall we go inside and eat?'

'Oh, yes,' Stevie agreed.

'Why not,' said Luchewski, his face slightly flushed with both embarrassment and wet sobs. 'Why not.'

The next few days of the case were spent filling in gaps and paperwork. Statements were taken, movements accounted for and data accumulated. It was the part of the job that Luchewski hated most. It was all very well saying something or doing something, but then having to write it all down and explain it ... it bored the living underwear off him.

Thankfully, Singh seemed to love all that shit. So he piled as much as was morally and legitimately possible onto her. He watched her closely though. Kept an eye on her. She'd had enough difficulties of her own over the last few months. He didn't want to add to them if he could help it.

One morning, Luchewski was standing over Singh's desk reading her notes while she tried to extract some sort of insipid coffee from the machine in the corner. He watched as she stuck the money in the slot, bashed away mercilessly at the unresponsive buttons and moaned at the lack of activity of the decrepit pile of junk.

'You OK, Singh?'

It was Green.

'Robbie,' she acknowledged as she gave it a kick.

'That won't help.'

'Makes me feel better though.'

'What you've got to do is ... may I?'

Singh stepped aside and Green got close to the machine. He put his ear to it like he was about to crack a safe before pressing and holding the button. A couple of seconds passed and then –

BANG!

Green rammed his shoulder hard into the machine,

410

making it wobble slightly back and forth. He stood back and suddenly a gurgling hissing noise came from it, spluttering undrinkable coffee and watery milk into the plastic cup that Singh had out there.

'Oh, wow. Thanks.'

'No problem,' he twinkled, wiping his jacket arm down with one of the blue disposable towels that sat on a nearby table. 'No problem at all.'

Singh took the cup and sipped, looking over the rim at Green.

'Robbie,' she asked. 'Can I ask you something?'

'Yes. Of course.'

'Would you like to go for a drink some time?'

Green seemed to grow an extra inch. 'Er … er … yes. Yes. I would, Singh. Very much so.'

Singh nodded, taking a small mouthful of the coffee. 'Priti.'

'Yes. Of course. Priti.'

She smiled at him and he half melted.

'I have to warn you, though,' Green said, a hint of seriousness in his tone. 'My life is very busy at the moment … so, you know …'

'It's all right, Robbie. I'm not asking you to marry me just yet. It's just a drink, yes?'

'Yes. Great.'

Singh wandered back to her desk and Green seemed to walk in a daydream back to Burlock's office.

'Cougar!' Luchewski taunted as she set the drink down on her Bridlington Sands coaster.

'What? I'm only a year or two older than him. Not exactly baby-snatching, is it?'

'Still …' Luchewski couldn't help himself. 'Grrrrr!' He clawed the air. 'Cougar!'

It still bothered him. Kept bothering him. Didn't stop bothering him.

It didn't make any sense.

Luchewski found himself staring at the ceiling in the early hours, Stevie fast asleep beside him. The occasional car drove past, and the lights moved across the ceiling as they did, sweeping an orange arc over the slightly uneven plaster.

He lay there and watched as his mind turned it all over in his head.

Arnold Richards.

Why would he admit to killing Caroline Merriman now? Why not just swallow it all down like all the other murders he'd obviously committed and wasn't admitting to? Why not spill them *all* out if notoriety was what he was finally after?

Why just this one?

And why now?

It was like having your arms tied behind your back and suddenly getting an itch on your nose. Try as he may, strain as he may, he just couldn't reach it. It just wouldn't come to him.

He rolled onto his side and watched Stevie's shoulders rise and fall, his chest swell and sink like the ocean. The inhalations and exhalations, a soft autumn breeze.

It was a strange sensation. Caring for someone. He'd always cared for his daughter. Always would. But not caring like this – for a partner. He thought he cared for Lily's mum a long, long time ago. But that wasn't true. It became unreal too quickly. Fell apart like Lego. This was different. How, he wasn't sure, but it was definitely different.

As he lay there, the thin slice of daylight slowly fed in through the curtains. Later that morning, Arnold Richards would be driven to Croydon Magistrates' Court for a preliminary hearing. There, a judge would determine if there was sufficient evidence to take things to a full-on media centric Old Bailey court case. The fact that Richards had confessed would be evidence enough, and the ridiculous charade would continue and spiral out of control from then on in.

Luchewski took a sip of the water on his bedside table, bashed some life into his pillow and struggled to get back to sleep.

Richards.

Being escorted.

Out of prison.

'For fuck's sake!' he muttered quietly so as not to wake Stevie. It was all going around his head too much. Richards. Merriman. Cassandra Shoneye. Stacey Graham. Bodies in dustbins. A courtroom. Lawyers. Police cars. Handcuffs. Geoffrey Chaucer. Alicen of Norwich. M C Escher. A prison van.

It spun around his head in a stupid, disturbing blur.

And he didn't understand why.

Arnold Richards was sat on the incredibly uncomfortable grey bench in one of the cubicles in the back of the van. They hadn't cuffed him for the journey – which had been nice – but they did tell him to put his seatbelt on. So he did, like the good law abiding citizen he wasn't.

Outside, two of the prison guards – Mr Allum, a sweaty, bald Man City fan with a surfeit of nose hair, and Mr Bickerton, a droopy-faced sack of spuds – were strapped onto their own bench talking about something too inane for Richards to even consider. As the van turned and twisted through the streets of Surrey, Richards could see the two men through the pane of reinforced glass, swaying and jerking, occasionally bumping into one another. They struck him as a pair of uniformed testicles, banging together in a jogger's underpants.

They'd given him a suit to wear to the initial hearing. He had no idea who'd picked it out for him, but it certainly wasn't anyone with any degree of taste. He'd had a look at the label on the inside of the jacket and saw that it was 80% nylon, 10% cotton and 10% elastane. The shirt wasn't much better. It had come straight out of a packet and no one had bothered ironing it, so two large stiff rectangles dominated his chest. As for the tie ...

Earlier that morning, before he'd been taken from his cell, Arnold Richards – convicted murderer of two young women, known to the tabloid press as *The Headmaster* – slid the three tiny needles he had managed to steal from the Governor's office into position just under his skin. Just below the epidermis. Two of them were on the back of each forearm, the third just above his left ankle. They felt awkward and unnatural, but nobody could see them. He had rotated his arms in the light of his cell window, checking to see if they were hidden well. Unless you were really looking, he decided, you wouldn't really notice them.

They were his insurance policy. Just in case things went wrong.

Of course, on the way out of Ashmoor, he set the metal detectors off, but a quick flash of his teeth reminded the guards that Richards – being fairly old – had a mouthful of metal fillings. They nodded and waved him on like the disinterested fools they all were.

Aside from the van, there were two police motorcycles and a police car. Not exactly the snaking convoy of security he hoped there might be for a killer of his status. But it was probably for the best. At least it would make his escape all the more simple.

The two men sat next to each other in the central part of the van laughed at some stupid pointless joke that Richards would never dare to deem funny. How he loathed the vast majority of mankind. With their pathetic, basic thoughts and their useless lack of ambition. So few of them saw the potential of their existence. So few of them realised that life was for soaring above clouds and becoming that which supposedly created us in the first place. To them, life was nothing more than a round of eating, sleeping, sexual congress, working, drinking and watching television. Round and round like hamsters on wheels, until eventually their weak and spiritless bodies gave up the ghost. They crumble into dust, instantaneously forgotten.

So it was down to men like him to try and skew the average.

Of course, he couldn't have organised this on his own, he had to admit. He was reluctantly indebted to *No1Fan* – his mysterious online partner in this escape. All those moments, those tiny snippets of time in the Governor's office pretending to hoover but instead checking his secret email account. And the messages that went back and forth between the two of them, the rest of the world blissfully unaware of the communication. Over months. Months and months. Piecemeal. Slowly. It all came together.

It was beautiful.

The window was set too high for him to peer out. It was also frosted. The number of times he'd seen footage on the news of prisoners being driven away from courtrooms, the press crowded together on tippy toe, cameras flashing at difficult arms-outstretched angles. Now here he was – again – the insider looking out, so to speak.

It was a lovely day in a way. Dry. Still. A glimmer of sun through the thin veil of cloud. Not too bright, hot and humid. Not too wet, cold and windy. A nondescript sort of day. An easy-to-lose-in-the-crowd sort of day. A perfect day, in fact, to escape.

Suddenly the van screeched aggressively, lurching to the left, and Richards found himself being thrown towards the wall, his seatbelt thankfully clutching him safely. The tyres rumbled beneath him and the van jerked hard before coming to a stop.

Richards pushed himself away from the side of the van, back fully onto his seat.

'WHAT THE FUCK …?' He recognised Allum's phlegm-rattled voice.

'JESUS!' Bickerton joined in.

BANG.

A gunshot from outside the van.

BANG. BANG. Two more.

'WHAT THE FUCK IS GOING ON OUT THERE?' Allum was panicking. 'WHAT THE FUCK …?'

Arnold caught his breath from the sudden stop and casually undid his seatbelt.

'OPEN THE DOOR!' A different voice this time. Muffled. Outside. 'OPEN THE DOOR OR I SHOOT HIM TOO!'

Richards watched in delight as Allum and Bickerton scrambled out of their seats like Laurel and Hardy and went to look out the rear window of the van.

'Oh, shit!' Bickerton sounded sick. 'Oh, shit!'

'I SAID OPEN THE DOOR!'

Richards felt frustrated that he was trapped in his little cubicle and that he couldn't see any of this.

'I'M GOING TO COUNT TO THREE,' said the man outside, 'AND IF YOU DON'T OPEN THE DOOR I'M

GOING TO SHOOT HIM. ONE …'

'Oh God, he's going to fucking shoot him!' Richards could hardly understand a word of what Allum said, his voice was almost bubbling with lactic bile.

'TWO …'

'What do we do?'

'Open the door.'

'We're not allow –'

'Just open the bloody door!'

'THREE.'

A loud clunk as the door was opened, and light enveloped the back of the van.

Allum and Bickerton seemed to suddenly disappear. Instead a square, stockinged face filled the glass window to Richards' cubicle. The dark eyes stared at him, as if making sure he was the right person, before Arnold could hear the lock on his door being sprung.

The man outside moved away and swung the door open.

'The Headmaster' stood up and smiled an almost uncontrollably wide smile to himself. He could feel and smell the cool air coming through the back of the van.

Freedom, he thought stepping out towards the sun.

Freedom.

At last.

The DI Luchewski Series

Mark Lock

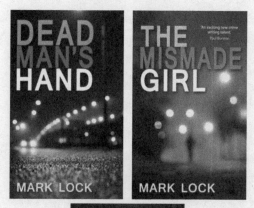

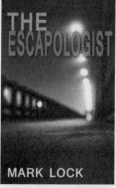

Dead Man's Hand
The Mismade Girl
The Escapologist (Coming 2018)

The Black Path

Paul Burston

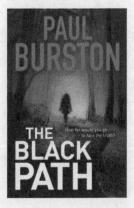

Helen has been holding out for a hero all her life. Her father was a hero – but he was murdered when she was ten. Her husband is a hero – but he's thousands of miles away, fighting a war people say will never be won.

Sometimes Helen wonders if Owen isn't the only one living in a war zone. She feels the violence all around her. She reads about it in the papers. It feeds her dreams and fills her days with a sense of dread. Try as she might, she can't escape the feeling that something terrible is about to happen.

Then one night on the troubled streets of her home town, Helen is rescued from a fight by a woman who will change her life forever. Siân is everything Helen isn't – confident, glamorous, fearless. But there's something else about her – a connection that cements their friendship and makes Helen question everything she's ever known.

Bad Catholics

James Green

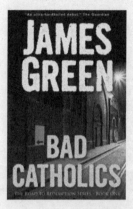

Meet Jimmy Costello. Quiet, respectable, God-fearing family man? Or thuggish street-fighter with a past full of dark secrets? Perhaps the answer is somewhere in between …

After Jimmy's wife dies the conflict inside him is too much and the violent assault he commits on a gangster forces him to leave London and his job with the police and disappear for a while. Now he's back, on what you might call a divine mission … and to settle a few old scores too.

Through the eyes of his hard-boiled ex-cop, James Green takes us on a thrilling journey from 1960s Kilburn, through war-torn 1970s Africa to the modern streets of a London that seems to have cleaned up its act … until you scratch the surface.

The Road to Redemption Series

James Green

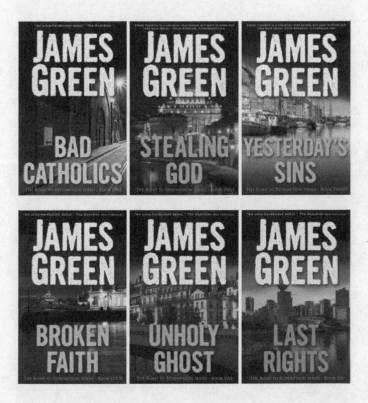

For more information about **Mark Lock**

and other **Accent Press** titles

please visit

www.accentpress.co.uk